I0788433

trials
and
TIARAS

Trials and Tiaras
Untouchable #7
Copyright © 2020 by Heather Long
Editing: Bookish Dreams Editing
Cover: Crimson Phoenix Designs

Trials and Tiaras/Heather Long – 1st ed.
ISBN-13 - 978-1-956264-80-7

For #TeamMadAtHeather
Sorry about that cliffhanger.
Well, no, not really.
Admit it, you loved it.

Foreword

Dear Reader,

Thank you for picking up *Trials and Tiaras*. If you haven't read the first six in the Untouchable series, I caution you to go and grab those right now and read them first.

It's funny, I have said for months that this would only be a ten book series. (Yes, yes, I know: *only!*) Yet, as I wrapped this book and looked forward toward the future, I considered how much of the story I had left to tell.

Could I do it all in three books? Would I have to sacrifice some of it? Or worse, would it all feel rushed and too heavy? I didn't want to do either of those things. So after some serious contemplation, and discussions, I've decided to add two more books to the series. This will let the story breathe.

The good news, books will continue to come out on schedule (still shooting for every 2 months). The even better news, you're getting more Frankie and the boys!

This series wouldn't be complete without the enormous support system I had in place from the Heathens in the pack to #TeamMadatHeather to my beta readers and editors to my friends who just cheer me on and occasionally kick my ass. The fact that this list has grown with every book is amazing to me and I couldn't be more grateful.

I have to take a moment to also say thank you to my family even though the chances are they won't read this. I know I'm a hermit, hiding in my office, lost in this world. I know you miss me and occasionally roust me out for human contact. I promise, as soon as the world gets back to some sort of normalcy, I'll still be exactly like this. So, good to know some things don't change, right?

Thank you to every single reader who has given this series a shot and to those who left reviews. Thank you to the readers who recommend the series to their friends and to every single person who has reached out to me about it. I see and hear all of you. Thank you to the readers who make the beautiful collages and cast who they see as the characters in this series.

I get such a thrill for every single one I see.

Thank you. Thank you. Thank you.

And now, as always, the housekeeping notes:

For those of you who have never read a reverse harem before, first let me thank you for picking this up and giving it a shot. Second, a reverse harem means the heroine will not make a choice in this book or any other between the guys in her life. It may take her a while to reach that conclusion, but it's the journey that drives it. There are many ways to frame this kind of relationship, currently reverse harem fits it very well.

Also, this is the seventh book in a series. If you haven't read the first six, I encourage you to pause here and go grab them. While there may be no specific happy endings at the end of each of these books, there will be one to the whole series, that I promise you. Some of these books will have cliffhangers, largely due to the size of the story, but the happy ending has to be earned as part of the journey.

Thank you again for reading Frankie's story and I truly hope you enjoy it!

xoxo

Heather

Chapter One
LIVING WITH LIES

ARCHIE

As soon as the car came to a halt, I slid over and opened the door without waiting for the driver. Jake exhaled as he followed me. I'd told him he didn't have to come with, but he'd just glared at me. Two plane tickets later, we were on our way to New York. With both of us gone, that left Bubba and Coop to keep an eye on Frankie.

My heart fisted as I headed for the main doors. I couldn't focus on Frankie too closely right now. My temper was still on edge, and if Bubba and Jake hadn't sat on me, I'd probably be in jail for murder. I had a plan. I just needed to stick with it.

Phillip, the doorman, gave me a nod as he opened the doors to let us in out of the frigid February air. Instead of spending Valentine's weekend with our girl, we were here in New York on a Sunday morning to track down my mother. Inside, I pulled a keycard out of my pocket and swiped it at the elevator before pressing the call button.

Jake let out a low whistle as the doors slid open to reveal a comfortably appointed elevator where no expense had been spared to make it appear as opulent as the building it served in. Inside, I pressed the penthouse button, then ran my swipe card again and entered the code. Only then did the doors close.

"You didn't have to come," I reminded him.

Arms folded, Jake shot me a smirk. "Fuck off."

"Right. So what?"

"Nothing, just forget how much money your family has sometimes."

"Good," I said. "I don't want to be known for the money."

"But you're more than willing to use it."

I shrugged. "It's an asset. Right now, it's a powerful one we have to protect her. You really complaining?"

"Fuck no," Jake said. "Just makes me think about our plans and I'm glad you're on my side."

I nodded. "Ditto."

Then the elevator doors opened to the penthouse. Express access never took long. The interior was lit from all the windows facing out over the city. Unsurprisingly, a butler greeted us.

"Mrs. Standish is still in her room, Mr. Standish…"

"Is she alone?"

"Sir?"

"Is she alone or does she have a guest over?"

"I'm afraid I couldn't—"

"That's fine, I know where it is," I said, waving him off. Whatever, if she had someone in there, Jake would help me throw him out so I could talk to her. "You should probably make coffee and get the vodka out if she needs a shot after this conversation."

Across the living room to one of the halls tucked just out of sight, I followed it to the master suite. I knocked twice and then gripped the handle.

Deep breath. It would hardly be the first time I walked in one of their dalliances.

It was how I'd figured out the Maddy equation in the first place. Not that they'd seen me.

The interior of the master was much darker, with only one window offering partial light through the drapes. Jake paused at the doorway.

"Archibald," Muriel said with an aggrieved sigh. "What is so urgent you can't even wait a polite fifteen minutes for me to make myself presentable?"

Robe on with her hair already coiffed, she held her phone in one hand and a cup of coffee in the other.

"This isn't a social call, Muriel, and I couldn't care less if you are presentable."

"Don't take that tone with me," she began, and I sliced a hand through the air to cut her off.

"Not in the mood, Muriel. We need to talk, and I have questions. You're going to answer them."

She arched a plucked eyebrow. "And if I refuse?"

"I can make life very unpleasant for you. I'm sure you want those accounts to stay accessible, but since they are part of a larger Standish estate funding, I can redirect that entirely or tie it up in enough paperwork, you'll have to jump through hoops to order a cup of coffee."

I'd come prepared.

She lowered her cup and eyed me. "You're serious."

"Yes, Muriel, contrary to your opinion, I'm quite often serious. But right now, what I want are answers and you have them. So the only thing you need to decide is whether we're doing it in here or out there."

"Let me get my coat and my shoes."

With that, she turned back into her closet, and I walked out to the hall to wait with Jake.

"Coat and shoes?" he asked.

I shrugged. "It's gotta be bad. She wants a cigarette."

Muriel didn't keep us waiting, surprise. She had indeed pulled on a heavy coat and warm shoes. I motioned for her to go past, and she barely even glanced at Jake. He mouthed 'Wow' to me, and I shook my head.

Sometimes, I forgot the guys didn't have as much experience with my parents as Frankie did. They were so rarely around. Just thinking of her sent a muscle twitching at the corner of my eye.

"…bring coffee out for all of us," Muriel said. "And do turn on the heating lamps for me."

"Yes, ma'am."

She had a thin silver case in her hand—a hand that now wore gloves. The wind outside might threaten her hair, but that was the price we would pay. Her butler was already carrying out a tray with large mugs of coffee. Jake grabbed two when I would have left it, but I took the second one from him when he glared.

Seriously, if he came to be my babysitter, I was gonna give him a black eye the next time we boxed. Once Muriel had her mug, the butler opened the doors to the patio. The wind was definitely brisk, but the alcove off this side of the building offered us a bit of shelter.

The heating lamps did the rest. Someone had already cleared away the snow and any ice accumulation. We paid people to take care of everything. For the first time in my life, it really seemed like a fucking waste.

At Frankie's, we all had chores and they sucked. But we did it, and I kind of liked the fact we all split up the work. It had kind of turned her apartment into *our* apartment. It had taken us a *long* time to get here, and I wasn't going to let anyone…

Fuck. I shook off the wandering thoughts, even as my gut bottomed out. No. Just fucking no. It was not all going to hell because Edward couldn't keep his dick in his pants.

Muriel lit a cigarette and then took a seat on the padded chair just below the patio heater, looking for all the world like we were on vacation and having the most pleasant time. "Well, are you going to send your friend away?"

"No."

"I would prefer to keep private matters private."

"Trust me," I told her as I set my cup down on the table and then braced my hands on the green marble monstrosity, "I would prefer if you'd all kept your fucking private matters private. But guess what, they aren't anymore…"

"Archibald…"

"Save it, you were a womb with a view and a name on my birth certificate. I spent more time with my nannies and my boarding schools than I ever did with you. So sit there, lose the attitude, and answer my questions. Believe me, when I'm done, you'll never have to see me again. I know what a chore that's always been."

Her lips compressed, and her expression turned icy.

I took her silence for compliance and began. "Why did Edward marry you?"

She blinked. "Excuse me?"

"Why. Did. Edward. Marry. You?" I ground out each word. "The truth."

Exhaling a stream of blue smoke, she eyed me and then said, "Because I was pregnant. We had a brief relationship, I got pregnant, we got married. It's what you do."

"Brief relationship is that what we call his flings?"

Another puff of her cigarette. "If you wish. I don't call them anything but inconvenient these days. And very shortly, they won't be my problem at all."

"You're divorcing now, why?"

"Are you seriously…"

"Muriel, don't make me repeat myself. I am asking the questions. You're divorcing now, why?"

I could practically feel Jake's gaze boring into me. I hadn't moved from where I'd braced my hands on the table. I'd done it as much to keep from throttling her as I had for effect.

Another drag and exhale. "The terms of the prenuptial are no longer in effect."

I frowned. Then… "Because I turned eighteen."

For a split second, something resembling regret seemed to pass over her features. Or maybe she had gas.

"Yes. When I got pregnant, I told your father. Three days later, he proposed. We were married a week after that in a quick civil ceremony and then a reception for the couple who eloped."

So that part of Edward's story checked out. I thought I'd feel something at the admission, but it barely even registered.

"You were a fling?"

She met my gaze evenly. "I was available and interested. He wanted to punish his girlfriend—he was quite honest about his intentions, and I was quite amenable to it. We were well-matched in that regard."

"Save me the gory details. What about the girlfriend?"

Her smile turned almost pitying. "I wondered if he would ever tell you."

"He didn't tell me," I informed her. "He told Frankie."

"Why would he tell that—"

"Choose your next words carefully."

Extinguishing her cigarette, she studied me. "Madeline Grayson, now known as Curtis, was engaged to your father for three years. The relationship blew very hot, and they were prone to their…mutual indiscretions. He was rather put out with her over something she'd done, and honestly, I didn't care. He was handsome and interested." After lighting another, she exhaled, then shook her head. "I didn't break them up, but I also wasn't opposed to the pregnancy tying Edward and I together…"

"Because you had your meal ticket."

"What? You want me to apologize for securing my future and, may I remind you, *yours*?"

"I wouldn't dream of asking you for an apology, Muriel. What I want to know is if you knew he and his ex-girlfriend hooked up *after* you and he were together?"

"He could have," she admitted with a shrug. "He had several affairs in the early years, and that didn't change. When I chose to move to Texas to get away from the city and your interfering grandfather, I did it because I'd found her and I wanted to put her in Edward's path." She flicked some ash away and then took a drink of her coffee.

"You moved there specifically so he'd run into her?" Who did that?

"Yes," she told me simply. "The prenuptial was quite clear, the marriage a contract for your father and for me. If he asked for the divorce, I got to keep my assets, or I simply had to maintain the marriage until your eighteenth birthday. I think we were all tired of the farce, yourself included. So I had to give him incentive."

My stomach curdled, and even the cold wind didn't register against the heat racing through me. I'd met Frankie because Muriel wanted to get a divorce.

Fuck, the world was twisted.

"But he didn't ask for a divorce."

"She put him through his paces. Played hard to get. I told you, they blew very hot back in the day. Considering she lives in that shitty little apartment with her—"

"Muriel. Not one word about her. I mean it."

"Archibald, you need to get over your crush on your little friend. She's—"

"Lady," Jake said in a clipped tone as I curled my fingers into fists. "He wasn't kidding, watch your fucking mouth where she's concerned."

"Fine, I won't warn you against her. But you have too much of your father in you."

"Thanks for the insult."

"Oh, grow up, Archibald. The world is an unpleasant place at times. Everything in this world is very practical. Business transactions. Investments. Allies. But the thing your father—even your grandfather—does is fixate, obsess over one person. That person for your grandfather was your grandmother. For your father, it was always Madeline. What does it matter if they're back together now?"

"It doesn't. It doesn't even matter that their affair has gone on for years. You always knew when he had a fling. We always knew. So if you always knew, did you know he and Maddy were together roughly four and a half months after you were married?"

I'd done the math. I had the window of time we needed to eliminate.

"Probably, I had a bit of a difficult pregnancy and it required rest. He grew bored with that, and for about three weeks, he was very busy. Then one day, he returned home and recommitted himself to you and I. He was very devoted for the next few months…"

How he always behaved following the end of one of his flings.

"I assume she threw him back out… Maybe she punished him by giving him another taste before taking it away. She begged him not to marry me, and he told her he had no choice. Which he didn't…your grandfather would have disowned him if he'd refused. Your grandmother expressed her own wishes and desires, but they wanted you to be born a Standish…"

"It's a fucking piece of paper," I reminded her. "Not some love story. They had the affair when?"

"I don't know."

"Yes you do. You hate her. Because he wanted her when he had you, and even if he was just a meal ticket, you also loved him. So every single affair was another nail being beaten into you, and you retaliated over and over, but he never cared."

I was so fucking tired of this.

"But you hate Frankie," I pushed out. "Because she looks like her mother."

"Yes," she admitted. "Though I was grateful to her for a long time."

"Why?"

After extinguishing the cigarette, she licked her lips, and for the barest moment, she seemed almost human. Then she gave a bitter little laugh. A scoff at herself. "Because you'd barely been at that school a week before she came home with you one day when your father and I had to leave for that trip."

My stomach sank.

"He found Maddy because I found Frankie." I almost didn't want to wrap my mind around it. It was sick and a little…

"Yes. I'd intended to make other arrangements, but that was the most natural and I could even feign the most mild of shocks when we *met* her."

And yet none of them revealed anything.

"The dates, Mrs. Standish?" Jake said, before handing me the rapidly cooling mug of coffee. I downed it.

"The first three weeks of July, he left just before the fourth and didn't come back until the twenty-seventh or thereabouts. He told me he had been on a business trip, but he was not in the office nor was he out on business. He'd told his father some lie and had taken the time off. I was feeling too poorly to care then, and I was actually relieved I didn't have to pretend around him." She gave another shrug.

The dates lined up.

"What is this about, Archie?"

"Don't call me that."

"I thought you preferred that…"

"I prefer my friends call me that. You're not my friend."

"Very well. What is this about?"

"None of your business." She didn't know, and based on her reactions, she would have spit it out just to get the dig in. But I had one more test…

"I would think it is my business, since it's my life you're asking about."

"Actually, Muriel, I'm asking about the components to a deal you negotiated that provided the tangible return of me. I was a means to an end and an investment. So let's not pretend there's some great emotion there. You may have loved Edward for all I know, but I don't care about that anymore."

"Fine. Then are we done? Do you know everything you need?" She rose then. "Because I will definitely have to adjust my plans to deal with this stress you've decided to throw at me."

The scuff of Jake's shoes sliding as he let out what had to be a swear word in a hissed breath filled the silence, I just shook my head.

"No, consider this information, not a question." I paused for a moment and felt the weight of Jake's gaze as he swung his head back toward me. We hadn't discussed this part.

But I needed a genuine reaction.

"Frankie and I are getting married."

Surprise flickered across her face. "Did you get her pregnant?"

"What?"

"Getting married at eighteen? Asking me these questions? Your father has informed you that you have to get married if you were so indiscreet you impregnated her."

"There are more reasons to get married than the mercenary ones."

"Fine, please tell me you're not having some huge ceremony where I would have to attend with that…"

No, she had no idea.

None.

"Trust me. You would be the third last person I'd invite to my wedding." With that, I turned and headed for the door. I pulled out my phone to text the driver to be back at the doors to get us.

"That's it?" Muriel said as she followed us. The heat from inside slapped against my face as we crossed the living room to the elevator.

We were already inside when she caught up with us. Thankfully, the doors closed on her glare, and then we were descending. Jake said nothing until we got outside and slid into the car. We had roughly an hour to get to LaGuardia to check in for our flight.

"Man…" Jake began, but I shook my head.

"It's fine Jake. It's not a surprise."

"I don't care, Arch, that's some fucked up shit. My dad's an asshole, and I'll never forgive him for choosing someone over my sisters and me. It's not even just about Mom, though it is about her too. Thing is, I get how complicated that whole situation must have been…but I didn't get it then, and I sure as shit shouldn't have had to. And that shit back there…"

He made a disgusted sound and fell back in the seat.

"Jake, they aren't my family."

"That doesn't make it better."

"Sure it does," I said as I pulled my phone out again and sent a message to Jeremy, asking him to put together a list of the best labs with the speediest turnaround times.

I needed the answer in hand when we got off that plane and drove back to the apartment. I couldn't take seeing that shocked and horrified look on her face again. Or how she'd recited what Edward had said in such a stunned and broken tone.

Ambushing her like that?

That alone made me want to kill him, but that whole story he'd dropped on her? The DNA tests made sense, but I still had more questions than answers.

"We're going to figure this out," Jake said quietly.

"I already figured it out," I informed him. "I figured it out that first day of ninth grade and every day since. I just want the answer for her."

"Yeah and for you. You need to know…"

"She's not my sister," I told him as I glared at him. "She's *not* my sister. Even if Edward contributed to her DNA, that wouldn't make her my sister. The only thing that affects is if we decided to have kids together or not. I can always pass on that. She's got you three. But let's be *explicitly* clear here—she's *not* and *never will be* my sister."

I didn't care.

I should have hit Edward a hell of a lot harder.

"For what it's worth," Jake said quietly. "You know we're on your side."

"It's worth a lot. Just tell me you're still on my side no matter what we prove."

He exhaled, and then he let out a grunt. "Arch, what's between you two, that's for you two to decide. We all made a commitment. Nothing's changed for me…well, except I always thought *I'd* be the one going to jail for violence. But man, you want to just keep one-upping me."

The silence stretched for a moment, and then a soft huff of laughter escaped from me. "I'm always the best, don't you know?"

"Yeah," Jake said easily, then knocked my foot with his. "Nothing's changed."

At the airport, we got out and headed straight in. We didn't have suitcases or anything else, and as we breezed through security as we neared the gate, I said "Huh."

"What?"

"I never thought you'd be the sappy one. That's always been Coop."

He laughed. "What can I say, I'm very in touch with my feelings these days."

Another laugh escaped me, not a big one but definitely there.

My phone buzzed, and I turned it over to see the message from Frankie.

I let out a breath. How the hell did she always know?

Frankie

Fuck.

Me

Soon as I get there.

The corners of my lips twitched. I could picture her face. When another couple of seconds went by, I typed another message.

Me

Too soon?

The middle finger emoji appeared, and I grinned for real.

Me

Love you, babe. See you soon.

Frankie

I love you too.

That helped.

That really helped.

Valentine's Day

It was raining by the time I exited the elevator and crossed the marble floor of the cold lobby to the main doors. I barely even saw it as I shoved my way outside. I couldn't stay in the building another second.

No.

Edward Standish was my father?

Everything inside of me rejected that statement. It was a damn lie. Bag slung over one shoulder, I folded my arms tight against my chest and tucked my chin down against the wind. Not even sure which way to go, I turned north and followed the sidewalk. There was a coffee shop at the end of the row, I could go there.

No matter what I tried to do, that thought and his words kept circling back around my brain like we were stuck on some merry-go-round and I couldn't get off. I was going to throw up.

A hand on my elbow stopped me, and I jerked around half-swinging before I found Coop's worried eyes staring down at me. "Hey…"

Chapter Two
DENIAL ISN'T JUST A RIVER...

IAN

Leaning against the door jamb to the bedroom, I stared at where Frankie slept. Coop was all arms and legs wrapped around her. Before Archie and Jake had left to go to New York, Archie had been sleeping on her other side. We weren't letting either of them out of our sight. She'd wanted to go with him to New York, but that wasn't a good idea.

His mother couldn't be trusted any more than hers. His words, not mine. Still…she'd wanted to at least take him to the airport, but he'd planned to just call a car. Jake joined her in bullying him to let me drive them. Still, he'd insisted she stay here.

What. A. Fucking. Mess.

Scrubbing a hand over my face, I shoved away from the door and crossed to the bed. The sun was up, theoretically, though the gray skies and continued chill after the freezing rain of the day before didn't promise much brightness.

I flicked Coop's ear first, and his eyes opened to snap up at me.

"How long?" I kept my voice low and soothing. If she'd only just gone back to sleep, then I'd leave her there.

Coop flicked his gaze past me toward his phone.

"It's just seven-thirty." It was a ninety-minute drive to get them to the airport, and their flight had been super early.

He pinched the bridge of his nose before rubbing his eyes, then glancing down at her. "She went back to sleep faster than I thought she would… What's up?"

"Let's get her up and go running."

Horror crossed Coop's face, and it took everything I had to bite back a laugh.

"She needs a distraction."

"That's not a distraction," he argued. "That's cruel and unusual punishment."

She yawned and stretched. Coop froze, and his attention went straight to her. Not that mine didn't. "Why are you two arguing?"

"Because Bubba the Brute wants us to get dressed and go running," Coop complained, and I shot him a look he totally ignored.

Frankie wrinkled her adorable nose and then scowled like I'd suggested we get rid of her cats. Then she huffed. "Why?"

Now for a little finesse. Because she needed to move. She needed to keep moving and accomplishing until we heard back from Archie, or she would worry herself into a frenzy. I didn't want a repeat of the day before, and I never wanted a Friday like that night again. "Because I need to take care of you," I told her, and I kept it simple.

Even rumpled, half-asleep, with a track left by drool at the corner of her mouth, she was still the most beautiful girl in the world. She studied me from beneath those half-lowered lids and then let out the softest of little sighs. "Okay."

Coop transferred that horrified gaze from me to Frankie. "What?"

With a little lift of her shoulders, she smiled at him, though the expression didn't quite reach her eyes, and that wrenched me all over again. "It could be fun."

"Like a hole in the head. We don't run. They run, we stay here and have sex." Coop nodded as if to himself. "Let's do that instead."

A laugh escaped her, weak as it was, but a real one. "Ian doesn't share that way, and he wants to run. He needs it and he needs to look after me, so we're going to run. You can stay here though."

Something settled inside of me when she acknowledged that I needed to look after her and acquiesced to it. In all our conversations, that play wasn't going to leave the bedroom or sex, but this right here? Her pain? This was not something I could ignore.

Even stopping Archie from charging back into that building and attacking his father had been damn hard. I'd done it for him as much as for her. So had Jake. Archie hadn't been rational, and Frankie had been a wreck. Not that Jake and I didn't share the same temptation, but right now, making sure they were all right overrode any other desires. We'd deal with them later.

His father.

Her mother.

The whole damn mess.

Coop shot me a mock glare. "Fine, I'll watch. You two have sex."

I chuckled. A month ago, I wasn't sure what my reaction to that statement might have been, but right now, it was both funny and a little charming. While he was going to some effort to make her laugh, he also wasn't kidding. He absolutely meant he'd watch.

"You never know," I told them both. "Maybe we'll revisit the idea—after we run."

Frankie pushed upward and dropped a quick kiss on Coop before she scrambled out of the bed. He stared at me dumbfounded for a second as she leaned up to kiss me, and I slid an arm around her to give her a hug. When she burrowed for a moment, I just soaked it up, then gave her ass a light swat to send her on her way.

"I'm just gonna pee and brush my teeth," she muttered on a yawn, and I tracked her as she paused at the bathroom door. "Their flight get off okay?"

"Yep," I promised. "Another couple of hours before they land. So we'll be back well before then."

The hint of tension around her eyes eased again, and she nodded before slipping inside. The second the door closed, I snapped a hand out and caught the pillow Coop flung at me.

"Are you for real right now? Or humoring her?"

"I don't know," I told him honestly before flinging the pillow back. "Get dressed, and we'll figure out. Right now, she's the priority."

He studied me for a beat. "Don't make yourself. If you aren't comfortable, just don't. Jake and I don't care. I think it's hot when he's all over her, and it's the same for him with me. So…if it makes you crazy, just tease her and I can always take a walk or you can."

"You don't even want to go for a run."

With a snort, he flipped me off. "Fuck no. But I guess I have to now." He pulled the covers up on the bed and headed over to grab some sweatpants. I was pretty sure those were Jake's. But we'd all ended up in each other's shit at this point.

"It'll be good for you," I said, and he flipped me off as he dug into the laundry basket for a clean sweatshirt.

Fifteen minutes later, and both of them were in sweats and sweatshirts. Frankie had on one of Archie's, and I appreciated that. Her worry over this whole scenario resurfaced at every mention, and he'd barely been able to take his eyes off of her. When she wasn't around though, he fucking seethed, and I had to hope Jake could make sure he didn't explode while he was gone.

She had her phone in her hand and checked it.

"They're still in the air," I reminded her, and she made a face.

"I know, I'm…"

"We get it," Coop said, wrapping his arms around her and pulling her back against his chest. "We're worried too. Well, Bubba is. Me, I'm still thinking about whether I can convince you both that sex would be a way better workout."

One sharp jab of her elbow elicited a comical if exaggerated 'oof' from him as a real smile flitted across her face. "Stop teasing Ian. It's not nice."

"It's fine, Angel," I assured her, and that earned me a solid blink. "It doesn't bother me in the slightest." It didn't. The teasing anyway. Whether the rest of it would…I wasn't entirely sure, but the kneejerk reaction to just say no wasn't there, so maybe? Maybe not?

"Really?" Interest flashed in her eyes and she bit her lower lip, and if I wasn't already a little curious about testing those boundaries, I absolutely would be now.

"Really. Now, let's move that beautiful ass of yours and, Coop, you really can sit this out, man, if you don't think you can keep up."

"Fuck you, Bubba," he told me cheerfully, and she grinned again, yet the moment she turned her back, he shot me a thumbs up and I nodded. First level of distraction achieved.

Archie, Jake, and I had mapped a few runs from Frankie's place at this point. If it were warmer, I'd have suggested we drive to the lake. As it was, there was an old bike trail about a quarter of a mile from the apartments, and it would be a good run, away from traffic but on solid surface.

I led the way at a walk, since I wanted to warm them up first. The fact Coop kept up a steady litany of complaints was hilarious. Sometimes, I wondered if he did it on purpose to distract her from any discomfort, or if he was so used to finding a way to make her smile, it just happened. Because Frankie didn't complain once, but her smile grew a little wider with every step.

Once on the trail, we started off slow, and despite all his bitching, Coop had no trouble keeping up. Course, when the pair of class clowns started hamming it up, I was torn between interceding and letting them wear each other out. As it was, they managed a respectable two miles, a mile out and a mile back, but the last half-mile, Frankie walked with one hand against her side and panting.

"I remembered why I don't do this," she commented, and I grinned.

"You did great," I promised her. "Coop on the other hand…"

He rolled his eyes and flipped me the middle finger, but Frankie laughed aloud, and that was worth just about any insult.

"You two are ridiculous, you know," she said as we left the trail for the walk back to the apartments. "I get it, you are trying to distract me and it's working and you're teasing each other and I think it's great."

"Us?" Coop sounded almost offended. Almost. Hard to sound too offended when you're cracking a grin. "Nah. This is foreplay. Remember what Bubba said about when we get back?"

"You have sex on the brain," I told him, not missing a beat.

"When it comes to Frankie?" He grinned slowly. "Not all of us need to control our urges."

Oh. That little shit.

Frankie, on the other hand, laughed. "Well, I tell you what, boys…" She skipped ahead and then turned to walk backwards as she looked from me to Coop and then back. "The first one of you back to the apartment gets to shower with me."

Then she pivoted and took off.

I cut a look at Coop and he stared at me, then we both surged forward. For all his bluster about not wanting to run, Coop was no slouch. He cut ahead of me and turned sharply instead of racing directly up the walk after Frankie. I debated it for all of about a split second and raced after him.

He knew the apartments better than we did. He knew the area better than we did. When he cut through a narrow passageway between the wall around the complex and the street, we bounced off each other. When he threw an elbow and I bounced into the wall, I laughed.

"Oh, it's on," I warned him, but he streaked away. I was just steps behind him, and I still conserved my oxygen for a final push as we weaved through the complex, and it didn't take long to spot Frankie as she circled down the drive. We were a hell of a lot closer to the apartment than she was, and since I knew where I was, I called, "Hey, Coop, don't forget…I'm still thinking about it."

He stumbled a step, and I shot past him and hit the backdoor with enough time to get it open before Frankie and Coop made it to the stairs. She was panting, flushed, with the wisps of her hair that escaped her ponytail clinging to her face, and she slid right up to me and wrapped her arms around my waist. Coop tried to slide around me to get inside, but I slammed a hand against the doorjamb and cut him off at the chest.

"Aww, you can't blame a guy for trying."

"Sure I can," I told him as I ran a hand down Frankie's back. She'd sweated enough that the shirt was damp. "You go shower in the other bedroom, and we'll talk after."

He laughed at me, but when I didn't grin or make a joke, he sobered. Better. With a nod, I tugged Frankie inside and flipped on the coffee maker on the way past.

"Oh, I love you," she enthused, still holding my hand, and I grinned.

"I know."

In the bathroom, I turned the shower on and then helped her strip out of the clothes. The flush on her cheeks added to the light in her eyes. Instead of climbing under the hot water, she turned into me. The hug at the door earlier had been one thing, but this was needing more, so I locked her up close and squeezed as she rubbed her cheek to my shirt.

"It's too soon for them to be there yet."

"Yeah," I told her. "We weren't even gone an hour."

She sighed.

"It's going to be okay, Angel," I whispered and pressed a kiss to her damp hair. "Come on, let's get you in the shower, and then you can have coffee and we'll find food."

"Ian." The soft demand in her voice had me hesitating, and I pulled back to meet her gaze. The skin of her arms was chilly beneath my fingers, so I rubbed my hands up and down her biceps. Her nipples were tight too, but the steam from the shower and the heat of the water had already begun to warm up the bathroom.

"What, Angel?"

"The thing with Coop…"

"Shh. I'm not making any promises, but I'm also not wildly opposed either."

Surprise skittered across her expression, and yeah, I probably deserved that.

"I'm a possessive bastard, we've established that."

The corners of her mouth tilted upward. "I kind of like that about you."

"Good. But Coop is very much what you need right now."

"I need all of you," she argued.

One finger against her lips, and I pressed my forehead to hers. "Listen to me, Angel. I'm not making any decisions for you here, I promise. But I'm also not blind. Coop is what you need right now, because he *always* makes you smile."

She sucked my finger between her lips and raised her eyebrows.

"Someone wants to be bratty."

A little shrug, and I chuckled.

"Frankie, really, I'm not saying yes. I'm not saying no. But let me ask you something…" I tugged my finger out because the swipe of her tongue was distracting as hell. At her wrinkled nose, I gripped her arms and then slid my hands down to her ass and lifted her up. She wrapped her arms around my neck and met my gaze without any shyness.

This right here was probably my favorite change. The directness that existed between us now. I could tell her anything, and I made damn sure she could say anything to me. We needed that communication. No more misunderstandings. Never again.

"When I said I'd think about it earlier…did you like the idea?"

Lips pursed, she considered me. "I don't want you to be unhappy."

"Not what I asked, Angel."

"But it matters," she countered, and I sighed because sometimes, I had to remember we were as important to her as she was to us. "It matters because no matter how much I might be thrilled by the idea, I can't enjoy it if you're not happy. Worse, if you're uncomfortable."

"Fair," I conceded.

"And I don't want you to push out of your comfort zone because you're feeling sorry for me."

I scowled at her. "Angel, one warning and one warning only. The next time you accuse me of doing anything because I feel sorry for you, I'm going to spank that sweet ass of yours red. Clear?"

"Not hearing a threat there, sir."

Dammit. I couldn't laugh at her, but the dare was right in her eyes. "You know what I mean."

"I do," she admitted, and I groaned.

"What am I going to do with you?"

When she kissed my chin, I smiled. "Whatever you want, I'm hoping."

"And if I decide to see how curious I am about having Coop in the room? Rumor has it he likes to watch."

"Then I'm okay with that."

"And if I decide to try for more? To let him play with you, too?"

She shuddered, and I swore her nipples pebbled tighter. I didn't know if it was the suggestion of me wanting more or the idea of him playing too. Her tongue flicked out to wet her lips. "I'm okay with that too."

"What if I blindfold you and then don't tell you which of us is doing what?"

Her eyes widened, and I swore her pupils dilated. That was an idea she really liked.

"Good to know," I murmured. "Shower, Angel." Because that little shudder had left her shivering. I carried her over and set her in the tub.

"What about you?" She'd gone a little breathless, and my smile widened. That idea rapidly gained merit with me. I liked the idea of teasing her senses and one way to do that was to take away one, but this reaction… I trailed my fingers up her arm, then touched her chin and leaned in to kiss her. She opened up so sweetly to me, and the delicate suck of her mouth against my tongue had my cock pulsing.

"I'm coming in, I promise. But you have to keep your hands to yourself."

She pouted. "The whole point was you are going to be naked in here with me…"

"Oh, Angel. I know what the point was, and I know what you were looking for. But I won fair and square. So my rules apply."

An impatient little huff escaped her, and I nearly ruined the mood by bursting out laughing. She was adorable when she wanted to push it. She was downright irresistible when she challenged the rules by being just this side of a brat. Of course, then she stuck her tongue out at me before she turned away, and the crisp slap of my hand on her ass earned a startled yelp and a laugh. I also didn't miss the way her thighs pressed together.

I stripped and joined her in the shower before she even had her hair soaked and then took over lathering the shampoo into her hair. As I stroked my fingertips against her scalp, she let out a little sigh.

"Archie's not my brother," she whispered. "That didn't happen, right?"

I pressed a kiss to her shoulder. "Angel, everything I know about your mother tells me she lied about something somewhere."

A shudder went through her, and she pressed her hands to the wall. I went from washing her hair to running my hands up and down her back.

"There were four tests, Angel."

"I can't lose him." Those words were so soft, they damn near broke my heart.

"You won't."

"You sound so sure." And she needed that certainty. Good thing I had it in spades.

"He's not going anywhere. He's one of the most stubborn people I've ever met. He can out stubborn you when he puts his mind to it. He can talk himself out of trouble and reshape any situation to make it work. Angel, trust this if you trust nothing else—he *loves* you, and there is nothing he won't do for you. Whatever the hell Standish said to you and whatever the hell your mother told him, that isn't changing a damn thing. We'll figure it out. I promise."

When she sank back against me, I wrapped my arms around her again and held her.

"I'm worried about him," she admitted. "I hated telling him. I hated hearing it."

"I know. Jake's with him, and you know Jake, he's going to be in full-on Pit Bull mode. He won't let anything get near him."

She laughed a little. "He's very protective."

"Yes, he is. And he's more than a little pissed off at how you two have been treated and extremely motivated to make sure they both get back here whole and hearty."

"Are you indulging me?"

"Just bit," I promised and smoothed a hand over her stomach. "Is it helping?"

"A bit."

"Good."

"Ian?"

"Hmm?"

"The idea of you and Coop doing things to me when I can't see you is really hot."

"Good to know." I tweaked her nipple. "Can I go back to bathing you now?"

A husky little laugh escaped. "You're really working at distracting me."

"Oh, I haven't begun to work on you, Angel." The clench of her ass against my cock was a clear sign she understood that promise.

Good.

Valentine's Day

"**F**rankie, what's the matter?" Coop's hands were hot against my icier ones, and the rain spattering me and soaking my hair registered as the honk of a horn pulled my gaze to the street. The familiar yellow SUV had pulled over, blocking a lane of traffic, and Archie and Ian both stared out at me. Jake probably did too, but I couldn't see him.

Another horn sounded, then the car behind them ripped sideways with a squeal of tires to whip around them. It was after five. The traffic was heavier, and they were just stopped on the side of the road. I glanced back at Coop.

"What happened?" He gripped my hands in his, and I swallowed. The sound of slamming car doors stopped the silent words that didn't want to leave my mouth, and then Archie and Ian were both there.

"Babe, what happened?" Archie had an umbrella in hand, and he snapped it open over me and Coop.

Fuck. I stared into his brown eyes, and I swore my heart broke all over again. It couldn't possibly be true.

"Angel." Ian had a hand on my back, and I tore my gaze from Archie to look at Coop and then Ian. Suddenly, Jake slammed out of the SUV and stalked over to us. They were all dressed nicely.

They all smelled great.

Fuck.

Valentine's day.

"Frankie, tell me what the fuck is going on so I can fix it," Archie said and dragged my attention back to him.

I really didn't have the words. "I had a meeting with…" I started to say 'your dad,' but I couldn't push those words out. I couldn't say his name either. "With Mr. Standish…" That sounded even worse. I really couldn't get it out. His expression turned to stone. How the hell did I tell him this?

My silence went on for too long, because Archie thrust the umbrella at Coop.

"I'll fucking kill him."

Chapter Three
ACTIONS SPEAK LOUDER THAN WORDS

COOP

I finished my shower first. No surprise. In the kitchen, I filled a mug with coffee and set the coffeemaker up to do a second pot when we finished the first. While sipping that coffee, I got out the cinnamon rolls from the fridge and popped a couple of containers open and got them in the oven. At least those were fast and easy to make.

They were also comfort food. The cats swarmed around me in search of food, but I was on to them. Bubba had fed them earlier before he woke us up. A yawn cracked my jaw as I went in search of the phone. No messages yet. I didn't think there would be, but always better to check. Bubba padded out into the kitchen, hair damp, and looking way more alert than I felt.

Course, if I'd just had a shower with Frankie, I'd be pretty pumped too. He glanced down at the oven window and nodded before grabbing a mug and filling it. When he didn't automatically fill one for Frankie, I raised my brows.

"She's on the phone with Rach," was all he said, and I nodded. Like me, Bubba had just pulled on sweats. We didn't say anything. The heat in the apartment had been turned up to chase away any lingering damp chill. After a couple swallows of coffee, he focused on me. "She likes the idea."

"She likes a lot of things." I kept it light and conversational, but I also wasn't playing dumb. "If you're not comfortable, it won't work."

"I'm aware," he conceded. He studied his coffee for a moment and then looked at me. "How comfortable are you with following instructions?"

I drained the last of my coffee, then glanced from him to the doorway and finally the stove. There was sixty seconds left on the timer. Nothing like the sense of being in the double Jeopardy round to make me laugh. "Depends on who you ask."

"I'm asking you."

Okay. I met his gaze head on as I stood. "Why? And before you get snappy, there's a reason I want you to spell it out. We're dancing around this, and I was serious earlier when I said if you're not comfortable, then it won't work. So be explicit on what you're asking me, and I'll try not to give you too much shit."

It was the least I could do.

"Also, let's be quick. She's gonna smell these in a minute, and if the coffee doesn't get her out here, those will…"

"You have a point," he agreed, heading to the coffeemaker while I got the cinnamon rolls out. He refilled my cup and his own. There was enough left for Frankie to get one big mug. Neither one of us would touch it until she'd had hers. "I like control," he admitted, never looking at me. "And I don't know that I could ask this with Archie or Jake."

I didn't know if he could either, particularly right now. Though Jake might surprise him. Archie remained a wild card.

"Can I ask how it works with you and Jake?"

I shrugged. "You can ask. We just…go with what works." We hadn't really discussed it beyond being okay with the other being there. Well, that and easing her into the idea of it. "Porn helped."

Bubba coughed and shot me a look.

"What?" The mild outrage on his face amused me. Not as much as the flare of curiosity though. "I know you've watched porn. I was there the first time we all watched it."

And turned it off like five minutes later 'cause Frankie had wandered back in and that was just not a place any of our fourteen-year-old minds needed to go while she was in the room. Not that it hadn't and often, but still, not with her there.

"Look," I continued, not needing him to answer. "We started with the making out. I liked watching her with Jake. He liked watching her with me. It took a little adjustment, not a lot. It's not like we haven't been around each other." Fuck, I'd seen Bubba getting a blowjob, and I damn well knew he'd seen me get more than that. Not that we needed to revisit the memories. "The point is, my primary concern was always Frankie's comfort. It was easy with Jake. And then he introduced her to porn."

Sorry Jake. Hopefully, the bus didn't leave skid marks.

"And it kind of went from there."

Bubba nodded once, and the sound of Frankie's voice neared.

"That said, if you want to experiment, I'm game. You get uncomfortable or need me to leave, say the word."

"Same for you," Bubba said.

Yeah, discomfort wouldn't be my problem, beyond a raging hard-on if I didn't get to play, but hell, for Frankie? I'd try anything once.

"Done."

I'd finished adding the last of the icing to the cinnamon rolls and watched as he poured Frankie's coffee before starting it brewing again.

"Bubba? Just…go with whatever feels natural. I'm easy." But on that note… "Although, if anyone spanks me, it better not be you."

He stared at me a beat, and then the tensions split right down the middle and we cracked up. Frankie arrived at that moment, and I was still laughing, though I had to be careful not to choke on my drool. All warm and flushed from the shower, she padded out in an oversized T-shirt with her long legs on display, and I swore the semi I'd been sporting for most of the morning flared to life.

"Sorry," she murmured as she gave Bubba a hug and kiss, and he passed her coffee over. I carried the big plate of cinnamon rolls to the table along with my cup. As soon as I sat down though, I had a lapful of warm Frankie. "Hey," she greeted me, and I smiled against her lips and curled an arm around her to keep her stable. I hadn't been intending to shove my erection in her face, but having her on my lap made that a moot point.

The shadows in her eyes were still present, but some of the swelling from all the crying she'd done on Friday had finally seemed to ease. No escaping the bruised or haunted look. I didn't often want to inflict violence on others, but I was with Archie on this one. Fuck his dad and her mom.

She cradled the coffee in her hands, and I slid my fingers up to comb through the damp curls. She hadn't dried it fully. "Everything all right with Rach?"

"I don't know," she admitted as she reached for one of the cinnamon rolls. Bubba gave her an approving nod and shot me a relieved look as soon as she bit into one. I'd made a ton just for her, and Bubba seemed to be doing what I was doing—waiting for her to eat.

Our girl, who loved food, hadn't done more than pick at anything the last couple of days. Archie had gotten her to eat the day before, but only because he kept picking up bites on his fork and holding it in front of her until she ate.

Bossy, but effective.

Jake had done the same thing later, going out to pick up a platter of potato skins. Still, not enough by Frankie standards. She pulled apart the cinnamon roll though and offered me a bite with sticky fingers. Nudging my coffee aside, I snagged one of the cinnamon rolls and pulled the still warm goodness apart and held up a bite to her mouth. Her eyes lightened a fraction, and when she opened up, and I pressed the bite in and then took the bite from her fingers at the same time. Only I made sure to suck her fingers in to clean them off.

It was the least I could do. Her pupils dilated, and she grinned before offering me another bite. Challenge accepted. From the corner of my eye, I kept an eye on Bubba, well aware that he was watching us. If he couldn't handle this, then it was a firm no for us to experiment. Then again, he'd seen all of us cuddling and kissing her, and that seemed to be less of an issue.

Still, baby steps.

Frankie sucked on my fingers this time and that pulse went straight to my cock, and she chuckled as she finished the bite before stuffing the rest of the cinnamon roll in my mouth. I'd been expecting it, even as she got the sugar all over my lips. Sliding my free hand into her hair, I tugged her back for a cinnamon and sugar flavored kiss that had her all but squirming and let me know that in no uncertain terms she had on no panties.

Fuck.

Me.

Bubba let out a little grunt of sound as Frankie lifted her head and grinned at me. There was still a bit of icing on her lips, but she turned to Bubba and he leaned over and kissed her, licking her lips clean.

When he leaned back, Frankie let out a little sigh and then recaptured her coffee mug. Running a hand up and down her back, I gave her a minute before I could switch tracks back to the earlier conversation. The flex of her ass against my very rigid dick wasn't helping, but two could play at that game.

"What's up with Rachel? Boy problems?" Was I really asking that? Sure. Why not.

Frankie made a face. "I don't know. She still doesn't want to talk about it. But she said she had a date tonight and I don't think it's with the same person, but then she was really, really vague. I don't know whether to press or to leave it alone."

"What would Rachel do?" Bubba asked.

Frankie and I both looked at him. He had a point. "But she's not me," Frankie said. "And even when she's pushy with me, if I tell her I really don't want to talk about it…she lets it go." She let out a little sigh and reached for her phone. It hadn't made so much as a twitch since she set it on the table, but she checked it anyway.

No messages.

"Okay, what do you do to us when we don't tell you things?" Bubba tried, then winced. I didn't mean to laugh. I swear, I didn't. But the chuckle escaped anyway.

Frankie pinched me, and I deserved that. "I'm getting *better* about calling you on it," she argued, and I agreed.

"Yes you are," I told her, and Bubba rubbed a hand over his face.

"Yes, Angel, you are. We're all getting better at this talking thing."

You'd think it was the one skill we'd mastered, but no, we had a learning curve, myself included. "I'll talk to her again," Frankie said finally. "But maybe I should save all the drama here for the next conversation."

"You haven't told her yet?" I wasn't fishing, not specifically, but Rachel had been enormously good for Frankie.

"No, I haven't talked to anyone but you guys." Some of the lightness in the air evaporated, and Bubba reached over to slide a hand over her leg, even as I hugged her. "Sorry," she murmured.

"Nothing to be sorry about," I said in nearly the same breath as Bubba released, "Angel, you don't have to be sorry."

She made a face and then wiggled a little—kind of killing me there—so she could look at both Bubba and me.

"You're both trying to distract me to keep me from worrying or obsessing or going to find Maddy and pummeling her."

That last one was new. "I'll help with the Maddy thing," I offered.

Bubba shook his head but surprised me when he said, "Me too."

A tremulous smile curved her lips. "You guys would, wouldn't you?"

"Yes." Not even a question. For either of us.

"Try to eat a little more?" Bubba nudged at her as he took her cup and mine to refill them. I tugged her a little closer and tucked my chin against her shoulder.

I loved the way she melted into me and leaned there like she needed me as much as I needed to be there for her. I hated everything about this situation, except us. The part with the five of us was good, and that wasn't changing.

"I'm scared," she said so softly, I thought I'd misheard at first. But she leaned her head back and looked at me. "I want to go back to Thursday. Or even Friday morning. Friday morning was good."

"Friday morning was great. And this sucked," I agreed with her. "But you're not alone. You remember that, right?"

She gave me a crooked smile. "Yeah I do. I just…"

"We know, Angel. Us too." Bubba set the coffee on the table. "And if you're still up for playing, then you need to eat."

I watched her as she glanced at him. The flare of hope on her face was hard to miss. But I still didn't want him pushing something he didn't want to or wasn't ready to deal with yet. "Are you sure?"

"Well, I'm positive nothing will happen without you eating at least one more cinnamon roll. Then I think we can work on making you hungry for real food later."

Man, I really hoped he was up for this, or I was going to get really intimate with my hand in the not too far distant future. We actually got her to eat two more cinnamon rolls, and she finished all of the second cup of coffee before all of our phones buzzed.

One word.

Landed.

From Jake.

She tensed against me, and Bubba shot me a questioning look. It wasn't hard to read it. Was I in or was I out? Because we had no idea how long it would take Archie to get to his mother's place and to deal with that situation.

Could I follow orders? What the hell, you only lived once, right?

I nodded.

He exhaled, and then his whole demeanor seemed to settle. Any sign of questioning or hesitation vanished. Fucking impressive if you asked me.

"Angel," he said, snaring her attention from the phone. "Give me the phone for now and then go into the bedroom and wait for us."

He hadn't been kidding about the orders.

With only a little reluctance, she handed him her phone. He caught her hand and squeezed it after she passed it to him.

"I'll make sure we have it," he promised. "You won't miss a word from them."

Relief rippled across her face, and she bent to give him a kiss before she glanced over her shoulder at me and winked.

Then she sauntered out of the kitchen.

"And, Angel," Bubba called. "Shirt off and eyes closed."

"Yes, sir," she answered, and I swore my jaw dropped. I managed to pop it closed before Bubba focused on me.

"Still in?" he asked in a quiet voice.

"Wild horses couldn't keep me away." That was probably one of the hottest things I'd ever heard. Okay, definitely in the top ten. "Just tell me where you want me."

"I'm blindfolding her," he murmured as he stood and drained his coffee. I followed suit. "I'm not sure I'm up for you touching her while I'm there, but I figure we'll go one step at a time. But once we're in there, not a word." Then he paused. "Not a single word. She likes the idea of not knowing which of us is touching her."

"Done. Anything else I need to know?"

"She likes to be spanked." And tied up apparently, but I wasn't going to bring that up. For the moment. "And she's still learning what she likes, so…we talk about new stuff first. So if you do touch, nothing outside of what you've done before."

"I can handle that."

"And, Coop? Thanks for understanding that this isn't easy for me and for not being a dick about it."

"Nah, man. We have enough problems, this is never going to be one. You want to test the waters, we test the waters. I'm good if you are."

There wasn't much more to say after that, and he led the way down the hall. The cats had scattered at some point. I caught sight of Tory darting into the old master suite and vanishing under one of the beds. Bubba paused in the doorway to her room, so I hung back a second until he beckoned me forward with a curl of his fingers.

Oh. Fuck. I got why he had to stop.

She sat on her knees in the middle of the bed, hands loose on her thighs with her palms up and her eyes closed. The wintry sunlight filtering through the blinds highlighted her fading tan from the summer, and damn, she was beautiful.

With a jerk of his head, Bubba motioned me into the room, so I headed in and started over to the desk. I figured if he wanted the space, I'd give it to them. Besides, I kind of wanted to know where this was going.

I leaned against the desk, arms folded, as goosebumps rippled over Frankie's skin. Bubba knelt on the bed behind her and used a bandana to cover her eyes and tied it gently behind her head. Then he leaned forward and pressed a kiss to her shoulder. Her nipples went stiff and peaked, and I swore my cock pulsed. Not saying a word, he trailed his fingers up and down her spine, then followed the motion with his lips.

Tracking Frankie's expression though held me riveted. The flush on her cheeks had deepened, and it stretched down her neck to her chest. She let out the softest of groans, and I shifted, doing my best to stay quiet, but my whole dick twitched at that sound.

Bubba had moved to her ass, and he was still petting and kissing, but I wasn't the only one getting turned on. Each time she started to squirm, she gave me a flash of her pussy, and it was deep pink, flushed, and very damp. Sweat dotted my brow and the back of my neck. Even the fact I was shirtless didn't seem to cool me off.

Her head tilted back, lips parted, as another sound escaped her. Another captivating part of being with Frankie was every reaction she had was so open and visceral. She guarded nothing. Held nothing back. And even those nights when I had to listen to someone else getting her off, I enjoyed the hell out of her pleasure.

Bubba had his hands on her breasts, massaging them, and each time he circled her nipples, he'd pause to squeeze them. Wrapped completely around her, he buried his face in her throat, licking and nipping, but the way he framed her put her on display. When he slid his hands down to her thighs and eased them apart, I was torn between staring at her nipples and where he was going next.

One of my hands flexed, and my palms itched to ease some of the strain in my dick. There was no way to hide the tent in the sweatpants now, especially not with Frankie's breath coming in short, hot pants. A cry fell from her lips, and I glanced down as he slid his hand between her thighs and speared two fingers into her. The rocking of her hips had me wanting to surge forward, but I stayed right where I was.

The whole point here was two-fold—giving Frankie pleasure and seeing if Bubba could handle it. God, my balls hurt watching this. They hurt in the best way. He slid his free arm up to catch her chin with his fingers and tilted her face. All at once, she stiffened as a sharper cry broke forth, and he kissed the sound right off her lips, chasing it with his tongue. Probably the same way I did. I wanted to swallow every bit of her pleasure.

Finally, he eased his fingers from her and spread her wide before he glanced over at me. The indecision on his face was utterly absent as he gave her pussy the lightest of smacks, then nodded to me and then down at her.

Fuck man, he did not have to invite me twice. I crossed the room in two strides and went to my knees, even as he lifted her and spread her thighs wider, cradling her against him, and I darted my tongue along her slick labia. A shout came from above, but I just canted my gaze up to where she and Bubba kissed with ferocity as I swirled my tongue through her soft folds and almost groaned at the sweet muskiness. I fucking loved how she tasted.

As much as I wanted to savor, my cock hurt and I wanted to make her come again. I dipped my tongue into her, keeping her thighs apart with my hands, then up to her clit. The swollen little nubbin strained at the first brush of my tongue, and a whimper ripped free of her. When I locked my lips around her clit and thrummed it with a combination of humming and tongue strikes, her hips bucked like mad and her cries grew more desperate. Another glance up, and I found Bubba had started tweaking her nipples in time with her gasps, and I had the perfect view of her falling absolutely apart.

Another few licks, and I wiped my cheeks against the covers. Frankie looked wrecked and flushed, and then Bubba shifted her again, and at this angle, I couldn't miss the way he lifted her leg and then pushed himself up into her. His sweats had vanished, and the first push of him up into her had her crying out all over again. Tears slid out from beneath the bandana, but she let out a stream of curses that almost made me laugh.

"Holy fuck, fuck, fuck…" It was beautiful and hilarious and perfect. Then she added, "Oh fuck, thank you…oh… Can I suck you? Can I please, Ian? Can I? I know you said quiet…oh…"

Frankie rarely asked for what she wanted, and fuck, I wanted to give it to her, but Bubba slowed his thrusting to look past her shoulder to me and then down at her. He pressed a kiss to her ear and then rolled them so they were on their sides. Snagging a pillow, he eased it below her head before he pushed her leg higher, bracing it out of his way for access, and then he looked at me.

He'd already let me play way more than I expected, but he just smiled faintly and then nodded to her.

Licking her lips, Frankie panted as Bubba started to thrust again. Holy shit? Fine, I shoved the sweats down and moved to kneel at her face. It wasn't going to take me long, I was fucking dying to come. A couple of strokes, and I'd be a goner. As it was, I fisted myself so I didn't just come all over her face.

She'd made a specific request about facials—as in never. I intended to honor that request. The moment I tapped my dick against her lips though, she smiled with such abandon, my whole heart constricted, and another cry escaped her as she opened up and wrapped her mouth around my cock.

Holy fuck.

Hot, wet heat closed around me, and I had to remember to be easy, to not choke her. I didn't brag about my dick, but I knew exactly how big it was. She didn't give me much choice as she half-swallowed me right toward her throat. The hot suction had all the liquid heat gathering in my balls.

Fuck. Fuck. Fuck.

When had she gotten so good at this? I wasn't sure I could keep quiet as I began to rock my hips in time to the rhythm she set, fisting her hair so I could help guide her. I swore she took more and more of me. The half-choking noises made me want to pull back, but she reached a hand up to my thigh and then fisted me as she worked me over, and I forgot how to think as everything drained down my spine.

Between the liquid furnace of her mouth and the slap of Bubba pushing into her and her own groans, I was a goner. I couldn't tell you who came first, but I tried to tug her hair twice to warn her, and then she pulled me deep and swallowed every drop.

Boneless, I drew back as she shuddered and cried out. Bubba had his hand on her clit, and I leaned down to kiss a nipple and suck on it until she was sobbing with her orgasm. When Bubba collapsed on her far side, I dropped down to stare at the ceiling. Then Frankie lifted a hand toward the blindfold.

Tugging it off, Bubba ran a hand down her side and then studied her face. The smile she wore was absolutely beautiful, and then she glanced over at me and the warmth in her eyes leapt.

Fuck yeah.

I'd call that a successful experiment.

Valentine's Day

"**A**rchie," I squeezed out before he took two steps away. The pop of the rain hitting the umbrella seemed so loud, despite the hum of passing cars, the occasional blare of a horn, and what might be some alarm in the distance. It all seemed to fade to this kind of blur of white noise. "He wanted to talk to me…about something they've wanted to tell me since that awful dinner."

"What?" He took a step back to me, his dark hair soaked, droplets of water running down his face. Kind of like tears.

No, I really couldn't think about tears right now. Coop still held my hand, and I flexed my fingers around his and then gripped for all I was worth. He returned the squeeze, not pulling away. He'd held my hand the same way the first time I'd been terrified when we'd had to stand up on a stage and do a presentation. I'd nearly thrown up behind the curtain while we'd waited, but he'd gripped my hand and hadn't let go.

When we walked out there, he'd held my hand the whole way, and he didn't care about the teasing we got for it. I knew he wouldn't let go.

"He said he was my father."

"What?" A frown tightened his whole expression as he stepped in closer to me. At least out of the rain, Jake and Ian huddled in closer, and I dug my nails into Coop's hand. I had to be leaving little divots in his skin, but he didn't flinch.

The whole story spilled out of me. I swore I was going to throw up with every single word, but they didn't move. They didn't interrupt. Not once did Archie look away. It hurt so bad to tell him this. It just hurt period.

When I got to the part about their affair, Archie snorted and then shook his head. "Babe…"

"I know," I told him. "I know it sounds like absolute bullshit, but he believes it. And for some fucked up reason, he says I'm his kid." I wouldn't take that to the next step. "The tests and now this…"

He shook his head slowly, then cupped my face. "You're not my sister. I don't care what bag of shit that…" He blew out a breath. "Sorry, babe, those bastards are selling. But you're not my sister. And I'm going with my first call on this…" He kissed me hard and then pivoted to stalk away. "I'm going to fucking kill him."

He was serious.

I would have followed, but Coop dragged me back, hand still in mine, as Ian and Jake took off after Archie.

"Coop…"

"They'll get him," he promised me and kept me close. His hand was still locked in mine. "We got you both."

Chapter Four
ANOTHER RED-LETTER DAY

JAKE

The flight back, Archie said almost nothing. I couldn't blame him. Not after that scene with his mother. I had my issues with Dad. Some days, I thought he was a real dick for choosing Klara over his kids, over Mom. But even at his worst? Yeah, I never thought he didn't love us. Just—fuck. I glanced over at Archie, who stared at his phone, reading something with the kind of intensity you reserved for a super villain you were planning on dismembering.

A glance at his screen had me looking away. He was messaging Frankie, so I'd leave him in peace.

"It's fine," he said quietly next to me, and I glanced at him. We were the only two in first class on this flight, which was fucking weird. But it also afforded us a measure of privacy, and he probably needed it. "She's just checking on me. I told her we needed to do a DNA test ourselves, and Jeremy's arranging something with a private clinic so we can rush the fucking results. It would be easier, but we're the same blood type."

"What can I do?"

"We land in…" he began, then paused to check something on the phone before continuing, "In about thirty minutes. I told Bubba and Coop to keep her busy and distracted." With a grimace, he motioned to his phone. "Currently, she's worrying about me."

"And you're worrying about her, so lay off on trying to wrap her up in too much soft cotton. She wants to be there for you every bit as much as you want to be there for her." Yes, I totally got the irony of me telling him to back off on the overprotective attitude. The snort he favored me with pointed out his feelings on the same.

"Bubba's gonna take her to the studio to work on practicing with her guitar and him on piano. Coop's gonna set up shop at the apartment and do some cleaning. Apparently, I should hire a maid because she started stress cleaning the bathrooms." Archie shook his head, and I didn't laugh, tempting as it was.

"She does that when she starts to feel out of control."

"Yeah well, we're going to fix that. I've got a car picking us up, and I know where Edward is. I plan to pay him a visit." He cut a look at me. "You in?"

This was a bad idea. "Fuck yeah, I'm in. What do you need me to do?"

The car took us from the airport to some country club. Considering it was still overcast but not raining, I guessed I shouldn't be surprised his father was at the golf course. Not that I had a lot of experience with them. My family didn't run in these circles, and with the exception of Arch, I wasn't finding all that much attractive about them.

"Wait for us," Archie instructed the driver as he pulled into the portico at the club. "We'll be thirty minutes max."

The man nodded, but Archie didn't even wait for the response. I got it. He had a goal and a target. I was right after him. At the front doors, a man stepped forward to greet us and give us the stink eye.

I guessed jeans and T-shirts weren't appropriate attire? I didn't really give a fuck. Archie waved him off. "We're not eating, just heading out to the greens."

"Mr. Standish," the man said, his tone chiding and prim. He started to block us, and I cracked my knuckles. That earned me a startled look. "If you'd like us to send word to your father, you could wait in the club or out here, until he comes in."

"I absolutely could," Archie told him in the most frigid tone possible. "And if that was what I wanted to do, I would have said as much. Now do us both a favor, get out of my way and don't make me put in a word to the club director about you hampering a member."

I swallowed a smirk, but it was hard. Archie didn't flinch as he stared at the man. The guy blinked first, then nodded and backed up a step. "Of course, sir." The last word was almost an afterthought, but I'd give the guy props. Archie wasn't in the mood, and he could read the room or at least the situation.

Archie flicked me a glance, and I nodded. I had his back. He led the way, and we headed through the club and out a pair of back doors. Outside, a fine mist had begun falling. I was over this shit. At least New York had snow, even if it had been cold enough to freeze my balls off. He slid right behind the wheel of a waiting golf cart. Apparently, they queued these fuckers up. My ass barely touched the passenger seat before we were off.

At my laugh, Archie shot me a look. "Go ahead," he muttered. "Say it."

"Fucking rich people, man," I told him, and he scoffed but didn't dispute it. Still, I braced my foot against the dash as he followed the path through the place like he knew where he was going. "How often have you been here?"

"A few times," he commented. "Mostly with Grandpa, offered to bring Frankie here with him. So she could play real golf. She actually said yes."

"Of course she did," I told him. "She loves mini-golf."

He grimaced, then laughed for real. "I'm going to buy her a fucking mini-golf place. Or maybe build her one of her own."

"Yeah, that might be taking 'fucking rich people' too far."

"Ha." But he didn't disagree with me.

We passed a few others still golfing, despite the drizzle. Apparently, very little stopped a real golfer. I'd stick to football. Maybe some hoops with the guys. A run.

"You ever play?" Archie asked after a couple of minutes.

"Plenty of mini-golf, none of this."

"You should learn," he said, and I didn't roll my eyes. "If you want. I could teach you when I teach Frankie. It's not so bad, with the right people."

Fuck me. "Sounds like fun."

"It's not a dental procedure."

"Fuck off," I told him with a laugh. "You want someone to go with, I'll give it a shot. Surprised you're not asking Coop."

That got a reaction. "He sucks."

"Eh…he fucks off a lot. He's better than he pretends, but he's not as competitive as the rest of us and it's easier for him to play that part up." It kept the rest of us even, especially since we could all be competitive as fuck.

"I'll take your word for it. We'll make a day of it. The five of us."

Okay, maybe Arch needed to make plans like this, and I got it. "Can't we do something like paintball?" Our Valentine's Day plans had been utterly obliterated after Frankie delivered that dick's bombshell and keeping her and Archie in one piece had become the evening's priority.

"We haven't done that in…"

"Years, exactly."

"I can work with that," he agreed, and I laughed. "I'll save golf for Frankie."

The smile that earned was fleeting. Soon, we came over a hill, and there was Standish Sr., lining up his shot. Archie hit the horn on the golf cart just as he went for the swing. Petty as fuck, but it made me laugh when the older man sent the ball careening off in what appeared to be the wrong direction. He and the pair with him turned to look at us as Archie drove straight up to their cart and parked behind it.

He was out of the seat and halfway to his father before I could follow. Yeah, this had bad plan written all over it. I scanned the other men standing with Edward Archibald Standish Jr., and I wasn't impressed. Both were older, one was paunchy and the other looked flushed, despite the chilly air and damp rain. I could take them.

"Archie," his father said in a warning tone.

"You better tell your buddies to play on or head back for a drink. You're busy." Every syllable carried an element of menace I'd never heard from Archie. Not this icy anger. His rage at Mitch had been white hot, and I'd been right there with him. As it was, I kept one eye on the other men and one on the older Standish. At the moment, I'd be happy to lay someone out. The nervous energy rolling off Arch made me itch for a good fight.

But I also didn't want to get either of us arrested. Not today. Not if it would mean Frankie and the guys had to come and get us. She didn't need the stress and fuck knew Archie didn't.

"Gentlemen," the older man called. "If you'll excuse us." He didn't offer a reason, and they didn't ask for one. Instead, they just nodded, waved, and moved on with their bags of golf clubs while "Eddie" slid his club back into his bag before he turned to face Archie. That right cross landed beautifully, and the older man staggered back a couple of steps.

"You just couldn't stop yourself from trying to fuck up my life and hers, could you?"

"Archie," Eddie said, shooting me a look, but I planted myself where I had Archie's back and ignored the drizzle. A trickle of blood escaped from his nose. "I understand you might be upset…"

"Might be?" Archie snorted. "I *might* be upset that you told my girlfriend you think she's my sister?"

The scorn in his tone was razor sharp and perfect. I swore I could see the skin he stripped right off the older man. As it was, "Eddie" paled and dropped his hand from his face as he stared at Archie. "What do you mean girlfriend? She's not dating anyone."

"According to whom? The lying cunt you've been fucking?" Every word rolling out of him carried a lash of anger and heat, but I'd bet money as much as he meant every word, he delivered them with purpose. "Or maybe in your own interfering and stalking ways, you hired someone to investigate? 'Cause let me tell you, if you did, you should get a refund. She's been my girlfriend for months, and I've loved her for a lot longer."

I swore the man looked ill.

Holy shit, he really hadn't known.

I didn't know whether to laugh or to spit.

"Wait," Archie said with a snap of his fingers. "I forgot, for you to know anything about my life, you'd have to give a fuck. We both know you couldn't be bothered. Until today, I always thought that was my fault."

"No," his father said slowly, though I loathed even calling him that. I couldn't help it. I studied him. The pallor of his face, the way his eyes widened, even the way he ignored the blood trickling from his nose. Nothing about him was like Frankie at all. There was a surface resemblance to Archie, but the guy lacked his directness or the ease of his charm. "It's never been your fault. But you can't date Frankie."

"She's not my sister."

"I understand this might be…"

"If you say difficult, I will take one of those clubs and beat the fuck out of you with it." The cold violence in that threat had the older man straightening and taking a step back. He believed Archie. Good. Because I didn't doubt that he would. "I don't care what you think you know. Tell me what that lying fucking cunt told you. I've seen the four tests. Only one is positive, and it doesn't have your name on it."

Expression rippling, Eddie frowned. "There were only two tests, and before you challenge that, yes, I was aware of Maddy's affairs at the time. It was why I had the affair with your mother."

"I really couldn't care less where you stuck your dick. I want to know exactly what she told you and what evidence she gave you that Frankie is yours, 'cause while you're not a fucking prize for a parent, I find it hard to believe that a selfish, narcissistic bitch like her wouldn't have come after you sooner."

Sighing, the older man pulled a fucking handkerchief out of his pocket and dabbed at his bloodied nose. "Archie, I understand you're upset. While I appreciate you may not care for Maddy, could you at least show her some respect?"

I couldn't help it, I snorted aloud, and that earned me a baleful look from his dad. Yeah, I met him stare for stare. I couldn't care less. "You want respect, you earn it," I told him flatly. "She's an abusive, neglectful, selfish bitch." That was about as kindly as I could put it.

"What he said," Archie agreed with a nod toward me. "What did she say to you?"

Seriously, I couldn't read the man's expression as he fixed a look on his son. "She asked for a sample so she could run the test. Largely because I needed proof. She wasn't certain about who the father was, she hasn't been."

Yeah, that didn't surprise me.

"To be fair," he continued, not that I had any fucking interest in being fair. "Maddy had a rather severe falling out with her family after our engagement collapsed and I married your mother. The ceremony was quick and efficient, it was important to your grandparents that you were born with our name."

Wow. My dad was looking better and better by the minute. What a douche.

"And before you decide that I'm a terrible person, I did want to be your father. I just didn't know how. I gave up the woman I loved for you." He actually looked aggrieved. "There's no pleasant way of saying this, and it's not a conversation we should ever have to have."

"No shit," Archie said. "But you're having it because I want answers, and at the bare minimum, you owe me this. Get to the point about the cunt's story."

"Call her that again—"

"And you'll what?" Archie dared him. "Please, throw a swing. I made you a promise, and I have every intention of keeping it."

We weren't alone out here, another golf cart had pulled up behind ours, so I just said, "We need to move this along."

Both men broke their stare-off to glance at me and then behind me. The others were still too far away to hear, but that didn't mean they were going to stay there.

"I broke her heart," Eddie said finally. "We were young and foolish and made bad choices, but we always chose each other until I had no choice other than Muriel. Afterward, I tried to keep her, to get her to stay, because I would have paid the penalty of divorcing your mother earlier *after* you were born. But she didn't want to wait that long, and eventually…eventually, she left. I tried my best."

Wow.

Yep. My dad was definitely looking better that this shit stain.

"Needless to say, she moved and changed her name, and I lost track of her. I never gave up on finding her, but her parents would have nothing to do with me and your grandfather was no help. When we moved here and it turned out you'd met her daughter—a child I wasn't even aware she'd had—it seemed like kismet."

The snort of derision from Archie actually made me wince. How the fuck was he putting himself through this and not beating the man with a club, I had no idea.

Well, that wasn't true. Of course I knew.

Frankie.

"At first, she still didn't want anything to do with me, but I made arrangements to take over the company she worked for."

Just when you thought it couldn't get any stranger…

"And while you may not think she cares, all she ever talked about was her daughter and how proud of Frankie she was. How Frankie would get to do all the things she never did. How she was cut off from her parents because she wouldn't have an abortion or be forced into a marriage she didn't want." He grimaced. "Unlike me, she stuck to her principles."

Did he really believe that?

"Get to the point," Archie urged him.

"We grew closer again. I know you don't like this and you don't want to believe it, but I care about her. I never stopped. Your mother agreed to the divorce because she was as tired of our sham of a marriage as I was. Both of us did wrong by you, I can admit that. Frankie even called me on being a terrible father."

Of course she did.

"But Maddy did the tests. She showed me the results. Frankie's my daughter—"

"Yeah, did those results have your name on them?" Archie just kept plowing through. "Did you get it independently verified? Did you bring in a neutral party to oversee it? Someone with no skin in the game, or did you just take her word for it?"

"Why would she lie to me? Why now?" his father challenged. "Why would she wait all this time when she could have been comfortable? I would have more than provided for them. Been there…even if…"

"Even if you were stuck with me. I get it. I'd pick Frankie over me in a heartbeat. But I'm betting she never came after you because she had no idea. Maybe there's a chance you're the father, but that's a one in four based on what I have, and I'll take those odds."

"Archie…"

"Don't," he said. "But I'd advise you to sort your shit out before she fleeces you for everything. Then again, you two deserve each other. Stay away from my girlfriend."

"She's your—"

"You heard me," Archie cut him off. "She doesn't want anything to do with you either. So you stay away from her, and trust me, we will be watching. You're going to make arrangements to get her out of that internship with full credit. Then you're going to stay as far the fuck away from her as possible. Muriel moved to New York. Not Paris. Shocked? Maybe not. Who cares? You could go to London or to South Africa or to hell, but what you won't do is go near her again."

With that, he turned to me and started walking. Edward stared at him for a beat, then said, "What if you're wrong? What if Maddy isn't lying, Archie? What then?"

"It won't matter," Archie said without slowing. "I'm not wrong. She's not my sister."

I let him pass me and kept an eye on his so-called father, letting Archie get some distance before I followed. Once back in the cart, he turned it and accelerated away like we were in a sports car. We were both damp, and I raked a hand through my wet hair.

He was dead silent all the way back up to where we picked up the golf cart, and as we walked through the club and back out the front to where the car waited for us. Once inside it, he closed the divider to the driver and slumped back in his seat.

It was already late afternoon, the weather outside looked like it wasn't going to improve anytime soon, and what light was left in the day would be gone before we made it all the way home. Exhaustion crawled through me, but I sucked it up. Today was not about me.

"Do you believe him?" Archie asked into the silence.

"I don't know him, Arch. What I know about him says he's a selfish jackass. So...does it matter what he thinks?"

Archie sighed. "No. But he wants Frankie to be his kid, you can see it all over his face."

"We love her and we know she's awesome, he's just a dick who wants to put his stamp of ownership on her. But I don't think it has anything to do with either of you." It had everything to do with her mother.

"Because she left him. She was the one who got away."

I shrugged. "Or maybe he loves her as much as someone like him is capable of. I don't see the appeal and I don't want to try. What I want to know is what you want to know. So that you can put this behind both of you."

That, and I wanted to knock his fucking teeth out.

I dug my phone out and checked it. No messages. I debated whether to send something. "Can I do anything?"

"You've been doing it all day, Jake. I'll be fine as soon as we have answers."

"You're going to be fine as soon as you see her."

He didn't argue.

I sent the message to let them all know we'd be at the apartment soon. My phone lit up with a message from Frankie almost immediately.

Frankie

Is he okay?

Me

No. But he will be when he gets there.

I could lie to her I suppose. A part of me wanted to, but he wasn't okay. Archie had pretty much cut himself all the way down to the bone today to get answers for both of them. She needed to know that, and he needed to let her help.

We all did.

Frankie

I'm here. Thank you for going with him.
For looking after him.

Me

Don't have to thank me, Baby Girl. He's family.

She sent me a kiss emoji, and I smiled.

Archie's phone buzzed next, and some of the darkness in his expression eased as he glanced at it. I knew exactly who was texting him.

She was waiting for us when we pulled in, and she was right there as soon as he got out of the car. I caught Coop's gaze as Archie scooped her up close, and they held on so tight. At his questioning look, I shook my head.

We still had questions.

Too many of them.

Now we just had to get answers.

Chapter Five
I DON'T WANT TO GET OVER YOU

FRANKIE

Waking up before Archie, I had a few seconds to just stare at his sleeping face and savor the soft sound of his breathing before reality crept back in. Those few seconds were the most peaceful I'd had in the last forty-eight plus hours since Mr. Standish dropped that bomb on me. Not that I hadn't escaped with Ian and Coop or been comforted by all of them, but that knowledge was always there, preying at the back of my mind like one of those slasher movie monsters that gave me nightmares.

The guys had left us alone the night before after dinner. They'd all gone home rather than stay in the other room. They wanted to give us privacy and comfort, but they'd all promised to check on us today and made us promise to check in with them. Archie hadn't said much as they left, and Jake whispered it had been a long day and to give him room.

When they were gone, I curled up in his lap and just held him. We didn't talk. Well, not much beyond what we'd discussed earlier. Neither of us were going to school today because we were going to get a DNA test of our own. Jeremy and Archie had made all the arrangements. I wasn't sure how long it would take to get the results, and I hadn't pressed Archie for answers.

He'd been on edge since Valentine's when I thought he was really serious about killing his father. The guys had all but wrestled him into the car, and Jake put me between Archie and Coop. It seemed to settle him when I was there. Coop hadn't let go of my hand though, he'd let me dig my nails in while I leaned on Archie's shoulder. It killed me to tell him.

Worse, it killed all our plans, ruining our first Valentine's. They hadn't cared, but I did. Sure, it seemed like a small thing in light of the rest, but we were gonna spend it all together. The five of us. It was supposed to be fun and light and loving and maybe even goofy, but I would have been with them, and then it was all just…broken. The guys were upset. Archie was hurting. And I had no idea how to fix it.

Tracing my fingers over his sleeping face gently, I carefully brushed the hair away from his forehead. He'd looked so damn tired when they got back from New York. He wouldn't tell me much about Muriel. "She doesn't know," was all he'd said, a certainty in his voice. "Grandpa hasn't answered my messages yet. But he will."

It wasn't the certainty that worried me, it was the hope in his voice. The hope that told me more than anything how scared this whole thing had left him. Who was I kidding? I couldn't accept that he was my brother. The thought just didn't compute. He was Archie. He was *my* Archie. My first time, my first…my first a lot of things.

Even asleep, he looked tired. The shadows beneath his eyes worried me. The hand on my hip tightened as his lashes fluttered. I kept stroking his scalp gently as he blinked sleepily at me. The lazy moment didn't last long, scant seconds before reality crashed in on him too. His fingers dug in but it didn't hurt, and his gaze clung to mine.

"Hi," I whispered, even if we weren't going to wake anyone up. I didn't want to disrupt the moment any more than it already had been.

"Hey," he answered in a low, sleep-roughened voice. He slid the hand on my hip upward to cup my face, and then he leaned in to brush a kiss. It was light. Barely there. While I might be aware of morning breath, I didn't care. The ache in my chest unfolded with the feather light touch. The moment I fisted his hair though, he dragged me forward and his kiss was like a drug—the drug my system needed.

The first stroke of his tongue against mine, and I was wrapping my arms around him. He tumbled me right onto my back, one leg slotting between mine as I curled a leg over him. I craved him like I craved my next breath. The connection between us seemed to sizzle to life, and then he was all lips and tongue and teeth. He sucked the air from my lungs and gave it back.

Tears burned in my eyes, even as I clung to him desperately. I don't know when the first sob broke, but he kissed the tears from my cheeks and then buried his face against my hair as he crushed me to him. "It's going to be okay," he swore. "I mean it, it's going to be fine."

The fine tremors shaking me had me holding on tighter.

"I'm going to make it fine," he promised. "Trust me? Please?"

That 'please' killed me, and I tugged at him so he would lift up and meet my gaze. "Of course, I trust you. That's never the question. I love you, Archie." None of this was his fault. None of this was *our* fault.

He exhaled, then pressed his forehead to mine. "I'm not giving up on us. I told you that before, and I meant it. I'm never giving up on us. This is just… another bump in the road."

"It's a little more than a bump." But that said… "But we're not letting them define us." That was something else he'd told me months ago when I first found out about Maddy and Eddie. "I don't regret us, Archie. I could never."

When he crushed me to him this time, he was the one who was shaking, and I held him as tightly as he held me. We probably left bruises on each other, but I didn't care. Rain lashed at the windows. February had turned into a damp, drab month, as though the weather seemed aware of our gloom.

Gradually, he pulled back and then pressed another gentle kiss to my lips. "Go shower," he told me. "I'll feed the cats and get the coffee started."

"When do we have to…"

"We have a couple of hours."

"Okay, I'll shower in a little bit then, and we can make breakfast together."

His grin was real. "How about I make coffee and you make breakfast?"

My chuckle might have been weak, but it was also genuine. "You're never going to master it if you don't at least try."

"Can I please be excused from potentially poisoning my girlfriend today?" He shot me a pair of puppy dog eyes, and I laughed.

"Fine. You're off the hook. I'll cook, you make coffee."

"Yes, you are the best." After another promising kiss, he nuzzled his nose to mine. "And I need to brush my teeth." One more nip of my lower lip, and he was up and out of the room.

I stared after him for a moment as I flopped back against the pillows. We could do this. It was going to be fine. Maddy lied.

A lot.

I repeated the mantra in my head before rolling out and straightening the sheets. Our phones were side by side on the nightstand, both plugged into chargers. My screen lit up with messages.

The guys. Rachel.

I sent the guys good morning replies and that I was fine. I'd check in with them later. To Rachel, I promised to fill her in later this week. She'd figured out something was going on and had been getting a little snippy that I wasn't telling her.

Me

You tell me yours and I'll tell you mine.

I could practically hear the huff in her answer of *fine, I'll wait*. After sending a couple of kissy-faced emojis in response, her middle finger answer made me grin. There was a message from Marsha about work, but it was just a possible schedule change. So I'd call her later and see what was up. I met Archie in the hall, and he grinned before giving me another kiss, this one minty fresh and sweet as he ran his hands up and down my sides.

Fuck, I was going to be a puddle before I even made it to the bathroom. "Coffee," I ordered as I gave him a shove away from me. Tiddles yowled at that moment, and we both grinned.

"I'll feed your pussy," he teased, and I groaned, but at least he was chuckling. It wasn't until after I'd brushed my own teeth that I caught the scent of brewing coffee and checked the last couple of messages on my phone.

Maddy.

I stared at her name and sighed. I debated just deleting the messages without looking at them. Then I frowned. Really, what the fuck could she possibly say to me *now*? I was done running from her.

MyBitch Mother

Your father told me he spoke to you. I thought I would have heard from you by now. I'm sure you have questions. Call me.

I snorted.

The second message actually made my blood boil though.

MyBitch Mother

I understand that your feelings may be complicated because Archie is your friend, but you can't take one boy's version of the story as gospel.

Lips pursed, I glared at the wording.
Yeah. Fuck it.

Bitch.

I stared at the message for a moment and corrected the spelling and typos. I wanted it perfectly clear with good punctuation. It didn't matter that I was shaking with rage. She didn't need to know she could get to me.

After hesitating a beat, I added one more line.

Then I hit send.

I glanced up to find Archie leaning against the wall next to the opening to the living room. His arms were folded over his bare chest, and his pajama bottoms hung low at the waist. It was the concern in his eyes though that drew me. "You okay, babe?"

"Just Maddy." And I held my phone out to him as I closed the gap between us. I rubbed his shoulder. "I'm going to grab coffee and get food started."

He took the phone, then caught my hand against his shoulder. "Are you okay?" The concern in his eyes darkened them, just like Friday in the rain when he'd been so worried about me.

"I hate her," I told him. "She ruins everything. She wants to ruin this, and

I bet she doesn't even know this exists." Or maybe she did and she didn't care. I gave a little shrug. "She really doesn't care about anything that isn't about her. That part sucks."

"She doesn't deserve you, babe. Not one fucking tear for her. For you? Yes, because fuck knows you were short-changed. But she doesn't deserve a goddamn thing from you." The savage tone and hard look in his eyes made me bleed. For him. For me.

For us.

"None of them deserve *us*," I told him. "I don't know what crazy pills they took. But they don't deserve you either. Your parents. Mine. None of them."

"Too damn right," he agreed. "After our appointment, I'm taking you out to a fancy fucking lunch and spoiling you like I didn't get to do on Friday. We'll make it up to the guys later. Then we're going shopping."

"We are?"

"Yeah. Prom is coming, and I want to get you a dress…my treat."

"Archie…"

He pressed two fingers to my lips. "My treat. I want you to get whatever you want. Silks, fancy, comfortable, strapless, lace. I want you to feel like a princess, and we're going to get our fucking night out at a fucking dance where we have a fantastic fucking time because you said yes and I'm taking you to prom. I'll even share the date, but you said yes to me first, so we get the hotel room after."

A laugh worked its way up my throat. "But what if…" I really couldn't ask that question.

"You're not my sister," he said. The savage note was back in his voice, and my phone hit the floor as he pushed me back to the wall. His hands cupped my head to keep it from hitting. "But you are *mine*." Then his mouth was on mine. The mintyness of the kiss was a cool accent to the heated demand in his lips.

The kiss took and gave in equal measure. His tongue swept in and dueled with mine, only to draw mine back as he sucked on it. A moan escaped my throat, and my nipples beaded as he slid his leg between my thighs. I had no idea who tugged at whose clothes first, but he pulled back only long enough to rip the tank top I had on up and over my head and then his hands were hot against my breasts as he devoured my mouth again.

Fingers hooked into the side of his boxers, I yanked them down. Every place his skin brushed mine left me needing. The pinch and pull of his fingers against my nipples, the way his callouses rubbed my breasts as he teased them. Then he kissed from my mouth to my jaw and along to my throat before he yanked my boxers down, and I had to wiggle to get them to fall the rest of the way.

The wall was cold against my overheated flesh, but Archie was already hauling me upward as I wrapped my hand around the heavy weight of his dick. The faint curve to it was so familiar, and I gave him a couple of warm pumps before he made a sound that was half-groan, half-growl as he sucked a stinging hickey onto my neck.

My core clenched around the emptiness as I began to tease the crown of his cock along my slit. I was already soaking. I had been since that first kiss in the bed. Lifting his head, he locked his gaze on me, and the naked desire in his eyes had the tension coiling in my stomach pulling taut.

"Do you remember what I said about all the ways I wanted to fuck you, babe?" he asked, his voice all dark, breathy, and hot.

"You wanted to fuck me from behind," I answered, stroking his tip back and forth until he was as damp as I was. "You wanted to see my tits bouncing as I rode you."

A slow smile widened his mouth. "Yes, and I *want* those things, just like I want to feel you come on my cock as you scream out your orgasm. I want to go down on you and eat you until you can't feel anything else. I want to come between those puffy, kiss swollen lips as tears run down your face 'cause I'm fucking your throat."

He shifted my weight, and in a move, pushed upward as his cock thrust into me, and we both let out a groan. I released his dick to grasp his shoulders as he buried himself in me.

"I plan to fuck your ass until I'm all you think about." Then his mouth was on mine, and his hips began to piston. I couldn't think of anything else. Just Archie and the way he filled me as he ran that illegal mouth of his. "I want to fuck you all the time, Frankie. I want to make love to you. I want to fuck you. I want to just touch you. Everything with you, babe. Fucking *everything*."

Then his mouth locked over mine, and between gasping, panting breaths, we tangled our tongues and I dug my nails into his shoulders. The friction of his chest to my breasts had me shaking, and the orgasm that struck caught me off-guard. I clamped down around him as a scream ripped out of my throat, but he didn't slow down.

Instead, he pulled out, and at my whimper, nipped my lower lip. "I have you, babe, I promise." Then I was facing the wall, the chill against my breasts a whole new sensation storming over me, and he pulled my ass back and gripped my hips, then he pushed into my pussy from the back, and I slammed a hand against the wall. The only pause came when he pressed his lips to my shoulder, and I damn well knew he was kissing his name on my tattoo. My heart sped up. It was like being too full, especially when he curved a hand around to tease my clit. Every thrust and rub combo had me seeing sparks, and I swore I came at the speed of light.

His fingers tightened against my hip as he shifted the angle of his thrusts, and we both cried out with that one. "I'm going to come," he warned me. "I'm going to fill you up because you're mine." He punctuated every single word with a thrust. "Mine. Mine. Mine."

Then his hips stuttered, but he didn't let go. He pulled me back against him and worked those magic fingers against my clit until I damn near sobbed because I didn't think I could come again when I was still spasming so hard, but I did, and then he gave a shout as he released.

I would have fallen if he wasn't holding me up. He sagged back against the wall, cradling me, my back to his chest. His cock softened slowly, but the pound of my heart seemed to echo in the silence. The warmth of his cum trickled down my thighs as he rubbed a hand against my abdomen slowly and then up to my breasts. It was all soothing caresses, and his breath was hot against my ear.

"Mine, Frankie, say you're mine."

"I'm yours," I promised. "I'm yours."

I swore I felt tears on his cheeks when I reached a hand back, but when I pulled forward to turn around, he seized me in another kiss. A minute later, he had me sprawled on my bed and his mouth was between my thighs.

"You're coming again," he told me like it was an order, and holy crap, he was right. I was a damn puddle by the time he finished, and when he played with my ass this time, working his fingers in and out while he sucked on my clit, I made a promise that he'd get that wish.

He'd get every damn one he wanted.

If we hadn't had the appointment, I don't know that we'd ever have made it out of bed. My legs were still jelly and my insides were quivering. My lips were definitely puffy, and I couldn't shake the trembling or the way my pussy clenched as it remembered the feel of him. I'd actually begged him to take my ass before he was done, and he told me next time.

But only because he wanted to take his time. Yet some of the darkness in his eyes had receded, and his smile had softened again. We managed showers, still playing with each other, and I did get to suck him off, though I swore he never once let go of my gaze as he fucked my mouth. The desperation and need in every touch weren't lost on me.

We ended up taking our coffee in travel mugs, which we finished before we stopped and grabbed breakfast with real coffee along the way. The lab was a private one, and it took us a bit to get there. We had an appointment and were shown in immediately. I really had no idea how to explain what we needed, but Archie didn't miss a beat.

"We're doing genetic matching for an assignment at school," he told him. "We need to do a full profile on both of us, demonstrating how we are not siblings."

I could have kissed him all over again. That was the most plausible explanation ever. I did not want to have to tell someone that I needed to prove that my boyfriend wasn't my brother. I just…couldn't make myself say those words.

"We can do buccal swabs and we can do blood. Do you have a preference?" The technician didn't seem to give a damn one way or the other.

"I'll pay for both," Archie told him. "We'll also pay any rush fees required."

"It can take anywhere from forty-eight hours to two weeks to run the full panel. But if you want us to rush, I can try to get you full results in seventy-two hours." He glanced from me to Archie. "That enough time for your assignment?"

Three days?

"Twenty-four would be better," Archie said. "And I'll pay whatever I need to to make it happen."

"Best case is forty-eight hours. But I'll see what I can do."

It was the best we were going to get.

So he used swabs to get the inside of our cheeks and marked the information down. "Can you tell me about the numbers on those?" Because our names weren't on the tubes. There were numbers instead.

"It's patient privacy and to eliminate any possibility of mixing up names. Everything is done by number. Even your results will be logged by numbers. Then when the reports are sent to you, the computer will add the name and we can access it by name only with your permission. Otherwise, no one knows who the samples are."

I glanced at Archie.

Great.

The technician had changed his gloves and had Archie roll up his sleeve and took the blood sample from him first.

"What if someone is submitting the samples?"

"There are home collection kits you can run, but if they weren't submitted by a physician or a technician, then they are generally only categorized by the information cards provided."

Information cards provided.

"So I could do a sample and just say it was from anybody?"

"Technically, although if you submitted several samples that were clearly different under the same name, that would probably raise flags. Then again, home collection kits don't usually have legal standing, so…I suppose. We don't process those here."

It wasn't long before it was my turn. And he was quick and almost painless about getting his blood sample. Once again, everything was marked with numbers. Archie paid him privately and paid the clinic. I didn't say anything as the technician promised to get the results within forty-eight hours or as close as he could.

"Though if you want finer detail work for the assignment, you may need the final report after that."

"That's fine," Archie said. "Just make sure you mark everything that proves we're not siblings. That'll be a great start for us."

Would it ever.

Outside, it was still drizzling as we walked to the car.

"Lunch and dress shopping?" he asked once we were in the Ferrari.

"How much money are you planning to spend on this dress?"

"Probably a lot. Then there are shoes and jewelry to go with it." He grinned. "I can play the pity card to get you to let me do it, but I'd rather you just say yes, Frankie. Let's go play for a while and let me spoil you."

"Dress shopping isn't exactly spoiling me."

"Ha," he said, and then his grin grew. "That's because you've never gone dress shopping with me. And I know a challenge when I hear one."

Chapter Six
I HAVE TO GO SHOPPING NOW

The waiter stopped at our table with an entire side of flank steak that he began to cut and add to my plate. It was probably my third helping of this particular cut, and he made sure to slice the medium rare section. "Thank you," I murmured as he offered the next cuts to Archie before moving on. "You know the boys are going to be annoyed with us."

"They won't," he said, then pressed a kiss to my bare shoulder. I'd shed my jacket when we'd been seated, and the sleeveless black top I'd worn was perfect for this place. No one would see anything I dropped on my shirt. "They'll be annoyed with me."

I rolled my eyes, but in spite of it all, I hadn't stopped smiling except to chew since we arrived at the Brazilian steakhouse. I think we'd come here the first time after Archie got his license. "That celebratory dinner for your license… that was a date, wasn't it?"

He chuckled. "Close, more just me stealing you away. Bubba got his license first, but he had to borrow his mom's car, and Coop farted around about getting his—"

"Because he went with me when I took my driver's test."

"Yeah, but I knew Jake wouldn't be so cavalier, so since I had a license and a car, I took full advantage of being able to steal you." The smugness in his tone just made me laugh. "And you loved this place."

"They feed you nonstop," I pointed out as the next waiter came by with bacon-wrapped chicken. There was a salad bar and plenty of vegetable sides, but I was here for the meat.

"The perfect Frankie dining experience." The playful look on his face softened the lines of tension that had tightened his expression at the lab. I reached over and traced a finger down his cheek. He caught my hand and kissed it. "Mine now."

"I thought it was yours before."

"Well, then too." He winked.

We kept the banter light as we ate. He graciously allowed me to borrow my hand back to cut my meat. It wasn't until I finally flipped my card from green to red to signal no more to the waiters that I let out a sigh. "Archie…"

"Babe, it's going to be fine. I don't give a flying fuck what those tests say. Seriously, I don't. If you do, then I'm really hoping you'll let me persuade you otherwise."

My heart skipped a little beat.

"I mean it," he said, holding my gaze captive. "I'm not giving up on us *ever*. If it takes me a week, a month, a year, or ten, I'm never giving up on us."

It was my turn to take his hand, and I threaded our fingers together. "Archie, I'm not giving up on us either. I promise. I know I'm dense and blind when it comes to that whole flirting and being asked out thing, but I know you want me and love me, and I'm not going anywhere. They aren't us. Whatever this crap is, is between bad meatloaf. They aren't us."

And he was right. I didn't care.

The relief that flickered across his face burned me a little. "Fuck I'm the worst girlfriend."

"Don't—"

But I shook my head. "You've been so charge ahead, and all I've wanted to do was make it all right for you too and I had no idea how to do it, especially since I was the one who had to tell you."

"Babe, stop. Seriously. You've got balls that clank, especially considering I found out about their stupid affair and didn't tell you, and you barely even slowed down to tell me something horrible."

I laughed "Oh my god, this is like some horrible Greek tragedy."

"No." He shook his head. "Not a tragedy. Tragedies end badly, we're calling this a comedy. Bleak and dark as it might be, but a comedy, because someone told me that's where the happy endings come from."

"Yeah…"

"And you have been there for me," he insisted. "I just get sick to death of them dragging *you* into their crap."

"And I hate how you are…left behind."

Stroking his thumb over my hand, he blew out a breath. "Honestly, the best thing they could do for both of us is to just forget us. I don't give a damn about what Edward wants or doesn't."

The knuckles of his hand were bruised. Had been since he got home from New York. I hadn't asked about them other than to kiss them gently, and he'd just pulled me in for a hug.

"I'm done with all of them," he continued. "All three of them. I just want *you* out from under them or having to deal with them. Wittaker's got that court date for you, so we sever you from Maddy and then you never have to deal with her again."

"Unless there's something with that trust." I made a face. "Wittaker left me a message about it, but I just can't muster up the urge to go in and talk to him about this sudden trust that appears from nowhere. That was what I wanted to ask you about anyway."

"The trust?"

"Sort of. Honestly, the idea that there's some big ass money fund out there for me just makes me uncomfortable. Yours has terms and conditions, right? Why else would Maddy keep it a secret?"

"Control." He shrugged. "If you don't know you have a lifeline, you'll never reach for it." The simple way he phrased it just made me angry at Maddy all over again. "And honestly, you don't need that trust. You have me. You have you. You're the most self-reliant person I know. But if there is something there that's yours, you damn well get to decide whether you get it. Not her."

That fierceness was such a part of him. Educated, cultured, brilliant, determined, and absolutely ferocious in his dedication to what he cared about. "I'm really glad you love me," I told him, and his sudden grin lit his whole face up.

"Can't possibly be more glad than I am that you love me."

"You might be right, you did shout it out to the whole world."

His laughter rolled over me and lit his whole face up, and for the first time since I'd had to tell him, the darkness was absent in his eyes. "And I'll do it again, I can do it right here…"

Oh. Shit.

I clapped a hand over his mouth, and his eyes practically danced. "I will promise you anything, just…let's not do that right now."

He kissed my palm and tugged my hand away as he repeated, "Anything?"

Yeah, it was a dangerous promise. I really didn't care. I meant it. I'd give them anything. Whatever they wanted. "Yes. Anything."

He closed his eyes as if he had to savor that for a moment. "Deal." Then after a little satisfied sigh that had me half-amused, half-intrigued by what he had to be thinking, he said, "Was the trust the thing you were worried about, babe?"

"A little bit, but more about the people who set it up. The Graysons."

The good humor drained away. "Them."

"You know them," I said, and it wasn't a question.

He nodded. "Let's get out of here and head to a couple of stores, and I'll tell you what I know."

I waited until we were in the car and on the road before I said, "You don't have to, you know…you don't have to talk about them. I just—are they good people?"

"I don't know if I'd call them good or bad. They're…stodgy, old school, real 'kids are seen and not heard,' very stiff upper lip, and old money."

That sounded delightful.

"And they're *Maddy's* parents?"

He gave a little shrug. "Like I said, I don't *know them* know them. I have met them a couple of times when I stayed with Grandpa and Nana. Clearly, if Edward and Maddy were engaged for three years, they all knew each other, but…I didn't sense any kind of bad blood between them over the fact their kids didn't get married." His knuckles whited on the wheel for a moment. "I'll be honest, I didn't know they had any kids."

"Well," I said slowly. "On the upside, that means I don't have any aunts or uncles I don't know about. Or cousins."

When he dropped a hand to my thigh and rubbed it, I leaned my head back against the seat. "I'm sorry, Frankie," he murmured. "Do you want to meet them?"

"Well I met her once," I said. "Not that we really spoke and she was very…distant, I suppose is the polite word." But I was curious now, except… "Archie, I didn't want to know about my father before because I know who I am *now*, I didn't need the past. That kind of applies to them too."

"Except?"

I grunted, and he squeezed my thigh.

"Babe, I know you. This is a bone you'll worry at until you have all the information."

"Do you think I should meet them?"

"Honestly?"

"No," I retorted. "I want you to lie to me."

His snort made me grin, and a moment later, we were both chuckling.

"You know what, don't answer that question. Let's stick a pin in all of that. We've spent more time on discussing the past than I want to. This is about you and me."

"Okay," he agreed slowly. "And I still have that 'anything I want' card to cash in."

"Yes you do."

"It's going to be a great day." He squeezed my thigh again, and I smiled as I watched him.

"It already is."

Thirty-five minutes later, I might have been revising my opinion, though the simple pleasure on Archie's face kept me from protesting as we walked into a boutique store that just screamed "you are underdressed and can't afford to breathe our air, much less shop here." We got the side-eye almost immediately, then Archie pulled out a credit card and informed the woman we needed to see the most stunning dresses they had in stock and those kept in the back, but only if they complimented me.

The woman about tripped over herself, and I had to bite back a laugh at the smug, arrogant look on Archie's face as he dismissed her. The sparkle in his eyes when he looked at me was just about irresistible. Which was how I found myself sitting with him on a white sofa as the woman hustled her staff into motion.

For such an expensive shop, they didn't have a lot of customers. Then again, I hadn't seen a single price tag on a dress. That usually meant "they cost too fucking much." They brought us drinks, and Archie had his phone out. There were a couple of messages from the guys, and he answered both.

Jake just had one question, *Okay?* And Ian's was an equally succinct, *Good?*

Head tucked against Archie's shoulder, I settled in as they not only brought out a series of dresses, but actually had a couple of the girls wearing them.

"Let me know which ones you like," Archie murmured as he kissed the top of my head. I was meat drunk and feeling pretty damn loved at the moment. The last few days slipped behind us, and I left them there.

"You tell me which ones you like, too," I said as we were treated to the parade of different dresses with everything from the little black dress to a pure white one that looked fabulous on the girl wearing it and I could *never* wear. I'd dump something on myself before I even left the bedroom.

There were body-hugging dresses and dresses with flared skirts. Strapless. Sleeveless. Halter topped. Spaghetti straps. Corset style that promised I'd look fabulous, even if I couldn't breathe. He curved his hand against my side and ran his fingers up and down as we watched. I had my hand on his thigh, and I stayed as tucked close to him as I could get without climbing into his lap.

I didn't want to be away from him and from the way he held me, he felt much the same. There was a dress in chocolate brown that made me think of Archie's eyes, and it was body hugging with ruching. No way I could eat much in that, but when I bit my lip, Archie raised a finger to choose that one. Then we were moving on. Teal colored dresses. Dark blue. Pale icy shimmering colors. Dark green. Red. So many red dresses. In fact, there were at least two red dresses for every other color they showed us.

"What can I say?" he murmured when I commented on this. "I love you in red."

Okay, red it was then.

It took over an hour to see them all, but I picked out three along with Archie's five, and it was my turn to head into the dressing room. Most of the dresses required losing everything but my panties to try on. When I walked out to model each one, Archie's smile grew. It was ridiculous and silly. The last time I'd done this, it had been with Coop and… Yeah, there went my smile.

Like Coop, Archie had taken snaps of me in every single one, but Cheryl had been there helping me pick out a dress when she knew the crap Mitch had been doing. The door behind me opened before I'd even closed it all the way, and Archie slipped into the dressing room behind me.

"What's wrong?"

"Just…my brain being weird."

Crowding me right up against the mirror, he tugged the zipper down on the dress. "Tell me."

It was written all over his face. Let him fix it, and I kicked myself for letting anything spoil today. When the dress spilled off me, leaving me in just the panties, he pressed his lips just behind my ear.

"Tell me."

Between his nibbling kisses against my throat and the way he stroked his hands down my sides until he hooked them beneath the band of my panties, I almost forgot. But the bite brought me back to the present. So I told him.

"Okay," he whispered. "Fuck Cheryl, but you liked the part about Coop, right?"

"Yeah," I said. "I was so tired that night, but…he was a lot of fun, and he made me feel good."

"You looked good," he continued. "You looked amazing. It took everything I had not to call that store and buy every dress you put on."

A soft laugh escaped me. Because that was Archie. "Your willpower and restraint are amazing."

"You jest, but I was a god that day," he told me before sucking on my earlobe and slipping a finger right along my slit. Oh fuck. "Shh," he whispered against my ear. "Don't make a sound and I can chase away any bad fucking memories." He plunged one finger and then another inside of me, and I had to grip his shoulders to stay upright. "When you think about dress shopping and trying on all those sexy dresses, you think about us peeling them off you and fucking you right here."

He hooked his fingers with every stroke, and his thumb circled my clit, a shark closing in, but not quite giving me enough pressure. I thrust my hips up to meet him, almost begging for it, and even as hard as I tried to keep quiet, a whimper started to escape.

"Gotta be quiet, babe," he admonished me with another bite, even as the pressure amped up and sparks danced through my system. I was riding his hand as he thrust it inside of me over and over. Then there were three fingers stretching me, and the tension went utterly taut as I was right there.

"That's it," he whispered. "Soak my fingers and come for me, Frankie. The only fucking people who matter are us. Just us. I love how wet you are for me, how you clamp down on my fingers 'cause you're so desperate for my dick. Do you want my dick? Do you want me to turn you around against this mirror and let you watch me fuck you until you're screaming?"

Fuck. Fuck. Fuck.

Every single word detonated through me.

The heat of his mouth on my ear, the sudden pressure of his thumb against my swollen clit, and the curve of his fingers, and it was over. I shook with the release, and before I could stifle my own cries, Archie kissed me. Even as he robbed me of breath, he wrenched every ounce of that orgasm out of me until I was a trembling mess and my panties were soaked.

Fuck. Me.

The heat scorching me in his eyes had me laughing weakly, even as he licked his fingers off one at a time, all the while watching me as I leaned against the cool mirror. My panties ended up in his pocket, and I tried on three more dresses.

Archie picked his favorites, which meant I got all of them and I didn't even have it in me to complain. Loose limbed and warm, I swore I could still feel his fingers as I dragged on my jeans. I figured we were done, but oh no.

The shop had shoes and jewelry. They accessorized every outfit, and with one single exception, I let Archie pick it all. The one thing I picked out was a simple gold bracelet with a metal gear hanging off of it. It was so elegant and plain, and yet the gear made me think of Archie and all the things he took apart to see what made them work. He didn't even hesitate to fasten it around my wrist.

And I had to admit, I did not ask about the final total because they never said a word, just charged his card and packaged everything up for us. First among his picks, the dress he took off me before he finger-fucked me in the dressing room.

He wasn't wrong, I wasn't going to think about anything else but that the next time I went shopping. Thank God the salespeople didn't say a word, but my face didn't cool even a little until we were back in the car.

"See, shopping with me is the best, isn't it?" he teased, all smug and satisfied, and I laughed.

"You're the best," I reminded him, because seriously, he wasn't wrong.

And I might have started running my hand up and down his thigh and testing how hard his cock was beneath the denim. I even offered a blowjob in the car on the way home, but he just held my hand against his stiff erection and grinned. The fact he kissed me senseless at every traffic light seemed to extend our drive back to the apartment.

Once there, he urged me ahead of him and through the cold and into the kitchen. The door closed, the dress bags landed on the dining room table, and Archie picked me up as we came together in a heated kiss. I swore I could still taste myself on him. We half-crashed our way against the counters toward the living room, stripping off each other's clothes.

The minute he had my breasts free though, he locked his mouth around one nipple and sucked so hard, I swore my pussy clenched and I was halfway to coming. I got my hand around his cock and teased the pre-cum on the tip with a thumb before I began stroking him. Almost frantic with need, I slid down him and started to suck his cock between my lips. He fisted my hair and pumped against my mouth a scant few times before he dragged me off and then up. With my jeans still hanging off one leg and his pants not even past his thighs, he slammed into me in one thrust that had us both groaning.

We didn't even make it all the way out of the kitchen. The force of his thrusts almost hurt, but he kept swiveling his hips and every strike had me seeing stars. I dug my fingers into his shoulders as I kissed him. The tangle of his tongue on mine as he mimicked the action of his body fucking me sent cries tearing from my throat.

I wasn't quiet.

I didn't want to be quiet.

And fuck knew, he wasn't as he told me every damn thing he wanted to do to me in between drugging kisses that had me tipping over and coming hard around his cock. His grunt as I clamped down on him just made it all sweeter at the first hot rush of him coming. The release just spread warmth through my whole system, and we hung there, panting, a sheen of sweat on our skin and sticking together.

It was dirty, raw, and more than a little perfect. As soon as I got the ability to use my limbs again, I was going to suck him as deep into my throat as I could. I wanted him to come as many times as he'd made me today.

Heart hammering, I stroked my fingers through his hair as he nuzzled against my throat. There was cum running down my thighs, and I just didn't care. He was still inside me, softening slowly. I ached in every delicious way possible.

Slowly, I dragged my eyes open and locked gazes with Coop over Archie's shoulder. Hair askew, lips parted, and a hand over his own dick that poked out of his boxers, red-tipped and hard, he grinned slowly at me and mouthed a kiss.

I licked my lips, and then a laugh escaped. I couldn't help it. It started out a chuckle, then turned into a cascade of giggles that had me flexing around Archie. He groaned at every squeeze until he eased out of me and leaned back to study my face. Then he glanced back to follow my gaze, and there was a long pause.

"Hey," Coop said. "Good day?"

Archie turned back to me and cast his gaze up and then huffed out a laugh. "You know, I don't even fucking care." Then he kissed me again. "It's a damn good day."

I didn't miss Coop's little fist pump or the way his hand flexed on his dick. "Good to know."

"Hey," I said to Coop as Archie set me down slowly. I was still clinging because my legs were pure rubber.

"Hey, beautiful," he answered me. There was definitely lust in his eyes, but also a lot of love. "Feeling good?"

"I feel amazing…and a little sweaty. I also need to go suck Archie off if he'll let me." Bold? Maybe. Coop's eyebrows rose. "And if you want to wait with that," I dipped my gaze down to his lap and then back up again, "I'll totally take care of you too."

Yep, I was feeling good.

He immediately let go of himself and dropped back on the sofa. Apparently, he'd been sprawled there when we came in. Slowly, it hit me the television was on and the cats were scattered around the room, all of them staring at us owlishly.

Huh.

I hadn't even noticed.

"I can wait," Coop said as Archie grinned at me.

"Where do you want me, babe?"

I laughed and, still on trembling legs, pushed him back to the wall. If he wasn't going to complain about Coop watching, I wasn't, and frissons of heat lit up my system as I could practically feel his gaze scalding me as I dropped to my knees. "Right here is good." I glanced up, holding Archie's gaze. Was this okay with him?

He gave me a slow nod, and then I gripped him. The sudden inhale of his breath promised me he was as sensitive as I was. Oh, this was going to be fun. It wasn't until fifteen minutes later as I licked my lips and Archie looked as wrecked as I was that Coop cleared his throat.

"So…is it too soon to ask about how you did that thing with your hips?"

Chapter Seven
IT MIGHT BE DIFFICULT

Back to school on Tuesday was kind of a surreal experience. Granted, the day before with Archie had been exactly what we both needed. There wasn't even a protest when Coop crawled into bed after us, and while I wasn't one hundred percent certain, I thought Archie had watched me give Coop the promised blowjob after our shower. I didn't see him immediately afterward, but there was a look on Coop's face that suggested he might have.

Honestly, I was just glad to spend the rest of the evening with them both and to fall asleep pressed right up between them after I talked to Jake and Ian on the phone. They were giving us the night, but we'd see them at breakfast. As promised, they were both there before we even got out of bed. In fact, Jake woke me with coffee that had Archie snarking that Jake was trying to steal his thunder.

The morning just escalated from there with playful one upmanship that kept me laughing all the way to school, and yes, we absolutely stopped for more coffee. I would never say no to two huge cups of coffee in the morning. We also had to get one for Rachel. Ian had new lyric sheets he'd been working on, and he brought me copies because we were going to the studio that night. Archie wanted to come and listen. Ian agreed, but Jake reminded Archie they had their own work to go.

"Secret project," I intoned, and Archie flashed me a grin.

"Maybe."

"Uh huh."

But neither he nor Jake gave away anything in their expressions. Coop, however, flung an arm over my shoulder as he leaned back in his chair. "I think Bubba and I should continue work on *our* secret project. You want to help *us* with *that*, Frankie?"

I almost snorted my coffee out my nose when Ian said, "Agreed. You want to come and listen to us tonight? We can get to work on it right after."

That earned me a pair of speculative looks, and I had to hide a grin as I took another sip of coffee. Though if today ended up like Sunday, I wasn't sure how well I'd be walking the next day. Particularly after Monday.

I guessed I could call that my own experiment, so I just grinned. "Whatever you guys want to do," I said, and that had Archie narrowing his eyes.

"Oh no," Ian told him, squeezing my shoulders. "You don't get to be demanding about our project if you're not sharing yours."

"Really?" Oh man, the light in Archie's eyes had me half-laughing, half-groaning. "That sounds like a challenge to me."

"My lips are sealed," Coop informed him, yet he still wore an amused look as he stared at the pair of them. "As you both know."

That's when both of them focused on me. Jake and Archie both grinned. "And on that note, I have to talk to Rachel."

Yes, I totally admit it, I escaped.

Well, fled. Yep, totally fled. Rachel was at a table three over from ours with a couple of other girls. One look at my face though, and she said, "Beat it."

I slid into the chair next to hers, not even caring that I'd displaced these other girls.

"What's wrong?" she asked.

"Nothing, everything. We need a girls' night."

She studied me for a beat and then slanted a look over her shoulder. I didn't even need to turn to know she was looking at the guys. "Do I need to destroy someone?"

I considered that for a minute. "Maybe, but not them. They're perfect."

The corners of her lips twitched as she focused on me. "I just threw up in my mouth a little."

Laughter escaped. "Sorry, Rach, they are perfect."

"Fine, fine. When do you want to plot this other person's demise?"

"Maybe tomorrow?" I had plans that night.

Rachel grimaced. "Okay, I have a sort of date. I can cancel…"

"You will not," I told her. "And what's a sort of date? I thought I was the only one who 'sort of' dated?"

With a snort, Rachel shook her head. "It doesn't matter. Chicks before dicks." Almost as soon as the words left her mouth though, she made another face, and I couldn't help grinning.

"You're going to tell me about him."

"There's nothing to tell really, yet. I promise. We're just…exploring the waters. Dipping a toe in, as it were."

I raised my brows. "It's okay if you like dick too."

"Ugh. Says the girl with four of them to juggle and doesn't let a little vag in on the action."

Okay, I'd spent way too much time with Archie because I burst out laughing. "My vag sees a *lot* of action."

That earned me a full-on smirk. "Details or it didn't happen."

"Bite me." But we were both grinning.

"Bare it and share it," she dared me.

Man, I loved Rachel. "You're going to tell me, you know you will."

"Maybe," she said and toasted me with her coffee. "Or maybe I'll make you beg for it."

It was such an Archie line I choked on my own drink. "I'll find a way to make you talk."

"I can't wait."

Still, despite the ease of the morning, some of the good cheer fled as the day plodded on. The guys were in full-on "distract Frankie" mode. I had make-up work from the classes I'd missed the day before, and there was a lot of talk about the upcoming AP exams. How weird was it to be talking about spring break too?

At lunch, Archie showed me the notice for prom tickets going on sale with a smug little smile. The theme was cheesy as hell—*fairy tale*. Well, *enchanted forest*, but still. I definitely had a dress to go for it. Also, the nomination form for prom king and queen was up. Only seniors were allowed to be nominated.

"And I'm totally nominating you," Archie announced, and I glared at him.

"Don't you dare."

"Anything I want, remember?" The look in his eyes, a cross between evil delight and playful tease, had me groaning.

"I love this idea," Coop said with a laugh. "I bet we could drum up the votes, no problem."

"Oh, you want votes?" Jake asked, phone in hand. "On it."

I covered my face with my hands.

"Tell Rachel," Ian said. "You know she'll help."

"I hate you all," I mumbled, and Archie tugged my hands from my face and grinned at me.

"No you don't."

No, I really didn't.

By the end of the day, fifteen people told me they'd nominated me for prom queen. Kill me.

After school, Archie kissed me soundly before dropping me off at the apartment and leaving with Jake again. "If I hear anything, you're my first call."

It had been twenty-four hours, not that I was watching the clock.

"Ditto."

"Okay, tell me you're not really annoyed with us for the prom queen thing," Coop ordered me when we got to the studio. The walk in, he'd been radiating curiosity as he checked out everything.

"Not annoyed," I admitted. "Not really. But do you have any idea how embarrassing it's going to be when I have to go up there?"

"Not embarrassing at all," Ian promised as he unlocked the door to the studio we used. I have to admit, my gaze went straight to the piano bench with a little shiver. "You're going to be stunning. Everyone is going to look and see how beautiful you are, and they'll do the speech thing and the crowning thing, and then you're back with us and dancing."

"Don't I have to dance with the prom king?" Wasn't that a thing?

"Only if it's one of us," Coop announced as he set my guitar case down. "Trust me, no one is going to push Jake at the dance itself, no matter who prom king. Besides, who knows? You could nominate all of us for prom king, then you'd be a queen with your court."

The wicked chuckle that escaped Ian gave me pause. "There is the one benefit to being out at school. *Everyone* knows better now."

Okay, I couldn't argue with that, even if my face was hot. Thankfully, they let me off the hook, and Ian pulled out the music sheets while I unpacked my guitar. I loved these lessons. I loved that Coop was here with us. I loved even more that Ian had invited him.

"Did you grab what I asked for?" he said to Coop while I studied the lyric sheets. I couldn't read music as easily as he did. To be fair, I couldn't really read it at all. I kind of still had to do the number game in my head. But he wrote the little notations next to each bar I had to play so I could find the right fingering.

"Yep. You want to do that *now*?" I wasn't sure if Coop meant to sound scandalized or teasing, but he managed both, even as he glanced at me with a grin. Oh, boy. What had these two decided to do?

Honestly, the excitement tingling through me had me agreeing without even knowing, and they hadn't asked yet.

"Depends," Ian mused, then glanced at me. "You up for a little play tonight, Angel? Or do you just want to work on the music and relax?"

"Can't we do both?" Because, um, yes please?

The smile in his eyes seemed to grow as Ian studied me. "We can, but this might be a little tougher on you tonight."

Like that was a deterrent. The last few days had been hell, except when I was with them. I touched my tongue to my teeth and glanced at Coop, who stared at us with an unreadable expression, except for the hint of curiosity in his eyes, and back to Ian. His expression was all infinite patience. He wanted to know what I needed.

Guitar in hand, I dropped to my knees and glanced up at him. "Whatever you want to do, sir."

"Fuck," Coop said almost under his breath, but he didn't add anything and I didn't take my gaze off of Ian to check on him.

"All right. Put the guitar down and come here, Angel."

Excitement shivered through me as I did as I was told, and that was how I found myself stretched over Ian's lap with my pants around my ankles as they loosened my ass with their fingers. When they had two each stretching me, tears sparked in my eyes, even as my pussy grew hot, slick, and needy. It ached beautifully, and then the pressure eased off and Coop moved around to kneel in front of me.

"You okay?" The soft question made me smile, even as a couple of tears escaped, and I nodded.

"Words, Angel," Ian scolded, and the warm hand he had spread over one curve of my ass delivered a sharp slap that was more noise than sting. But it grounded me. How the ache could feel so good, I couldn't explain, but being right on the cusp of pain had me panting for more.

"Yes," I whispered. "Very okay… It feels…like too much and not enough."

"Good," he said softly and rubbed the spot he'd slapped gently. "Go ahead and kiss her, Coop. You've waited long enough."

Coop needed no further encouragement. He gripped my face in one hand and then kissed me with such soul-searing sweetness, I almost sobbed all over again. The moment was a perfect counterpoint to the sudden pressure as Ian removed his fingers and replaced them with a well-lubed plug that stretched me nearly as much as their fingers had. Fuck, I was so full that I rolled my hips and groaned. The soft, sharp slap had me holding still, ass clenching, until Ian soothed me with a gentle murmur, and I relaxed to let him finish pushing it in.

"Good girl," he said, stroking my ass in slow circles. "Such a good girl for us. Need another kiss from Coop?"

I laughed between my tears, because yes, it stung, and oh God, I was so full and stretched and aching and needy, but also…"Yes please?"

Not even waiting, Coop claimed my mouth again with a slow tongue-stroking, nipping kiss that promised to consume me, and I didn't even care how exposed I was over Ian's lap or the thickness of Ian's very interested dick pressing at my belly. Ian kept rubbing slow circles against my ass as Coop lingered in the kiss, and I hung on for every single moment.

After, they helped me sit up and, much to my disappointment, pulled up my pants. The plug wasn't terrible, but it also wasn't the most comfortable thing. Ian and Coop took turns going to wash their hands before they settled back in and handed me back my guitar.

I wanted to ask, but at the same time, I wasn't sure I was supposed to.

And the look on Ian's face told me he knew it and was just waiting to see what I'd push. I could do this. I'd said whatever he wanted, and if this was what he wanted, I'd do it. The pleased grin that graced his lips as I sat gingerly, intimately aware of that plug and the soaked state of my panties, tickled me. The weight of his attention flooded me when I braced the guitar against my knee.

Keeping my focus on Ian, I waited, though Coop's warm gaze shivered over me from where he'd taken a seat against the wall. They were both focused on me and it had everything inside me clenching at the same time.

"Good girls get rewards, Angel," Ian told me, and I grinned.

"Being bad does have its perks too."

He laughed. "You can absolutely do that if you want, but I think you'll like this reward."

"Okay," I agreed, then dabbed at my eyes 'cause they were still damp. I wasn't entirely sure why this worked so well for me, but even with all the tension and the needy state they'd left me in, I felt *better*.

"That was easy," Coop said quietly.

"Frankie's a good girl," Ian said, more to him than to me.

Pleasure suffused me, but Ian didn't leave me long to bask in it because he nodded to the music and we started practicing.

I thought it would be impossible to focus, but all of my normal nerves when we started working on a new piece of music vanished. I was a lot huskier when I sang the new lyrics, but even the chords came easier. Ian switched over to sit behind me at one point and then adjusted my hands. With his over mine, we played through it again, just my parts, but we sang the whole thing and it sounded amazing.

More, it *felt* amazing. As the last notes faded away, I let out a little sigh and Ian nuzzled a kiss behind my ear. "Perfect."

"Yeah?" I glanced back at him, delighted at the note of pride in his voice.

"Oh yeah, Angel. That was perfect. I want to record it just like that. You up for it?"

I was up for anything, and when I kissed the corner of his mouth, he slid his hand up to my throat and tilted my head a little more so he could take control of the kiss. I swore my whole body sighed at the feel of his lips on mine and the way his thumb tilted my chin to give him greater access.

The pressure made me dizzy, but the kiss just seemed to go on and on. I lost myself in the way his tongue stroked mine and how he'd ease back, only to change the angle and then plunge his tongue back inside. I swore my pussy clenched like his mouth was on me and his tongue thrusting into me. The moment my hips started to rock though, Ian bit my lower lip and dragged his teeth over it with a hint of warning sting that brought me right back to Earth.

Heat flooded my whole body, and soft whimpers filled the room. I didn't even care that the hungry sound came from me.

"You can last a little longer for me, Angel? You can do that, right?" His voice had dropped into a deeper range. My nipples tightened at the dark promise kissing each word, and I nodded. "That's my sweet angel." Another kiss, and he pressed a last one to my temple before he stood and moved back to his own guitar.

A shudder rippled over me, and I shivered as I tried to find an easier way to sit that didn't have pressure increasing or my panties so damn wet I worried about soaking through my pants. Who knew that would be a problem?

I found Coop staring at me, all flushed, eyes dilated and nostrils flared. I hadn't forgotten he was here, if anything, I think it just made me hotter knowing he was watching and that Ian was letting him be a part of this.

Craving these connections, all of them, was like a living, breathing thing inside of me. "You ready for us to record?" Wow, I didn't even sound like me. I swore need drenched every syllable.

"Oh yeah," Coop said as he leaned forward. "You have no idea how sexy you are, do you?"

"I know you are, but what am I?" The tease just flew effortlessly, and Ian let out a real chuckle as Coop grinned.

The actual recording took another hour before Ian was happy with it. Minor adjustments and exacting requests demanded every ounce of my attention. I swore my voice got throatier with every note, but when we played back the last bit, he wore the most satisfied expression.

"Give your guitar to Coop, Angel. Time for your reward."

Oh hell.

In no time at all, I was naked and kneeling in front of the piano bench. He stretched me over it, and the cool wood against my flushed skin was almost too much, but any time I squirmed, I earned a sharp slap and he slowed down even further.

The torture was real. When a blindfold wrapped around my eyes, I let out another full body shudder as Ian's words came back to me about not letting me know who was doing what. Only after that was secure did he lift me and urge me to lie with my back on the bench. It wasn't the most comfortable of positions, but it left my legs open at one end and my head tilted slightly off the other. Something soft was bunched up behind my neck to keep the edge of the bench from pinching in.

The softest of ties went around my wrists, then my arms were bound behind me but under the bench, and it forced my back into this curve. They didn't say anything, not one word as they moved around me, and it was definitely both of them because one was tying and the other traced fingers over me in a touch so light, I swore I was going to go mad.

Warm hands spread my thighs wider, and I bit my lip as they rubbed up toward my pussy and then away without ever touching it. The last time the two of them had me like this, Coop had eaten me out until I was sobbing. The first brush of breath against my clit had me clenching in anticipation, and I gripped that plug even tighter. A groan broke free at the competing sensations.

Music started up, and it was us, our voices twining together in a sex-drenched and needy duet that washed over me and pulled at every emotion. I wasn't ready for the mouth that closed over my nipple or the sudden push of a cock thrusting into me.

Oh. Fuck.

Every single inch filling me seemed to push me out of my body, and there was no patience to the motion after that first thrust. Ian, a part of my brain identified before his movements pushed away all other thoughts. The mouth on my breast nipped and sucked at my nipple like it was his favorite treat. Then he continued kissing his way up to my throat and back down again. Warm hands on my thighs pushed my legs higher, and then Ian was striking so deep, everything faded to just feeling.

The music.

Our voices.

The feel of him pulsing inside of me.

The first orgasm rattled through me and left me screaming—a cry that Coop swallowed into his hot mouth. When Ian pulled out without coming, I wanted to weep, but they didn't give me any time as Coop moved, and then Coop pushed into me and I was clenching around him in desperation as Ian kissed me this time.

I swore they took me apart between them, and I couldn't stop coming. Every orgasm seemed to trip into another, and when the music started again, I wanted to sob. The tap of a cock against my lips had me opening immediately to him, and they fucked me back and forth until the only thing left of me was the feel of them and the pleasure splitting me open. Ian thrust deep against my throat, and the pressure of Coop coming finally just sent me spiraling. The first jet of Ian's release was almost as much a relief as it was a delight.

I did this to them. Or their playing with me did it to them.

I lost track of how many times we heard the song, but I would never forget it. I swore it was ingrained into my bones. Ian kissed me as he pulled the ties from my arms, and Coop rubbed his cheek against my thigh as he worked the plug free. Somewhere in there, I blacked out. Or maybe I had blacked out and came to and then blacked out again.

I roused, shaking like a leaf, all wrapped up in Ian's lap with Coop pressed right up against me. Ian nuzzled my hair as Coop held my hand.

"Hey," he whispered. "There she is."

The light in the room seemed almost too bright, but I blinked past it as they kept me warm between them. I had no idea who brought a blanket, and I didn't care. It was warm and kept the chills away.

"Talk to me, Angel," Ian ordered. "You okay? You drifted away on us there."

"I'm fine," I said in a trembling voice. "I promise." My cheeks were damp, and Ian tilted my face back until I looked up at him. He studied me for so long, I worried something might be wrong, but he nodded.

"Did you like both of us having you?"

"I loved it."

He smiled, and my heart fisted at the open affection in his eyes. "Maybe next time, I'll let you tie up Coop and you can figure out what kind of playing you like to do."

Coop coughed, and we both looked over to find him staring at us with an actual blush on his face.

Laughter swelled through me. "Maybe," I said. "If Coop wants."

He coughed. "I'll think about it," he told me, and I grinned at the redness on his cheeks. I extended trembling fingers to touch him, and he smiled. "I'll think about it, I promise. I kind of like getting to play with you, and I don't want to push my luck."

"Anything you want." I really didn't have to be in charge of this one. There was tons of time to play later. "But…truth?"

He raised his eyebrows.

"Are you really okay with us doing this?"

He glanced from me to Ian, then back. "That's not even a question. I'm down for however you guys let me play or not. Bubba is in charge."

"Sir Ian," I corrected, and he snorted.

"I'm not calling him that."

Against my back, Ian chuckled. "You will if she insists."

"Bite me."

"I'd rather bite Frankie."

And then we were all laughing, and I snuggled back into Ian while clasping Coop's hand. It took another hour to regain some normalcy, and it was late by the time I was cleaned up and dressed again. There was no escaping how well fucked I looked, because one glance in the studio bathroom revealed that, but I honestly didn't care.

The drive back to the apartment was filled with gentle touches and soft laughter. The sight of Jake and Archie's vehicles made me smile, and I would have skipped up the steps but my ass was just a bit sore.

Inside, Jake and Archie were both in the kitchen, and they turned as I walked in. Archie had his phone in his hands.

"I was just about to call you," he said. "The results are in."

Chapter Eight
LIFE IS WEIRD

"Holy shit." Rachel stared at me as she lowered the soda she'd been about to drink. "That's fucked up."

I shrugged and slumped back against her bed. A storm raged outside, and her whole house smelled like rich, spicy stew. A stack of laundry waited to be put away at the end of the bed, abandoned once I'd started telling her about the last week.

"Honey," she said as she set the soda down and came to sit on the edge of the bed next to me. "Are you okay?"

I slanted a look at her and shrugged a second time. "Yes and no. He's not my brother. I knew that and he knew that, and I didn't care what his asshole of a father said…"

"But for five days…" Rachel grimaced. "Holy shit, that really is just all kinds of fucked up."

"Yep," I agreed with her. "But we got our own test done. Archie and I don't share enough common alleles to be siblings. The report is pretty explicit, and Archie and Jeremy both trust the lab so…there's that." The depth of relief in Archie's eyes had only been matched by the fury kindling within them when either of our parents were mentioned. "He's going after his father now. I don't think I've ever seen him so angry or determined."

"Good, sounds like someone needs to stab him. Repeatedly. In non-vital places. So it hurts more." The viciousness in her tone pulled a smile from me.

"Aww, Archie will be touched that you care."

She snorted and pinched me. "Rich Boy is a lot of things, but he redeems himself in my eyes every time he looks at you. No one deserves a prick like that for a parent."

I grinned wider. "Your softer side is showing."

"Pfft. I trust Archie to take care of his father and that ice bitch of a mother. What about *yours*?" With the way her dark eyes focused on me, I didn't have anywhere to go to escape the studying gaze. Fortunately, I didn't want to.

"My emancipation court date is in a little under two weeks."

"Okay, and that's fantastic. Hopefully, you stick it to the bitch when you cut ties." Rachel braced a hand on the bed. "But what are we doing about *her*?"

"That's the ten-thousand-dollar question." I pursed my lips. "I have an idea. But I don't know if it's as cruel and manipulative as something she would do because it definitely serves my interests and not hers." Even as I said it, I hesitated, then grimaced. "It's not even about my interests, it's about getting Eddie back for Archie as much as it is getting back at Maddy."

"Color me intrigued," Rachel said with a slow grin. "And I'm all in. What do you want to do?"

It was the middle of the day. The guys had all had school today and I was technically still on internship hours, but I had promised Archie and the boys I wouldn't go anywhere near Standish. Archie guaranteed it wouldn't be a problem for the internship, and to be honest, even if it was, I didn't care. I wasn't sure what I would do or say if I saw Edward Standish again.

I would have to, sooner or later, but I still didn't know what I would say. Or to be correct, what I would say beyond telling him what a cataclysmic asshole he was.

"My grandparents," I said slowly. Archie and I had talked about them a little, but that conversation had upset him on some level, and after the last few days, I wanted to keep things lighter for him. Fuck knew how we'd do that, but I still wanted to.

"I'm listening." Rachel pulled a pillow around to hug it as she leaned forward and focused on me.

"Patience," I said with a half-snort, because talk about irony, "and Eugene Grayson. As far as I know, Maddy is their only child. When I did an internet search, I found them living in New England, although they have a home in California as well as another in Europe and vested interest in places in the Caribbean."

"Okay." Nothing in Rachel's expression changed. She was letting me work this out aloud, and it was the first time I'd actually tried talking about them since I'd brought it up with Archie. When I'd emailed Wittaker, he'd also sent me a two-page letter summarizing them. "So they're rich."

"They own resorts and hotels all over the world. A lot of them."

"So, they're filthy, stinking rich."

I gave a little shrug. "I guess. Their net worth is in the billions."

"Holy fuck."

Another shrug. "I don't want to think about that part, because Maddy came from that kind of money and I grew up with her living paycheck to paycheck and shopping at discount stores and using duct tape to hold my shoes together when I got holes in them and she couldn't afford to get them fixed."

I had no shame about that. I could stretch a dollar. I was self-reliant. I could support myself.

"Girl, do *not* tell me you are feeling sorry for her?"

"I don't—I don't know what I feel exactly. But how do you go from that kind of money to living how we were?" I spread my hands. I'd kept some of the pieces out of the story, the pieces that were personal to Archie. Like the fact his parents were made to get married or whatever. "And she always throws that thing in my face about how she could have given me up for adoption or had an abortion. Is that why? Was she exiled for having me?"

"I don't care if she was given fifty lashes and tossed out on her ass," Rachel said, expression tightening into a frown of disbelief. "Parents are supposed to love and take care of you, not inflict their emotional damage onto you or make you responsible for their bullshit."

True. Eddie was a fucking moron. He blamed Archie because Eddie got caught with his dick out and had to marry Muriel. At the end of the day though, that was a choice, right? What if he'd refused? He'd have been cut off.

Had Maddy been given a similar choice?

Fuck, this whole thing gave me a headache. "I don't feel sorry for her." I didn't. "I just don't understand her."

"Well, if you look up 'raging cunt' in the dictionary, I'm sure you'll find her picture next to it."

I laughed.

"I'm serious," she deadpanned. "Because fuck that woman. Please tell me she's the one you want to fuck with because I am so down for that."

"Except I don't even think we can fuck with her, except to point out to Eddie that she lied." Which, we were going to do. Maddy only cared about what she wanted, what affected her, and I guessed telling Eddie I was his kid was her in. Well, fuck her and that plan. My life wasn't her damn toy to play with. "But the rest of it?" I rubbed my hands against my face. "Rachel, I don't know. Do I try to meet these people? Do I care?"

"Didn't you say your grandmother came once when you were a kid?"

I nodded.

"But you really didn't talk to her?"

"No, she was pretty cold. Like, you could freeze ice on her ass cold."

Rachel shot me a comical look, and I shrugged.

"What? She was? She and Maddy argued, that I remember, but it wasn't heated or anything. It was cold and distant and just impersonal as hell, and then she was gone again. I don't think she gave two shits about me then, so I can't imagine she'd care now."

"But you want to know," Rachel concluded softly.

"I'm an open book, huh?"

"No." Her smile was almost wistful and a bit teasing. "Well, yes, but more you have a big heart. That's always been you, Frankie. It's why those idiots are so possessive of you, because you love so fiercely and openly. You really are feeling bad for Maddy, even if it's only on some abstract, intellectual level because you can't fathom how a parent can do that to their child, even if *your* parent did it to you."

I spent the rest of the afternoon with Rachel, but headed home to meet Jake after school let out and to go do some deliveries. While I'd seen him over the last few days, we hadn't really had any us time and I'd missed him.

Of course, he laughed at me when I told him that. "Baby Girl, you never have to miss me."

"Pfft," I said, sticking my tongue out at him. "You know what I mean."

"I do." He was driving because we were going to work a couple of hours for him and a couple of hours for me. We'd tried using both of our apps at the same time and that just got complicated as hell, so it was easier if we did it one at a time. The point was to spend time together. "You missed me. So that means you should spend the whole weekend with me."

I laughed. "I would, except I'm sure your 'secret project' with Archie will keep you both tied up." Not that I was complaining. I liked that Jake had been there for Archie, especially over the last few days.

"Nah, he can take care of it. You and me, we'll lock ourselves in the bedroom and make Coop deliver us pizza whenever we want a little change in the sexual menu."

I died. Seriously. Died. Laughing, I leaned against the door. "Change in the sexual menu."

He grinned. "I don't hear you saying no."

"And you won't. Because you love it too."

"Hell yes, I do."

We kept it light and playful for the first couple of deliveries, but it quieted after the third one. He pulled over into an empty slot near a row of restaurants. They were typically the most popular ordering spots, so it was as good a space as any.

"You doing okay, Baby Girl?" He coiled a lock of my hair around his finger and tugged gently. "It's been a long few days."

"It was," I said. "And I still have to figure out what to do about the internship and the trust and all that other stuff, but a big part of me wants to just blow it all off and focus on graduation and the future, you know?"

"Then do it. You know we're going to back you on anything you want to do."

I did know that. "But isn't that just running away?" One thing Archie had said to me the other day had been playing on a quiet repeat in the back of my mind. I had *me*. I was the most self-reliant person he'd ever known. He didn't think I needed any of it—the family, such as it was, the trust, the history, and with all of it, the baggage.

On the one hand, I loved that he believed in me like that more than I would ever be able to express. But on the other...

"Talk to me, Baby Girl. I'm not Coop, I don't have magical insight into what's going on behind those stunning eyes of yours, but I'm right here. If I can fix it, I will. If you just need me to listen, I can do that, too."

"You'll call it like it is, though." Because Jake had never pulled his punches with me. Except, you know, asking me straight out to be his girlfriend.

He tugged my hair gently. "Yep, so tell me what you want."

"I want to understand." And I thought that Jake, of all people, would get that.

"Okay, let's start with the pieces you want to understand—why your mother told Archie's father what she did?" He ticked it off on his fingers. "Why did your grandparents and mother cut ties with each other? Why there's a trust fund? Who are your grandparents?"

"Who is Maddy too," I added to that list. "How much do I take after her?"

"Fine, to the first one, and not a fucking bit to the second. She's a selfish bitch, and you don't have a selfish bone in your body."

I cut him a smile at the resoluteness in his voice. "I love you too."

"I know." He winked. "Do you want to add who is your actual father or not to that list?"

"I have *no* idea." That nagging headache resumed its dull thump behind my eyes, because that was exactly one of the issues I'd been having. "I didn't want to know before, remember, when we found the tests?"

"Was that you really not wanting to know, or you not wanting to be disappointed, Baby Girl?"

"Does it matter which?" Sitting sideways in the seat, I stared at him, and he reached over and shut off his availability on the phone.

"Yes," he answered. "Lately, I've been thinking more about my dad and Klara. About the choices he made that I don't understand, and that I made choices in response to those choices."

Pulling my knees up, I reached over to catch his fingers. "Yeah?"

"Yeah. The thing is—I've been pissed at him for so long, all I saw was what he didn't do. I never thought about why he did what he did."

I frowned, but didn't interrupt as he tangled our fingers together, then turned my hand from side to side as he stroked his thumb over the palm.

"I resented that he didn't choose his kids. That he didn't choose Mom. I mean on one level, I knew he couldn't just leave his commission. That's one thing about being in the military—you don't get to decide where you go. You go where you're sent. I don't know if I'll ever understand it," he admitted. "But at the same time, I never tried. When he calls, I avoid the conversations and just let the girls talk to him. When it comes to going to see him, I pass."

I hadn't even realized that he'd had the opportunity, and that surprise must have shown, because he gave me a wry smile that was clear, even in the darkness of the front seat.

"Yeah, there's been a couple of chances over the last few years. The girls went over to Germany last summer."

Oh.

"But I passed on it, and not just because I was hoping a certain someone would come out of hiding." He reached over to trace his free hand down my cheek just before he tweaked my nose. "But also because I didn't want to understand him."

I swallowed. "But now you do?"

"Yes and no. I mean, that ship might have sailed, but the other day, I went with Arch to see his dad and…" He shook his head slowly. "I don't get that about him. He's an ass to Archie."

On that we agreed.

"And my dad's choices might be inexplicable, but he's never been an ass to me. Even when I was being one to him. Granted, I didn't really give him the chance, but…but when you say you want to understand, I get that, and it's why I know you're nothing like your mom, Baby Girl. That big ass heart of yours is looking for something to forgive."

I made a face. "I don't know that I like thinking I have a big ass heart."

"I do," he told me, his smile growing. "That big ass heart found a way to forgive all of us, and it still managed to love us, even when we were being asses. It's made room for all of us and loves us so fiercely, we don't want there to be a time when it doesn't."

My face heated, and his smile softened.

"You showed us it was possible, and while I think we all competed for a long time, it only really started working when we worked together to win you."

I laughed. "I'm not a prize."

"Hush, you're the best prize there is." He pressed a kiss to my nose and then rested his forehead to mine. "What I'm trying to tell you is don't be afraid to try to understand. The last thing any of us want is for you to be hurt, which means we'll be with you every step of the way and if they look at you cross-eyed, well…you don't worry about it. We have your back."

"If you want to go and see your dad, I'll get a passport and go with you."

He blinked at me.

"What? You didn't think this road goes two ways? You've avoided talking about your dad for years. Now you've brought him up twice in a couple of weeks. I'm absolutely on your side. If you want to go and see him, I'll go with you and we can see Germany together." Hopefully, we could afford the tickets. "Or at least, I'll be there to buffer if you need it."

A smile widened his mouth slowly as he cupped my cheek. "You would, wouldn't you?"

"In a heartbeat. Though, can we wait until after AP exams? Or if not, I guess we could go spring break. If I can get a passport that fast." I actually had no idea how long that would take. I'd done research at one point. I was pretty sure it would cost extra, but if Jake needed it, we'd find a way to make it work.

"I adore you, Baby Girl." Then he was cupping my face and kissing me. The soft brush of his lips was so tender, it had me gasping a little, and then I sighed into the sweetness. I teased his tongue with mine, and his seat slid back as he pulled me out of mine and onto his. The seatbelt slid free because someone had already unlocked it.

"Smooth," I teased him as I straddled his lap. He chuckled before claiming my lips again, and I ran my fingers through his hair as we played, nibbled, and tasted each other.

"I like to think so," he answered, nuzzling my chin. "And thank you for offering to go with me. But if I stole you away to Germany over spring break, there would be a riot."

I laughed. "The boys would understand."

He gave me a look that said I was fucking nuts, but I tapped his nose gently.

"They would. If Archie needed me to go somewhere, or Coop or Ian, you would understand."

Grunting, he made a face. "I wouldn't like it. I'd hate the idea of you being far away where I couldn't help either of you."

"But you would understand," I reiterated.

With a sigh, he nodded. "Yeah. Thank you, Baby Girl. Maybe not yet, but we should look into getting you that passport. Maybe Archie will want to take you to Paris or something."

I knew he was joking, though with Archie…okay, maybe not. Still, I couldn't resist tweaking him just a little. "Well, if we went to Paris, I could say hi to Mathieu."

Honestly, the pinch he gave my ass hurt, even through my jeans, and he caught my lower lip in his teeth as he scowled at me. Finally, he said, "No Paris for you."

I laughed.

While we should have been working, we didn't. I stayed cuddled in his lap, and we kissed and nuzzled and just held each other. If I hadn't been wearing jeans, I had a feeling I'd already be riding him, but Jake scowled at the lights all around us and then back at me.

Yeah, this was a little *too* public for him. On the way back to the apartment though, I decided I'd just wear a skirt and no panties next time. I'd surprise Jake, and the thrill of the idea left me tingling all over.

My life was so weird sometimes. I loved all four of them. I loved the time we spent together. And now I was actively planning how to seduce them. Not that I thought it would be hard, but they all loved surprising me and I adored it.

Now I wanted to do the same for them.

"When do I get to hear this new song of yours and Bubba's?" Jake asked as he locked the car and we headed inside, hand in hand. "Coop said it was hot."

I stumbled a step, and Jake let out a little whoop, even as he caught me and pulled me to him.

"I knew it! That lucky bastard worked his way in with you and Bubba."

Clearing my throat, I thumped him. "I'm not having this conversation."

"You can tell me," he whispered. "You know you can tell me anything. Bubba talked to me about the classes, and I've been reading your books."

The earlier heat had nothing on how my face caught on fire.

"And in case you were at all curious," he whispered into my ear. "I'm all in, Baby Girl. That next class of yours, I want to go."

Holy shit.

That thing about surprising them?

Yeah.

I needed to get on that.

Biting my lip, I pulled back and canted my head. "You show me yours, and I'll show you mine."

"Trust me, Baby Girl. You will see ours soon enough, and mine is always yours."

A shiver went through me.

He definitely showed me his when we got inside, picking me up and utterly bypassing Archie and Ian in the living room and *locking* the door when we got to the bedroom. I was still laughing when he dumped me on the bed all caveman style and then pounced me for a tickling that nearly had me peeing my pants.

Chapter Nine

LITTLE BOY BLUE AND THE MAN IN THE MOON

ARCHIE

The host led me through the club's dining room to a private table. While Grandpa hadn't arrived yet, they weren't going to make me wait. When the host asked me if I'd like something to drink, I resisted the urge to ask for whiskey or a bourbon. They wouldn't serve me here no matter how much money I had. They liked their liquor license. Course, once Grandpa got here, he'd probably take care of that for me.

"Just a Coke," I ordered and pulled out my phone as I checked to see if there were any messages. I was early, but I wasn't worried. Grandpa had been on the move for weeks to deal with Edward. He was literally getting all his pieces in place so that when we sprang the takeover, it would be a smooth transition and not hostile.

Well, at least not the kind of hostile Edward stood a hope in hell of fending off.

I grinned. My smile grew wider when she sent a selfie of her puckering up and blowing me a kiss.

Fuck, I loved this girl.

There were a couple of messages from Bubba.

Holy. Shit.

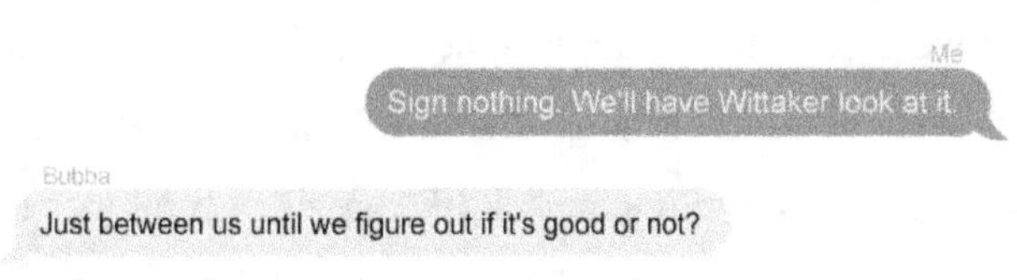

I totally got that.

Fuck. A contract. The producers liked the recordings he'd sent in. I really needed to up my research on the music business, and they needed a full-time entertainment lawyer if they were going to do this. If they wanted to do this, then they were damn well going to do it. Text sent, I checked for any other messages. Most were things I could ignore, the guys were busy.

Jake was at the house and working until I got there. We had most of it figured out, now we just had to put it all back together and run some tests. Coop had family stuff tonight, while Frankie was working. She'd text us all when she was done, and whoever was closest would head back to the apartment.

After the last ambush, she didn't stay there alone. We were trying to be subtle about it, but Frankie recognized it. She wasn't an idiot, the knowledge flickered in her eyes along with the acceptance. She'd acquiesced to my desire that she *not* return to Standish, and that was as much for her as for me. I had every ounce of faith she'd confront Edward, and I didn't want her anywhere near him.

Not until I made sure to cut off all avenues of retaliation, at least within the company. Then we'd deliver that blow—and it would be a blow—and hopefully, that would swing his focus to Maddy. I couldn't think of anything more fitting than dropping the two of them into a sack like a pair of feral cats to battle it out.

Though, I avoided that particular analogy with Frankie.

Grandpa arrived at six promptly, and I rose as the host arrived, escorting him.

"There's my boy," Grandpa greeted me with a wide grin and clasped my hand. He gave me a side hug, patting my back. "How are you doing, Sprout?"

"I'm better," I admitted, and I was. I hadn't given a damn what those results said. Neither of us had, but the relief that what we knew was true had been proven? That was profound. All it left behind was considerable anger at the two people who had been the architects of far too much pain. "I'm glad you're back in town."

"I would have been here sooner, but courting board members is a lot like herding cats, and half of them wanted to 'talk' on the golf course." His laugh carried equal elements of humor and sarcasm. Grandpa liked golf, but he'd never favored bringing work to the course. Nana used to make him leave work at the office too. Better for everyone, she'd say.

And I had to believe she was right. Grandpa was a hell of a lot happier than Edward. The waiter interrupted to ask about drinks and to go over the specials. Grandpa asked if I wanted one, and while I did, I was also driving, so I just waved it off for now. He got a small bourbon and some water. Then once we were alone, he leaned back in his chair and fixed those eyes so like my own on me.

"Tell me what happened." No preamble, no dancing around it. Another reason I loved Grandpa—he didn't need to be lulled or coaxed into a conversation. He'd much rather get the worst of it out of the way before the food arrived.

He nursed his drink as I laid it all out. I didn't mince words. Told him exactly what Frankie had told me about how Edward approached her and what he'd said. Then I added the details I'd gotten from Muriel and Edward in the aftermath. For a brief moment, I considered holding the DNA test in reserve. To test him. But I didn't want to do that.

Not with Grandpa.

He'd never given me a reason to doubt him, and I refused to let this poison the well. I'd finished my Coke by the time I filled him in on the last bits and then downed half the water.

Sighing, he rubbed a hand over his mouth as I finished, and for the first time in a long time, he looked *old* to me. The silvery-white of the stubble on his face, the deeper wrinkles around his eyes, and the weariness on his face. "You have questions."

"Some."

"Well, let's see if I can address these in order." He only waited when our drinks were touched up and then our salads arrived. I was in no mood for mine, so I just ignored it and kept my focus on him. "First, were Junior and Maddy engaged? Yes. They knew each other at school, had grown up around each other. Were practically inseparable. But both her parents and your Nana and I felt that they were too young, and they were both required to finish college and establish themselves, at least a year, in whatever field they would choose to go into. That didn't stop the engagement, but it was informal."

Fuck.

"That said, they were both very temperamental. They broke up and got back together a dozen times between their junior year at Blue Ivy Prep and their third year at college. Honestly, it was so regular that Patience, Gene, and your Nana and I didn't pay much attention to it anymore. It simply proved the point they weren't ready to get married."

"Until he had an affair with Muriel."

"Yes," Grandpa said, not shying away from it. "According to him, they did use protection, but it failed. Six weeks after their indiscretion, she came to him about you, and he was on the cusp of reuniting with Maddy once again. That's when he came to me." With another heavy sigh, Grandpa leaned forward as he nudged his plate out of the way. "To be perfectly clear here, Sprout, you were always wanted. By me, by your nana, by Junior and by Muriel. Despite their terrible behavior toward each other and you, *you* were wanted. But it became clear to me over the years that what they didn't want was each other."

That…that I got.

In spades.

But I didn't say anything. I needed the facts here, and I was already well-acquainted with their disdain for me as just another piece in their never-ending war.

Well, I supposed it was over now. At least for them.

"That said, when Junior showed up at my office in a panic, I sat him down as I would you and got him to tell me what was happening. In my day, if you got a girl in trouble, you did right by her. Don't hold your nana accountable for what comes next, because ultimately, I'm the one who laid down the law. Maddy and Junior may have been crazy about each other, but they were also hell on each other. They encouraged and brought out the absolute worst in each other. That wild impulsiveness is why we insisted they finish their schooling before they got married, and frankly, neither one could stay true to the other. They kept finding ways to hurt each other more, and I was tired of Junior being hurt by that girl. Her parents are good friends, but she's always been…all about herself."

He downed the last of his bourbon and shook his head.

"So you basically told them if he didn't marry Muriel, you'd cut him off?"

"Yes." He grimaced as he stared into the empty glass. "As much as I wanted to fix things for them and I wanted you, if he'd truly fought me and fought for Maddy, then I might have relented."

Holy shit.

I flopped back in the chair. "It was a test."

Grandpa tested people. He always had. He liked to know what their character was made of. He'd done it to Frankie at our dinner, and she'd rallied to my defense so swiftly and with such fire, Grandpa had liked her immediately.

"He failed."

Another nod from Grandpa. "So, I dictated the terms of the prenuptial. If he could blow so hot and so cold about a woman he loved so much, I needed to make sure he secured the home he was bringing his child into. Strong arming? Yes. But I thought, given time and forced proximity, your parents would find a way to love each other. Arranged marriages used to happen all the time, just because you don't love each other in the beginning doesn't mean you won't in the end."

Nice thought. Definitely didn't work out.

"You could have let them drop the prenuptial when it wasn't working out." Only a blind man wouldn't have seen how unhappy they were. Then again, it might have been screamingly obvious to one too.

"He never asked, Sprout. And to be fair, after your nana died, I didn't much think about it. I kept my eye on you. That was enough. We tried to have you with us as much as possible when it became clear they weren't just a terrible couple but failing at being parents." He frowned again. "I tried to talk to Junior about that once, but…your father and I don't get along much."

Understatement of the year.

I waited for our appetizers to be taken away and our dinners to arrive before I hit the next segment. "You knew who Frankie's mother was the moment you met her." It wasn't a question.

"Yes, I did, and that was the other reason I tested her that night." He grimaced. "If she was at all like her mother…I couldn't risk having her in your life. Not after everything with Maddy and Junior."

"She's not."

"No, Sprout. She isn't. I figured that out in five minutes. And I know you're crazy about her. I wish…I wish I'd gotten your call sooner. I could have told you she wasn't Junior's."

"Wait…" I frowned, hesitating before cutting into my meat. "How would you—of course. As soon as Maddy got pregnant."

Grandpa nodded. "Patience and Gene were beside themselves. Junior was already married to your mother, and Maddy wouldn't tell them who the father was. They had a huge fight, but she wouldn't budge on it and then she shocked everyone by walking away. Gene threatened to disinherit her, and she left. Packed a bag, took her car, and moved out." He looked thoughtful. "It was your nana who tracked her down first. She always was good with reading people. Maddy had taken an apartment not far from the school. She had only a semester left, so she was trying to finish it up. She befriended, helped pay for things, and kept her close until she was ready to move, and then when she went to California, we kept tabs on her until the baby was born."

"And you arranged a paternity test."

"I paid the right people. If that baby was Junior's, we'd have had to wrestle her away from Maddy or pay her off. But she wasn't, and that closed that chapter or so we thought. We gave her enough money to get by and then cut off contact."

I wasn't sure whether to laugh or not. "What about her parents? Did she really cut all ties with them too?"

"Apparently, as far as your nana and I knew, they never heard from Maddy again, and to be honest, I hadn't heard her name in fifteen years or more when you messaged me about her."

"Do you know who Frankie's father is?" Because right now, I was trying to figure out whether I would have rather they had been able to take her from Maddy, at least she would have been raised with love and caring. At the same time, I'd have had a sister and not a lover, and I couldn't see her in that role. I couldn't let go of what we had.

"There were a couple of possibilities, but I'm afraid I didn't investigate them all that far. Sordid business really, and to be fair, it could have caused problems for the men involved. If she wasn't pursuing it with them or with Junior, then I let it go as well. I'll be honest, with everything I'd known about her, it didn't seem her character to walk away from all that wealth, yet she did.

Your nana said that being a mother can change a girl."

Not from what I'd seen, but maybe it had and then it went wrong.

"I have to wonder if Junior coming back into her orbit sent them both back down that path again." He'd finished his fish and some of his vegetables, but like me, he'd picked at the food. This wasn't the most comfortable of talks. "Is your girl all right?"

I cut him a small smile. "She's a survivor. Edward seems to really believe she is his. Maddy has him completely snowed, and he was thrilled to think of her as being his."

Grandpa's expression tightened, and I waved off the fierce tirade I could almost see in the storm of his eyes.

"Frankie already ripped him a new one about being a dick, and I don't really care that he wants her like he never wanted me. She represents what he thought he had with Maddy, like evidence they would have worked out. I think he really wants it to be true, wants to believe her lie. I'm just not entirely sure why she's lying to him."

"When the girl graduates, Maddy will get some of the monies in a trust set aside by her own grandmother. It's a tidy sum. Not extensive wealth. I know Gene changed the terms of the other trusts, put them in Frankie's name. I did call them about that after I met her."

And that was the other thing. "So they really do know about her? And they've done fuck all where she was concerned?"

"Sprout, I know you're angry and I'm not going to tell you that you shouldn't be, but again, it was a different time, and I think Gene and Patience hoped that Maddy was growing up. Particularly when she never came back, never acquiesced to their demands. That kind of stubbornness, it requires a certain amount of strength."

Right. I didn't expect to be handing out any medals anytime soon. "But Frankie has met her grandmother once."

"Yes, Patience approached Maddy a few years ago, seeking to heal the rift if possible. Gene had a heart attack, it was during the week we were supposed to all go to Italy. I sent you and your nana ahead, and I stayed back to help Patience a bit before I joined you."

That seemed so long ago.

"As for the details of what happened, I know very little. Patience and Maddy had another disagreement, and that was that."

And that was that.

Fuck these people.

I rubbed a hand over my mouth. "This is like some really bad PBS melodrama. Or *Afterschool Special* thing."

"How do you even know about *Afterschool Specials*?" Grandpa gave me an amused look, and I shrugged.

"Frankie has eclectic tastes." And researched *everything*.

"Sprout, all of this, it's a lot, but you know it's not on you kids, right?"

On that we would have to disagree. "Frankie's been paying for their choices for a long time. And they seem intent on making her continue to pay for them."

Scratching at his jaw, he nodded slowly. "But your Wittaker has that well in hand. She'll be emancipated soon, and even if she wasn't, she's almost eighteen. We'll look after your girl and we'll protect her."

"Edward? Maddy? We just let them get away with this?"

"No," Grandpa said slowly. "No, we do not. I promised you my help in dealing with Junior at the quarterly meeting next month, and there will be a vote. I'd like your proxy. But we'll be removing him as CEO."

"Okay. You're going back in?"

"Interim," Grandpa said slowly, eyeing me. "Contingent on your graduation from college in the next five years. At which point, I'd like you to take over the majority of the day to day. I have a couple of candidates in mind who can help me with the workload and also be in a position to shepherd if anything happens to me in the meanwhile, but I've all but secured the votes we need to make this a reality."

If something were to happen… "You're fine, right?" The bottom of my stomach dropped out. "I don't want you stressing yourself…"

"Sprout, I'm healthy as a horse, as much as my physician hates to admit it. I'm hardly a decrepit old man. I can more than handle getting back into the swing of things. I retired more because your nana wanted me around more often and Junior needed a kick in the ass to be more responsible."

Fuck. Me. "Great, but if that changes, I better be the first call and not the one who gets the call after."

I didn't even want to contemplate what losing him would be like.

"I'm good, Sprout," he promised me and gripped my shoulder. "Look at me."

I met his gaze and blew out a breath that shook more than I wanted to admit.

"We're going to take care of all this, but that company, I built it for the future on what my father left me. You're that future. If you don't want it, you tell me now and I'll make other arrangements so that you are secure. But I'm not forcing you into anything. I've learned my lesson…" He frowned. "Maybe if I'd done that sooner, you wouldn't have been trapped between them for so long."

"Grandpa, I'm fine." Weirdly enough, that was true. Sure, it sucked back then, but… "Everything that happened, their wars and arguing, it's what brought me here and what let me meet her. Meet my friends. Fall for Frankie. I don't want to be anywhere else. We're lining up school for next year, and we're going to get a place together, all of us. And I'm going to take care of her."

He gave me a small smile. "Are you planning on marrying Frankie?"

"If I was?" I dared him to tell me I had to wait until after college. Not that I was in a raging hurry. I didn't need some piece of paper to tell me what I already knew. Hell, I'd told Muriel just to test her.

"I'd ask you to wait until both of you were settled and sure, but I won't forbid it. She's a good girl. Smart. Capable. I've heard about her work at Standish.

I've seen her grades. I even had a talk with Harvard about her."

I blinked.

"If she wants that school still, I think we can secure her a spot."

Fuck me.

"Grandpa."

"No, what good are connections and nepotism if you can't use it to make someone you love happy?"

I laughed. It sounded like the same kind of argument I would use. Had used. "I do love spoiling her."

"Then you let me know what she wants, Sprout. We'll take care of it."

A half-laugh escaped me, and I sagged in the seat as he gripped my shoulder tighter. He didn't say anything. He didn't have to. Somehow, Grandpa got it. It took me a few minutes and the steak was cold when I got back to it, but I managed to finish the whole thing. When we were done, we walked out together. He had a car waiting for him, and the valet went to fetch my Ferrari.

"Next time, bring your girl. I think we should look at having family meals, maybe once a month? I know you kids are going to be busy."

"I'd like that, and I did promise to take her golfing with us one day."

"You said she liked that mini-golf." Humor flared in his eyes. "Your nana was pretty good at it too."

Yeah, she was. "She loves it. A lot like Nana did."

He nodded. "Then we'll see how she likes the greens. Give you a break."

When he offered me a hug, I took it, and he gripped me tight before kissing my cheek.

"Love you, Sprout. It's going to be all right."

"Love you too." I couldn't pretend my voice wasn't tight. As much as I'd needed to hear it from him, knowing he was part of the reason a lot of this happened the way it did still ached. He meant well. But the road to hell was paved with good intentions.

After promising to keep in touch and to get him my proxy, I waited until he drove off before I headed to my car.

Inside it, I checked my phone, and there was a single message from Frankie on it.

Frankie

I love you. Come back to the apartment tonight if you're not staying over with your grandpa somewhere?

Me

Just finished dinner and coming home. Kick out whoever is sleeping on your right. That's my spot tonight.

Frankie

Coop's just waiting for you to get here. Promised he'd 'fuck off' after. His words, not mine.

I laughed.

Me

I'm surprised he doesn't want to watch.

My phone buzzed.

Coop

Of course I want to watch, but I'm not an asshole. Besides, be hard to beat your performance the other night.

The laughter that escaped me was sharp but real, and it knocked some of the jagged bits loose. I fired off a middle finger emoji to him.

Me

Just for that, you're definitely not invited.

Coop

Shit, there was a chance before?

I smirked.

His middle finger emoji followed by a couple of crying ones made me laugh harder. I wiped the hint of tears from the corners of my eyes and then called Jake as I backed out. I needed to let him know I was heading to Frankie's and see where we were. We had time, but we also wanted to make sure it was perfect.

Something to Talk About

"**A**nger at your mother is normal," Erin said. "You've been working on expressing that in these sessions."

"Yeah well," I admitted as I leaned back in the chair, fingers interlocked over my stomach, "I have no problems expressing it at the moment." How long had I defended her? "I just can't even begin to understand what the hell she thinks she gets out of lying about who my biological father is."

"Do you want to understand it?"

I stared at Erin and then went back to tugging at a loose string on my ripped jeans. "I'm not sure there's a point in understanding it. At the same time…" I'd been talking in circles on this for the last few days since we got the test results back. Honestly, though, I'd talked about it even before. "I don't know what to do with it all."

"All right, let's put a pin in that piece for a moment and come at this from a different angle, shall we?"

One of the things I liked about Erin, she didn't always push, even when she did push. She made it sound like I had an option. I hadn't really pushed back, not since the first couple of sessions. Weirdly, even when I wasn't sure if talking helped, it helped to get it off my chest. I could and had talked to the guys, but this was different. Coop was right—she was unbiased, and what I told her didn't hurt her or fill her with the need to fix it for me.

She wanted me to fix me.

"Frankie?"

Blinking, I tugged at the thread. "Yeah, sorry. Just thinking."

"You okay to try and take this from a different angle?"

"Are you handling me with kid gloves today for a reason?" I frowned.

"Not kid gloves. In a very short period, you've been hit with a lot of information. A great deal of it has been emotionally challenging. Processing that is going to take time."

Well, she wasn't wrong about that. "What angle do you want to tackle this from then?"

"Do you want to know who your father is?"

Chapter Ten
THIS COULD GET AWKWARD

IAN

"Thank you," I said into the phone as I walked around the far edge of the pool. Mom and Dad had added a heater to it a couple of years earlier so we could keep the pool open in winter for me to train. After days of on and off drizzle and icy rain, I'd just left the cover on. "I can forward the email with the PDF files over to you."

"All right," Mr. Wittaker said. "According to young Mr. Standish, this contract would also be for Miss Curtis as well?"

"Yes, sir, and she knows I submitted the recordings and the demos. If I'm reading the information correctly, it's for both of us, but there was something about nullifying if one or the other of us decided to quit. I don't want her to be bound by something if I am. I know this is kind of pushing her out of her comfort zone. There was also some stuff about band work and we're not a band, just a pair of singers."

"I understand, Mr. Rhys. Entertainment law is not my specialty, however, contracts are. I will review this contract and reach out to a colleague if I believe you would be better matched with someone who specializes in these types of negotiations. That is one thing you need to remember, this is not the final offer. This is the first offer, the opening gambit. No matter how promising, you never take the first offer."

That's part of why I asked Archie about the contract. The email had been a shock. The attachment and the subsequent follow-up phone call had all been a lot. The one thing I hadn't done though was agree to anything. As tempting as it had been, I wouldn't sign anything without verifying every sentence, punctuation mark, and legally binding clause.

They'd included Frankie in the offer, but since I was the point of contact, they'd also asked for her information. Right. They'd get that when we were ready to give it to them and not a minute before. She had enough on her plate between the paternity drama and trying to hold it together for Archie.

My angel needed good news only, and while I fully intended to tell her, I also intended to control this particular flow of information. I refused to get her hopes up and watch them be dashed again.

By anyone.

"How soon were they expecting an answer?"

"I asked for a week." Not just to think about it, but we were still trying to get through the latest bombshell, and I wanted Frankie to have time to bounce back from that.

"Excellent. I should be back in touch within forty-eight hours. If I do refer you to a secondary attorney, I will sit in on that meeting with you to help address any concerns you or Miss Curtis have."

After going over a couple more details, we ended the call and I forwarded the email. The backdoor opened, and I glanced over as my mother stepped outside. Arms folded against the growing chill, she frowned. "Why are you hiding out here?"

"Not hiding," I told her as I made sure the email and attachment sent before firing a message off to Arch thanking him and another to check on Frankie. Coop was hanging out with her tonight because Mom and Dad wanted to have dinner and we were still "discussing" my choices. "Just making use of some privacy. Dinner ready? Or did you need help?"

"No, it's fine. Your dad is on his way home from the office. He ran late with a patient, so I have everything warm in the oven."

Uh huh.

"No Frankie tonight?"

"No," I said. "I want us all to be on the same page the next time she comes over for dinner."

"Ian," Mom sighed. "We've had this discussion. Your father and I aren't going to treat her differently or badly."

"You say that now," I told her as I pocketed my phone and narrowed the distance. "But neither of you are happy with the decisions we're making."

"You're all so young," she said, and I could practically hear the words she didn't tack on.

"I know," I told her as I kissed her cheek and then motioned to the door. She didn't have a coat on and was shivering. "You've told me several times."

Scoffing, she slapped my arm but hurried inside. "You know what I mean."

"I do," I agreed as I walked over to the sink to wash my hands. "I have listened to every objection and point you've made."

"And none of them are changing your mind."

I glanced at her reflection in the window over the sink. "I love her, Mom." It was that simple.

"Sweetheart, I know you do. You've loved her for a long time."

Done with washing my hands, I dried them on the small hand towel and turned to face her. "But…?"

"But you're young. Both of you. All of you. While I'm not necessarily a fan of unconventional relationships, there are enough challenges when there are only two people, much less five. This is too young to be making life altering decisions."

"What exactly do you think we're deciding to do?"

"Choosing your colleges, for one thing," she said. "I know that you changed up your applications, and I even understand it. Your father and I both do, but have you told them you've been offered a full ride right here in Texas?"

"Nope," I said with a shrug. I'd been offered a couple of them. But they were football scholarships, and I wasn't even sure I wanted to concentrate on football in college. More and more, I leaned on no. I wanted to work on my music. I wanted to be with Frankie. I wanted to work on us. "The plan has always been for the five of us to target the same schools or at least the same area so we could share a place."

Mom huffed out a sigh, but the sound of the garage opening quelled her for the moment. Without her asking, I grabbed the oven mitts and started pulling the food out to take to the table. Family dinners always involved us sitting around the table, no phones, no work, no television, just the three of us talking.

"Sorry I'm late," Dad called as he let himself in from the garage. "Smells good."

"It's fine," Mom told him.

"No Frankie?"

I almost snorted as I set the bowl of pasta on the table and then the bread followed by the sauce. Spaghetti was one of Frankie's favorites, and Mom had definitely made more than enough.

"Apparently, our son doesn't trust us with his girlfriend." The sharp bite in Mom's words made me turn.

"I didn't say I didn't trust you," I corrected gently. "Frankie has just had enough on her plate. She adores both of you, and your approval or lack thereof would mean something to her. I don't want her hurt. So until I've answered all your questions satisfactorily, I'm not bringing her over here."

Dad met my gaze and pursed his lips a moment before he nodded once.

"Let me wash up, and then we can eat and discuss this. I have a feeling this is my fault."

"I never said it was," I answered—because it wasn't—as I pulled out Mom's chair. She paused to study me for a moment as Dad washed his hands at the sink.

"You know we love her, right?"

Glancing down, I smiled. "I do, Mom. Just like I know she loves you."

"And you still want to protect her from me?" She wrinkled her nose.

"Mom, I want to protect her from everything." After the last few months, I wanted to do it more than ever.

Dad waited until after we'd all settled on helpings before he dove in. "This is because I warned you about pursuing something with her when she was already on emotionally unstable ground."

"Partially," I admitted. "But not wholly. I understand a lot of what you 'saw' as an issue, but I don't agree. Not anymore."

Studying me for a moment, Dad nodded. "I'm not going to offer you some platitude or insult you by saying sex clouds things."

"Thanks."

"But sex clouds things," Mom added into the conversation. "It's human that it clouds things. When your father and I started having sex, it complicated a lot of things. He had his duties, I had classes…"

"Sara," Dad said with a chuckle, "Ian doesn't want to discuss our sex life."

"I'm aware," she said without an ounce of shyness. My parents had never been the type to shy away from a subject. "And I don't even object to you and Frankie having sex, I'm sure you're both sensible."

I downed a full glass of water before I started shoveling the pasta in my mouth. If I kept my mouth full, maybe I wouldn't have to keep up my part of this. Mom liked to embarrass me into talking about myself. It was a very effective technique and I had to admire her, but not going to let it work tonight.

"That said," Mom continued as she broke apart the bread, "a poly relationship with four boys and one girl is bound to lead to some strife." She paused, almost considering. "Ian, the fact you would need to balance not only your needs, wants, and desires but theirs… She's not even eighteen yet—"

"She's more mature than all four of us put together," I told her flatly. "And she'll be eighteen in a few weeks. Age isn't the issue, Mom. If it was, then the fact I'll be nineteen in the not too far distant future would have some impact."

Dad chuckled. "He has you there."

"I thought you agreed with me on this," she argued, focusing on him. "You expressed reservations from the beginning, particularly with the boys fighting so much."

Yeah. The fight with Jake. The fight at the party. The fact Jake slugged the asshole who 'slut-sneezed.' Hell, Mitch's family had actually tried to sue us. It had gone absolutely nowhere, and I'd kept that part to myself. The pending criminal charges helped.

I'd break more bones in him if he ever came anywhere near her again.

"I do agree with you, but I also know the harder we push, the harder that he'll push back," Dad said with a nod toward me, and I almost snorted. "He's your son, Sara. He got all of your stubbornness."

"Ugh," she scoffed and then shook her head. "I just want you to be happy."

"I am happy," I promised her. "I'm right where I want to be. I made mistakes, Mom. I made mistakes, and I almost lost her. I'm not risking that again."

"But one person cannot be responsible for the happiness of another," she stressed.

"I get that. It's why we're all working together. We talk, we communicate, we coordinate. The guys are my best friends, I trust them with her and they trust me. She trusts us all. I know it's not conventional."

"Well, it's less about conventions than the fact that age and circumstances can often dictate relationships as much as anything at your age," Dad told me.

"We know. It's why we are even more firmly committed to no long-distance relationships. Jake did the math." I didn't quite smile when I said that, but Mom had to smother one, even as her eyes danced. "Like I said, we wanted that, even before we were dating."

"Fair," Dad conceded, but he pinned me with a look. "Now tell me it wasn't because all of you were still hoping for a chance with her."

"I won't lie," I told him as I straightened in my seat. "But Frankie is more than just some girl to date. She's always been more than that. She's our friend, I'd count her as one of my best friends. I'm lucky, I got four of them. But she's also the girl we love. And yes, Dad, I said *we*, because I'm not the only one in love with her. Truth is, we all have been for years."

I'd finished enough of my food that I set my fork down and focused on them.

"Look, you're worried I'm going to make a decision I regret someday. Right now, the only decision I'd regret is if I didn't choose to be in this relationship. I'm not fooling myself. I know she is in a relationship with the other guys. We're all very up front about it, and when we went to Colorado for Christmas, I got a firsthand taste of what it would be like with just the five of us without the stress and the trauma of the last few months."

I held both of their attention now.

"I loved it. I loved having my best friends right there. I loved spending time with her. I loved that Frankie relaxed and we talked. I know you think we're all too young. But we're not getting married…"

"How would that even work?" But even as Mom asked, Dad caught her hand and shook his head. She sighed. "Sorry, sweetheart. I worry."

"I think that's in your contract." Moms were supposed to worry about us. I just wished Frankie's mom hadn't defaulted on hers. At her quick smile, I nodded. "Like I said, we're not getting married. We're not taking anything for granted or lightly. We've had a lot of discussions. School is important. We all have goals, we're all keeping those in mind. But it's more important to us that we stay together. If that means we don't go to a first pick school, because our second or third pick has not only the classes we need but the added benefit of all of us attending? Then that's where we go."

"All right, so no football." Mom gave me an expectant look, and I nodded. "You're going to pursue your music more vigorously."

I nodded again. "That's the plan. Depending on how things work out, I thought I might minor in business or accounting. Something I can use to pay the bills while I work on my music."

"And in a few years, you graduate. Then what?"

"Then we do what other graduates do—we work on getting jobs and into our careers."

"What if—"

"Mom?" I reached across the table and put my hand over hers. "I get it. You're worried. I can't answer every single possible scenario with anything other than—we'll work it out. Together. I'm not planning for failure, though. We're a team, the five of us. That means sometimes one of us will sacrifice something for the others. But that doesn't mean the end of the line, it just means getting creative so that once they get what they need, the others get it too."

Dad had gone curiously quiet, so I looked at him after I squeezed Mom's hand and sat back in the seat.

"Sir?"

"The axe forgets, but the tree remembers."

I frowned, and even Mom gave him a look.

He shook his head. "Why you won't bring Frankie here—the axe forgets, but the tree remembers. Our choices bothered her before. You don't want them to bother her now because she has enough cuts to heal over."

I nodded once.

"We'll put the axes away."

"Joe…"

"We'll put the axes away, and we're going to respect your choices."

"Thank you."

"Don't thank me yet," he advised. "We'll respect your choices, but you're going to respect ours, as well. We love that girl. Maddy's never done right by her, my worries about her mental health and emotional stability are honestly earned."

I couldn't argue that, except…

"But I'm not *her* psychologist. You said she is seeing one."

One nod.

"Then I'm going to work on putting that hat away and just try to be her friend."

"I'd appreciate that," I told him honestly. "I think she would, too."

"Good. If she needs any help at that emancipation hearing, I'll be glad to lend my expertise."

I grinned. "I really appreciate that. I think we have it covered, but if it becomes an issue, I'll let you know."

"Excellent. Now, family dinner nights, we'll set one aside, and you can bring Frankie and the boys over. We should all get used to that. I think a couple of times at least before graduation. But I would like you to bring Frankie weekly if she's free."

"I'll work on that."

After that, the air at the table relaxed some as talk shifted to their work and some things they wanted to do around the house. A couple of the projects would eat up a few weekends, but we could probably get it done and still leave me time on other stuff.

"You should draft your brother boyfriends in to help, that will make everything go much faster," Mom suggested as Dad and I cleared the table. I wasn't the only one who paused to stare at her, and she gave us a look. "What? They aren't your boyfriends, but you're all dating the same girl, and if they want to call it sister wives when it's the other way, I think brother boyfriends fits."

I wanted to argue that so bad, and at the same time, I wanted her to never ever mention that around the guys.

Coop would have a field day.

"We'll work on it," Dad promised me. "The terminology. Just…understand the feeling is there."

I laughed. "Thanks."

"Anyway," Mom continued as she rinsed the plates we stacked up. "If we draft your brother boyfriends into helping, you could fix the siding in no time and then get that new workbench finished up. Archie is good with tools, right? Maybe he could look at the lawn mower."

By the time I was able to excuse myself to go to my room, I'd begun to regret ever mentioning this to my parents. They'd gone to the den to do research on poly-family dynamics. In my room, I checked my phone for the first time in hours.

Archie was back at the apartment. Frankie and he were tucked in for the night. Coop had gone home, much to his chagrin and complaints. Jake was giving him shit, and Frankie had flipped them off twice in the group chat before she'd stopped answering all together.

I sent her a quiet, private message. I wasn't too worried about her not seeing it tonight. Like I'd told Coop the other day, she really needed him right now. She also needed Archie. That was how this was going to work. We all had our needs, and some of us would need more than others at different points.

My phone buzzed with her response, and I chuckled.

Frankie

How did dinner go? It ran late

Me

We talked a lot. You up for a family dinner here next week?

Frankie

For real?

So I told her. The laughing and crying emojis made me grin. Finally though, I had to ask, because we'd been chatting for nearly an hour.

That it had.

Flopping back on my bed, I stared up at the ceiling and started to laugh.

Brother boyfriends.

Only my mom.

Laugh a Little Too Loud

"It's not about whether I want to know who he is…not really."

"Why would you say that?"

I tugged at the loose string, toying with the frayed end. "I've never had a father. It was always just Maddy and me. I didn't really think about the fact I didn't have one until first or second grade."

"What happened to make you question it?"

"Father's Day. Coop wanted to make something for his dad for Father's Day, and he wanted me to help him find some stuff to do it. Anyway, it was normal stuff. It must have been second grade."

"Okay."

I shook my head. "I just—Jake was here. We didn't meet Jake until second grade." I could almost see the three of us. It was after the end of the school year and the beginning of summer. Jake came over every day because we had the pool and his place had sisters. Including *baby* sisters. Coop only had Trina, but the three of us could run around on our own as long as we stuck together.

"We were always in and out together, hanging out, playing, but on Father's Day weekend, they were both busy and I asked Maddy about why we didn't celebrate Father's Day."

"What did she say? "

A laugh worked its way free. "That it was just her and me. We didn't need a father. Either of us." I glanced at Erin. "Weird, right?"

"I don't know, do you think it's weird?"

I exhaled and then stared up at the ceiling. "Looking back, now? Yes. Then? No. The guys never really asked me about my father, I think they thought he was dead maybe. Or maybe the fact I never brought him up. It's…how do you talk about someone who doesn't exist?"

"Parental relationships are more than genetics and blood."

"Oh boy, do I know that. But there were four DNA tests, and one was positive. She wanted Mr. Standish to believe it was him. It wasn't about *me* knowing. It was about him knowing. She didn't seem to care what it did to my relationship with Archie. To be honest, I kind of wonder if she even knew Archie and I were involved. Or would she have tried to stop it if she had known?"

Ugh. The thought gave me a headache.

"And now that you know it's not him, it means you still have a potential bio donor out there."

"Yeah."

"You don't have to know if you want to meet him."

Well, that was something. "I want to laugh. Because this is like my own damn soap opera, only it's not my storyline, I'm just getting jerked around in hers."

"Then laugh."

I blinked. "What?"

"Laugh," Erin advised me. "Laughter and tears are both cathartic. If you want to laugh, laugh."

A chuckle escaped me, and I shook my head again. "What if I want to find this guy, but it turns out he's no better than Maddy? I mean, she told me once my father didn't want me. Another time, she said he told her to get an abortion.

Another time…" I curled that frayed string around my finger. "Each time it came up, her story changed."

Maddy had always said she'd wanted me. Her. No one else had wanted me, and I should be damn well grateful for it.

"What if you find him, and he's none of the things your mother has described?"

What if…

Chapter Eleven
DON'T FORGET TO REMEMBER ME

COOP

The last week had been crazy. I'd been trying to spend more time with Trina when she wasn't blowing me off. I'd even taken her out with me while I worked a delivery shift. That had been a fucking joy. The icy silence punctuated by bitchy comments. Sign me up for more of that. But it wasn't my first rodeo, and I did what I could.

Now, sitting outside of the family therapy office while Mom and Dad talked to the therapist, I scrolled through my phone. Trina hadn't said much when I picked her up from school, and she'd said even less during the session. As much as these sessions were about helping her address her anger and getting all of us to talk, I had to wonder how much good they could do her until she was willing to be helped?

She released a long sigh. And I didn't look up from my phone. Social media wasn't that interesting, but sometimes, Jake and Archie posted pics of what they were working on. Not always specifics, but the tools they used or something equally vague. Couldn't hurt to look for clues.

Another heavy sigh escaped Trina, and she shifted her weight. I didn't glance at her or smile. I got it, she wanted my attention. Well, she needed to use her words. Not that I could miss her exaggerated complaints. At the same time, she'd been pretty much in the treat me like crap category, so I wasn't feeling a lot of intense sympathy, even if I understood the actions.

The hardest thing in the world to do was not reward bad behavior. Then again, I wasn't going to let her ghost me either. Learned that lesson with Frankie. I drew back and let her set the terms last summer when I should have pushed.

So here we sat, and I endured these sessions with Dad for her sake. Maybe it would help me to get my anger into perspective. Maybe not. Who knew?

"Coop?"

Still not smiling, I glanced up from my phone. Jake and Archie were being less than helpful in my quest to figure out what they were up to. "Hmm?"

"Do we *have* to wait here?"

Shooting her a look, I studied her a bit. She had her head down, and she seemed intent on picking at a seam in her pants. One foot tapped and the rest of her kept shifting subtly in her seat. "Nope," I said, rising. "Texting Mom to let her know we're going to grab food and we'll see her at home."

"Oh thank God," she said in a rush and grabbed her bag from the floor. When had Sis started carrying a purse? It was weird 'cause Frankie mostly stuck to her wallet that was just like mine and used her backpack. Shaking that off, I pushed open the door for her and hit send on the message. We all had our phones off in session, so they'd get it after they were done. Considering how frosty it had been between them, that might take a while.

Once we were in the car, she reached for her phone, even as the Bluetooth system picked up mine and started on my playlist. The number of Torched songs on it might have climbed recently, but at least Trina didn't complain. She didn't look up as I pulled out of the parking lot, her attention on the phone.

I slanted a look at her when we were at a traffic light. The first week we'd started these sessions, she'd been talking nonstop. The more we went, the more distant she grew. Clipped. Downright bitchy at times. My little sister knew how to be a brat, but this was different. This was like I was being punished for something, only I didn't know what that something was.

Yeah, fuck that. I did that with Frankie last summer, let her dictate the where and the when. Let her shut us out when she'd been hurting. At the next traffic light, I turned us around and headed back the way we'd come. There was a Mexican restaurant that Trina loved. An all you can eat buffet and endless sodas.

Frankie discovered it—because Frankie—but she'd introduced me and Trina, and it had become Trina's top pick whenever we asked her about going out. Sis didn't even look up from her phone until I parked, and then she frowned.

"Why are we here?"

"Because we're going to get food and talk."

"What if I don't want to talk?" The belligerent tone in her voice dared me to fight her.

"Then we'll sit at a table and stare at each other while we eat. Just chew your food with your mouth closed."

"I don't want to eat."

"Get out of the car, Sis," I ordered. I got out, and she continued to sit there, all mutinous. Oh, fuck my life. Opening the passenger door, I glanced in. "Out. We need to eat. You like this place."

She sighed and dragged herself out of the car like I was killing her. Holy fuck, fourteen wasn't that long ago. I did not remember being this dramatic.

Frankie would have socked me.

Inside, I paid and then went through the buffet line and loaded up. Trina didn't get as much as usual, so I got extra and I grabbed chips and queso. She filled our sodas and got diet for herself. I grimaced. When had she started drinking diet?

Adding it to the mental list of things we needed to talk about, I let her choose the table since I'd chosen the restaurant. She picked one of the quieter booths on the side where the tall backs gave us an illusion of privacy. Once we were seated, I dug in while she moved the food on her plate more than actually ate it.

True to my word, I waited her out.

"You're really going to sit and stare at me while I eat?"

"I'm staring, but you're not actually eating." I pointed to her plate with my fork. "You keep moving your rice from one side of the plate to the other."

The baleful look in her hazel eyes made me shrug.

"I notice things, Sis."

"When you want to," she muttered.

"Okay, what have I not noticed that you're clearly pissed at me about?"

"If I have to tell you, then clearly you haven't noticed things." She made a face, and I leaned back in the booth and kept staring at her.

It took fifteen minutes, but she cracked.

"Stop," she said with some force. "Now you're just being creepy. How does Frankie put up with you?"

"You should see what she does when I won't tell her what's wrong," I pointed out. "All I do is stare. She'll start singing."

"You like her singing."

"The worst, drunken and repetitive songs ever over and over… It's definitely a form of torture." I grinned. "We could try that if you want."

"Don't. You. Dare."

I chuckled. "You're lucky I'm not Archie, or I'd take that challenge. Now, eat and tell me what's going on with you."

She scowled at her food, then stuck a fork full in her mouth. Two more bites later, and she tried to wash the food down with a sip of her diet crap. The grimace on her face had me grabbing her drink and mine.

"Hey…"

"I'll be right back."

I dumped her soda and got her a regular one, even as I refilled mine, and then I carried them back and set hers in front of her. "I'm trying to lose some weight."

"Right, well, run more or something if you want to burn a few more calories, not that you have a lot spare there, Sis. But don't drink the diet stuff if you hate it."

"Run more? That's your suggestion?" She glared at me. "Not all of us are Frankie. We can't all be human garbage compactors."

Not an unfair assessment. Still… "Be nice. She isn't the one you're pissed at." And after that scene in the parking lot, I had zero tolerance for letting her vent in Frankie's direction. "You're scapegoating onto her to avoid whatever it is you don't want to talk about. If it's a weight thing, I'll listen, but you're adorable, Sis. And you're not fat. Not even close."

"I barely have any tits or ass." The rise of her eyebrows dared me to contradict her. "In fact, I don't have a shape at all unless square is a shape."

"Square is a shape, and you're not a square." I skipped right past the rest of it. "You'll get there. Every girl is different, but starving yourself is not going to give you curves."

"I'm eating for fuck's sake," she snarled and then stuffed another couple of bites in her mouth. I dipped a chip in some of the lukewarm queso. Her scowl deepened and then vanished as she slumped in the booth. "You are such a pain in the ass sometimes."

"Only sometimes?" I mused aloud. "I must be falling down on the job."

She snorted and then sighed. "You guys are really going to move, aren't you?"

At the abrupt subject change, I paused with the chip halfway to my mouth. "Yeah, we're going to for college, but it's not like we won't come back to visit."

"So a couple of weeks here and there? And will you come back if Frankie cuts all ties with her mom?"

"Frankie still loves you too," I reminded her. "And Bubba and Jake both have families here too. Besides, even if they didn't, I'm not going to not be here."

"You weren't here for Christmas," she stated, glaring at me. "This is like Dad all over again, only in slow motion."

I stuffed the chip in my mouth to chew rather than answer her right away. The therapy sessions had been peeling the scabs off a lot of emotional wounds, most of them infected and refusing to heal. "Sis," I said slowly. "The game plan has always been us going off to college. It's what you do after you graduate high school if you have specific plans."

"I know."

"And we were always planning on going to school out of state."

"I *know*." She glared at me. "But you spend *all* of your time with Frankie. You spent Christmas with her. You're going to move away with her and then she's gonna be your family, and where does that leave us?"

"First of all," I said, holding her gaze. "Frankie was already family. Frankie has been family for years."

Expression crumpling, she let out a miserable, "I know. I'm not really mad at her but…this whole thing with Dad. He left and we barely get to see him. Now you're going to leave. Then it's just me and Mom."

"Sis, I don't care where we move or go to school, I'm still your brother. You can call me or text me, we can video chat. Though based on your recent schedule, you're usually too busy to hang out with me without a lot of arm twisting."

Her cheeks pinkened, even as she swiped at the tears.

"And Dad leaving—that's between him and Mom. You still see Dad every other weekend, and if you want to spend more time with him, then say something."

"You don't want to spend the time with him though," she pointed out. "So if I say I want more, then it's like I'm having to choose between all of you."

Deep breath. I fisted my temper and shoved the whole thing in a box. I could punch my dad and his wandering dick right now, but that wasn't what

Trina needed. Nudging my plate out of the way, I rested my forearms on the table and leaned forward. She needed one hundred percent of my focus and to know I heard her.

"We're your family, for better or worse, and we're always going to be your family. Saying you want more time with Dad doesn't mean you want less time with me or Mom."

"Except that's exactly what it means. If I spend more time with him, it's less time at home. Mom always looks so sad when I go, and so does Dad."

"That's because they both love you. Do I look sad when you go?"

She glared and threw a chip at me. I picked it off my shirt and crunched it with a smile.

"They aren't sad that you're leaving one of them to go hang out with the other, they're just sad you're going at all. I expect full on waterworks at graduation, and fuck me, it's going to be bad when we're packing to go."

Her eyes welled up, and she sniffed almost indignantly. "Why are you being an ass?"

"I'm not being an ass," I told her, and I meant it. "I know you're going to miss me. Even with the way you're scowling at me right now. Did it occur to you that I'm probably going to miss you and Mom too?"

That earned a slow blink, and she took a long drink of her soda before swiping carefully at her eyes. The hints of black eyeliner smudging with her fingers made me want to sigh. When did she start wearing make up?

"I'm going to be a thousand miles away and some boy is going to ask you out, and I'll have to find a way to fly back here and kick his ass and get back in time for classes. It's going to be a whole thing."

A real laugh escaped her, even as she rolled her eyes. "You'd totally send Jake."

"Probably," I agreed. "But I'll always be a phone call away, and if you really need me, I'm going to be here."

She sniffed. "I guess you going will help my dating life."

"That's it, you're coming with us. We'll get an extra room for you so I can keep an eye on any boys. Though we may need to get you earplugs."

"Oh God, you are so *gross*." Any sign of tears vanished as she flung another chip at me. "I take it back, I can't *wait* for you to move out."

Chuckling, I nudged her plate toward her. "Awesome. Do you want to try and finish that, or do you want me to go grab us some hot plates since ours got cold?"

"Hot plates?" She looked so hopeful, I just grinned.

"On it."

When I slid out of the booth, she called, "Tamales and rice—and guacamole."

"I know," I said over my shoulder. I knew exactly what she liked. I went through the line again and got her a little extra of each, including some refried beans. I wanted some myself, but Frankie would kill me so I left them. For now.

Back at the table, she put her phone down as I set the new plate in front of her. "Everything all right?"

"Yeah, Mom just wanted to know where we were since we weren't at home."

"She wants us to bring food home for her."

Trina pointed her forefinger at me and cocked her thumb like a gun. "Yep." This time at least, when she dug into the food, she ate it with some actual gusto. And she talked about a lot of stuff and nothing. School. Her friends. What she'd like to do with her weekends with Dad. Saving up for driver's ed. What they were going to do for a car when I left and wasn't there to ferry her around.

It was nice. I offered helpful suggestions, mostly involving the boys she listed on her friends list, but the tears were gone from her eyes and she was definitely more upbeat. Only when we were in the car and on the way back with dinner for Mom did I bring us back to the topic.

"I need you to do me a favor."

"Depends," she answered. "I don't want to clean the bathroom this week.

It's your turn, even if you use Frankie's more than ours."

"That's fine, I already said I'd stick to my half of the chores, though you'll have to get used to doing without me soon enough." It was testing the waters, and she shrugged.

"I'm starting to see the upside of it."

"Brat."

"Pfft. What's the favor?"

"Don't bottle this shit up," I told her. "Don't suck it in so deep and not say anything that you make yourself miserable. You've been upset about this for weeks, and instead of talking to me or to Mom or even the therapist about it, you've just been stewing on it and hurting yourself. I need you to talk to me before things get bad. Yell at me. Throw something at my head. But talk to me and let me help. Can you do that?"

A long, almost thoughtful sigh, and she didn't answer me immediately. I'd rather she took the time to think about it, so I didn't push her. She made me wait until I parked before she answered too.

Little shit.

"I'll try," she said finally. "I don't think I really knew what was upsetting me before you made me go eat and I didn't want to be there. Then I was mad at you for making me spend the time, and that didn't make any sense that I was mad at you for leaving and for making me spend time with you." She shot me an apologetic look.

"It's all good. I'm your brother, I have to love you, even when you're a brat. It's in my contract."

"Ass," she growled, laughing as she got out of the car. I walked her to the apartment with the food.

"Piece of advice," I offered as I held the food over for her to take. She didn't even question it. I was going to go check on Frankie, period. "Go in there and talk to Mom like you talked to me. Tell her how you're feeling and listen to her if she tells you how she is. Then do the same with Dad."

Our breath was visible in the chilly air. "Are you going to talk to Dad?"

"I have," I told her. "He knows exactly how I feel. But my relationship with Dad, or Mom for that matter, isn't yours. You are entitled to the relationship you want with them. Just don't shut us out. We're here for you, Sis, all of us."

She threw herself at me, and I wrapped my arms around her for a hug. Trina hadn't wanted a hug from me in a long time. While she shrugged away soon enough, I still ruffled her hair.

"Love you, Sis."

"Only because you have to," she teased, and I grinned.

"I know," I retaliated. "What's your excuse?"

That earned me a real laugh, and then she let herself into the apartment and I waited for the door to close before I headed toward Frankie's place. Our place really. We'd all pretty much half-moved in. Archie had been there every night that week, and none of us said a word about it. He needed her. Right now, she needed him. Like I told Trina, it didn't mean she wanted less time with the rest of us.

Inside, I caught the scent of her shampoo and a hint of Chinese takeout. There was a note on the fridge that said there was plenty if anyone was hungry. I dropped my shit on the sofa and headed back to the bedroom. Most of the lights were out, and it was quiet. Frankie and Archie were sound asleep when I glanced in.

It took me no time to shrug down to my boxers and brush my teeth before I eased in on her other side. She stirred when my leg brushed hers, nose crinkling.

"Cold."

"Sorry," I whispered. "Go back to sleep." But instead of scooting away from me, she curled closer and tucked her head against my chest. My heart squeezed as I buried my nose in her hair.

Home.

Thinking About It Every Day

"I don't know what to do with that," I admitted. "I like most of the parts of my life right now. Do I want to disrupt that with adding someone else?"

"That's a question only you can answer." Erin set her pen down on the pad she often took notes on and folded her hands together. "When you first started coming here, we talked about your attack, how you were recovering, the upheaval with your mother, and your relationships with the men in your life."

Men in my life. I almost smiled. Not once had Erin been judgmental on that front. And while I still thought of them as the boys, I guess men was more appropriate. "It feels like we've talked about a lot in the last few months."

"That's part of what these sessions are for," Erin offered with a small smile. "Your emancipation hearing is next week?"

I nodded. "That's why I canceled the session for that day. I don't know how long it will take."

She nodded. "I'm going to keep the hour set aside, even if you just want to call me and have the session on the phone."

"Thank you."

"Of course. Normally at this point, I like to gauge whether a client wants to continue and to assess how far we've come. But I think I'd like you to answer that for me. Are these sessions helping you?"

"You don't think they are?" My gut dropped as I frowned.

"I didn't say that," she scolded in the gentlest tone. "I'm asking you if you find these sessions helpful."

"Even when I leave with more to think about than when I came in," I said slowly. "Yeah, I find them helpful. The guys are great about never asking me about what we talk about. I know they'll listen if I want to talk, but sometimes… sometimes I feel like I complain a lot. It's hard, because I don't want to be the one they always have to fix things for."

Archie loved to fix things. Coop was always there with a smile and comfort. Jake charged through my defenses and dared me to step outside my comfort zones. But never alone. They were always there. And Ian…

I blew out a breath. He blanketed me in this feeling of security I didn't fully understand and let me just let go. "I feel like I should be doing more for them. They do so much for me, and they…they agreed to this unconventional relationship." A little laugh escaped. "You know, I think about that every day, about how lucky I am that I didn't lose them. That they didn't give up on me. Some days, it's harder to balance than others, but the last few months would have been unbearable without them, and even in the middle of all this paternity drama…"

When had my life become such a soap opera?

Hands spread, I lifted my shoulders. "They make me laugh. They let me cry. They hold my hand when I need it and let me punch things when I need that. Sometimes, they're just there, and my day is better because I know they're there."

"How would you feel about having them come in for a session with you?"

What?

I blinked at her. "Like all four of them?"

"You're in a relationship with all four, so yes." Nothing in her relaxed manner changed. "I like to meet with the significant others of my patients from time to time, because it helps me get a feel for where you all are and how that affects you. It also…it's also sometimes easier to tackle some of these subjects you're hesitant about in a controlled setting."

"Erin? How did we go from talking about my paternity drama to whether I wanted to do a group session with the guys?" And nope, I did not just say that 'cause I swore my mind flew straight to a much dirtier place than this office. Despite the flush creeping up my neck and super heating my cheeks, I resisted the urge to hide my face.

The quirk of her lips told me she didn't miss the suggestion, but thankfully, she was way too professional to tease me about it. "Because you've been making life decisions and you take their feelings into account on several of these issues. Bringing them in for a session isn't my way of suggesting something is wrong, but rather another tool in your toolbox of support. You don't have to bring them…and before you ask me why not bring them one at a time, it's because this relationship you've built rests on the foundation of all five of you, of the friendship you share."

I put my hands over my mouth as I leaned forward, elbows on my knees. They'd come if I asked them. No doubt existed within me. "Can I think about it?"

"Absolutely, and now, for some homework since I won't be seeing you next week…"

Oh.

Goody.

Normally, I liked homework.

Chapter Twelve
PELVIC SORCERY AND WICKED TIES

JAKE

"This isn't going bowling," Frankie chastised me from the backseat, and I shot a grin at her over my shoulder before holding a hand out to Bubba.

"Five bucks, pay up."

He laughed and slapped the cash against my palm. "Jackass."

"What bet?" Frankie asked.

"I told Bubba you wouldn't let me get away with it for five minutes, and he thought you'd indulge me for at least fifteen."

"Oh, I hate you both," she declared before flopping back in the seat, arms folded.

"Now, Baby Girl, you know you love us." I grinned, flicking a look at her in the rearview mirror. She stuck her tongue at me, even as her eyes danced when the headlights from traffic illuminated them. The demo class at the club was the first one we'd all been available to attend. "Anyway, Bubba already went over the rules earlier. We'll be on our best behavior *when* we get there."

Before then, everything was fair game. While I might be teasing Bubba, I had no intentions of making her feel bad about anything. It had been a long couple of weeks since our aborted Valentine's Day date and the wrecked few days that followed. Even after getting the DNA test results, there'd been something infinitely fragile and strained about the air around Frankie and Archie.

We all felt it. Archie had spent nearly every single night with her, and none of us complained. Though Coop, the fucker, had started sliding in there too. I'd managed a couple of nights, and Bubba had gotten one. Most of the time, we slept in the other room, but some nights, I just wanted to be next to her. At the same time, I couldn't begrudge Archie holding on quite as tightly as he was. The fear of losing her had been real.

The fear of what those fuckers would pull next was also real. That was the other thing, the unspoken thing—since our visit to New York and his mother then his father at the golf course, we hadn't heard from any of the parents in the equation.

They could have tried to call Frankie, I supposed, but she'd blocked their numbers. At least the numbers we had for them. Considering the Standishes could probably afford a phone company, I doubted those were the only numbers they had.

The court date, however, was in three days. If they were going to do anything, it would probably be then. All of us were blowing off school to go with her. Spring break was right around the corner, and Archie had already made plans. Shocker, right?

"Are you sure they're meeting us?" Frankie asked from the backseat, and Bubba twisted to glance back at her.

"Yes, Angel, I'm sure. Archie had something he wanted to finish, and Coop was getting in a partial shift before they head over. I made sure they had the address and," he continued, holding up one finger, "I checked twice."

"And Archie doesn't mind?" There it was, that note of worry that crept in. It was almost adorable how much those two worried about each other, as if it wasn't also brutal for them. I glanced at Bubba, but his expression didn't tighten or change. If anything, it just relaxed more.

"Not that he told me, Angel. He said he'd come and listen and learn."

"Okay."

But that okay lacked a certain amount of confidence, and I flexed my fingers on the steering wheel. Punching women was not okay. That said, I wanted to punch Maddy for every single uneven note that left Frankie's lips. Archie was waiting on going after his father, even if every ticking second wore at him. He waited. Frankie waited with him.

I knew the plan. I even agreed with the plan.

Emancipation.

Corporate crap.

Kick them in the metaphorical balls.

Cut them off.

Great plan.

And I still wanted to punch that bitch.

"Angel," Bubba continued, "we don't have to go to the class tonight."

Wait…

"I want to go." Something in her voice shifted. The sadness lifted, and there was a spark there. Ah, got it. He was pushing her out of that bad mood. I was all for that. "I'm sorry, I had a long meeting with Wittaker today about the hearing and my trust fund and all of that stuff, and it makes my brain hurt."

It made more than her brain hurt.

"Like I said, we don't have to go tonight. There will be other classes, and we can go torture Archie with mini-golf if you want."

I can't help it, I laughed at that idea. No matter how much she wanted to play or how much he hated it, Archie would show up every time. Her chuckle deepened, and I grinned wider.

"No, I don't think Archie needs that tonight. Besides, you got him to agree to come, and I know Coop is dying to learn more."

Uh huh. I bet that lucky bastard was. Still couldn't believe he'd managed to swing an invite with Bubba. Then again, why shouldn't I believe it? It was *Coop*. If Archie could talk his way out of any kind of trouble, Coop was a master of getting himself into the middle of it—the good kind too.

"If you're sure," Bubba said, pushing it once more, but Frankie leaned up between the seats which meant she didn't have her seatbelt on.

"I'm positive. I'll stop being so gloomy."

"You don't have to stop anything, Baby Girl," I said before Bubba could respond. "Except the part where you took the seatbelt off. Now put it the fuck back on." I was a safe driver, I still wasn't risking her.

She laughed and brushed my cheek with a kiss but sat back, and the snap of the seatbelt buckle engaging settled me down.

Even though Bubba warned me about the place being in an industrial area, I still had some trouble wrapping my head around the fact we were heading into a 'club' of any kind here. Though I supposed they had techno clubs in similar locations. It didn't take long to navigate through the warren of streets to the right building where I pulled in to park.

Still, Frankie tucked herself between us, hooking her arms through ours once we were out of the car. There was no sign of Archie's Ferrari or Coop's car, but I didn't think they'd beaten us here. Inside, I got to fill out the paperwork and got a dog tag to wear like the ones both Frankie and Bubba had on.

Again, not sure what I expected, but the fact the place had a sitting room and a little kitchen and conversation area kind of gave it this air of community I hadn't been expecting.

"Different, huh?" Frankie murmured in my ear. She'd taken the seat between us, and I had a hand on her thigh, while Bubba held her hand. I'd have taken her hand too, but she was drinking a soda.

"A little," I admitted, murmuring my answer into her ear before kissing just behind it. When I'd discovered her stash of books, I'd borrowed them to read up. Even before Bubba talked to me, I got the impression this wasn't an intellectual exercise for her. The flash of her smile pulled one of my own.

The door to the lobby opened, letting Archie and Coop in. Frankie's thigh tensed under my hand, and I scanned both of the guys. Coop wore his normal, laidback expression, but there was just the faintest hint of a furrowed brow, like he was smoothing it over before he got in the room. Archie, on the other hand, looked as tense as Frankie felt under my hand, until he locked his gaze on her.

Fuck me. They needed to heal from this. Another reason I wanted to punch that selfish bitch. Archie's meeting on the golf course convinced him his father really believed Maddy. She was the source of the misery for both of them as far as I was concerned.

We'd saved seats for them, and I almost rose to surrender my spot to Archie, but Bubba was already on his feet. He moved to stand behind Frankie and rested his hands on her shoulders, even as she took Archie's hand. Fair enough.

It wasn't long before we were invited into the dungeon proper and to the chairs they had set up. Tonight's demonstration would be followed with open time in the "dungeon" and the "playrooms" if we wanted to use them. Yeah, I wasn't sure how likely that was to happen. There were way too many people here to see Frankie naked, thank you very much.

Coop elbowed me, and I cut a look at him.

"Lose the scowl," he murmured, lips barely moving. "There's restrictions on sex on the property, not to mention you look like you're going to kill someone."

I would kill someone if they saw her that way, but fine.

"Good evening," a petite blonde woman said as she walked out wearing what amounted to a leather corset, the tiniest lace panties, and a pair of stiletto heels. My gaze cut upward and stayed there. Lady had great legs, and I focused on her face because the corset took her boobs and pushed them high enough they were still visible, *even* when I focused on her face.

Fuck.

A soft giggle from next to me had me glancing at Frankie, and her open grin teased me. Yeah, yeah. I was a guy. I noticed things. But I wasn't watching the chick in the skimpy clothing, even if she was the one talking.

"For our newcomers, I'm Lyssa, and this is Master Richard."

Master Richard.

I didn't scoff. I really didn't. But at the same time, I had to choke back a laugh.

"I know we have some newcomers tonight, so welcome, and we have some who are new to the lifestyle as well." I swore, she looked right at me. Fuck. Called out. Wait…

No, Lyssa focused on Frankie. Yeah, okay.

"Tonight, instead of a full scene, we're going to talk a little bit about the romantic dominant and the power exchange between dominant and submissive. What one gives and the other takes."

The man behind her stepped forward and slid a hand up to rest against Lyssa's nape, and her whole body seemed to relax at the contact. Okay, that was pretty cool.

"It's not a one to one exchange," Richard explained. "It's a cycle. The dominant commands the submissive, and the submissive takes those commands and crafts a response. The dominant then takes the response to craft into their next commands."

"For example," Lyssa began as she moved to her knees and bowed her head. "Master Richard gripping my neck is a command, it's a nonverbal one, but it also offers me the opportunity to play if I want or just to relax if I want."

"Not all commands are going to be an open discussion, though you should have good communication in any dominant and submissive relationship," Master Richard said, picking up the thread. "Lyssa's response communicates that yes, she would like to play. She is open to the commands. Now I can take this a step further…"

And so it went. For the next thirty minutes, they walked us through the dynamic of a full power exchange that had almost nothing to do with sex and everything to do with how they interacted. In fact, it was both interesting and entertaining. While Richard stressed listening to and responding to both verbal and nonverbal cues, Lyssa, in turn, discussed being open to those responses and fearless in offering them.

"Romance is a co-created reality," Richard said. "It doesn't just fall from the sky. It takes effort. When you add romance to dominance, you get dominance that cares, dominance that's loving, dominance that puts the needs of your submissive before your own. It's still intense, but it can be very fulfilling."

The conversation segued into transition into scenes through micro rituals and how the communication and choices made could dictate a scene. Even if they'd previously decided on one thing, that they may change their minds, because organically, that's not what the submissive needs or what the dominant can offer.

By the time they opened it to questions, I had a lot of thoughts in mind. Not to mention a lot of ideas. The micro rituals they discussed, we did a lot of them. At some point during the demo, Frankie had interlocked her fingers with mine. She had her head tucked against Archie's shoulder, and her free hand locked tight in his.

"So, when you talk about micro rituals," Coop asked, and I wasn't the only one who twisted to look at him, "and that exchange, is it possible in a relationship with more dominants than submissives that there can be conflicting messages, or more positively stated, more specific messages to communicate different needs to different dominants?"

"Well that's kind of a two-part question," Lyssa began when Richard glanced at her. The interesting thing was the dynamic when it came to who answered what. They deferred to each other, not always on the relationship dynamics in the question that was answered, but maybe the one who had more experience? Maybe? "So let me address one part. A submissive, no matter who they are, will never have the exact same relationship with more than one dominant. Just like in life, in a power exchange, our relationships are unique. What a submissive may ask of one dominant, she might not of another."

"Alternatively," Richard answered, "the relationship requires a lot of trust, communication, and negotiation. So depending on whether it is a lifestyle—where you live it twenty-four-seven or you are only engaging in scene play—will also play a part in it, because a sub could send conflicting messages to two different dominants without intending to. So ahead of time, there needs to be a decision on who is the final arbiter. Being a Dom is about control and giving, but multiple people can't drive a car, even if a passenger can help with the directions."

"Fair enough," Coop said, satisfied, and I half-listened to the other questions being asked. Frankie didn't ask any, but I caught her and Lyssa locking gazes. I had a feeling she would want to talk to the other woman before we were done.

Sure enough, when the "class" ended, everyone was offered a chance to make use of the different scene areas, and there were others present who were members of the club who were prepared to help or act as guides.

"I'll be back," Frankie told me and the guys before squeezing my hand and letting it go as she stood. Yep, straight to Lyssa she went. I tracked her, and I liked that Richard backed off when Frankie got there with a small smile and nod to her.

"Stop glaring," Coop advised as he clapped me on the shoulder. I didn't elbow him in the gut, but I thought about it. I wasn't glaring.

Archie chuckled, and I sighed.

Okay, maybe I was glaring a little.

"Well?" Bubba asked as he folded his arms and moved to stand with us. The four of us were more in a horseshoe than a circle. The opening perfect for Frankie to rejoin us.

"Interesting," Coop said. "I'm definitely down to learn more."

"Not sure I'm into all the play," Archie admitted, though he divided his attention between Frankie and the sessions starting up around us. Thankfully, clothes seemed to stay on—and never mind. One woman was out of her top. "Not like this."

"No," Bubba agreed, thank fuck. "Though she doesn't mind if you guys watch."

Coop grinned, and I snorted softly.

"What?" Bubba asked as he glanced at me, and I shook my head.

"Nothing, just…processing all of it. It's a lot more complicated than it sounds, and at the same time…"

"Kind of straightforward and simple," Archie finished for me. "Communication. Observation. Giving."

"We do all those things." We had been, particularly the last few months. We'd all been more open about what we needed or wanted. I'd definitely been paying more attention and not just to Frankie.

"Yep," Coop agreed, hands tucked into his pockets. Frankie and Lyssa were deep in discussion. "Any idea what that's about?"

"Five bucks it's research or homework," I offered.

"I'll take that bet," Archie said. "She's asking for advice."

"That could be research," I countered.

"No, research is when she wants to understand a topic, advice is when she's looking for solutions for herself." He smirked at me, and I frowned. He had a point.

"You're both wrong," Coop said. "She's asking about future classes, or that one on one coaching they had on the board up front."

I must have missed that. But as one, all three of us looked at Bubba. He just grinned and folded his arms. "I don't need to bet. I know what she wanted to talk to her about."

Lucky jerk.

I scratched at my jaw. Still, I had to admit the whole intrigued me. But I wasn't sure about the punishment aspects. Then again, I did like slapping her very sweet ass, and I loved how she wiggled it when I did.

"I've got one request," Archie said, sobering. "This can't be a twenty-four-seven thing."

"No," Bubba agreed immediately. "It's not for either of us. Right now, we're exploring and we're playing and we're testing what we like and don't like. But the dynamics of who the five of us are isn't going to change."

"Unless we're playing too," Coop supplied, and Bubba gave him a look.

"Unless *we* are playing," he conceded. "But that's still an ongoing trial and learning curve."

"But it's not a no all the time anymore?" Maybe this wasn't the right place to have the conversation, but I was still curious.

"It's more of a maybe," Bubba admitted. "Under some circumstances, but not all the time."

I glanced at Archie, but he wasn't listening to us so much as watching her. Yeah, he wasn't there yet. Frankie gave Lyssa a quick hug or maybe the other woman gave it to her, and then she headed back over to us. With a little hop, she joined our circle.

"And what are you four plotting?"

"Betting on the conversation topic," Coop told her, not missing a beat. "Advice? Homework? Research? Or asking about some private tutoring?"

Frankie grinned wider. "A little bit of each, but more about whether there's a right or a wrong way to learn some things. Like should we have a guide or should we just keep doing what we're doing, and was there something on when you have multiple people involved."

"So, we're all right," Archie said with a slow nod. "And you want us to do the one-on-one class?"

The hopeful look flaring in her eyes was unmistakable. "You don't have to. Ian and I already discussed it. I like the idea of being tied up, but he really wants to learn how to do it the right way so it doesn't hurt me."

I agreed with that thought one hundred percent.

"But if you'll notice, not everyone here is shy, and I wanted to make sure I didn't have to be naked even for the one-on-one stuff. I mean, if it was just Lyssa there, that would be fine, but Ian's going to need someone who is a master of ropes, and he gets to learn how to tie others up first."

Bubba grimaced, but Frankie's smile didn't waver.

"And I get to watch."

Coop laughed.

She hooked her arm through Bubba's and leaned up to nuzzle his jaw. Whatever she told him settled him almost immediately because he relaxed, and then Frankie's gaze locked on mine and I raised my brows.

Outside, Frankie slipped away from us to walk with Archie over to his Ferrari. I leaned against the SUV to wait with Coop and Bubba, only half-listening to their conversation on ropes and why it interested him. I'd seen some of the pictures in the books, I got it.

"Hey, you think she'd mind if you took pictures when you had her all tied up?" I mean, if I wasn't going to be there.

"We'll discuss it," Bubba offered. "But maybe not right away. Not while we're learning."

Yeah, fair. That might be a little too intimate.

Still…

Frankie wrapped herself around Archie and then kissed him before he slid into the car and she headed back over to us.

"You guys okay with everyone coming over tonight?" Frankie asked us. Well, she focused on me. "I know we haven't had a lot of time together…"

"Baby Girl," I said, wanting to stop her right there, "we have all the time in the world. If you want everyone to come over tonight, I'm in. Archie grabbing food?"

"Yeah, he's gonna grab pizzas. Then I'd like very much to just spend the night like we did in Colorado, just us and playing games and hanging out and not thinking about the rest of the world."

Because she had court looming over her.

"Whatever you need," Bubba said. "I'm going to ride with Coop, you ride with Jake and talk. I'll even concede him the spot in the bed tonight."

"Generous," I said with a faint smirk, and he just grinned.

"I know."

Then Coop pressed a kiss to her temple and they headed for his car, leaving me and Frankie alone in the cold.

"Jake…"

"Baby Girl, I meant it. I'm fine." But when she plowed into me, I wrapped her up close. "We're fine," I murmured into her hair. "I know you love me."

Voice muffled against my jacket, she said, "I really do, and I've missed you. It's just been so…crazy."

That was a word for it.

"Well," I assured her as I pulled back and caught her gaze with mine, "then it's a good thing crazy is my specialty."

I could almost *see* the worry evaporating off her.

Yep, I'd totally punch that bitch in the face.

"C'mon, pajamas, pizza, and video games sounds like a perfect night to me."

Chapter Thirteen

ALL RISE

FRANKIE

The weekend sped past, despite all our best efforts to block it out. And by best efforts, I meant the video game marathon, movie marathon, and even YouTube video marathon we engaged in. I also got homework done. I worked my way ahead through two of my classes, including writing up the last two French papers I'd need for the year. Our AP classes would pretty much switch to drilling for the test itself after spring break, along with final projects, if any.

There were also a few weeks of graduation practice. The walk at the elementary schools. The preparation of speeches. Final class ranks would be posted, and the valedictorian and salutatorian would be picked. The top twenty students in the class would be awarded grants and scholarships. There would be more.

I had every item written down. I'd been tracking all of this for years, prepping for the final senior stretch, and here we were, not even nine weeks away, and I couldn't care less. Wittaker had called the evening before to confirm our court time. He wanted me there at least thirty minutes early. Rarely were times pushed up, though they could be delayed. However, the number of cases rolling through the court meant we had to be in the courtroom and ready to go when it was our turn.

Positive thoughts. Focus on them right now. My homework for Erin included making notes when my mood dropped and why it dropped as well as what I did to recover. The weekend had been all but perfect, and my mood had seesawed so wildly, I wasn't even sure if what I wrote down would be useful.

It was still dark when I woke, well before the alarm. Ian slept on one side and Archie on the other. Hopefully, today would help purge some of the demons for him too. At least when he slept, the tight lines between his eyes smoothed. Tiddles moved as I shifted my legs, and I crawled out from between them. Shockingly, neither moved. They had to be even more tired than I thought.

Smothering a yawn, I went to the kitchen and fed the cats before they woke up the whole house. After getting the coffee maker brewing, I headed for the shower. Better to start the day right. I snagged my phone off the charger and pulled the bedroom door mostly closed before I got the shower started. Once the water was on, I brushed my teeth real quick while the water heated, then cued up Torched's latest album. By the time I was shampooing my hair, I was singing along.

I was really jamming out to the third song and pivoted to find Jake leaning against the interior bathroom door, eyes bright and a smile on his face as I sang. Heat flooded my face, and I faltered on a note or two, then just went for it. Jake's grin widened when I curled my fingers to beckon him.

He shed his shirt, and his boxers landed right next to it before he slipped into the shower with me. I was already warm and soapy, so I contented myself with a good morning—Oh hello, he tasted all minty and fresh. His groan answered my own, and the stubble on his cheeks stung a little. I didn't care, except…

"Can I shave you?" I asked as I leaned my head back, and Jake gave me a sleepy look.

"Shave?" He scratched at his stubble. "I guess it's probably not too pleasant."

Biting my lower lip, I fought to keep my smile tucked away. "I don't mind it, though I don't want beard burn today and I want to shave you." I kind of always had wanted to. It was a little thing, but the guys had helped me with my legs when my wrist was broken. Not something I ever imagined having them do, but Jake hadn't even cracked a joke.

"Sing me one of your songs with Bubba, and I'll be putty in your hands."

This time, the heat hitting my face was scorching. The guys had all listened, but I hadn't been able to watch them listening to me. Of course, after the evening at the studio with Coop and Ian, I didn't think I'd be able to listen to myself sing again without getting turned on.

"One sec."

I leaned out of the shower and wiped my fingers on a towel before grabbing my phone. I switched to the list of songs Ian and I had recorded. I had all of them on there, since he always made sure I had copies when he was done mixing them.

After hitting play, I snagged the razor and shaving cream from by the sink. "This one okay?" The sound of the first strum of the guitars sent a needy little wave through me. That, coupled with the cooler air, had my nipples tightening.

"That's fine." He moved back a little and leaned against the wall. It put his shoulders and head a little lower. I took the time spreading the foamy shaving cream over his cheeks. "Down first," he murmured. "Follow the grain. Up second, if it's not smooth."

I grinned. "Trust me?"

He didn't even blink. "Absolutely."

I had no idea why that settled my jangling nerves, but everything quieted, and while I'd only been half-listening, I caught the part in the song where my voice was supposed to come in and started singing. Jake never looked away as I worked the razor over his cheeks and along his jaw. He tilted his head back so I could get beneath his chin and just to this throat. The mustache area was tricky, but he rolled his lip down and stretched it, then winked when he stole a kiss that left me with shaving cream on my face.

We made it through two full songs before I had it almost as smooth and soft as he could make it. He ran a hand over his face, then rinsed it off before he took the razor from my fingers. One moment, we were standing there, and the next, he had me lifted up and pressed against the now much cooler than my back tile.

A hiss escaped me, but it had nothing on the wave of heat crashing through me as he rubbed his very interested dick against my slit. "Baby Girl," he murmured against my lips as he stroked one hand down my side and fisted himself so he could adjust the angle.

"Yes." I didn't even care how he wanted to ask the question. I had missed Jake a lot the last several days. Timing and opportunity hadn't been on our side. More than once, he'd just slipped aside because Archie needed me or I needed him. More than once, it had been Coop that tucked in with us at night, Coop whom Ian had insisted I needed, and they were both right. "I need you."

Between one heartbeat and the next, his mouth slammed down on mine as he pushed in, and we both shuddered. I didn't know where his groan ended and mine began. Slick and wet, I locked my thighs around his hips and trusted him to not drop me as he thrust his tongue in time with his dick. The pressure was perfect, and the angle even better.

Cupping his smooth cheeks, I rocked forward to meet his thrusts, and he lifted me a little higher and then dragged me down so he controlled the speed and the force of the thrusts. Little syllables escaped me in a litany of curses because it hurt in the best possible way, striking sparks across my vision as I kissed him with the same consuming force he used to try and devour me.

The bite of his fingers on my hips and the surge that pressed me into the wall over and over held a frantic edge that didn't slow as he pushed me up and over. I came with a scream he couldn't even smother with a kiss, especially when he grunted and pushed against me clamping down on him twice more before he came in a rush.

Panting, we clung to each other, and Jake pressed a kiss to my shoulder. "I love your voice, Baby Girl, and you can shave me anytime you want."

A laugh bubbled up, and I giggled. The hot water had gone warm, and even as Jake eased me down and we cleaned up, we interspersed it with little kisses and gentle touches. He didn't even slip out while I dried my hair. Instead, he parked himself behind me and took over the back, combing it.

"Up or down?" Fair question since I had court.

"Half up, half down," I said, meeting his gaze in the mirror.

"Braid?"

I hadn't considered that, but now that he mentioned it, I liked the idea. He tapped my fingers out of the way and braided the single long strand in the center so it pulled my hair back from my face but left the rest to fall in neat lines. The blowing drying it straight helped. Though, if it got rained on, it was going to be unruly as hell when it dried.

When we finally left the bathroom so I could get dressed, the scent of coffee and something far sweeter assaulted my senses. My mouth was watering by the time I scooted into panties and a bra, then pulled on a pair of nice slacks and a button-down shirt. I even had a blazer to go with it. The dark green looked great on me, and though I didn't wear it often, it definitely fell in the professional category.

Jake dressed silently while I did, and then he attached the clasp on my bracelet before sliding the class ring on my finger.

"How do I look?" I still had to put on shoes, but I was starving. Thankfully, the top was black and I had a jacket to wear with it.

"Like a million bucks," Jake told me. "Come on. We have a surprise for you."

"That is French toast I smell," I said with a little squeal and then hurried around him and down the hall, tugging him with me. Sure enough, the guys were all crammed into my kitchen with Jeremy.

I paused on the threshold at the sight. Jeremy had been in here cooking while Jake had been getting me off in the shower and I'd been screaming.

Ian watched me from across the room as he sipped his coffee. His bright blue eyes were warm and full of humor. Coop practically smirked next to him, but it was Archie who said, "Come and eat, babe. Jeremy wouldn't let us have a damn thing until you got yours first. No matter how much we yelled at him."

Relief swarmed through me, and when Jake chuckled next to me, I jabbed my elbow into his stomach hard enough to make him 'oof.' "Just be glad I don't have my shoes on," I warned him, and he grunted.

"Duly noted." Even if he rubbed his stomach, I doubted I hit him that hard. He was carved out of stone.

"Good morning, Jeremy," I greeted him as I moved past, and he smiled at me.

"Good morning, Miss Frankie. I've prepared your favorite, as well as bacon. Do you want fruit with your French toast, or powdered sugar and syrup?"

"Hmm…yes please?"

He chuckled. "The works it is."

On impulse, I went up on my tiptoes and kissed his cheek. "You're the best, Jeremy. Thank you."

The indulgent smile he gave me made the action seem a lot less awkward, thank God. "My pleasure, truly. You sit, and Mr. Archie will get your coffee. The boys will finish making a space."

"On it," Ian said as they shifted the chairs around. Jake was still laughing as he followed me over.

"Can Mr. Archie get my coffee as well?"

"Considering you took your job to an extreme?" Archie told him with a bland look. "You can wait for the next pot."

I laughed but took the chair next to Coop, who leaned over to nuzzle a kiss and then sighed when I gave him a real one. "Good morning," he murmured.

"Hi."

"Good shower?"

"All out of hot water I think," I told him without an ounce of apology.

"Good thing we used the other one." He winked, and I laughed.

It wasn't long before we had stacked plates in front of us. Despite his teasing, Jeremy had most of it ready, so I had three thick pieces of the perfectly cooked French toast, dusted with powdered sugar and a lovely dollop of butter, as well as a plate of strawberries with bacon. Yeah, I'd pretty much died and gone to heaven.

There was coffee and juice and even eggs for the guys. Far more food than had been in our fridge, because we'd skipped shopping this weekend while I indulged Archie's ordering in fetish, and the five of us had dug in and just made the most of our alone time.

Across the table, Archie smiled at me and I shook my head, but I couldn't hide my own smile. This right here was the way to kick off our day.

"Now," Jeremy said, "you finish up, and let me know if anyone wants seconds. I'm going to take care of the housekeeping here today…"

"Jeremy, you shouldn't have to—"

But he didn't let me finish, instead, he fixed me with a very stern look with those gray eyes. "There is nothing about shouldn't. I have offered, Mr. Archie accepted on your behalf, and I would be very pleased to do these tasks because you have enough to think about. Also, you provided me with excellent pictures of Mr. Archie cleaning the bathroom last month."

Laughter circled the table, and I spread my hands. "Well, when you put it that way…"

"Excellent. If there is anything specific you all require from the store, please add it to this list." He set the pad and paper on the table. "Otherwise, I shall just stock the usual."

The usual.

I fixed Archie with a look, but he gave me a look of such innocence that I rolled my own eyes and then let it go. After this was settled, *Mr. Archie* and I would be having this argument. It could wait until then. For now, I'd accept the gifts and the offers exactly as they'd been made—with love.

It didn't take long for us to finish up. I glanced at the list and pursed my lips. There were a couple of things I needed, but I wasn't adding tampons or pads to the shopping list. I just wasn't. It was bad enough he had my brand of deodorant on the list. Thankfully, we weren't buying condoms anymore. I didn't want to even think about that one.

Nope.

Nope.

Nope.

It wasn't long before I had my wallet tucked into the inner pocket of my jacket. I snagged my backpack. I had no idea why I might need it, but you never knew. Ian dropped his letterman jacket over my shoulders, and Archie had his umbrella.

Oh look, it was drizzling and gross outside.

I was over winter in Texas. It wasn't even pretty. Just gray, gloomy, and wet. All at once, I was homesick for Colorado. How bizarre was that? I missed the lodge and the fire and all the snow outside. I missed how cozy and warm it was, and most of all, I missed how safe it had been for all of us.

No bad meatloaf. No hearings. No stupid DNA tests or paternity questions.

"Almost to the finish line," Archie murmured to me as he caught my hand, and I blew out a breath.

"This is just one finish line," I reminded him. We had a plan. He and his grandfather had a plan, and I was going to do my part as best I could. It didn't mean I didn't want to slap his father though.

"Just the first of many," he whispered, then kissed me. "No more worrying. We got this."

Even as much as I believed him, I couldn't stop the quivering on the inside. Nerves. Jitters. They were all bouncing around inside me. We took Jake's SUV, and I was in the back between Coop and Archie, while Ian sat shotgun and Jake drove.

We stopped for coffee, and we played the music loud. Ian actually put us on and grinned back at me as I laughed. Coop squeezed my thigh when it played the song we'd recorded the other day.

"You guys sound amazing," Archie admitted during one lull.

"Don't they?" Jake agreed, and I blushed for real, all over.

I caught Ian's gaze, and he winked at me. Yes, he was right, we sounded good together, but I didn't think I would ever sound that great. He could probably do so much better without me, but at the same time, I loved that he wanted to do this *with* me.

Just as long as I didn't hold him back. Though I wouldn't say that aloud again. The last time had earned me a spanking of the stinging kind, and it had been far less fun than the others. For the drive, at least, I was able to forget about where we were going or why we were going there.

For the drive.

The minute we pulled into the parking garage across the street from the courthouse, all of my nerves resurged. Even though Coop clasped my hand and let me squeeze his tight, I couldn't quite shake the trembling. Jake took charge of my backpack, and Ian moved in front of us as Jake came behind, while Coop and Archie flanked me. I swore they moved in a way that meant no one got near me.

We had to go through security one at a time, and then waited while they scanned my backpack. Mr. Wittaker was already there, waiting for us in the lobby.

"With fifteen minutes grace," he said almost as a compliment. "Well done, Miss Curtis. Let's go sit and talk, shall we?" He took the lead and found us a small bench across from a courtroom, and the guys formed a barricade of sorts as Mr. Wittaker and I sat together.

"All right, Frankie, this is what's going to happen. We're going to go inside and sit. We're on the docket for Judge Andrew Novak. He's in his fifties, married—second wife. He has two children from his first marriage and two from his second. His oldest, a girl, is pregnant with his first grandchild."

I opened my mouth to say something, but Wittaker shook his head.

"Just listen for now." He didn't wait for me to nod, just continued on. "His oldest is in her last year of college. He's a blunt-spoken, straight shooter, who sees more abused kids in his courtroom than he can help. While he's not a man on a mission, he does do what he can when he can. This is all good for us, because he's going to like you. When we get in there, we'll wait until we're called, then you and I will move up to the table at the front. He has a copy of the briefs and the affidavits, and he will likely have questions for you. Just answer them. Don't worry about how it sounds or trying to make it sound better, just tell him the truth."

Okay.

"As of…" He checked his watch before continuing, "an hour ago, your mother's attorney had not withdrawn their objections, however, they have also not filed any evidence or briefs on why they want to deny you emancipation."

So, Maddy wasn't fighting me per se, but she wasn't helping either.

"The judge will be looking for her in the courtroom. If he calls for her, don't react, don't get upset. He's going to have questions for her, and if she isn't there, that's even better for us."

I knew we'd talked about this a few times already, but the quick pace of his recitation actually settled my nerves.

"In all likelihood, it will be fifteen minutes from start to finish, but don't be dismayed if the judge wants to take longer or if he postpones making an immediate decision."

My stomach sank. "Why would he postpone it?" Coop asked, and I glanced up to find him focusing on us grimly.

"To give it all due consideration, or he could simply want to have a couple of hours to think about it. He has been known to withhold judgments until the end of the day. Not always," Wittaker cautioned me, "but it does happen."

That sounded awful. "Do we have to wait?"

"No, the court clerk will call me. Once we've been excused from court, you're done here. Now, if things don't go our way for whatever reason, I've already got a second brief ready to file and keep your temporary emergency order in place," Wittaker said. "So, no panic. We're going to take care of this, Frankie. Are you ready?"

Not even a little. My nerves had nerves. I glanced up to find the guys all studying me. Each one had a confident look on their face, but Coop managed to cross his eyes and Archie stuck his tongue out at me.

Real mature.

"I can do this," I said. Ready or not.

"Excellent, as for you gentlemen," Mr. Wittaker stated as he stood. "I don't care what the judge asks or what is said in there. You four stay quiet. No outbursts. No rushing to her defense. No cutting off anyone else. Allow me to do my job. You are here as silent but very helpful support. Understood?"

One by one, they nodded, save for Archie, who just shrugged. Yet when I squeezed his hand, he summoned a smile and said, "Just make sure you do protect her."

"Be nice," I teased him and leaned up to brush a kiss to his lips. There was a scrape of shoe that seemed to cut right through the sudden silence, and I glanced over to find Maddy and Edward standing there.

They both wore shocked looks.

I didn't smile.

I didn't say anything. I just kissed Archie again and squeezed his hand.

Bad meatloaf didn't move as we walked past them and into the courtroom. It was a lot more crowded than I would have expected, but Wittaker directed us to a couple of rows that were four seats wide. Ian and Jake grabbed the seats directly behind us, while Coop and Archie flanked Wittaker and myself. They had me as close to the corner as I could get.

The weight of Maddy's stare bore into me, but I didn't look at her. I didn't say a word.

It was the longest ten minutes of my life before a clerk called out, "All rise."

Chapter Fourteen

IF I DENY YOUR REQUEST…

Judge Andrew Novak seemed a huge man when he walked in wearing a black robe, but I didn't think he was as tall as he appeared. His pate shone under the lights, and a faint half-coronet of graying brown hair wrapped the back of his head. The hard expression on his face eased as he smiled at the court reporter, then the bailiff, but the warmth drained away when he glanced out at all of us.

The courtroom was pretty full. My pulse rabbited at the look he wore. "Call the first case," he said, moving a stack of folders to the side and pulling one down to open as two people were called and they went up with their lawyers.

It was an evidentiary hearing, and even though we were all in the same room, I could barely hear the people presenting to the judge. When he asked them questions though, I heard those just fine. It didn't take him long to decide on that case. He gave an order, signed something in the folder, handed it off to someone, and those people were out.

"Next…"

And so it went for the next hour. At some point, my right knee began to bob as hot and cold flushed through my system. I wanted to take off the jacket, but I had a feeling sweat stains on my underarms would be far less attractive than the warmth. Even the air in here had started to turn stale. Had I even put on deodorant that morning?

A hand settled over my knee and the gentle pressure eased the dancing, and I glanced over to find Archie studying me. He didn't say a word. He didn't have to, it was written all over his face. Fixing this whole situation was high on his priority list, but I wasn't alone. They were all here with me. The quivering inside me didn't go away, but it did slow down, and I blew out a breath.

Archie squeezed my knee gently, and then I linked my fingers with his again. My palms were sweaty, but then so were his. Neither of us let go. If I turned around, I'd see Jake and Ian. If I looked left, I'd find Wittaker and Coop.

I wasn't alone.

It was another hour before they called my name, and I'd been digging half-moons into Archie's hand by then, but he didn't pull away.

"…Francesca Curtis."

Fuck, I hated that name.

Wittaker moved with me, and Coop brushed my leg with his as I passed him. We stepped out into the center area and up to the table.

"Is the minor's legal guardian or parent present?" the judge asked, looking at the latest file folder in front of him rather than at me. To be honest, I hadn't looked back to see if bad meatloaf had stuck around.

"Yes, Your Honor," Maddy stated as she arrived.

Fucking great, she stood at the same table where we were, along with a man in a suit who was presumably her attorney. Honestly, I didn't look over at him because my stomach was roiling, and I didn't need to embarrass myself by throwing up.

"Is it Mrs. or Ms. Curtis?" the judge asked, still studying the paperwork in front of him.

"Ms."

"And the other gentleman you attended with today?"

Holy shit, the judge noticed that?

"My fiancé," she stated, not missing a beat. What? Not going to call him my father, Maddy? The question was on the tip of my tongue, but I stayed quiet.

"Is he involved in any of the custodial arrangements?" The judge seemed to focus on her now. Man, he had resting asshole face. I was really glad he wasn't looking at me.

"No." One answer, short and clipped. There was just an edge to that single syllable too.

"I'm not seeing anything in the paperwork about a legal father," the judge said as he continued to flip through the papers. "Mr. Wittaker, when you filed this with the court, I am assuming you did your due diligence."

"I did, Your Honor." Wittaker spoke with confidence and ease. "If you will look in the exhibits section, I have included certified copies of Miss Curtis' birth certificate, as well as every school enrollment from pre-school through her current year. There is no father identified on any of the documentation."

The judge frowned, then glanced at Maddy before he focused on me. "Miss Curtis? Or do you prefer Francesca?"

Great. He asked me a question. "Honestly, sir, I would prefer Frankie." Fuck. "I mean, Your Honor. Sorry."

He smiled, a bare flicker, and it eased some of the sternness in his expression. "Sir is fine, Frankie. Is it all right if I call you that?"

"Yes, sir."

"Frankie, have you ever met your father?"

"No, sir." I didn't hesitate, and I didn't turn around to see what Eddie's reaction was. I also ignored Maddy. Thankfully, Wittaker stood between us so I didn't *have* to see her.

He nodded once. "Do you know his name?"

"No, sir."

The judge glanced at the paperwork in front of him. "So you have no relationship with anyone who fills the role of father?"

"No, sir. It was always Ms. Curtis and myself."

Yep. Not even going to call her Maddy right now.

The judge nodded again.

"Ms. Curtis," he said, and I almost sagged at being out from under his focus, even if it wasn't as bad as I expected. "You were not married at the time of Frankie's birth?"

"No, Your Honor."

"You have never been married." It wasn't a question.

"No, Your Honor."

I kind of wondered where the judge was going with this, but I couldn't exactly ask.

The judge wrote something down. "Ms. Curtis, are you aware that your daughter has filed paperwork to legally sever herself from you and that an earlier court granted her emergency and temporary emancipation ahead of this proceeding?"

"Of course I'm aware."

Oh, someone didn't like that. I sucked my upper lip between my teeth.

"And you didn't contest the emergency order?"

"No, I was not present in the state when the order went through, and I only found out about it after the fact." Yep. She was pissed. Maddy did not like to be made to look bad. "Your Honor," she tacked on, almost as an afterthought.

Another half-nod, then the judge looked at me. Pen down, he folded his hands together and leaned forward. The scrutiny in that gaze had me standing up a little straighter.

"Frankie, do you think you are doing well enough to be in charge of your own life?"

"I do, sir."

"Can you tell me why you think that?"

"Because I've been in charge of it for a few years now. I've certainly been in charge of it for over a year, particularly after Ms. Curtis' frequent absences for 'work' that began last spring and escalated over the summer. "

"You traveled yourself this past Christmas."

"Yes, sir."

"Where did you go?"

"To a place in Colorado owned by a friend's grandfather."

"A boyfriend's?"

"Yes, sir."

The judge nodded. "What did you do during your time there?"

"Learned how to ski. Talked about college. Played video games. Read books. Hung out with my best friends. Celebrated Christmas. Got away from the crazy."

The judge smiled. "Sounds like a lot of fun."

"It was."

"You've also been awarded at least two considerable scholarships in the last few months, one from a place you work?"

I blew out a breath. "Yes, sir."

"Tell me about the scholarship?" He framed it like a request, but I got the impression it wasn't one, and since Wittaker didn't interfere, I answered it. It didn't take long, but then he wanted to know about Mason's, how long had I worked there, the hours I worked, then he asked about the second job with the food delivery and why I'd needed that.

Finally, he said, "While I'm not going to ask you to go into too much detail, your records also indicate you are in therapy. In fact, your psychologist has written a glowing recommendation for you with regard to your independence and maturity. She's not alone. I have recommendations here from your manager at Mason's, several teachers, and friends of the family, as well as the parents of all of your friends."

Wait, what?

All of them?

"I have to say, young lady, this is an impressive list of accolades and character references. If I deny your petition for emancipation today, what will you do?"

My gut dropped, but I kept my focus on the judge. "The same thing I'll do if you grant it, sir. I'll go back to my apartment, catch up on my homework, and get ready for school tomorrow. I might be a little upset and vent to my friends."

The judge gave me another one of those smiles.

"Your Honor," Maddy said. "May I speak?"

"No," the judge said. "You may not."

Shock locked me in place, because the judge barely looked at her.

"Your Honor," her attorney tried.

"I said no, Mr. Alden," the judge stated. "Ms. Curtis has had ample opportunity to be present in the last year. According to all records, she moved out several months ago. She has ceased all support, financial or otherwise. Her legal address was changed with the postal service. I have notations here that during a hospitalization for Frankie following an assault, Ms. Curtis was unreachable. She also did not pay any of the hospital expenses."

That, I hadn't even thought about. I hadn't seen any hospital bills at all.

Archie.

I blew out a shaky breath.

"Frankly, I don't see why I should deny the petition at all when clearly Frankie has been living independently and managing very well, based on grade point average, scholarships, and college acceptances, and all the while, maintaining employment."

I bit the inside of my cheek. I turned eighteen in a month. If he denied me, I'd be okay. I'd made it this far, I could make it a few more weeks.

"While I find Frankie's determination and, dare I say, 'grit' commendable, I find it absolutely appalling that someone her age has had to fend for herself when she has the reasonable expectation of parental support. You were a single mother, Ms. Curtis, and while you may have been the only parent she had, that was a choice you made and a choice you then abdicated. Frankly, I think you should be ashamed of yourself, and if I had the power to charge you with neglect, I would."

Holy.

Shit.

"As it is, all I can do is free your daughter from any legal obligations you've already walked away from and give her the freedom to make decisions she may need to make with regard to her colleges and future. My only other regret is I couldn't give it to her sooner." He looked at me with a nod. "Frankie, I'm granting your request for emancipation. Good luck, young lady. I think you've got a bright future in front of you."

He said something else, but there was a small cheer behind me from the guys, and he glared past me a moment, even if the corner of his mouth twitched.

"All paperwork will be processed, Mr. Wittaker. I'm assuming you can take it from here?"

"I can, Your Honor. Thank you."

He nodded again, and that was it. We were being motioned away, but I hesitated and the judge looked at me. I mouthed 'thank you,' and he gave me the first real smile I'd seen since he arrived. Then Wittaker was taking my arm. As I turned, I met the full wrath of Maddy's icy glare, but I ignored her as my attorney guided me over toward a clerk, who was motioning to us.

Maddy snagged my arm, but her attorney grabbed her wrist and there was a frigid three seconds of a stand-off. Eddie appeared as I tugged my arm free, and he frowned as he glanced from me to Maddy, but I ignored them as Wittaker urged me away. They were already calling the next case, but I barely heard any of it.

It was done.

I was emancipated.

Free.

I signed where Wittaker gestured for me to sign and then accepted the packet I was offered. I was still a little dazed when we left the courtroom a different way from how we'd come in, and I frowned until Wittaker motioned up the hall where the guys were waiting.

"Yes!" Coop said, both arms high. He scooped me up as soon as I got to them, and then Jake tugged me into a hug and finally Ian. Archie was the only one who lagged back. I clung to Ian for a long moment, the shakes seeming to rock me, and he rubbed my back soothingly. Finally, I lifted my head to look for Archie and found him glaring at bad meatloaf, who also stood there waiting.

"Archie," I said, and even in the busy hall with all the people and background noise, he heard me and pulled his gaze away to look at me. I raised my eyebrows. We'd discussed this. He and his grandfather were waiting for the right time.

Was now the right time?

His eyebrows dipped briefly as he looked from me toward bad meatloaf and then back. His eyebrows raised. Was I up for it?

Even if my insides shook like a fucking leaf in a tornado, I was ready. I had his back.

I nodded.

"Guys," I murmured. "It's time."

"You be careful," Ian answered in the same quiet tone. "We're going to be right behind you."

I nodded and then grinned at Mr. Wittaker, even as Archie approached bad meatloaf. "Thank you," I told him. "For *everything*. You're my hero."

He chuckled. "You're very welcome, Frankie. It helps that I agree with the judge. You've more than earned the right to call your own shots. I'll take care of everything from here, and once the final papers come through, I'll make sure you have copies. Though you won't need more than what you have right now."

I hugged that little packet to myself.

"Want me to hang onto that?" Coop asked, and I handed it over as he pressed a kiss to my cheek. "Also, we have plans tonight."

We did?

Jake just grinned and nodded, though the smile didn't quite reach his eyes. He was watching bad meatloaf behind us.

"We do," he confirmed. "Archie knows, and you'll have plenty of time to change. Just keep that in mind."

"Go on, Angel," Ian urged me. "Go rip this Band-Aid off so the two of you can be done with this once and for all."

I gave him a quick kiss, then pressed another to the corner of Jake's mouth before I pivoted. Shoulders square, I headed for Archie. He held out a hand just as I arrived, and I clasped his hand in mine.

"All right, Edward," he said. "We're ready for that conversation."

"I don't see why we need to have this," Maddy sniped. Yep. She was still pissed.

"Because, Maddy," I told her. "It's time we were all on the same page. You. Me. Archie. Mr. Standish."

The older man nodded. "Agreed." He took Maddy's arm, and I swore his knuckles whitened. "Shall we?"

"After you," Archie told them, and Edward gave us a nod before he moved and hauled Maddy with him. The look she shot me over her shoulder was pure venom. Tugging me closer, Archie said, "Still time for you to get out of this, babe."

"She doesn't scare me anymore," I promised him. "And after what we just went through? I'm looking forward to paying her back."

He grinned. "I love my little badass."

I snorted and bumped his hip. "You haven't seen badass."

"Yet," he teased as we followed them. Behind us, Jake, Ian, and Coop followed us. I didn't know where they'd decided to do this meeting, but the guys were going to be there for us, and a part of me hoped Maddy was ready.

Because no way was I pulling this punch.

She fucking deserved it.

Chapter Fifteen
THEN SHE SAVED HIM RIGHT BACK

We followed bad meatloaf through the courtroom halls and outside. The cold air hit me and reminded me of all the sweating I'd done. For a split second, I really hoped I didn't stink. I had put on deodorant, right? But I dismissed those thoughts before they could take root. There was a limo waiting for us. Maddy was already sliding inside, but Archie's father waited for both of us to get there.

"It's all right," Archie murmured against my ear. "They know where we're going."

I nodded and let him help me inside first, while not paying one ounce of attention to Mr. Standish. I wasn't alone with Maddy for long. The limo had a long U shape seat that curved all along the other side. Maddy sat at the curve nearer the driver, so I took the bench at the back. Archie followed me inside and planted himself next to me. Edward was the last inside, and he took a seat next to Maddy. The driver closed the door, and then we were alone, the four of us, in the close confines of the stretched car.

Archie leaned over me and snagged the seatbelt, then dragged it across and clicked it in. I gave him an amused look and grinned before repeating the process with himself. Then with one thigh pressed against mine, he interlocked our fingers, and only then did he glance across to where our parents sat.

They weren't touching. If anything, there was a clearly defined space between them. Trouble in paradise, Maddy?

"I'm still very—"

"Wait," Mr. Standish said, interrupting Maddy before she could say another word. "We agreed to keep this civil."

Oh, that glare she sent him had me sliding a look at Archie. He wore the faintest of smirks, but while his fingers were tight on mine, he glanced out the window. The stroke of his thumb along the side of my hand helped soothe my nerves. To be honest, I was curious about the details of what Archie got his father to agree to and the destination. Still, I didn't ask.

We were a united front, so I'd trust whatever Archie had arranged. The fact the guys were following us or would meet us there and be close so when we decided to walk out, we could? Even better.

The drive took almost thirty minutes, and I managed to not bob my knee as the tension inside the car dragged taut. Every time I glanced at the pair opposite us, Maddy glared and Eddie looked troubled.

Our destination surprised me.

Standish.

I hadn't been back here since Valentine's Day, despite the fact I still technically had an internship.

Bryan had texted a couple of times. I couldn't even begin to explain the twisted path this had all taken. I'd ended up just telling him there'd been a change in plans and left it at that. Mollie had reached out too, but she seemed to be pretty busy, so our texts had been hit or miss.

The limo slowed as it pulled into the circular plaza of the building. The parking garage was on the other side, and I rarely came in this way. Made sense that the Standishes would. When the driver came around to open the door, I had to resist the urge to bolt. Archie didn't let go of my hand as he slid over and out, taking me with him.

As soon as we were outside in the icy air, I sucked in a deep breath. I didn't realize how much the interior smelled like Maddy's perfume until I was free of it. At Archie's searching look, I summoned a smile. "I'm okay," I told him.

He nodded, flicking a look behind me. "C'mon, they know where we're going." We moved inside together and across the marble floored lobby. Archie didn't even glance at the security as they nodded to him, and we bypassed the elevators I'd normally used and went straight to the executive. By the time I turned around inside it, the doors were already sliding shut, leaving bad meatloaf on the far side of the lobby to catch up with us.

Blowing out a breath, Archie rolled his head from side to side.

"Are you okay?"

He lifted our joined hands and pressed a kiss to the back of mine. "I'm fine, babe. Just needed to get my temper leashed. I really fucking hate how she looks at you."

"She's trying to intimidate me. She doesn't want me to argue with her." The technique had worked for years, but no matter how pissed she looked right now, I didn't care. The elevator opened to a familiar floor, and I glanced at Archie. "Here?"

"Trust me?"

"Always."

He guided me out onto the level that housed his father's office as well as his grandfather's, and I thought Archie mentioned he had his own. Did this mean Grandpa Ted would be here? Oh, that would be an explosion. There were no secretaries, not even the really sweet lady Archie had directed me toward.

Once inside the conference room, he pulled out a chair for me. Belatedly, I realized he had my backpack, which he also sat down next to the chair out of sight. I hadn't even realized he had it when I walked over to join them. I'd been too focused on making sure he wasn't alone in facing them.

"Really," Maddy snapped as the door opened. I thought she was talking to us, but nope, she had her head turned. "Eddie, this is patently stupid, and you can't expect me to keep putting up with this crap."

"You're part of this *crap*, as you put it," Mr. Standish answered. "Stop being such a bitch about it."

I swore I forgot how to breathe. In any other world, I was pretty sure Maddy would have torn the face off of someone who called her a bitch. But in Eddie's case, she just made the most indignant snarling sound before she turned and our gazes locked.

Oh. Yeah.

"Speaking of little bitches."

Archie tensed as Eddie glanced at the ceiling.

"I'm not the one he called a bitch, Maddy. Maybe you should check yourself before you hurl any more stones." My voice didn't waver for a second. Go me. Her eyes went positively glacial, but I refused to flinch. Archie hadn't taken a seat. Instead, he stood next to me.

"You might want to control your girlfriend, Edward," Archie warned. "There's already one judge that wants to throw the book at her for child neglect. I don't doubt assault charges could be arranged."

"Maddy," Mr. Standish said in a tone damn near as harsh as hers. "This isn't helping anything."

"Of course it isn't," Maddy argued, swinging around to face him. "You already sided with her against me when you sent that letter to the court. Not that it scored you many points with our daughter, did it?"

Sliding his hands into his pockets, Mr. Standish gave her a look I recognized. Archie wore that look when he was about to argue his points, but he didn't want you to know just how prepared he was.

"I did what I felt was necessary," he said patiently. "Much like you have been." Easy. Even. Not an ounce of harshness. Then his mouth compressed. "Or so you claimed."

"Don't you dare accuse me of being the problem here, I wasn't the one who went and knocked some slut up—" She practically vibrated, she was so angry. Wow. Here I thought I was the only one who infuriated her that much. "Then went and married her. I didn't *leave* you. I didn't *abandon* you."

All of sudden, Maddy cut all that venom toward me.

"And as for you…"

"I wouldn't," Archie said, ice slicking each syllable. "Because as entertaining as you may find your melodrama, we don't. We're not only not interested, we're sick of it. Not to mention the only slut present in this room would be you with your penchant for going after married men."

"Let's walk this back," Mr. Standish tried. I'd give him that. He tried. He actually looked like he wanted to have this conversation, but Maddy just wanted a fight. "We came here to sort this out." Suddenly, he focused on me. "As much as I know Archie didn't have to come here, I'm aware you didn't either. The fact you're both willing to talk to us—to me—it means something."

"It really shouldn't," I told him, and maybe I should have let him defuse things with Maddy, but honestly, I didn't care if she was comfortable. "I only came here to close the last door on Maddy."

"Frankie," he began, paused, seemed to collect himself, and then continued, "I know we got off on the wrong foot, and you weren't wrong about your accusations where Archie is concerned. But I really do want to get to know you. I should have been a part of your life." He grimaced and then looked at Archie. "I should have been a part of yours, as well."

"Too little too late, old man. As for Frankie, you don't need to have anything to do with her life. You're not her sperm donor."

Maddy pivoted. "Don't speak to your father that way."

"Shut up, Maddy." Those three words landed in the silence and yanked her furious attention back to me. "Every word that comes out of your mouth is a lie. Every story you've ever told me. Every piece of garbage you try to sell about the life you lead or the life *we* lead has been a lie. I'm tired of it."

Grabbing my backpack, I pulled open the front pocket and pulled out the four DNA tests. I slapped them onto the table one at a time.

"Four tests. So I'm assuming four candidates. Must have been a hell of a party if you weren't sure which it was." Yeah yeah, I had four boyfriends. She could still fuck off. I was on birth control, and even if there was an oops, I wouldn't wait eighteen years to try and figure it out.

That thought gave me pause for a moment, but I put it away. It was very much a discussion for another day. One that would take place nowhere near these two. Mr. Standish—you know what, fuck it. Edward moved to the table.

"Those aren't important," Maddy said. "I have the test that mattered."

"Really?" Archie said slowly, then pulled a form from inside his jacket and unfolded it. "Because unless you want to try and sell that he and I aren't related, what you gave him is a pile of crap." He slid the results across, and Edward snagged it before Maddy could. "Frankie and I went to the lab there and they drew blood and did swabs. They did full panels on both of us. We're not related. At all."

Maddy sucked in a breath. I could almost see the thoughts racing through her mind as her aggravated expression smoothed and she put a hand on Edward's arm. "She was supposed to be yours."

And there it was.

"You fucking cunt," Archie muttered, and I glanced up at him, even as I put my hand over his on my shoulder.

"Archie," Edward said, but there was no reprimand in his voice, "I'll handle this."

"Will you now? Like you've been handling everything else so well. She *played* you. She has been *playing* you, and she used her daughter to manipulate you."

The bite of Archie's fingers tightened on my shoulder once, then he eased his grip and I slid my fingers between his before I glanced back to find Edward staring at Archie. Maddy glanced between them before she finally glared at me.

Yeah, I was waiting for that.

"You couldn't leave it alone," she said to me.

"This isn't my fault," I told her. "It's never been my fault. You've reminded me continually that you could have had an abortion or you could have given me up for adoption. I don't owe you anything."

"I chose to keep you!"

"Do you want a medal?"

"You don't get to talk to me that way—"

"I'll talk to you however I please," I said, but I wasn't yelling. If anything, I was just tired. Tired of this. Tired of her. Tired of this farce between us. "You're a shitty mom. You've been a shitty mom for a long, long time. I just didn't know any better. I've spent *years* making excuses for you. Trying to understand, trying to be a better kid so that you would love me."

"Of course I love you." She even managed to say that with a straight face.

I laughed. "I don't think you even know what that means."

"And you would?" Maddy stared at me. "You, who was too scared of your own shadow to grab life and live it? You just focused on your books and your cats? You had all those boys for years, and you don't express any interest until *now*?"

"I've got a response for that," Archie said dryly. "Fuck off."

Edward sighed, but he was still staring at the DNA test results that had mine and Archie's names on it. We'd gotten them to give us more than just numbers.

"I only want one thing from you," I said abruptly, because I was done. When I stood, Archie pulled the chair away and then moved until he had me tucked against his side.

"Oh, *now* you want something?" Maddy all but threw her purse on the table. "And that would be exactly what? Not that I plan to give you anything, since you not only humiliated me in that courtroom, you're killing yourself to sabotage the one relationship that has ever meant anything to me."

"I want the names of the other three men."

Maddy snorted and folded her arms. "They aren't important."

"Bellville," Edward said abruptly. "She had an affair with Roger Bellville."

"Eddie…" Maddy stared at him. But he ignored her and focused on me and Archie.

"That was before I met your mother," he said to Archie. "She'd been seeing him for months, and it went on for a few months after. They were seen frequently at parties. As far as I know, he's an attorney these days. Still in New York."

New York.

"This is hardly necessary," Maddy tried again, but he shook off her grip.

"There was a teacher too—humanities professor at Harvard. Well, he wouldn't have been a full professor then. He was an assistant or in training. Might have been working on his master's degree." He rubbed his jaw. "Jackson? Jackson Something or maybe Something Jackson."

"I didn't have an affair with him." Maddy folded her arms. "I can't believe you paid attention to those rumors."

"You made sure I saw you with him, Maddy," Edward said without looking at her. "You always enjoyed rubbing my face in it. As I recall, you also came straight to my bed after leaving his."

I flinched, and my stomach rolled. There were some things I really didn't want to know.

"With that disgusting thought in mind…" Archie stated. "That's two names. Do you have a third?"

Edward shook his head. "There were a few in those days, and then I made a point of not rising to the bait and stopped paying attention."

I swore Maddy almost looked hurt. Or maybe she was just embarrassed.

"But you might try talking to Amber Van Dien. She and Maddy were the best of friends before Maddy slept with her boyfriend."

"Eddie." Now Maddy rounded on him. "What are you talking about?"

He barely spared her a look. "If I think of any others, I'll call you…" He hesitated a split second, then glanced at Archie. "If that's all right with you."

"Email will be fine. By the way, you can keep that copy. We have our own." He picked up my backpack. "And keep a leash on your girlfriend. I'll get an injunction if I have to, but I don't want her anywhere near mine."

"Archie," Edward said as we rounded the table. While my hand was in Archie's, he still moved to block Edward from getting anywhere near me. "We should talk."

"We had eighteen years to do that. My calendar is pretty booked with *my* family." He squeezed my hand, and then we were out the door.

"Don't you dare, Maddy. Sit your ass down. I want an explanation, and I want it *now*."

We didn't even make it a full step beyond the door before Edward's voice reached us, and it was so icy, I flinched. As much as she deserved the man's ire, there was a small part of me that felt for her. I had no idea why. In the elevator, Archie pulled me right against him and wrapped his arms around me.

"It's okay, babe," he whispered against my hair as I gripped him. "They're supposed to be the fucking adults. Let them deal with the fallout. It's not our mess to clean up."

Edward's voice rose over Maddy's more strident tones, and both cut off as the elevator doors snapped shut.

"Your father is an asshole."

"Your mother is a bitch."

I don't know which of us started laughing first, but he pulled back and cupped my face.

"You okay?"

"I'm emancipated. And I just told Maddy to basically go fuck herself."

"You did great," he said, grinning wider. But still, there was a shadow in his eyes.

"Your father really is an asshole…and I'm pretty sure he's beginning to regret a lot of things." Maybe they could patch it up. I had no idea how, but Archie deserved a win.

"I don't care, babe. I don't care what he regrets. I don't need him. I have no regrets. I have you, Jeremy, the guys, and Grandpa. I'm set."

I laughed. Maybe there were some tears too, but the internal shaking was gone and I almost felt giddy. "I care about you. I love you," I said. "But we did it."

"Yes, we did." Then he wrapped an arm around my shoulder and turned as the elevator opened. Out in the lobby, sitting next to the fountain, were three beloved faces, all belonging to men I adore, and who all rose as we headed straight for them.

They'd been waiting for us, and I squeezed Archie's hand before he let me go and half-skipped over to them. Coop caught me first, and I got a big hug.

"You good?" he whispered against my hair, and I nodded. "Arch?"

I hesitated a second and glanced over to where Archie shook hands with Jake. There was a lightness there, despite the shadows. No matter what happened next, we were really done with them. Let our parents kill each other.

"I think so," I murmured. Coop squeezed me and then gave me a gentle nudge toward Ian, who enfolded me into a tight hug, and I closed my eyes as I took a deep breath. A real one. The tightness in my chest was gone. While I wanted to change, the clammy feeling of cold sweat was gone too. Ian didn't say anything, but he didn't have to. When he let me go, I turned straight into Jake, who picked me up with his hug, and I laughed because my stomach gurgled.

"The monster is hungry, guys," Jake said. "We need to feed Baby Girl before she gets hangry."

"Hey," I protested and swatted him as he set me on my feet. "I do not get hangry."

"Oh yes you do," all four of them said together, and I glared, then sniffed before flipping them off and heading for the exit. I didn't make it three steps before I was tucked right up against Archie, with Jake on my other side.

Right where I wanted to be.

Chapter Sixteen
CELEBRATE GOOD TIMES, COME ON!

"The red or the green?" Archie asked as I tilted my hair back in the shower. His excitement was infectious. After hitting a Japanese steak house for an amazing lunch, we'd adjourned back to the apartment where I'd been all but chased into the shower. Though no one joined me. Brats. Well, Archie was standing in the open doorway, and I shifted to look out to see him holding up two dresses.

The green was a cocktail dress, and it had these sweet little lace inlets. The red was a lot dressier and even had a sparkle encrusted waistline. I knew which one was Archie's favorite. "I want to wear the red to prom," I told him, and his eyes lit up. I swore they practically gleamed.

"Done and done. I think they included shoes for this."

"No heels," I called.

"Heels are fine, we're all going to be there." His voice faded on his answer as he moved farther away.

"Don't worry, Baby Girl," Jake said, sticking his head in and giving me a sweeping once over. "We won't let you fall. And you look fantastic in heels."

"She looks fantastic in everything," Archie said as he passed behind him.

"And nothing," Coop yelled from somewhere, and I stared up at the ceiling before ducking back under the water. It was a little nuts to be having this conversation like this.

When I shut off the water, I found Ian waiting for me with an oversized towel. I stepped right into it, and he wrapped it around me.

"I'm okay, you know," I told him, and he pressed a kiss to the tip of my nose.

"I still want to look after you, you know." He tugged me into a full hug and didn't seem to care that I was still soaking wet.

Eyes closed, I leaned into the contact. They'd all been cuddling close all day. While not quite hovering, one of them was either holding my hand or had an arm around me or one hand on my knee. I had no idea how they were working out the transitions from one to the other, but they'd all been handing me off so smoothly, it seemed coordinated.

Ian brushed a kiss to each of my closed eyelids as he wrapped the towel a little tighter and tucked a corner between my breasts. He nudged me toward the toilet, and I sat on the closed lid as he worked a towel gently against my wet hair.

I glanced up to find Coop watching us with an indulgent smile, and he winked. "Want something to drink? We were debating coffee."

"Hmm…" I was tired and we were apparently getting dressed up to go out, so… "Coffee, please."

"On it."

Ian chuckled and then took his time toweling me off and being very thorough to the point he left me panting a little. When I squirmed, he slid his fingers right down the seam of my labia and raised his brows. "Hurting, Angel?"

"Wanting," I said, through little gasps. "But I can be good."

His sudden smile warmed me, and then he slid two fingers into me and curved them, even as he pressed his thumb down. I hadn't even realized how on edge I was until I came, and I clung to him as he pulled a second orgasm out of me right on the heels of the first.

Lips against my ear, he whispered, "Told you I liked taking care of you."

Laughter swelled out of me as he pressed a kiss behind my ear.

"Now finish drying your hair and get dressed. We have plans."

Before I could prompt him for more, he surrendered his spot to Jake, who came bearing coffee and a wide grin. I should probably be blushing from my head to my toes, but the flush of warmth cascading through me had everything to do with being loved.

After a very thorough kiss—payment for my coffee apparently—Jake passed over my cup and then settled in while I dried my hair.

"Up or down?" I asked him.

"Down," came three answers from beyond the bathroom.

"Thank you, Jake," Jake answered them. "I'm so glad you could answer my question without the peanut gallery."

"You're standing in here with her naked and you want her hair up?" Archie asked from the doorway, even as I laughed.

"Well," Jake mused, "she would raise her arms—can you show him for me, Baby Girl?" There was no mistaking that twinkle in his eyes as I gathered up my hair and lifted it with both hands. "Right there," he said as I had my arms up and my chest forward.

"I see what you mean," Archie said slowly, and I snorted.

"And it's staying down," I said, dropping it and shaking the length out. "Especially since you're not telling me where we're going."

"We're going to have fun." Archie hooked an arm around me and dragged me forward for a kiss. "Trust me?" he murmured against my lips. "Trust us?"

How did one argue against that?

I'd never been so grateful for the earlier orgasms Ian had given me, because Jake and Archie were both very *helpful* as I headed for the bedroom. "I can get dressed on my own. I'm sure you've picked out the panties and everything. Now shoo."

"Aww." Archie mock pouted at me, but Jake just laughed as I shut the bedroom door. I turned and collided with Coop, who pinned me to the door, one thigh right between my legs as his mouth locked over mine, and I forgot how to breathe or even think.

The sweep of his tongue went on and on as he cupped my face in one hand and my hip in the other. Even the coolness of the door against my back couldn't temper the heat he aroused. A low groan escaped me, and then there was a hard knock on the door.

"Let her get dressed, Coop. No cheating." Jake sounded like he was having way too good a time.

"No cheating," he murmured against my lips before lifting his head to say, "Fuck off. Bubba already cheated."

I leaned against the door and stared up at him. My nipples were so tight that even the softness of his shirt left me tingling. Running my thumb over his lower lip, I said, "We keep this up and we're never going anywhere, because I'm going to end up shoving one of you down and climbing on."

"I volunteer as tribute," Jake said through the door, and Coop threw his head back and laughed.

A giggle escaped me as he gave me another quick kiss. "Trust me," he said, "if we weren't excited about this surprise, I'd totally drop my pants and let you ride whatever you wanted."

"That would be me," Jake contributed from the other side of the door, and Coop slammed his hand against the wood. There was a muttered, "Ow," from our audience, and my giggles just increased. Coop's eyes warmed and his smile grew when I slid my hands up under his shirt to teased across his abdomen.

"When do we have to leave?" I hooked my fingers in the waistband of his jeans, and it was Coop's turn to groan.

"Not enough time to do all the things I want, beautiful."

"*Fine*," I said with a long-suffering sigh, and he chuckled. "Then stop teasing me." I gave his dick a good squeeze through his jeans, and his breath stuttered. "Not so funny when you're the one getting riled up, is it?"

Jake's barely muffled laughter carried through, and Coop raised his hands in surrender as he fell back to lie on the bed. I opened the door so Jake could join us, and Archie was right behind him. I'd never had almost—wait, there was Ian—so all of them watch me get dressed before since the day we left for Colorado.

Panties pulled on, I paused and looked at them. "We're not going on another sudden trip, right?"

"Nope," Archie answered, but despite all of them shaking their heads, they all wore shit-eating grins. And they all looked really nice too. I skipped the bra because I didn't want to wear the strapless one—it bunched—and the dress didn't need it. It had cups sewn into the bodice, and sometimes, not having big boobs paid off.

Coop and Jake were in jeans, but Archie and Ian both sported slacks. Archie had rolled up the sleeves of his black button-down shirt, revealing his forearms. Ian had on a white one, also rolled up. But Coop and Jake were both in a black T-shirt and white T-shirt respectively. I swore they'd coordinated.

I glanced at my dress and then at them. "I'm going to be overdressed."

"Yes," Jake said solemnly. "You're going to have clothes on."

And on that note, I gave up. No fishing for me. When they decided to plot together, it was better to just hang on for the ride. I pulled the dress on, and Ian made it to me first to zip it up in the back as I pulled my hair out of the way. Then I was sliding my ring on, but my bracelet wasn't on the dresser where I left it.

Archie held it up by two fingers, and they were all grinning again.

"Couldn't really find something that said 'emancipated,'" he explained as he turned the bracelet to show me the newest charm added to it—a gavel. "But I thought this would work."

Oh man, I was going to cry.

"Congratulations, babe. We're still celebrating your big one eight next month, but as of today, you are officially free and clear." He slipped the bracelet on and clipped it into place, and when I wrapped my arms around him, he hugged me tight. Coop locked his arms around me from the back, then Jake came at us from the side, and finally Ian.

"Group hug," I said, almost breathlessly as they caged me in.

"Huddle," Jake corrected with a chuckle. "But group hug works too."

I didn't cry.

But it was a damn close thing.

As it was, I was reluctant to let go, but as we pulled apart, I caught Archie's gaze and smiled. This was our family. I swore he must have been thinking the same thing, 'cause he winked.

Even with all their "help," it still took another fifteen minutes for me to finish being ready, and yes, I was in the damn heels. I was also wearing a buttery soft leather coat that was way too expensive and did not belong in my closet. I knew better than to leave Archie alone in a store, especially after I'd admired the coat for all of about fifteen seconds.

Still…it was really soft, and the smile he wore when I ran my fingers over it shut up my objections before I could even make them.

Finally, we were all out in the car—Jake's as usual when it was all of us—with the music cranked and singing along. The cats were probably glad to be rid of us. The guys had taken care of making sure they had food and water, and I'd even noticed the new cat tree in the living room. Not to mention the whole apartment had been a lot neater.

Jeremy had really done way too much.

But I put that away. I put it all away. Tonight, we were celebrating.

And apparently, we were going to the Liquid Lounge. A squeak escaped me.

"We didn't make it on Valentine's," Ian told me. I was sandwiched between him and Archie in the back. "So tonight, we're going to make up for that *and* celebrate your freedom."

"And that whole 'we're not siblings' thing," Archie said. "'Cause while I didn't care…"

"It's still good news," I agreed with him in a rush. Because to be honest, I hadn't cared either. But neither of us wanted that out there. "No more bad meatloaf."

"Yes!" Jake yelled from the front as he pulled up to the curb with the valet. "Fuck off, bad meatloaf."

The whooping increased until I was smiling so hard, my face hurt. There was a cover charge to get in, and we all had to get stamps on our left hands—no alcohol because we were under age—but I didn't care. Inside, there were singers on the stage already doing "Summer Nights" from *Grease*. Archie had made reservations, so we were shown right to a table.

I danced along to the music as I followed Archie and the hostess. Jake's hands were on my hips as he followed. The interior of the club was gorgeous. It was all art deco and dark colors, save for the splashes of neon. It was so outrageously over the top that I loved it. We got a round of drinks ordered, and I settled in the center of the booth with the guys sliding in on the edges.

Coop was the last one to the table, but he wore a grin. We toasted my 'freedom,' and then Ian pulled over the music catalog and pushed it to me. "Pick one," he said.

And I grinned at him. I'd asked for this date, and not only was I getting it, I got it with all of them. There was a steady stream of performers, some awesome, some terrible, and a lot in between. But they were all having fun. When one group got up to do "Bohemian Rhapsody," we were all singing along.

I'd picked a song, and when I showed Ian, he grinned wider and gave me a thumbs up before he slid out of the booth to go and sign us up. When he came back, he winked, then finished his drink before he lifted his chin toward Archie. He nodded, and there was that silent communication thing the boys all did as they exchanged looks.

As the last group finished and left the stage, they all slid out, but not before Archie pressed a kiss to my lips and said, "This is for you, babe. Happy

Valentine's—you know what, fuck it. Happy every day."

I grinned as the four of them streamed up on the stage. What were they going to…

Then the music started, and I swore my face caught on fire as all the blood rushed to my cheeks. The fact that Ian started it off had me grinning from ear to ear. Then the guys backed him up, and I died laughing as they even added the moves to "The Best Song Ever." I would kill Coop later for betraying my One Direction fascination.

It had been a year-long obsession that I outgrew, but I had to admit, this was one of my favorite songs. Jake took the next stanza, but the fact they nailed the chorus had me laughing, crying, and dancing in my seat.

When Archie sang about having a dirty mouth, I lost it as I clapped along. I wasn't the only one. They'd captivated the whole damn club, and they were all focused on me as they sang. I raised my arms and kept dancing in my seat, even as tears blurred my eyes and my face hurt.

And our night was really only getting started. When they finished, everyone applauded, and I whooped, whistled, and fangirl-screamed, just for them.

By the end of the night, Ian and I had done "Under Pressure," "Shallow," and I let Jake talk me into doing "Cool Rider" from the second *Grease* movie.

Best.

Night.

Ever.

We closed the bar down and totally blew off school the next day.

Yeah, we were rebels.

But we were celebrating freedom, right?

Freedom and family.

Chapter Seventeen
GOOD VIBRATIONS

The Queen Isabella Causeway was stunning to look at as we made the two-and-a-half-mile drive across the connection between the mainland and South Padre Island. Archie and Jake had talked about the steel cantilever beams and main span of it when we'd stopped for lunch, and I could totally appreciate the engineering.

Even more, I loved the feel of the sun on my back as I pressed against Ian. When we set out earlier that morning, the guys had surprised me with the fact Ian was bringing his bike, and I'd alternated on breaks between the SUV with the boys and the bike with Ian. I wondered if he'd be too exhausted by riding all the way, but even if my ass and legs vibrated, I love that we were on his bike.

Jake was directly behind us. Even when I was in the SUV with them, he didn't let anyone get between his car and Ian's bike. Despite a few breaks and the stops for lunch, and the dog museum in Waco, we'd reach the *house* Archie rented for our three days in Padre before sunset. Crazy museum date was officially checked off our list. The fact they remembered delighted me on every level.

I should have known they were up to something when Rachel took me swimsuit shopping. Course, she made no pretenses when she said the more scandalous the better. The bandage style bathing suit I'd picked out was probably going to get me in trouble. I couldn't wait. While the ride had begun somewhat cooler, it was in the upper seventies, low eighties this far south, and the breeze coming off the ocean teased me.

Honestly, I couldn't wait to hit the beach. Jeremy had the cats again and had already provided two shots of them setting up in the sunroom at Archie's house and sprawling over the elaborate cat tree he'd set up for them. They were in heaven.

I resisted the urge to stretch my arms out and ride like I was flying. I'd done that earlier, and Jake nearly had an aneurism, even if Ian had laughed. I didn't want to scare anyone, so I settled for squeezing Ian and just savoring the closeness as he followed the streets to the gated community where the rental house awaited us. The place was gorgeous, unsurprisingly, and Archie gave it an assessing once over as I stretched.

The guys were laughing and shoving at each other as they grabbed our bags and carried them in. The house had five bedrooms, four bathrooms, a huge heated swimming pool, and a series of terraces off the house, with the back of it facing what was ostensibly a private beach meant for the homes in this little community.

"Get changed," Archie called. "We can get some beach time in and then grill some food. The house should be stocked."

There were shouts from Coop and Jake, but I walked out onto the deck that a big pair of French doors in my room opened onto. The view was…amazing. The ocean rolled in—well the gulf, but it smelled like sand and salt and warmth.

The last ten days or so since the emancipation hearing and facing off with Maddy and Edward had been surreal in some ways. The guys stayed close, and no matter who I went to bed with, I always woke up with one extra in the morning. Ian and Archie had been having these intense, quiet conversations that they thought I wasn't paying attention to, but like the secret project Archie worked on with Jake, I let them have it.

Did I want to know? Sure. But something in me settled over the last few months. I *trusted* them. I had private time with each of them, time when we talked about everything and nothing. Those moments belonged to us, and the guys deserved the same courtesy and respect.

Besides, the shifting we'd all been doing since Colorado seemed even more comfortable now.

"Hey," Coop said from behind me, and I turned to find him standing in between the open doors dressed in a pair of swim trunks and nothing else. The sun gleamed off his skin and seemed to highlight his fading tan and sinewy muscle. He'd added a little bulk and tone.

The running Ian had dragged us out on had actually begun to grow on me, much to Coop's chagrin, so we joined the guys two of three mornings, but I made sure to stay in bed with him at least a couple of times a week.

Leaning against the railing with the breeze pulling at my hair, I pushed my sunglasses up and grinned at him. "Hey."

"You planning on changing?" Just a hint of concern in his eyes and the dip of his smile. He worried. They all did.

"Yep," I told him as I pushed away from the railing. "Want to watch?"

Laughing, he spread his arms, and his expression lightened again. "Duh."

Five minutes later, he'd surrendered his amusement for outright lust, and I had to admit, my nipples beaded at the way he raked his gaze over me.

"I changed my mind," he said. "I say we stay in."

When I'd first tried on this suit, I'd been uncertain, even as I loved the way the black bandage suit fit me. It was snug and high on my hips, with two bands of thin fabric connecting it to the top that cupped my breasts and made them look a bit bigger than they really were. It bared just as much skin as a bikini, maybe a tad less, yet it looked way sexier in my opinion. Coop's reaction just cinched it.

Laughing, I pivoted to grab my sunglasses off the dresser, and his groan sent shivers up my spine. "You're killing me."

With a teasing look over my shoulder, I said, "You'll live."

"Mean," he called after me as I headed out of the room. "Really mean."

Downstairs, Jake yelled, "What's mean?" He appeared at the bottom of the stairs, mouth open to say something, and then seemed to freeze as I descended. Oh, they definitely knew how to make me feel good about my choice. Rachel had been extremely complimentary, but this was a whole new level. "Fuck. Me."

"Later," I promised as I reached the next to the last step and brushed a kiss to his jaw. "Beach first."

"Hot, right?" Coop said from above as I circled around Jake. Him in swim trunks was a good look, all hard packed muscle that rippled along his back as I trailed a finger over him. I made it three steps before Jake's groan sounded almost as agonized as Coop's had been. "I already called dibs," Coop continued, and Jake laughed.

"You don't mind sharing."

"No, I definitely don't," Coop said, and as I grinned at Archie and Ian, who were both standing next to the doors leading out to the path that would take us to the beach. They had towels and looked damn good in their own swim trunks. "But I have a feeling it's gonna be a race tonight to see who gets there first. Or our girl is going to get a hell of a workout."

Not for the first time, it hit me that I got all four of them. They all loved me. I loved them. I got to touch them. They touched me. And while I was always aware of how attractive they were, I didn't think about just how hot they really were until right this moment. My pussy clenched tight around the sudden feeling of emptiness, and my already beaded nipples grew almost painful.

Maybe Coop was on to something, but I'd just put on the suit. I figured we should see the beach at least once, because currently, I was considering how I could work out holding all four of them hostage. Somehow, I didn't think it would be all that difficult.

"You look great, babe," Archie told me as he did a little twirl with his finger, and I paused just out of arm's reach to do a little spin. Their groans of appreciation bolstered my ego, no lie, and I grinned as I faced them, just as Jake plastered himself to my back.

"She looks better than great. I don't know that I want to share just how good she looks."

"We're not sharing," Ian told him firmly. "She can wear whatever she wants and the rest of the world can look, but they don't get to touch."

"Hmm." Jake didn't sound like he disagreed as he pressed a kiss to my throat. "You guys head on down, we'll join you later."

"Uh uh," I scolded, despite how interested I was. "I wanna see the beach." Spring break. The five of us away together. The sun. The sand. The ocean.

"Fine," Jake grunted as he walked us forward. "Can you see it from here?"

Laughter rippled through all of us, and I elbowed him. His exaggerated 'oof' just made me smile though. "C'mon," I said, catching his hand as I pulled away. "I've been dying to see this since Archie announced we were going to run away like normal teens for the holiday." The beach and spring break went hand in hand, right?

I hadn't bothered with shoes. The swimming pool was beautiful, but didn't hold the allure of the water or the sand. While the beach wasn't empty, it wasn't crowded either. Another perk to a semi-private beach, I guessed. Either way, I didn't pay attention to the other groups as I reached the gate. Archie made it a half-step ahead of me and popped it open. He snagged my fingers, interlocking them before we stepped over the warm sidewalk and then onto the sand itself.

As soon as I hit it, I curled my toes against the coarseness. It wasn't super soft, but it wasn't hard either. It was definitely warm after being in the sun. The guys trailed along with us and we dropped our towels and a bag down about ten feet from the water.

Head tilted back, I let the sun hit my face, and I couldn't stop smiling. Not when Archie lifted my hand to kiss, or when a pair of arms wrapped around me from behind. All the tension of the last few weeks kind of melted away.

"Stay just like that," Coop said, and then there was a telltale shutter sound from his phone. When I opened my eyes, I found him grinning at me as he snapped photos of us.

"You done?" Ian asked.

"Yep. I'll upload it to the cloud later."

"Fantastic." Suddenly, Ian scooped me up, one arm beneath my knees and the other wrapped around my back. I gripped his shoulders and stared up at his wild grin. "Ready, Angel?"

"Ready for…?" The answer to my question hit me, even as he started moving. Oh shit. He didn't slow until we plowed into the surf rolling in, and I landed in the salty water. It was bracing and a little chilly, but I couldn't stop laughing. We hadn't gone that deep, but the water foamed where it hit us, and I wrapped my arms around his neck.

"Perfect," he murmured and then dipped his head. I arched to meet his kiss, the soft caress of his lips on mine a delight. He'd brushed his teeth, the minty freshness sweet as he swept his tongue in to stroke mine. Hot palms cupped my ass as the water buffeted us. "Hold your breath," he warned against my lips a split second before someone hit us lightly and we went a little deeper and then under the water.

I was laughing and spluttering as I emerged. Jake and Ian were wrestling in the water, and I laughed as I climbed to my feet. It was still chilly, but I didn't care. We were at the beach, and I threw my head back and whooped before I leapt on Jake's back. It didn't take long for Archie and Coop to join us, and then it was a five-way tussle for dominance. Or maybe a four-way tussle for who had me on their back while they wrestled with the others.

My sides hurt from laughing by the time I stumbled back onto the warm sand. The breeze was a little chilly on my damp skin, but I didn't care. I staggered over to the towels and sank down to sprawl against the oversized one they'd pinned down. Eyes half-closed, I soaked up the last few rays of the sun.

"Hey, gorgeous," an unfamiliar voice greeted me, and I glanced up to find a stranger with a smile grinning down at me.

"Taken," I informed him, and then pointed to the ocean without looking. "And my boyfriends aren't fans of strangers."

He raised his hands. "Damn, just being polite."

"Great," Jake called. "Be polite somewhere else."

Right on time. My hero.

I grinned, and the guy above me backed out of sight. "No harm, no foul."

A moment later, Jake replaced him in my view, and he gave me a once over before glaring off in the direction I suppose my erstwhile visitor had vanished toward.

"I told him I was taken," I informed him. "No need to look so fierce. He didn't push his luck."

"Pfft, he pushed it the minute he made a beeline for you." Raking a hand through his damp hair, he dropped to sit on the oversized towel blanket. The scatter of cool drops hit me as he traced a finger down my cheek. "You good?"

Oh, I was more than good. "Where are the boys?"

"Still swimming."

A shiver raced through me. "Want to go back and shower?" I looked at him from beneath my lowered lashes, and his grin was fierce. One minute, I was on my back, the next, I was over his shoulder and he was racing up the sand.

I laughed so hard that I worried I was going to puke. There were whistles from the guys and a half-hearted "Hey," but Jake didn't slow down except to wipe his feet on the mat. Upstairs, he only set me down in the shower, then ducked in with me, suit and all, as he turned on the water.

The first spray was cold, and I yelped, but Jake swallowed the sound with a kiss, all fierce teeth and tongue. My suit vanished along with his. The water was barely warm before he had us rinsed off, and then a rough run of a towel over each of us. I did my best to help, but I got caught up exploring the dips and lines of his muscles as I alternated between rubs of the towel and tracing my tongue over his skin.

Every part of me shivered and tensed. I couldn't get over just how beautiful he was. They all were, but for some reason, it delighted me on this primitive level and I wanted to mark him up as mine. Abruptly, I pushed my hands against his chest, even as he cupped my breasts and teased my aching nipples. My whole body vibrated with need for him.

"What's wrong, Baby Girl?" The roughness in his voice echoed the feeling in my soul, but I just shook my head and tried to manhandle him into turning around. Bless him, he did, and I groaned at the way the muscles in his back bunched and shifted and then fixed on the dark lines of the tattoo with my name in the center.

I pressed a kiss to it and then scraped my teeth against his flesh, sinking them into the muscle just below it. His groan punched right through me. "You bite me again, Baby Girl, and I'm going to bite you right the fuck back."

Taking that offer, I let him go to turn around and then stared up at him as I laved my tongue over one of his flat nipples before biting down just above it and sucking a hickey into his flesh. At his harsh, indrawn breath, I grinned and ran my hands up over his chest. I didn't get another bite in because Jake settled his hands on my hips and lifted me.

Wrapping my legs around him, I groaned under the sensual assault of his mouth plundering mine, even as his dick rubbed against my damp pussy. Oh, the clench was back, and the bite of his fingers into my flesh had me grinding against him with every step on the way to the bed. He fell backward, one hand sinking into my wet hair to keep me still as I writhed against him.

I wanted more. Everywhere my skin rubbed against his, I wanted more. The ache inside of me had turned into a violent need, and he barely let me get a breath as his tongue thrust against mine. When he kissed a path down my throat, I let out a cry, but it only escalated when he urged me higher, and then one hot hand cupped a breast as his mouth closed over the other nipple. The combination of hot, wet sucking with laves of his tongue against the pinching twist of his fingers made me want to scream.

I stretched a hand between us and wrapped it around the thick length of his dick. I swore it pulsed against my palm as I cupped him and then began to stroke. His moans encouraged me to squeeze him a little tighter, even as he sucked my nipple against his teeth with a force that had tears filling my eyes, while my pussy clenched and a rush of warmth and wetness raced between my thighs.

With one stroke of his head along my labia, I teased my own clit, but Jake didn't let go of my breasts, and my cries were coming in shorter, sharper bursts, then he ran a hand down to my hips and pushed me down. I didn't need any other encouragement, I sank all the way down on him.

Even as wet as I was, there was a burn and a stretch. Mouth open, I tilted my head back as he filled me, and then his hand landed with a crack against my ass. I clenched down on him so tight, he finally released my nipple with a wet pop as I gave a little scream.

"You like that?" he asked on a hot breath as he slapped my ass again and earned the same result. Yes, I liked that. I sank my fingers into his damp hair as I began to rock against him. Every roll of my hips brought me up, and the slap of his hand against my ass had me sinking back down. The sounds escaping him were as desperate and hungry as my own.

We seemed to take turns kissing each other, alternating between a harsh exchange of breath and a soul-searing plunder of each other. Need for him turned into a violent pulse that drew tighter and tighter until I slammed down, and the cracking sound of his palm lit me up nearly as much as the sharp heat and sting on my flesh.

When Jake ripped his mouth away, I tilted my head back and let him go so I could brace my hands behind me on his thighs. The corded muscles in his thighs clenched as I dug my fingers in. The change in angle sent sparks up my nerves as he dragged me back down with every pump. It was wild, frenetic, and desperate in a way it hadn't been in a while.

Every thrust sent another cry out of me, and when he circled my clit with his thumb, I tripped over the edge. The scream I released was raw, and then I was on my back as he powered into me. Even the soft feel of the sheets against my ass added another layer of stinging sensation. When he pinned my wrists, I swore I came undone, lifting my hips in desperation, and the world turned into nothing but sensation, heat, and the feel of him pulsing over me and inside of me.

He came with a harsh cry of his own. The warmth of him filling me sparked a fresh wave of tears, but not as many as how the harsh bite of his kiss turned soft and tender. The moment elongated, suspended there for a breathless length of time before he collapsed with a shudder and buried his face against my throat. I clenched around him, my internal muscles spasming.

The eddies of pleasure left me languid and replete. Some distant part of my mind acknowledged the fact my ass still stung and my thighs burned. Jake was heavy but in all the best ways, and he stayed inside of me, even as he began to soften. I didn't want the moment to end. A breeze carrying the scents of sand and salt cooled my sweaty skin.

Belatedly, I turned my head toward the double doors I'd left open. A bird cried in the distance. A faint hum of voices accompanied the steady rush of water to shore, and a laugh fell out of me.

"I hope our neighbors didn't mind the show," I whispered, and Jake began to shake, the huff of his laughter against my throat a delight.

"Coop probably got popcorn," he teased.

"Nope," Coop said, and I turned my head toward the open door where he, Ian, and Archie stood, all still in their swim trunks, damp and delicious from being outside, and I clenched around Jake again, even as he hissed. "Didn't want to miss anything." Coop's absolutely unrepentant grin delighted me almost as much as the fact both Ian and Archie were still there.

More, they both wore naked want on their faces. They weren't Coop, watching wasn't normally their thing, and yet they hadn't moved away. Jake rolled off me slowly with a groan, pulling free with another hiss as I tightened. The clenching came with its own wave of spasms. Coop dipped his head to look over me, and when I curled my fingers, he grinned.

"Player three entering the game?"

"After player three takes a shower," Jake told him, sprawling next to me with an air of smug satisfaction and repletion, utterly unconcerned by his nudity or mine. As much as I'd begun to treasure that possessive nature of his, I loved even more that he put it away when it was just all of us. Me and the guys I loved.

When Coop vanished into the bathroom, I looked back to where Archie and Ian stood, and then Archie pushed away from the door to walk over to the bed.

"That was hot, babe," he told me before planting a hand next to me, and then his mouth was on mine. There was no hesitation or reticence, he chased my tongue with a fervor. The salty kiss had me curving upward, ready to chase him, but he sucked my lower lip out and then let go. "Play with Coop," he whispered. "Bubba and I are going to get the grill fired up." Even as he spoke, he traced his fingers down to my breasts and toyed with them.

The weight of two other stares on me was a very present thing, but even more was the fact Archie seemed even more turned on than off.

"Then I want to test our video game theory after dinner."

Oh.

Fuck.

"I'd like that," I said with a shuddering breath as he slid his fingers between my legs. "Do you want me naked or in a dress?"

I didn't miss either Jake or Ian's indrawn breaths. Archie circled my swollen clit before he dipped his fingers lower, and I swore he was playing with Jake's cum, pushing it deeper into me as he speared his fingers inside.

"Dress," he decided after a moment, curving his fingers until my whole body lifted from the bed. "Just be naked under there so when that hot pussy is wrapped around my cock, I can feel every inch of you. They can imagine what it's like to have you clenching down on my dick like you are my fingers, all warm, wet, and swollen. I bet Jake takes you again after Coop, or maybe they both will." Every word sent a pulse through me. "So you'll be so hot and tight when I fuck up into you. Then we'll see who the better player is…or maybe I'll just fuck you nice and slow while they have to keep their focus on the game."

Had I mentioned how much I loved his mouth and the fact that he kept pumping his fingers into me? When he applied pressure with his thumb, it was like we were back in that dressing room as he fucked me with his hand and his words, seducing me, and when I thrust up to meet him, he grinned. "That's it, babe, make yourself come on my hand while they watch."

Heat scorched every inch of me, but I did exactly what Archie asked, aware of Jake stroking his dick next to me and Ian watching me with fire in his eyes.

I really didn't think I'd be seeing that much of the beach this weekend.

When the orgasm I'd been chasing crashed over me, Archie swallowed my scream with a lingering kiss before he raised his damp fingers to my lips and I cleaned them.

"Fuck," Coop said from somewhere in the room, and I shivered.

Yes, please.

Chapter Eighteen
BE GOOD TO YOUR DAUGHTERS

I leaned back against the seat of the rental car. Archie had arranged for two vehicles to be waiting for us when we arrived so we would have options. The flight from Texas to Connecticut after three pleasure-and-fun-soaked days at the beach seemed a lot like spiraling back to reality. The delicious ache invading every single muscle had made sleeping on the plane easier.

We'd arrived before lunch, and instead of a rental house, Archie had gotten us the honeymoon suite at a really expensive hotel. I wanted to argue about the money so bad. This whole thing was costing him a fortune, but he just kissed me and reminded me it was his money to spend. Now, sitting beside him in the convertible as we followed the winding and picturesque roads toward our final destination, I made a promise to myself.

Someday, I was going to be the one who spoiled him. I was going to make sure he was okay. And I was going to make him feel like a king. The air was a lot chillier here, and I was back in my buttery soft leather coat, jeans, thick boots, and a dark cable knit sweater. I'd even pulled on a little knit cap, not only to protect my ears but also to keep my hair from getting windblown.

The car had seat warmers, and the soft kidskin leather gloves kept my hands warm. The only problem with them was I couldn't wear my ring, so Jake had slid it onto a chain and tucked it around my neck. It nestled right between my breasts beneath the sweater.

"How much farther?"

"We're not scheduled to be there for another hour," Archie said, and I was impressed the wind didn't steal his words. "I wanted to show you something before we got there, if that's okay."

"Anything you want." I had no problems with delaying. I couldn't make up my mind if I was excited or terrified or somewhere in between. I couldn't even say why I wanted to do this. Yet, the night I explained it—or tried to—all four of them had understood and shifted our spring break plans to cut our time at the beach short.

He grinned. "Don't tempt me when I know how sore you are."

I groaned and tilted my head back. Who knew it was possible to have too much sex? I thought I'd strained my vagina or something. Telling Rachel on video chat had been hilarious. Her reaction still made me smile. She also suggested that I add more variety that didn't insist on stretching me so much. It was cute, but I reminded her she had a secret boyfriend of her own, not to mention a girlfriend. And how did I know that second one? I'd caught sight of the bare leg out of the corner of her video camera as she'd scrambled out of bed.

The flushed look and over-bright eyes were another dead giveaway. Those and the hickeys on her throat. They got darker and more numerous about every five days. Fading just in time for her to see him again.

"I promise," Rachel said, holding up her hand. "I'll introduce you when you get back. But you have to promise to leash your boys."

"I can't guarantee it, they like you now. You're going to be stuck with how overprotective they are. But if he isn't treating you right, or she isn't, trust me when I say I'll be the one kicking their asses."

"I love you too, now go away." Rachel had winked before she'd ended the call.

But when I asked Jake later would he kick a guy's ass if I told him it needed kicking but didn't tell him *why*, he just looked at me like I was adorable. "Baby Girl, you want me to beat someone's ass, all you gotta do is point. If you want their ass kicked, it needs to be kicked."

Yeah, maybe that shouldn't turn me on, but it so did.

We'd debated whether the guys should come with us, but everyone decided that it should just be Archie and me, at least for the first meeting.

"Honestly, Baby Girl, I kind of hate the thought of them," Jake had confessed. "They knew about you, knew Maddy, and they left you there. That makes them assholes in my book."

Coop had nodded grimly, but Ian's reaction surprised me. "I get why you need to meet them and I want that for you. But I don't like them, and I don't want them anywhere near you. So the compromise is Archie goes because I know he'll tear them apart if they try anything. Then you can make the call, Angel. This is your life. We just want you to be happy."

Then again, if anyone—say, Archie's asshole parents—treated them the way Maddy had treated me? Yeah, I'd be ready for blood too. Decision made, Archie and I had stayed at the hotel long enough to change into warmer clothes before heading down to the rented convertible. He followed a twisting road that bypassed a pair of great iron gates into an isolated section that looked so forlorn, with only a hint of green amidst the sparse foliage.

Winter still held a fierce grip on New England, even though a weak sun had warmed the day up to the upper fifties, low sixties. My cheeks burned a little, chilled from the drive, but as he took the long winding route through the sparse woods, the wind abated.

"Where are we?" As if summoned by the question, the trees parted to reveal an old gothic style structure of a building. It was huge and imposing. There was a circular drive leading up to the front and huge wings jutting off to the sides. I wasn't sure if I was supposed to be impressed or terrified. It was both fascinating and cold all at once.

Archie followed the circular drive around, then backed into a parking slip I hadn't even noticed so that we could face the building. After he put the car into park, he said, "Welcome to Blue Ivy Prep, my home away from home for a few years."

Surprise speared through me, and I glanced over at him. "I thought you went to a boarding school."

"This is it," he said. "Generations of Standishes and Graysons have gone here. If Maddy hadn't left and broken off with her family, we might have met here instead of in Texas."

I stared at the building. It was…cold. Unfeeling. I mean, it was just a building, but it seemed…isolated and alone.

"I know it looks bad, but that's just the outside. C'mon," he slid out of the car and walked around to get me. "Kids are probably away on their spring break, which is why it's so quiet. But it's perfect for an impromptu tour."

"Aren't we going to get into trouble?" I stared at him.

Archie laughed. "Babe, this is one of those times where our last names open doors, and here, our money built at least a third of this place."

Our money.

We made it three steps as I lagged, and he glanced at me with a question in his eyes.

"It's not my money," I reminded him. "I'm not even sure they're my family."

"No," he murmured softly and cupped my cheek. "But I am. What's mine is yours."

Some of my reservations melted away. "I love you."

He grinned slowly and with more than a little smugness. "Luckiest bastard in the world right here."

I snorted. "I'm the bastard in this relationship, remember?"

A snort followed by a groan met my declaration, but we set off again. The big doors looked like they'd been created out of hammered iron, but they were just heavy and wooden, yet Archie pulled the door open easily. The interior was all dark cherry wood and elegant looking. If the outside was cold and forbidding, the interior was warm and inviting.

Portraits lined the walls of stuffy looking individuals, yet they all seemed extremely expensive oil paintings. "School founders," Archie murmured against my ear. "This is the main hall. Food court is down there." He pointed toward one of the myriad of halls jutting away from this building. "Upstairs are administration offices and counselors. This way…" He grinned at me as he tugged me along. "This is the way to the boys' quarters. Girls are quartered on the other side, though there is a courtyard between them."

It was a whirlwind tour that included seeing a communal shower, bathroom, and a library that I wanted to stay in until Archie told me there were two of them—this one and then an identical one in the girls' wing. Why two? He shrugged. Probably sex in the stacks in the sixties and seventies. Free love had changed how Blue Ivy did business.

When he eyed one of the shadowy areas in the shelves then me, he winked. "Next time. When you're not so sore."

They were all intimately aware of my current status, and my blush was not for that, so much as for the promise of next time.

Next, we plunged deeper into the boys' side, and he took me to a room at the far end. Only then did he let go of my hand to work something against the lock.

"Archie, what are you doing?" I hissed. So far, we hadn't seen anyone, but that didn't mean we were alone. There were cameras in some of the halls. None up here, though.

At all.

"It's fine," he said as the lock gave. "This thing is so stupid easy to open if you know what you're doing." Inside, we found a tidy room with a private bathroom. It was a single, apparently, about as big as my bedroom, maybe a little bigger. There was a bed tucked in the corner under the window with a desk next to it and a big fat arm chair in the opposite corner.

It definitely *smelled* like teenage boy in here.

"This," Archie said. "This was my home away from home for four years. Started at Prep in fifth grade. Left after eighth. This hall has changed some, but they quartered by year when I was here, so all my neighbors were in my class. Facilitating cooperation and closeness. Not that it worked. They were just kids who went here, not my friends."

My heart twisted.

"Nana and Grandpa lived about twenty-five minutes from here. Pretty close to where your grandparents live. Grandpa sold the house after Nana died." He'd told me that.

"You spent weekends with them."

"Every chance I got," he told me as he turned in a slow circle. "This room though, was basically my world for four years. I spent a couple of holidays here when Edward and Muriel were too busy to make it back. That was the first year. After that, Nana always came to get me."

"Did you go to boarding school before here, too?"

He nodded. "A couple of different ones. Jeremy would collect me at the end of terms and bring me back in the spring. He always made sure to send care packages too. I never ran out of contraband. But it was easier when I decided on public school."

Pivoting, he faced me and grinned.

"Best decision I ever made."

I laughed. "I don't know if I can even imagine going here." Our parents had. Was that why they were so messed up? Had Maddy saved me, inadvertently or not, from this life? Had Archie saved himself by leaving?

What if his nana hadn't died?

What if…

There were too many of them.

"I'm glad you came to Texas," I told him, and I really was. When he dragged me into a hug, then glanced at that kid's bed, I whacked him.

Laughing, he kissed me before leading the way out and locking the door behind us. "Can't blame a guy for being turned on around you, babe. You're everything and more."

"Smooth talker," I teased, even if I was grinning. We finished our sneaky tour and had just made it back to the car when we got busted by security. Unsurprisingly, Archie talked our way right out of the trouble, particularly after the security guard recognized him. After a handshake and a flash of cash vanishing from Archie's palm to the security guy's, we were back in the car and on our way to the Grayson Estate.

Estate.

Ugh.

A chill raced through me, but I did my best to cover it as we left Archie's old school behind. I really couldn't picture him there. Or maybe I just didn't want to. When he talked about that time to me, all I heard was the loneliness in his voice. Reaching over, I covered his hand on the gear shift, and he glanced at me with a grin. The sunglasses and ruffled hair gave him a rakish edge, but did nothing to hide his inescapable charm.

Never lonely again. Not like that.

Despite the fact I'd done an internet search on them, I wasn't prepared for their house when we arrived. It really was an estate with a fountain in the front. The brick work was brighter here than at the school, but the building was equally imposing. It looked easily as big as our high school. Holy crap.

"And Maddy has no siblings?" I hadn't found any in the search. Archie parked in the circular round right in front of their main doors.

"Nope," he told me. Granted, Archie lived in a huge house too, but that seemed almost cozy compared to this museum. "Still time to bail, babe. No questions, no judgment."

No, I had questions and a lot of judgment. I wasn't doing this for Maddy or for Patience and Eugene, whoever they might be, I was doing this for *me*. I *needed* to know. I needed to put these questions to rest so I could move on with my family.

I tugged off the knit cap and stuffed it into my pocket before checking my hair in the mirror in the visor.

"You're beautiful," he told me, waiting patiently for me to step out, and I grinned up at him.

"You're biased."

"Absolutely," he winked. "I'm also right."

Blowing out a breath, I gathered up my courage and stepped out the door he held open. We didn't even make it to the door to ring the bell before it was opened by a stately looking elderly gentleman wearing a suit. He didn't look like the picture of Eugene Grayson, I'd seen.

"Miss Curtis, Mr. Standish, please, come in. You're expected." Well, that confirmed it. He stepped back to allow us inside and then closed the door behind us. "May I take your coats?"

Archie had already shrugged out of his and then helped me out of mine. With care, he passed them over to the man, who hadn't introduced himself but seemed to be some kind of butler. A woman bypassed us and headed for the stairs. Unlike the butler, she was dressed in a pale blue uniform of some kind. She kept her eyes down but gave me a polite if quick smile before hurrying on.

"Mr. and Mrs. Grayson will be down directly. If you'll follow me to the sunroom. Lunch will be served in thirty minutes."

The sunroom turned out to be a huge glass enclosure filled with foliage, flowering plants, and another fountain. It was much warmer in here and just a tad humid. Not enough that I wanted to shed my sweater, but I was definitely glad to be out of my jacket and gloves.

A table awaited us, all set for serving four. I guessed they'd prepared when Archie confirmed our arrival time. I'd been a bit of a coward on that front. I had no idea what to say to them right now, when I was about to meet them face to face. Calling them seemed impossible. What do you say to grandparents who might as well be strangers?

"Can I get you a refreshment?" the butler asked.

"A couple of sodas would be great," Archie told him. "Coke, if you have it. If not, coffee."

"Of course," the butler said, then gave us the briefest of nods and left us alone.

"So. Weird." It was almost creepy. I mean, the sunroom was gorgeous, and I could imagine sitting out here to read in the middle of winter would be amazing if there was snow outside and it was still warm in here.

Arms folded, I made a slow circuit, not quite ready to sit down. The fountain was a total surprise. Not that I had expectations, but the fact there were literally dozens of brilliantly colored koi in the water and the fountain was more of a water feature that wound through all the plants, including little bridges to create footpaths over it, was incredible.

"Holy crap, Archie." I turned as he cleared his throat and stared right into a pair of intensely familiar eyes. They should be familiar. I looked into them every single day.

Patience Grayson with her near perfect white hair, streaked in silver and dressed in a neatly tailored blouse and what I imagined were riding pants—did they own horses too?—stared at me with the same green eyes I possessed. Her eyes. Mine. Maddy's.

"You look like Madeline."

Well, that was a greeting.

"So do you." Two could play that game.

Perfectly manicured eyebrows raised, the woman—yeah, not leaning on a title for her yet—said, "Touché." Then with a little more warmth, she extended her hand as she crossed to me. "Patience Grayson."

"Frankie Curtis," I answered and gripped her hand in a brief handshake. Her fingers were warm, almost papery in texture, but her grip was strong.

"Not Francesca?" There was a note of disappointment in her voice.

"Not if I can help it," I told her simply. "Francesca is a little too fancy for my tastes, and I'm a pretty simple girl."

"You're dating a Standish, and you come from a prestigious line that can trace its roots back to the Mayflower."

She probably didn't mean that to sound as pretentious as it was, but I gave her a little shrug and a smile. "I'm dating Archie because he's Archie. That he's a Standish just happens to be a small part of the equation. As for my 'prestigious line,'" I continued, making sure to emphasize the air quotes, "I grew up in a two-bedroom apartment in Texas, cutting coupons and buying stuff on sale. Bloodlines don't mean much because they don't really make sure you eat."

Patience Grayson frowned at me, her eyes cooling but not turning frosty. If anything, they seemed disappointed.

"She sounds like Madeline," a male voice announced a moment before the older man came into view. Like Patience, he had white hair, though more of his was steel gray than white. His eyes were a shocking shade of blue, somewhere between Ian's deep blue and Jake's much paler color. Still, he fastened those eyes on me with an assessing look. "But more direct, and with far fewer digs."

I shrugged. "Unfortunately, you can't choose your parents."

The man surprised me when he laughed. While he moved slowly, he didn't seem to have any balance issues. In some ways though, he seemed ancient. Like a lot older than Patience. Maybe I should have checked on their ages, but there were some things I didn't want to know and others I avoided. I had enough preconceived notions about them.

"Archibald," Eugene called. "Good to see you boy."

Archie grimaced but inclined his head. "And you, sir."

Laughing, Gene glanced at me and then surprised me with a wink. "Boy hates when we use his full name, but he's far too polite to correct us. He's a good boy though, we like him. Ted did right by him, and he seems awfully fond of you." Eugene Grayson gave me a piercing look before he held out his hand. "It's been a long time coming, young lady, but I'm Eugene Grayson."

"Frankie Curtis," I answered him exactly as I had his wife. His grip trembled faintly and took what seemed like a robust man and made him seem a little frailer beneath the surface. That was the only reason I bit back my next comment. My nerves were fluttering like mad, but I was also on guard. These were Maddy's parents, the people who cut her off and ultimately, cut me off.

"Shall we sit? Pat, let's get the kids some food, and then we can talk like civilized people."

"Of course," Patience said smoothly as she accepted his arm. "Please, join us. I know you must have questions."

Questions?

Oh, I had questions. But instead of leading Patience away, Eugene offered me his other arm, and I stared at it a minute, then Archie swooped in to wrap an arm around me. "Excuse me, sir, but I'd like to be the one to escort her to the table."

That earned us a pair of assessing looks from both Eugene and Patience. They nodded and moved ahead before Archie pressed his lips to my ear. "Good?"

I glanced at him and gave a slow if uneven nod. But even as he pulled out my seat and I took it, the scrutiny from the other two at the table weighed on me. What did I want out of this meeting? That would be what Erin would ask me. Was my anxiety misplaced? Did I want to blame them? Did I want them to answer all my questions and tell me they'd wanted me, even if Maddy cut them off too? Or did I want them to just tell me they hadn't cared because Maddy had broken all their conventions? What did I want to know?

Or was it that I simply wanted them to like me?

Once we were seated, someone brought out the drinks Archie had asked for. The woman who served us turned out to be someone else from the one I'd seen earlier or the butler. But instead of quiet reserve, she wore a bright smile and radiated warmth. While she didn't say much, she seemed pleased to see me. Only after she'd served the salads and excused herself did Patience sigh.

"Martha is going to gloat at me for weeks after this."

Eugene laughed. "And rightly so. You've been worried about meeting her and fighting the urge to call her for two years out of fear she would be too much like her mother."

Patience flicked a look over to me. I raised my eyebrows. What did she want me to say? Thank you for not lumping me into the same category with Maddy?

When the silence stretched out, Eugene glanced between Patience and I before he opened his mouth, but I had one question and I wanted to know the answer before we went too far down this road.

"I met you before," I said abruptly and pulled the focus of the whole table. "You came to Texas. You and Maddy had a big fight and then you left, but you didn't say two words to me then. So you knew where I was, where we were, and you knew her. So all I want to know is why? Why did I never hear from you?" Not to let Eugene off the hook, I glanced at him. "Why didn't I ever hear from either of you?"

Chapter Nineteen

I'LL BE YOUR ALLY THROUGH ALL YOUR BATTLES

ARCHIE

The silence at the table grew, but Frankie didn't back down. My little badass met their stares evenly. She'd asked that question in a strong voice, one that commanded respect, even if she didn't realize it. Fuck, I loved her, but more than that, I was proud of her. Frankie despised confrontation. She could handle it, but she'd never liked it. Another mark of Maddy's influence. Yet in the months since she'd unloaded at us at the apartment, there'd been a noticeable shift in her demeanor. She didn't back down, and if anything, all the knocks that kept hitting her had made her stronger.

I flicked a look from her to the grandparents, who both wore controlled expressions, even if Eugene's slipped a little at her question. She'd scored a mark on them. Considering she'd only just met them and wasn't as familiar with this world as I was, she may not have seen it. But I had.

At the same time, if they compared her to Maddy again, I was going to rip them a new asshole. Frankie was *nothing* like Maddy. Polite courtesy only went so far.

Eugene cracked first and leaned forward, focusing on her. "I don't know if our explanation will ever be enough."

"Maybe not," Frankie agreed as she lifted her chin. The determination in her eyes seemed to gleam even brighter. I needed to tell her later just how stunning she was in that dark green sweater, jeans, and boot combo she had on. Maybe when I peeled it all off. "But I'd like to hear it one way or another."

With a glance at his wife, Eugene sighed. "Your mother—Madeline…" he began, then hesitated again. "A parent never wants to talk ill of their own child." His lips turned down, but the droop to his shoulders disappeared as he sat a little straighter. "She was a difficult, demanding, and very competitive child. These are not negative traits, not really."

"We encouraged it," Patience admitted, and while Eugene could hold Frankie's gaze, she couldn't. She kept looking away. "Perhaps too much. I had… three miscarriages while Madeline was young, and each time, she grew more agitated with me for trying to have another child. I thought at first she was just trying to excel to prove to me I didn't need to have another one. Selfishly, I wanted to think the best of her that she didn't want me to be sad."

Eugene put a hand over his wife's. "When we couldn't have more children, we accepted it and focused all of our energy on Maddy. She was such a happy child for a long time. She excelled at school, at home, in all of her extracurriculars. She was charming, delightful, and won the hearts of everyone who knew her."

Yeah, I might have to throw up if they keep this line of the story going. Rather than comment, I kept my focus on Frankie. From the moment she'd asked the question, I'd settled a hand on her thigh. Our legs were pressed together, but I wanted her to remember she wasn't alone.

"Again, I have to stress she was happy. Or so we thought. When we enrolled her at Blue Ivy Prep, we did it because she wanted it. The agreement was initially, she would say there during the week and come home on the weekends. By the time she reached seventh grade, however, she wanted the full immersive experience, so she alternated weekends she came home. By the first year of ninth, she stopped coming home except for holidays." Patience looked so troubled. "We thought it normal. She was a young lady, she wanted to assert her independence." When she flicked a look at me, she didn't have to tell me that was also the year she and my dad had probably started dating.

"We've always been close with your family, Archie, as I'm sure you're aware," Eugene said, taking up the thread, even as Frankie's hand slid over mine. I turned mine over, and we interlocked our fingers. "She and Edward practically grew up together, but I don't think they really noticed each other until that year. The relationship accelerated at an unseemly rate."

"We don't really need those details," Frankie said with a faint grimace.

"Good thing, because I don't particularly relish sharing them." Eugene's voice had grown stronger. "That was also the year she began to act out. We heard through sources of her throwing her weight around at school. She'd gotten access to a small trust fund set up by my mother. It was for incidentals, pocket change."

If it was anything like the one I came into, then it would've been a lot more money to Frankie than they realized. Fortunately, they skipped ahead and didn't focus on that.

"She began to host illegal parties," Patience said with a sigh. "The headmaster tended to overlook these infractions because we contributed a great deal of money to the school."

Frankie shot me a look, and I gave her a little shrug. I couldn't help it if our names did that. To be honest, that onus wasn't on us. Yes, I had taken advantage of the fact more than once, but again, I wasn't the one who created the situation.

"In their junior year, it all came to a rather unfortunate and disturbing head when two students overdosed at one of her parties. While no charges were filed, the school had done what they could to mitigate the circumstances, and we had to fight to keep her in because they wanted her to withdraw."

But no way could they have forced the issue. "You paid to keep her in," I supplied, in case Frankie didn't understand why they would have asked but not forced the issue.

"There was no proof," Patience said. "That other than those two students attended her party. There was no proof that Maddy supplied the drugs. There was no proof that Maddy had anything to do with them. It could just as easily have been a case of wrong time, wrong place."

Right.

"Still, Maddy promised no more parties. She did stop throwing them." Eugene sighed. "That was when Eddie started hosting them for her."

Of course he did. Then again, would I really tell Frankie no if she wanted something badly?

"When they graduated, Eddie proposed," Patience continued as she lifted her cup and took a sip. "They were both far too young, but Maddy threatened to elope if we forbid it. Fortunately, we weren't the only ones opposed, and Ted had much firmer control over Eddie. They had to graduate college, and they had to be in their careers a year. That was the agreement. For that, we sanctioned the engagement."

"No offense," Frankie said abruptly. "I am trying to understand what indulging her every whim has to do with ignoring me."

"We weren't trying to indulge her whims," Eugene stated. "Though ultimately, we did, because Maddy never took denial well. She often found a way to make what she wanted happen. In the beginning, we thought it was luck or just her perseverance, but later…later we learned the hard way. Her relationship with Eddie was always troubled. They fought, almost constantly. He wanted them to move in together, but she wanted her own place. After all, they were going to be engaged for years, they should embrace their single, committed lifestyles."

I swore Eugene was going to roll his eyes, but he caught himself.

"What he's trying to say tactfully is that Maddy wanted a place to see other boys. She enjoyed winning the hearts of those who seemed impossible. Like it was a personal challenge." Patience's lip compressed. "She began with a business acquaintance of ours when she was just sixteen. We found out much later, or I assure you, that would never have happened. At college, this need to conquer others only grew, and it became something of a competition between her and Eddie."

The whole concept was nauseating. The one-upping each other in the shitty to each other department, the need to assert herself…

"When Maddy threatened another student with a pair of scissors because she'd had an affair with Eddie and nearly shaved her head, we insisted she see a psychiatrist." Eugene looked a hundred years old all of a sudden, and Patience looked away.

Frankie's fingers suddenly tightened on mine, and the bite of her nails dug into my skin.

"She refused at first, but when she faced actual criminal charges, she made a deal to seek psychiatric help if the charges were dropped, and unfortunately, we made sure that happened—the charges being dropped."

I didn't know whether to feel sorry for these people or throttle them. "What happened?"

When Frankie started to pull her hand away, I tightened my grip and glanced over to find her mouth whitening as it compressed. She was probably biting the inside of her lip or her cheek. Either way, I didn't want her focused on Maddy's actions, they were taking a long roundabout way of answering her question, which left me suspicious as hell about what their answer would be.

"She saw a psychologist for a few months, and I thought it was going well, but I should have known better." Patience sighed. "The next year or so, things escalated with Eddie and they escalated here. Her acting out took on an entirely different kind of flare. There was a far meaner edge to it. Eventually,

Eugene told her if she couldn't be respectful, she couldn't return here. Then… Eddie got the girl pregnant." She cast me a look. "I'm sorry, Archie."

"Well, I'm here, I can't be too upset about it." What did they want? An apology? It was Frankie's turn to grip my hand.

"Maddy seemed to be truly devastated," Eugene admitted. "She tried to kill herself the day after Muriel and Eddie married."

Frankie flinched.

"We kept it quiet, swept it away so no one would know, and insisted she go back to her psychologist." Patience looked away. "Unfortunately, that man was part of the problem. Maddy had seduced him at some point. Then she just ignored us, went back to school like everything was normal, but she was in the social columns constantly, a new man every weekend. She went after all of Eddie's friends. She was acting out her hurt. And then she got pregnant herself, and I'm afraid that was the final straw."

"Young lady—Frankie," Eugene said in a weary voice. "You asked why we didn't do anything, but we did want to do something for you. At first, we wanted her to marry the father, but she refused to identify him, and then we were quite afraid she'd gone and gotten herself pregnant with Eddie. But that came to naught. When I told her I'd cut her off if she didn't at least contact the father, she emptied her bank accounts and walked away. She refused to speak to us. The only reason we knew about your birth was because Ted told us."

That lined up with what Grandpa told me.

"I did try to reach out to her," Patience said. "After you were born, but she refused to take my calls. Then she disappeared entirely. I found out later she changed her name." She glanced at her husband. "She used my maiden name—Curtis. We paid a private investigator to find her, and it took time to even realize she had changed her name. That day I came to visit…that was after Eugene's heart attack. She'd refused all our calls, sent back our letters as addressee unknown, even when we sent them to you. I wanted to try and repair that relationship, but she refused to listen to anything I had to say. What she wanted was for me to apologize and admit we'd been wrong. When I threatened to take you from her, she told me she would kill you first."

The fuck? Frankie flinched, and I stared at them.

"That is why we withheld contact, because I believed her. You were hers and only hers. The only thing in her life no one could take from her, and she'd kill you before she allowed it." A distinct fog of tears touched her voice as Patience spoke. "I love Maddy very much, but there is something deeply wrong with her. We should have done more, but…"

"But we were afraid," Eugene said slowly. "She wanted nothing to do with us or our money. We told her about changing the terms of the trust fund. I'd hoped that would encourage her…"

"Because you thought she wanted your money," Frankie said in a raw voice that had me wanting to strangle everyone involved. Her nails dug crescents into my hand, but I didn't let go. She could draw blood if she needed.

"She wants control," Eugene admitted. "For us to surrender everything to her because we were wrong. After she threatened you, though, we couldn't risk it, so we backed off. You seemed happy and healthy according to Patience."

Frankie snorted as she fell back in the seat.

"We hoped if we gave her what she wanted…"

"You know, it sounds to me like you gave her what she wanted all the time," Frankie said slowly, and I glanced over to find her not looking at them but looking up at the sky. It was coolish outside, but the sun shone down on their warm little room, giving them an illusion of a much warmer spring. "And you decided that it was better to leave me with someone who threatened to kill me if you interfered. That seemed reasonable to you."

"She did like to exaggerate," Patience said quietly, but there was no mistaking the devastation in her voice. They had believed her. It was why they'd retreated.

I could leave it alone, but I wouldn't. "You don't believe that," I said flatly. "You were afraid of her. You have been for a long time. You couldn't control her, not even with money or power or emotion. You tried to get her help, but she sabotaged that. You covered up her crimes, bought her out of trouble, and then when a child was involved, you distanced yourselves."

"Frankie is fine," Eugene said in a firm voice, then glanced over at her as if making sure. "We had every intention of reaching out to you on your eighteenth birthday, when she couldn't interfere. When you called…we were relieved."

Relieved.

I pinched the bridge of my nose as Frankie withdrew her hand. "Okay." Just that one word, two simple syllables, but her expression was so guarded, I had zero trouble seeing the walls going up. "Do you know who my father is?"

"No," Patience said quietly. "We tried to find out, but it would seem she'd been very promiscuous in those last few months. Losing Eddie cost her something deeply, and I don't think either of us realized how bad it was."

"My grandfather said you cut her off," I interjected. Because right now, I believed them, but I also believed Grandpa.

"It's what you told people," Frankie answered for them, and there was so much empty disdain in her voice. "To cover up her choices again. You erased her bad actions by shifting the blame of her departure to something you decided, not her. I guess appearances were very important."

The fact Patience paled and Eugene couldn't look at her pretty much confirmed it. "Well, good to know that you didn't really care what happened to either of them as long as it happened far away." Yeah that earned me a dark look from Eugene Grayson. Sorry Grandpa, he might've been your friend, but I wasn't impressed. My parents sucked, but Grandpa hadn't distanced himself from me, even when they fought.

At least I'd always known he was out there.

"There's a trust for you," Patience said, scooting forward as though those words were an olive branch to repair the breach between them.

"I don't care," Frankie told her. "Money can make things easier, but it definitely doesn't make people happier. If there are some crazy terms to it, I don't want it."

"The terms are not…" Eugene paused, then gave me a grim look. I raised my brows, even as Frankie gripped my hand again. "They are not crazy. They do require you complete your education and avoid—"

"Avoid marriage? Children? Standishes?" I was spit-balling.

"Of course not," Eugene said. "But we would prefer she focus on building a strong life for herself…"

The minute she started to rise, I was on my feet. My napkin hit the table alongside hers. "I don't care about the money," Frankie repeated. "And right now, I'm not sure about either of you."

"Of course not," Patience said in a sad voice. "We must seem like unfeeling monsters."

"Maybe not quite that bad, but…I need some time to think. I'm sorry to just leave abruptly, but I really don't want to be here anymore."

We were almost to the door when Patience called out to us. "Please…"

I only paused when Frankie did. If she wanted out, we were out. We could discuss this between us somewhere else.

"I know you don't know us, and maybe you don't want to," Patience said, and she seemed far more approachable than she had when we first met her. Though, I had to admit, her eyes were just like Frankie's. If I'd seen her at all in the last four years, I'd have recognized the connection immediately. "And I'm truly sorry for my part in that," she admitted. "I must have seemed so cold to you when I was there."

Frankie didn't answer her and Eugene didn't join us, so I waited, giving the women a moment.

"Please don't disappear from us. We may not have earned it, but we do want to know you. I'll talk to the lawyers about the trust, the terms can be amended. We want you to have the money, even if you want nothing to do with us. I want to know you're okay and that you can take care of yourself."

"She can take care of herself with or without your money," I said abruptly and focused on her. "What she wants is to understand you and have you understand her. This isn't about money, Patience. It's about family."

And maybe I overstepped, but Frankie shot me a grateful look before she squared her shoulders. "I'm not saying never, I just can't do it right now. I know you may not know everything that's happened, but I'm trying to figure out my place in all of this. I didn't want this whole piece of the past, but it keeps taking swipes at me…" She hesitated, and then said the words I'd known she would say, whether it was now or a week from now. "But I will call you again. Maybe…we can spend some time talking and get to know each other."

She glanced back to the table where Eugene stared at all of us, but he looked so weary and defeated. They really were afraid of Maddy. And Edward was in bed with a psychopath. Great.

I'd never been more grateful that we'd gotten Frankie away from her.

"All of us," Frankie said. "But maybe one step at a time?"

"I'd like that," Patience told her. "Very much."

It took another ten minutes, but we were finally back outside at the car and alone. We'd retrieved our coats, but Frankie didn't jump inside. Instead, she stared up at the house. And I couldn't imagine what she saw. The walls, the architecture, or the strained family relations.

"She threatened to kill me," was all she said. "I'm not sure what's worse—that she told her parents that, or that I don't doubt the fact she actually said it."

Nor did I.

Leaning back against the car, I watched her. Frankie needed to work this out, and I needed to be patient. Even if Maddy was thousands of miles away, the urge to make sure she couldn't get anywhere near Frankie again was a driving force in my gut. There were ways to take care of things, I wasn't blind.

We had the resources.

I'd already taken advantage of it once, and I just had to bide my time until it was done.

"If she's crazy," Frankie said slowly and then turned to face me, "what does that make me?”

“Not her,” I told her firmly.

“Are you sure? They seemed to think…”

“They’re old.” My tone was flat, inflexible, just the same way my viewpoint on this subject was. “They see what they want to see. There’s a physical resemblance, but that’s just DNA. The same way I look like Edward. Doesn’t make me a carbon copy.” No matter what Muriel said about me having too much of him in me. “Nor are you. You have a heart a thousand times the size of that house. You care about everyone and not just yourself. You’re standing here trying to decide if you should feel sympathy for her because on some rough level, you already do. You feel for the girl you think she could have been.”

“Don’t make me sound so predictable,” she grumbled, even if she flashed me a small smile. The tears in her eyes pissed me off. We’d just gotten her free of her fucking mother, I wanted to cut those cords entirely. But Frankie, despite it all, loved her. Fuck, what had Jake said? Her big ass heart. It was that big ass heart that let her forgive us.

But we couldn’t afford for her to forgive Maddy.

She couldn’t afford it.

Especially if the woman really had threatened to kill her.

“I know you,” I reminded her and pushed away from the car. Cupping her face in my hands, I ignored the house and the surroundings and the history. All I focused on was her. “I *know* you, Frankie Curtis. What you said in there about your past was right—this is all the past. This isn’t about you. You want to know so nothing more ambushes you, and I agree with that. But what we’re finding out? That’s not on you. That’s on them. Hell, it’s on Grandpa, Edward, Maddy, the Graysons. It’s not on us.”

She let out a shuddery sigh. “I just…I feel bad for her, and at the same time, I’m so damn angry. Erin would tell me that conflicting emotions are normal and I’m allowed to be angry.”

“Damn straight.”

Frankie had asked us to do a group session with her psychologist, that the woman had wanted to meet all of us. I'd been reticent. Not anymore.

"Be angry, babe. Be sad, if you are. Be frustrated… You are entitled to your feelings. I'm right here. We all are. We're here and we're going to do this with you. Then when it's done, it's done."

She glanced back at the house, twisting out of my hands, but then she leaned back, and I wrapped my arms around her at the unspoken request. Setting my chin on her shoulder, I cradled her tight.

"Do you know what I see when I look at that house?"

"Too much money? Too much focus on image? Prestige?" Frankie sighed. "No wonder she always said I made her look bad. She couldn't just sweep me under the rug like every other problem."

I begged to fucking differ, since that was exactly what that bitch had been doing. We, however, could argue about it another time. "I see loneliness and bad choices, but I don't see regret."

"Because their bad choices led to us," Frankie whispered, and I squeezed her.

"Exactly."

"You're not a bad choice, Archie."

"Right back atcha, babe."

She sighed again. "What if we find out my father is some epic douche?"

"Well, since I have some experience there, we'll just put a pin in that and I'll share Jeremy and Grandpa with you."

A real laugh slipped out of her, and I smiled. We stood there for a little while, probably long enough to make the Graysons nervous, but they didn't come out and they didn't ask. Maybe they were giving her the time she needed.

Good.

Finally, we climbed in the car and she looked so tired, I had to fight the urge to hit something. Back to the hotel and the guys, we'd look after her. My phone buzzed as I started the car, and I pulled it out to check to see if the guys were checking in.

It was Grandpa.

I snorted.

Too bad. The old man should have made better choices.

I stared at the message and then over at Frankie before I turned the phone to show her. "See," I said. "Not alone."

Her smile warmed her whole expression. "I love you."

My heart fisted just like it did every single time she said it. That night in the hotel when she'd told me that on my birthday, it had left me wildly elated. Seriously, I'd always known she cared. She'd shown it with every act, every smile, every daring chance she took. But it wasn't the same as hearing it.

"Best thing I've heard all day," I answered. "Love you more."

"Ha," she said with a real laugh.

"What?" I challenged as I put the car into gear. "Don't think I love you more?"

"No," she told me as she tugged the knit cap over her hair. The sun was still out, but I'd put up the roof because it had gotten colder. "I think you love me best. I think you all do."

Well all right then, I wasn't going to argue with her on that point.

"Then let's get back to the hotel where we can do that, shall we?" I gave her a playful leer. "Still sore?"

This time, the laughter rippling out of her held just a little bit of a scandalized note.

"'Cause…" I said, pressing my luck, because why not? "I'm sure there's something we could do about that, and I would love a little Frankie dessert…"

That earned me more laughter.

"Hmm, that sounds like you're covering me in chocolate syrup and whip cream."

Well, that was an idea. "Never say never," I told her. "I bet your nipples would be great under a little whip cream."

The flush of pink sweeping up her face and the sharp indrawn breath told me I was on the right track.

"Shall I tell you all the things I could eat off of you before I ate you out?"

Yeah, I didn't wait for her to answer, I just went there.

I might have been hard as a stone by the time we got back to the hotel, but Frankie wasn't pale or shaky anymore. At least not from shock or worry.

And how sore was too sore? I bet we could figure that out if we were real, careful like.

Chapter Twenty
WE'LL FIGURE IT OUT

IAN

After meeting her grandparents, Frankie had been quiet, and while not quite withdrawn, there was no missing how lost in thought she'd been. More than once, she'd retreated to call Rachel and talk. When Archie proposed we divert and drive to Cambridge, I took all of five minutes to agree with him. One thing Archie and I had both been doing more over the last few weeks, we discussed options before either of us made a move.

It helped.

I wanted to look after her and so did he. We didn't always rely on the same methods. A trip to Harvard wouldn't even have been on my list of possibilities, but he pulled up directions and a map. It was roughly two hours north of us.

"If I change our flight plans, we can fly out of Boston. And we'll get her up there and take a good look at it."

"She's on the waiting list…" But I had my suspicions.

Especially when he grinned and spread his hands. "It's me."

Yeah, it was him.

"You know what, fuck it. Let's do it." I wanted to see her smile. Really smile, not the shadowed smile she'd worn for the last forty-eight hours. I wanted the triumph and the light back in her eyes. I wanted the giddiness she'd worn like a sparkly dress when we'd been at the karaoke club after she won her emancipation.

Before I could head back inside from the chilly balcony where we'd taken our coffee to talk, he'd put up a hand. "Have you talked to her about the contract yet?"

While we had discussed it briefly, Archie had been letting me sort it out with Wittaker and the entertainment attorney he'd hooked me up with. It was a slow-moving process, but I'd rather take my time and understand the nuances before I pulled Frankie into it.

"No," I admitted. "I wanted to have all the answers before I got her hopes up, and after the last few weeks…"

He nodded slowly. "Agreed, but don't take too long. She hates when we make decisions without her, and while she's reeling at the moment, she's relying on us to keep her steady."

Something we'd definitely been doing, but he was right. "I'll talk to her this week."

"It might perk her up," Archie suggested, smiling faintly. "And if you and Wittaker don't trust these guys, we send your demos elsewhere. Hell, I'll provide the finance, and we'll find someone to produce it for you. Go indie and keep all the control."

The thing about Archie, that grandiose plan might sound like he was just making it up right now, but I was on to him. He'd done his research, and he wouldn't make the offer if he didn't have faith in us.

As if reading my mind, he locked his gaze on mine. "I've listened to you both. You're really good, and you bring out something spectacular in her."

It wasn't hard. Frankie had a gorgeous voice, it held every bit of her heart when she sang. "Thanks, man, I really want to make this happen. Maybe the hard way first."

"You think I'm not the hard way?" But the laughter in his voice told me he got it.

"No, I think you're every bit as invested in her happiness as I am." While Coop and Jake had found a near perfect balance with us on their own, it had taken Archie and me a little more work and finessing. The fact I punched him the day after he first had sex with her probably hadn't helped.

"Good," he said, one corner of his mouth kicking a little higher. "Best investment ever, in my opinion."

I chuckled. "You think more about her birthday?"

"Yep."

"And?" I raised my eyebrows. We'd gone back and forth on this for four weeks. Negotiation, discussion, limits—everything. He'd seemed even more interested after the visit to the demo, but I'd put money that was more based on Frankie's reaction than anything else.

He lifted his coffee. "Count me in."

"Yeah?"

"Yeah," Archie said. "Why the hell not?"

"Why the hell not…"

Laughter carried through the glass doors from inside, and we both turned almost at the same time. Frankie was squealing where Jake had her pinned on the sofa, tickling her, but he couldn't see Coop coming behind him.

"Oh that's not going to end well," Archie said.

"No," I agreed, just as Jake jumped to the side and Coop dumped the water he'd been holding. It missed Jake by a mile and doused her.

His eyes went comically wide, and Frankie was off the sofa like a slingshot and after him. Jake threw his head back and laughed before trailing behind the pair where they vanished into the bedroom. Archie glanced at his watch.

"We have time for more coffee and probably time to talk contracts if you want."

I chuckled. We definitely weren't going to be leaving anytime soon. "Yeah, let's do that. Maybe downstairs," I suggested as he opened the door and her sudden groan echoed from down the little hall toward the oversized bedroom the honeymoon suite boasted.

"Yeah, I'd rather not spend the whole drive to Cambridge with a hard-on."

We set the mugs aside and grabbed room keys and wallets before we were out the door. The last time Jake and Coop disappeared with Frankie it had been easily an hour. "Ninety minutes?" I suggested.

"More than fucking fair," he agreed as he hit the elevator button, and I grinned. He shot me a look, then shook his head. "Don't tell me."

"Didn't plan on it." But I had to admit, I was looking forward to her birthday more and more.

We'd turned in the second rental car and just took the oversized SUV to make the drive to Cambridge. It had two rows of seats in the back, and Frankie ended up curled up against me and sleeping. Not that I minded. She'd been flushed and brighter eyed by the time we made it upstairs and in a very cuddly mood. In fact, convincing her to head to Harvard had taken no effort whatsoever.

Pliant Frankie was sweet, but always made me a tad wary. Jake gave me shit about overthinking things, but I never wanted to take advantage of that heart of hers.

Ever.

I woke her as we got close, and she gave me a sleepy smile. "Sorry, I didn't mean to pass out on you."

Pulling a strand of her hair away from the corner of her mouth, I grinned. "I didn't mind. Feel better?"

Archie shifted in his seat to glance back at us. Coop was still conked out in the far back. Him, we left sleeping. Jake could probably have used a nap too, but he'd been in an insufferably good mood by the time they were done, so Archie threw the keys at him.

"We're almost there, Baby Girl," Jake said over his shoulder. Frankie smothered a yawn and stretched before she tucked her head back against my shoulder.

"Cool, are you sure we're going to be able to do a tour?"

It irked me that she hadn't gotten to come up here over the summer like she'd planned. Like so many other things, we were going to find a way to make up for it.

"Of course, I'm sure," Archie said with a sly grin, then held up his phone. "Did you know you can download an app from the school to do a self-guided tour? We may not get to meet with professors or counselors, though I bet we could find a way to make that happen. But we can see the school and learn about the programs."

Which allowed us not only the freedom to wander the campus, but also to take our time and linger where we wanted. Her whole face lit up. Yes, this had been an excellent plan.

"I did the virtual tour online and I did, like, three of their information sessions over the summer."

"Three?" I didn't laugh. Jake didn't laugh.

Archie? Yeah, he laughed, but the grin he sent her was more proud than teasing. "Of course you did. I bet you could give us the tour yourself."

"Maybe," she said with a sniff. "Of course, I'm not the snot who got accepted. Why didn't you do your homework?"

"Who says I didn't, babe?"

"Prove it."

"No betting," I said before Archie could respond, and he flipped me off with an easy smile.

"Killjoy."

"That's my name," I drawled. "Don't wear it out."

Frankie cracked up, and Archie grinned as he faced forward. From behind us, Coop let out a groan. "What's so funny?"

"We're almost to Harvard," Frankie informed him. "Wakey wakey."

The pure excitement in her tone was contagious. My only concern about the trip up here was that she'd been waitlisted and that had been a hard pill for her to swallow. Yet she displayed none of that reticence now.

If anything, she was bouncing in her seat, and I wasn't the only one laughing. Then again—Holy shit, look at this place. From the moment we got there, she waxed and waned between awed and amazed to adorable and enthusiastic.

I was glad we'd all brought heavier coats and gloves. There was still snow on the ground, not a lot, but enough to make it picturesque. And enough for a few snowballs. Our breath was visible in the air, and the nip of it kept Frankie's cheeks red and cheerful. Nothing quite matched the shine in her eyes. It was hard to miss the wistful expressions she gave some of the buildings.

The tour on the phone offered us a lot of data, and I swore Frankie and Jake were a pair of nerds about it. Particularly when the tour offered history behind a building or the architecture or pretty much anything about the school. We kept going until almost nightfall, and we still hadn't seen everything.

"We can come back tomorrow, babe," Archie promised. "We've got a hotel a couple of miles from here, and we don't fly back until the day after tomorrow."

Frankie bit her lip, and then she glanced back at the building we were standing outside of. To be honest, I'd kind of lost track. They all looked the same. Not that it wasn't cool, but they weren't exactly palatial.

"Come on, Angel," I said, holding out my hands. She let me pull her to me and tuck her under my arm. "I wanted to talk to you about some stuff tonight, anyway."

"Oh, that sounds ominous." She blinked wide eyes at me before she crossed them and wrinkled her nose. A chuckle rumbled up from my chest as she cracked up. "Sorry. I couldn't help it."

Coop and Jake had started slinging snowballs at each other behind us, so we slowed to let them burn off some energy. A part of me kind of wanted to join them, but I had Frankie and I wanted to talk to her more.

"It's not," I told her as I pressed my lips to her temple just below the knit cap she wore before tugging it down a little more securely. "It's about a music contract we got offered."

You know, it was important to me to have all the answers, and Archie and I had discussed a lot of it. I had a fairly good understanding of what they were asking us for. It didn't just affect Frankie and me. It affected all of us.

"Wait," she squeaked. "What?"

I grinned down at her, even as Coop slid to a halt and Jake dropped the snowball he'd been about to fling. "Did you just say contract?" Coop asked.

"Yep," I answered both of them, but I kept my gaze on her. It was twilight, and the sun had begun to vanish rapidly, taking the daylight with it. The temperature was dropping, so I squeezed her shoulders and got us moving again. "The producers who listened to the demos really liked them and they are offering us a contract—us, as in you and me, not you one and me one."

"So, like a contract for us together?" Her voice took on that breathy quality it got when something baffled and surprised her.

"Yes, Angel. For us together. I told you, we were doing this together, and as it turns out, the producers agree with me." So as we made our way back to the car, I told them about the deal we'd been offered.

It was for twelve to fifteen original songs and possibly the recording of three different covers. They had suggestions, and we could offer our own. They had song writers we could work with or do our own stuff. Once we submitted the songs and they signed off on them, we'd have to do studio time to record them.

Then there was information about promoting and selling and possibly touring with another band or doing some local spots in Los Angeles and New York. It had all seemed like a lot when I'd first gotten the deal. But now, after going over it a few times with Wittaker and Archie, it seemed the producers were demanding a great deal. Like what we were being asked for didn't match what they planned to do for us. "It sounds like a lot…"

We were back at the rental car, and Frankie stared at me, mouth slightly agape.

"I know it seems like a lot," I repeated. "It is. But we just address it one step at a time, and we're not signing anything until the attorneys are done looking at it. Wittaker's consulting an entertainment lawyer, who also can serve as an agent to protect us and make sure we're not screwed if this doesn't work out."

"Or I buy out the contract," Archie said. "Either way, both of you are protected."

Frankie hadn't said anything, she just stared at me and then at Archie and then back to me. "Ian Rhys."

I straightened like someone had yanked my strings. Frankie *never* used my full name, and I couldn't decide if that was hot or terrifying.

I leaned somewhere firmly in the middle.

"You got a contract offer from an actual music company, label, thing?"

"*We*," I stressed that word. "*We* got an offer. There's no me if there is no you. Not for this."

Lifting her gloved hands to her lips, she steepled her fingers and stared at me. "*We*," she said slowly, the words just a little muffled, "got an offer from a record label thing?"

"More or less," I answered slowly. "I know it's probably not the best timing and you probably have a hundred questions…"

I didn't get to finish the rest of that thought. I had an armful of excited Frankie, who gripped my face and dragged me down. The cool press of her lips beckoned to me, so I was not going to argue with the lady. I half-picked her up and dragged her against me as I let her own the kiss. The happy little sounds she made went straight to my dick, but the layers of clothing kept that fact to myself for the moment.

When she lifted her head with a breathless laugh, I eyed her. "Good news?"

"Good news?" She thumped me, and I laughed. "That's the best news, you jerk. Why didn't you tell me sooner? We should have been celebrating you."

Behind her, Coop and Jake let out twin breaths of relief, and Archie chuckled as he put his phone to his ear and paced away from us. Knowing him, he was planning a celebratory dinner.

"Celebrating *us*," I reminded her. "And I wanted to have all the information before I told you, but…we had to get through the rest first. You had enough on your plate. If this turned out to be some bogus idea or bullshit offer…"

Touching her tongue to her teeth, she studied me and then pressed her lips to mine. "I love you, even when you suffer in silence by yourself when you should have been shouting it from the rooftops."

I chuckled. "I wasn't suffering in silence, Angel. I promise. And I talked to Arch."

"Cause Archie fixes everything." She glanced over her shoulder to where he'd gone with the phone. "Five bucks says he's planning a celebration for the hotel."

"No takers," Jake answered with a laugh before he clapped me on the back. "Congrats, man, congrats to you too, Baby Girl. This is *awesome*."

I let Frankie go for hugs from the guys, and then Jake started urging us toward the SUV that had been running and warming up while we talked. Coop stole into the backseat with Frankie, but Jake gripped my arm before I could follow.

"Tour?" He looked at me.

"Yeah, that's one of the things I'm asking about. And before you flip a switch, I don't want to take her away from you guys…"

"Fuck that," Jake said with a laugh. "I wanna go. So I can beat the hell out of anyone that tries to hit on her."

Oh. Fair point.

"You don't get to have all the fun."

All the fun.

"Dude, you got a potential recording contract. That's huge. You're allowed to be excited."

I was excited, but at the same time…

"Wait until they start recording," Archie said as he walked back to us. "He'll be insufferable. Until then, we celebrate for him."

At the hotel, I pulled her back to me as the guys headed inside. "We'll be up in a few," I told them, and they waved. They got it, and Frankie turned to study me. "Do I owe you an apology?" I'd been thinking about it on the way over. I'd expected a lot of questions, but all she'd asked was how I was feeling about it.

"Why would you?" She frowned. "Because you didn't tell me right away? Or because you're not even letting yourself feel this yet?"

Gathering her hands in mine, I glanced around. The air outside was damn frigid for March, and we were thinking about moving to the frozen tundra of the north for school. We were nuts. Then again, I'd live in Barrow, Alaska, where it didn't see sunrise for months in the winter, if it meant being with her.

"I want it to be perfect, and I don't want anything to bite you."

"Take me out of the equation for a minute…"

"Impossible."

"Please?" She tilted her head, and with one simple gesture, she had me in the palm of her hand. "Just take me out of the equation. If it was just you getting offered this deal, what would your reaction be?"

I tried. I really did. "Moderate excitement and probably dread."

"Dread?"

"If it was just me, then going to record or touring would mean leaving you. I wouldn't drag you out of school. As it is, I'm worried about how to balance all this against school for you."

"And if we could sign it tomorrow and I said it didn't matter, we're doing this together because it's important to you?"

I grinned. "I'd love that." More, I'd revel in it. "I know I've been twisting your arm for this, so if you don't want this—"

She stopped me with two gloved fingers against my lips. "I want you and everything that entails. I love singing with you. I can't believe how I sound when we do, but…that's an us thing."

Yeah, it was. "Then you get why I can't take you out of the equation."

"Are you happy? I know you're trying to be strong and maintain because you're worried about getting my hopes up. But what about your hopes?"

Considering her for a long moment, I let out the smile I'd been holding onto. "I love the idea of doing this with you. I love the idea of showing you off on stage and singing with you. But whether this becomes a career or it's just something we do because we love it, you're the only one I want to do it with."

"I don't know, I think you and the guys could have a future as a boy band."

At that, I snorted and dragged her close. "Bite your tongue."

"Nah," she grinned, nose wrinkling, and the glint in her eyes seemed to brighten. All those shadows we'd been worried about had been chased away. One day soon, we would eliminate them altogether. The world didn't get to keep hurting her, not without going through us first. "I'd rather bite yours."

"And you say that when you know damn good and well Archie's pulled strings for us to celebrate upstairs."

"Something else to look forward to later?" She raised her brows, and I pressed my forehead to hers. "I'm so proud of you." She breathed the words, but I felt every single syllable imprint on me. "This is amazing, because you're amazing. If you want to do this, I'm in. Even if it terrifies me, maybe because it does."

"We'll figure it out," I promised her.

"Yes," she said with a grin. "We will."

I needed to get her out of the cold, but I kissed her first, and I tried to pour every feeling I had on this. The excitement. The caution. The thrill. The adventure. Most of all, the love. None of this would be possible without her, and

I didn't think she understood how much. The tangle of her tongue with mine and the grip of her fingers against my neck answered my own urgency and desire.

I nipped her lower lip as I lifted my head, and her smile warmed my fucking soul. "I'm really proud of you and I'm more than a little in awe of you, but that panty rule? That stays in effect."

"I'll collect yours in a little while then."

She threw her head back and laughed. The open sound was so damn joyous, it made my heart hurt. And enough of this, I needed her out of the cold. Hopefully, Archie got us multiple bedrooms again. I needed her tonight, and I was going to stake my claim. They could have her back in the morning.

"Tonight, you're in my bed," I told her, nipping her ear gently before turning her to head into the hotel.

"Yes, sir," she murmured, and that bolt definitely went to my cock. Okay, new plan. Quick celebration, early night, Frankie tied to a headboard.

I wasn't sure what we had that would work, but I'd figure it out.

Chapter Twenty One

LIFE IS MORE FUN IF YOU PLAY GAMES

COOP

Spring break might go down as one of our most different vacations, but for our last escape from high school, I'd take it. Fuck knew I was bored as shit being back now that we were. We'd been accepted into college, most of us were just marking time. NYU was still at the top of our list, but we were cutting it down to final decision time.

We'd been back for a few days, and so far, it had been quiet. To be honest, I didn't think any of us thought it was going to remain quiet. Mom had started bugging me to bring Frankie around for dinner. Bubba and Frankie had gone for family dinner at his place, and she came back in an upbeat mood, so that seemed well. Apparently, the next one they had, they wanted all of us there.

I checked the clock on the wall and tipped my head back. Today had been a practice exam, and mine was long finished. At the moment, I was just counting down the minutes until we could bail. April was right around the corner, and we had Frankie's birthday right up front, then the week after that, we had to do the elementary school walks, and there would be an assembly to begin awarding the senior achievements.

Was it wrong that I just wanted this over and done with?

Frankie and Bubba were going to pursue that recording deal, but their entertainment lawyer had done some push back on the terms so we were waiting on that.

"Sixty seconds, class. Anyone still taking the test, you have sixty seconds."

A chorus of groans followed her announcement, but I tuned them out. The minute the bell rang, I was up and out the door. Today was going to be interesting. At least it had gotten warmer, so by the time I hit the door for outside, I shifted my backpack and stripped off my sweatshirt, dragging it over my head one armed before shrugging the rest off.

My T-shirt rode up, and a couple of people wolf-whistled. I ignored them and tossed the sweatshirt over my shoulder before dragging the backpack over it. I'd worn a plain white tee under it, and it was easily kissing eighty out here. Damn near perfect weather.

I made it to my car first. Jake and I had brought Frankie today. Archie had been out late with his grandpa, and Bubba had some breakfast thing with his dad that he'd stayed home for. Since it was just the three of us, I drove for a change.

Archie pulled up behind me and flipped his sunglasses up onto his head. "We still on for this afternoon?"

"Far as I know. No one changed any plans on me."

"Cool, I'll let Jeremy know we're on our way, and I'll meet you guys at the house."

"Hey, Arch…" I threw a glance toward the building, but there was no sign of Frankie or Jake yet. Bubba had brought his bike since he pulled it out on every decent day to ride. "You said your grandfather had it covered, right?"

"Yep, but it's up to her to accept it. You too. Bubba can pull it off academically, but he's still waiting on the conservatory."

Not to mention, he was seriously debating full time college versus full time recording. His interest in other careers wasn't there, and I got that. Still, he wanted to go where we were, and the visit to Harvard had been so much fun for her. At the same time, she hadn't gotten upset or complained about her waitlisting, she'd just enjoyed the trip.

"We've got a couple of other things to go over too," Archie reminded me, and I nodded. Yeah, we'd gotten word at lunch that Wittaker had an update on the names that Archie's dad had given them. There was also more from the lab. "Chin up, Coop. We're almost done. Six weeks from now, we test and then we're outta here for good."

I chuckled. "I'd be fine if it were tomorrow."

"Same," Archie said, then whistled, and I glanced back to find Frankie and Jake heading toward us. Bubba was right behind them. "I'll catch you guys at the house."

"Yep," I told him as I patted the side of his car and backed off. Frankie blew him a kiss, even as she reached me, and then she wrapped her arms around me and gave me a real kiss. "Hey, beautiful, you look beat."

"G is drilling us daily now," she said with a groan. "And we're practicing essay questions this week, so it's been two essays a class."

Jake chuckled and tossed his bag and hers into the backseat. The rumble of Bubba's motorcycle pulling up interrupted his answer. Frankie grinned at him from where she cuddled up to me. I kept an arm around her because she didn't usually demand a lot of affection at school. Pressing my lips to her forehead, I frowned. It was definitely on the warm side. I glanced at Jake, but he shook his head.

"You feeling okay, Angel?" Bubba asked, turning off the engine so we didn't have to shout over it.

"Just tired," she admitted. "Long day."

"You want to go for a ride? It's warm enough and might make you feel better."

As much as she was leaning into me, I opened my mouth to object, but Frankie shook her head. "I forgot my jacket, and I'm not feeling up for it."

That had Bubba's eyebrows up, and Jake's. He slid a palm under her hair to the back of her neck. "She's been pretty tired since lunch."

"Horny boys don't let me get enough sleep," she teased and poked me in the side. In all fairness, we really had kept her up last night.

Bubba frowned, and I found myself agreeing. I didn't totally buy that it was lack of sleep either. Still, we'd play it by ear. "We'll meet you at Archie's," I said. "Unless you want to drop the bike off and ride with us."

He gave me a look, then her. "Let's do that. Follow me back to my place. Supposed to rain tomorrow, so I want to put the bike in the garage."

"Sounds like a plan."

Jake climbed in the back with Frankie, and I didn't complain because I wanted to keep an eye on her. By the time we got to Bubba's, she was sound asleep. When I looked back at him, I murmured, "What the hell?"

"She's really warm," he said.

"Think it's a fever?" Frankie didn't get sick that often. Not really. I swore germs were scared of her, because when she had the flu in ninth grade, she'd missed almost a week of classes and had been *pissed* about the sheer amount of make-up work she had to do after.

I sent a text to Archie about Frankie not feeling well. Bubba didn't keep us waiting, and Frankie groused when we got to Archie's 'cause Jake was all set to pick her up.

"I'm tired, not an invalid," she complained and poked him.

"You don't have to be an invalid for me to want to get my hands on you."

Nice save.

Not that we had to really do any arguing to check on her, because Jeremy had a touchless thermometer waiting for us as soon as we got inside.

"Really, guys?" She made a face but didn't argue with Jeremy. Archie shot me a small smile and folded his arms.

"You definitely have a touch of fever, Miss Frankie," Jeremy told her. "Go make yourselves comfortable, and I'll get you some cold medicine and some tea. Then you can eat. Any other symptoms?"

"Just tired."

He nodded, then shooed us off to make ourselves comfortable.

"We can have this discussion later," Archie offered.

"No," she said. "I want to know what Wittaker found, and we really do need to lock down our decisions for the fall. We've been putting it off and putting it off, but I don't think Harvard is changing their mind anytime soon. And it doesn't matter where we go as long as we're together."

She raked a hand through her hair as we headed upstairs, and I hadn't missed the note of stuffiness in her voice. In fact, she'd had a huskier quality to her voice all day, but again, thinking with my dick and not my brain. The smoky voice was a fucking turn on. Bad Coop.

We headed into the entertainment room and the big sofa. Archie snagged her a blanket, and when she would have curled up by herself, I slid in and pulled her into my lap.

"You're gonna get sick," she complained, and I chuckled as I stroked her hair back.

"Frankie, I ate you out last night for an hour, not to mention Jake and I were both fucking you. I'd say we were already as exposed as we're gonna get."

Her lower lip jutted out, and she sighed. "Crap. I don't want to get you guys sick this close to AP exams. We have too much work to do."

"We have plenty of time, Angel," Bubba told her as he sat at the end of the sofa and pulled her feet to his lap. He stripped off her shoes so he could massage them. "Right now, we focus on getting you better and sorting all this out."

"Blegh," she said, and Jake laughed.

"I forgot how crabby she gets when she's sick."

"I do not get crabby," she informed him, and I swore it was like watching a rapid decline. She'd been flushed on and off all day, but we'd been flirting like hell. So it was pretty normal.

"Tell you what, let's just whiteboard it." He motioned to the other side of the room, and sure as shit, there was a white board set up. "We'll do all the pros and cons while you sit and rest. Then when we're done, we'll pull that final pin."

Bubba worked his thumb against her instep, while I ran my fingers through her hair. "Okay," she murmured. "Has anything changed about other schools? Aren't you waiting on your auditions qualifying you?"

"Not anymore," Bubba told her. He let go of her foot long enough to snag his bag and pulled out his phone. "I've gotten emails all day."

"And?" Not even feeling crappy could diminish the excitement in her voice. To be honest, I was dying to know too. Also, I was going to start calling him Iceman, 'cause I used to think I was cool under pressure, but I hadn't even realized he'd gotten any news. This after what he did with the contracts.

"All of them," he said with a grin. "Well, except for Julliard, but I only did that because you insisted."

"Fuck Julliard then," she said with sniff. "Their loss."

Laughter circled the room as Jake and Archie added Bubba's data to the board. Jeremy came in with a huge tray of food and drinks. There was hot tea, soup, sandwiches, and more. He also offered her more cold medicine and a handful of other pills.

"Vitamins, minerals, and homeopathics to help nip that in the bud. We also want to get your fever down." He gave her a firm look, and she took the meds without argument. Man, Jeremy and I needed to talk. Getting Frankie to slow down took an act of congress, and he managed it with a look and gentle word. "All of the tea, and there's honey in case your throat gets scratchy. You can have a soda after you finish it. The hearty soup is for you, and the boys will leave it be until you've had your fill."

Yeah, I knew an order when I heard one, and I wasn't the only one saying "Yes, sir," in response.

"There will be dessert if you fancy it in a little while. Who is looking after your cats this evening?"

"Trina is," I told him. "She already texted that she went by and fed them." She'd been working hard on communication, and one of the things the counselor suggested was building trust. So we'd given Trina access to a spare key but only to be used with our permission. I hated to say that Archie had set up a couple of surveillance cams at the apartment and we'd used them just to check in when she volunteered to feed them, but we'd tried to find a reason a couple of times a week for her to do it.

So far, so good.

Jeremy nodded. "Let me know if I need to go and fetch them. You, Miss Frankie, will be staying here. I'll make up Mr. Archie's room for you, and he can sleep in the guest room."

"Hey," Archie said. "What the hell, Jere?"

The look Jeremy gave him would peel paint. "Miss Frankie needs rest, not boisterous boys she needs to comfort or will feel bad if she ignores. In the meanwhile, Mr. Coop and Mr. Jake will look after the cats this evening, and you and Mr. Bubba may switch with them tomorrow if she isn't feeling better." Then he fixed a look on Frankie. "Of course, if you want Mr. Archie or Mr. Bubba to sleep with you, that's fine, but I would imagine you want to sleep and not worry about getting them sick."

She hid behind her tea and shot Archie a smile. "I don't want to get you sick."

"I don't care," he muttered. "I'd risk meningitis before I choose to sleep somewhere else. At least if one of us is there, we can get you what you need when you need it."

Biting her lip, she did a terrible job of not laughing, so I just said, "Sounds like a plan to me. Though if you send them over to watch the cats tomorrow, Jake and I can sleep in Archie's bed with her."

Yeah, that got me a look from Jeremy and Archie's middle finger salute from behind Jeremy's back.

"Thank you, Jeremy," Frankie interceded before we got further scolded. "I'm fine going back to the apartment. The boys will take care of me."

"Hmm, I would prefer you stay here until that fever is taken care of. If you cooperate, I'll let them stay in the room with you." With that, he nodded to the tea. "All of it, and then the food."

He didn't wait for our answer before he headed out. Jake thumped Archie on the shoulder. "Damn, you got told."

"Right?" He laughed, then looked over at Frankie and his expression softened.

"You did say you'd share him and Grandpa with me," she pointed out all reasonably in a thick, almost stuffy voice that was equal parts adorable and miserable.

"I did," Archie admitted with an almost sorrowful note. "Which means I have to behave."

That did it. Jake cracked up, and so did Bubba. I buried my face in her hair, but that didn't stop my laughter. Even Frankie laughed, though a cough cut her off, and I pressed a kiss to her hair.

"Better get on that tea before Drill Sergeant Jeremy gets back up here."

"Be nice," she chastised me, but she kept sipping her tea. She was most of the way through her soup when she noticed what the guys had on the board. "Harvard's not even an option, guys. I mean, I'm down for you going, and I can look at community college there or even take a skip year and work on the album with Ian."

"That sounds great, Angel. Except…"

"Harvard's back on the table, babe." Leaving the board, Archie moved to perch on the coffee table in front of us. She lowered the soup cup to stare at him.

"I know I'm sick, but that doesn't make sense. Did they move me off the waitlist?"

"Not yet," he said. "But we know people, including your grandparents and mine, who are connected. Harvard's an option. For all of us. It won't just be you we get in. Jake and I are in, and Bubba got in with the conservatory, so that's gonna lend weight to getting him at Harvard. That just means you and Coop. It's totally doable."

"But that means someone else will get skipped that might have been ahead of us in line."

And that right there was what I'd said she'd do. Archie blew out a breath.

"*May* get skipped, babe. May. They don't have a precise number of applicants they accept or decline each year."

"Their admissions are based on programs, and even if someone got in and didn't take their spot and that spot opened up, then it would go to the next person on the list. You're talking about skipping me and Coop over other people who may not have those connections. That's not fair."

She let out a little sigh, and when she tried to shift, I helped her slide over to sit on the sofa, and Bubba rescued the nearly empty soup cup before she took Archie's hands.

"I know you are trying to fix this for me. But I want to get in because I earned the spot, not because Maddy is my mother. I don't want anything from her. Not that name." She swallowed hard. Over the past couple of weeks, she'd talked to her grandparents twice. Both times, it had been a stilted conversation, but she was trying. "I don't know them. Some of what I know, I don't like. You… you have been you your whole life. Your name opens doors, and you deserve to have them opened because you're brilliant. You don't coast—"

"And you do?" he challenged, and I caught Jake's eye. We'd all argued this already, but Archie thought he could convince her, and if he did, fine, we were in. Harvard had been her dream. "'Cause you work twice as hard as anyone I know, and you've never had a door opened for you that I know of. If anything, they've been closed or you didn't even know they were there. Babe, even if Grandpa and I open that door—just us, not your grandparents—you're still the one who has to walk through it."

She blew out a breath, and the flushed look to her cheeks had cooled some, but her eyes were still a little glassy as she gripped Archie's hands. "I let go of this dream. We started talking about New York and, with Ian recording, I know the city is expensive."

"Don't think about cost right now," he advised, and on this, I agreed. We'd figure it out.

Jake moved in closer. "Archie's right, don't think about cost, don't think about who is opening the door. Think about the school and where you want to be in the fall."

With a look to each of us, she said, "Did you guys fall that hard for Harvard while we were there?"

Bubba shrugged, and I rubbed the back of my neck. "It's a good school," I said.

"Kind of stuffy," Jake pointed out. "But the history is on point."

"It's a school," Archie admitted. "It's not where, it's who. Right now, you're the who. You wanted it. Do you not anymore?"

"Don't be mad," she said softly.

"Hey," I said, sliding an arm around her. "No one is mad. If you changed your mind, you're entitled."

"It's not so much that I changed it, but…I let it go. When we were there, it was great. I loved getting to see it with all of you. But I like the idea of New York. If Ian and I start recording a lot, then we can do it there in the city, and it means less time away from all of you. There's the park and the concerts and Broadway. There's skiing not that far away in Pennsylvania and Maryland. Though, I'm really rather fond of Colorado too. I just…I just want to be where you guys are and where we can do this together."

Archie dipped his chin and nodded. "Then New York. If it's what you want, we all said it was leading before."

"What about you?"

"New York works," Jake said. "And one of the schools you got was NYU, right?" The last he directed to Bubba.

"Yep," he said, and he wore a small, very proud smile on his face, and I knew why. Frankie said when *they* recorded, not just him.

"All right, Arch, I guess you need to look at New York real estate, because we're going to need an apartment that will take the cats."

He laughed. "I think we got that covered." When he pressed a kiss to Frankie's forehead though, he wore a worried look and then brushed her hair back. "You want to put off the call to Wittaker and take a nap, babe? You're still hot."

"Well, I've been hot for a long time, according to you guys, don't sound so surprised."

That earned another round of laughs.

"And I don't want to put it off. Too much has been put off, and we have plans to make."

Fair enough. Jeremy brought up more drinks, including tea for Frankie, and some acetaminophen. He also took her temperature again. It had actually gone down some, so we settled in, and Archie called him. It was late, but the attorney had been waiting for us apparently.

"Well, I have good news and interesting news," he said. "What would you like first?"

We all looked to Frankie. "Good news," she said before taking a sip of her fresh tea.

"The good news is with the information provided by Mr. Standish and the sources he identified, we reached out to all three of the other possibilities. All of them agreed to the test, and the results are in."

Oh boy.

"I have the name of your biological father, and he would like to arrange a time to speak to you, if you're willing…"

Chapter Twenty Two
THAT'S WHAT MAMAS DO

JAKE

"She's been sick, Mom," I told her as I set the table. I swore it had to be the flu, but Jeremy hustled her off to a doctor on day two of her fever, and the doctor said it was just a cold. So, she'd basically been convalescing at Archie's for three days, and we'd all taken turns looking after the cats and spending time with her.

Missing four days of school was not making her happy. If anything, it had made her crabbier. Which was so fucking cute, but we'd stopped telling her that after she threatened to bean Coop with a textbook. Still, we'd been bringing her homework, and I drilled her with G's notes and teased her about getting out of essay practice. The fever finally broke the day before, and Archie said she slept like the dead. That gave her the rest of the weekend to convalesce.

Much to Jeremy's chagrin, she insisted on going home. Coop had picked her up a few hours ago and promised to drop her off here for dinner with Mom.

I'd offered to get her out of the dinner, but she'd said as long as she was feeling better, she wanted to come.

"Is she feeling better?" Mom paused in the doorway between the kitchen and the dining room. "We could have rescheduled this."

"Yeah, she's doing a lot better. Just a little cranky, and she wouldn't let me reschedule." Fortunately, or maybe unfortunately, none of us had gotten sick too. Frankie waxed back and forth between being happy she hadn't made us ill, and grumpy that we got out of having to suffer.

See? Adorable.

Mom chuckled. "That girl works too hard."

"Yes, she does." Mom would get no argument from me. In fact, Coop was pretty sure that cold probably hit her so hard because she was so stressed, and after Wittaker told us about her biological father, including his name, she hadn't brought up the subject again. At least not when I was there.

The man had waited almost eighteen years, so it hurt nothing to let it sit a few more days or weeks. I wasn't sure what she wanted to do yet. But I wasn't going to push it.

"Where are the girls?" I'd done deliveries all morning and into the early afternoon to sock away some cash because I'd been lightening my load in the evenings this week to help look after Frankie. We'd all done our NYU acceptances and gotten that process started.

"Becca and Blake are doing a lock-in at the dance studio with their class and movies all night. Louisa is at April's, and they're having a sleepover. So it's just the three of us tonight."

She disappeared back into the kitchen, and I paused to stare after her. After putting the last fork into place, I circled the table and followed her. I waited a beat as she opened the oven and pulled out the pan of stuffed peppers. The smell had my stomach growling. There were huge planks of bread ready to go in the broiler, and she'd made ratatouille.

No wonder the girls weren't here. Mom and I loved all of this, but Becca acted like we were killing her when the stuffed peppers came out. She would eat the stuffing in the peppers but not the peppers.

"I made banana pudding too," Mom said as she set the pan on the stove top and then switched the oven over to broiler. I waited until the planks of bread were in before I folded my arms. Not even looking in my direction, she said, "Don't take that attitude with me, Jacob. Go wash up and brush your hair before your girlfriend gets here."

I made a face, but before I made a step, she patted my cheek and gave me a smile.

"It wouldn't kill you to shave, too. Girls don't like the burn when you get intimate."

I cringed. God. "Mom!"

She cracked up and snapped a towel out to swat me. "I have four children, Jake, I assure you, I know what that burn feels like, and while you might not mind in the throes, it's not always fun after."

I was out. *Fuck.* The word played over and over in my mind, like it got stuck on repeat, and she laughed at me as I beat a hasty retreat to my room for a clean shirt. Nothing wrong with what I had on, but after that little performance, I didn't hesitate to hit a quick shave.

Fuck. Me.

There was not enough brain bleach in the world to get that image out of my head.

The smell of garlic and hot bread filled our place as I checked my jaw, then I did a quick brush of the teeth. Better to have minty breath to start with, even if we both ended up tasting like garlic afterwards.

I'd just made it back to the living room when the doorbell rang. "I got it."

"Dinner in five," Mom answered. "So no sneaking off to test that shave."

I groaned, but I was still laughing when I opened the door. Frankie stood there looking absolutely adorable in a pair of jeans and one of her Torched T-shirts with a jacket over her shoulder. I lifted a hand to wave to Coop, who was backing out before wrapping an arm around her and pressing a kiss to her lips.

"Hey, Baby Girl," I murmured as I tugged her inside, even as I took her jacket from her. It wasn't that chilly, but it might be later. Good call to bring one. Her hair fell in a pile of silky soft waves, like she'd blown it dry but hadn't worried about straightening it. The glassy look to her eyes was gone, and she was nowhere near as flushed. With my lips pressed to her forehead, I checked her temperature. While not accurate, the fact she wasn't burning up was a good sign. "Still feeling good?"

"Yeah, I sound worse than I am." She sounded stuffy. "And before you get bossy, I promise, I took a nap. Coop insisted."

I bet he did. But she curled into me, so I wrapped my arms around her and cradled her close. Yeah, Coop was right about one thing—when Frankie didn't feel good, she got super cuddly. Never going to hear me complain about it. "All up to date on your cold meds? Don't make me call Jeremy on you."

She giggled against my chest, then patted me before wiggling away. "I am. Took them before I came over, and my next dose is at bedtime. So I'm good for food. I brought my appetite too." Course, she also made a face. "Too bad I can't smell what's cooking, I bet it's awesome."

"Stuffed peppers," Mom called as she carried the big platter out to the table.

"I can get the rest," I told her as I draped Frankie's jacket over one of the chairs. Mom smiled at me and patted my cheek. I stared at her, hopefully communicating 'do not fucking bring up the intimate burn again.'

Dammit. Brain bleach.

I needed brain bleach.

She laughed at me as I headed for the kitchen. Mom was going to kill me at this rate. Death by embarrassment.

I carried out the bread and ratatouille and found Mom and Frankie still chatting in the living room. Mom had an arm around her, but Frankie didn't look remotely embarrassed or upset.

Winning.

If anything, she was smiling.

My heart did a little high five with my ribcage. I loved that Mom and Frankie got along. There was a genuine warmth there. Hell, Frankie even liked my sisters, and I couldn't say that three out of every seven days.

"Food," I said. "Did you want me to get your wine, Mom?"

"Thank you, sweetheart. Frankie, we have soda, or do you want water?" Mom looked at her. "There's iced tea in the fridge too, I think, and lemonade."

"Ooh, lemonade sounds good."

"On it."

When I got back, I set out the drinks and slid into my spot next to Frankie. Technically, I could have sat across from her, but I'd rather sit where I could put an arm around her or press my leg up against hers.

"I forgot how much I loved these," Frankie admitted as she added two of the stuffed peppers to her plate. I passed the ratatouille to her and broke up the bread, while Mom grabbed hers. After their plates were full, I grabbed some for me.

Another perk of the girls not being here—we didn't have to share, and there was going to be more than enough for everyone to have seconds.

"I'll make sure you have the recipe for it before you kids move," Mom told her. "In fact, Frankie, as soon as you're feeling better, Carly and I both want to go over some recipes and anything else you might need."

"Hey," I complained. "Why don't I get the recipes?"

Mom snorted. "Because you'll eat just about anything, Jacob. But if you want, come along. Coop too. I don't suppose Archie and Bubba cook?"

"Ian does," Frankie told her. "He's got a lot of the basic stuff down. Archie's kind of hopeless."

I snickered. "He's not hopeless, he just gets distracted. If you put it to him like a problem he has to solve, he'd nail it every time." Maybe. Firm maybe. To be honest, it was good there was something he wasn't the best at. We all needed our humbling moments.

"Well, we'll figure it out," Mom said. "But Carly and I still want to get you set up. Living in New York will be different from here—different weather, different demands. Have you kids decided what you're doing with your cars once you're in the city?"

We were most of the way through dinner before it hit me that Mom had pretty much pulled every single plan out of us for what happened after graduation, including the potential recording Bubba and Frankie were going to do over the summer before classes started in the fall. Frankie had even picked out her first round of classes, and she was only waitlisted for two of them.

Personally, I hoped she stayed on the waitlist for those two. She signed up for seven classes, and even coordinating, different degrees meant we only had core classes similarly, so we'd managed to get all five of us in three of the same classes together.

Archie and I would likely be running parallel tracks, but Bubba and Coop would be diverging, and Frankie was still undecided on her final major. She had a definitive interest in business of all things, but also in social work.

That made phenomenal amounts of sense. So, she didn't have to lock that in first year, and she wanted to audit some classes before she made her final decisions. I had my personal bets on what she would end up doing.

It wasn't until we'd made coffee and served up dessert that Mom brought out the big topic change. One I hadn't been expecting when Frankie offered to start on clean-up, and before I could tell her no, Mom beat me to it.

"Not at all. I'll take care of it later. I want to talk to you both tonight about something I wished I'd understood when your father and I got married and when we brought Klara into the relationship."

I froze.

"Don't look so worried, Jacob," Mom said as she refilled her wine glass. "I promise to keep this as painless as possible." But she flicked her attention to Frankie. "But I want both of you to understand a few things, to take from my experiences what you can, because I know how determined you all are."

"Okay," Frankie said slowly as she cradled her coffee cup. The stuffy nose sound was still there, but she still seemed pretty upbeat. "How painless is this going to be?"

The teasing note even pulled a grin from me, and I pressed a kiss to her hair in thanks. "Yeah, Mom. Because trust me when I say there are some conversational topics I don't want to have with you, and I'd really prefer you didn't have with my girlfriend." Case in point, see what happened in the kitchen earlier.

Swirling the wine in her glass, Mom shook her head. "Nothing like that. Let's just say that unconventional relationships require as much care if not more than a conventional one. In a standard relationship, there are two people who each have their own hopes, dreams, likes, and dislikes. It can be a challenge to balance those competing needs and desires, even when you adore the other person. The more people you add, the more complicated it gets."

"Fair," Frankie responded, and when she shifted to lean against me, I curled my arm around her. "We've worked on that. We're always working on that. Talking, figuring things out, being honest."

"That's good," Mom told her. "That's really good. Communication is going to save all of you. But there's also things like jealousy. Expectations. Boundaries."

"I think we've got the jealousy handled," I told her. "Not that it won't happen or we don't get a little envious if someone gets a little more time than others, but I think on the whole, we all know we're welcome." Most of the time. Bubba was coming around, and so was Archie. To be honest, I didn't mind that they were less inclined to share her in bed. That was fine. Coop and I didn't want to share her all the time either.

"What about you, Frankie?" Mom focused on her, and I frowned. I wasn't alone.

"What about me? I'm not jealous of their friendships."

"Do you have rules or boundaries in place for if they want to see someone else too?"

"Woah," I said before Mom went any further down that path. "We're not seeing anyone else. We're not going to." I'd cut off my arm before I cheated on her. We'd hurt her enough with seeing other girls because we were stupid.

No more stupid in my future, thank you very fucking much.

"No?" Mom actually looked surprised, and if I wasn't mistaken, pleased.

"No," I said firmly and squeezed Frankie. "It's us and Frankie. That's the relationship. It's not open to anyone else."

"Jake," Frankie said, and the look she gave me curbed some of my irritation that Mom would even suggest that. "It's okay. It's not an unfair question to ask." Maybe not, but still… "And I'm glad your mom is comfortable enough to ask us rather than trying to guess or assuming the worst."

"Exactly," Mom said, leaning forward with her elbows on the table. "This is why I wanted you to all be honest with the families. We can be supportive, I intend to be supportive. But it's important to know your boundaries, and that everyone knows them."

"Trust me," I promised her, "we know them, and I make sure anyone who thinks they can interfere knows them too."

"Good. Something else to keep in mind, going to college is going to seem like you're just extending your high school careers. You're not. Frankie, you have been living independently for far too long, so you're going to adjust probably with greater ease than the boys. Not that I expect their adjustment will take long with as much time as they spend at your apartment."

I snorted. "Thanks, Mom."

"You still technically live here, Jake," she reminded me. "And you are quite versed in looking after yourself, but this isn't just a ten-minute drive away. It's moving to a huge city that you don't know, with its own personality and culture. It's new schedules. New jobs. New everything."

"Except us," Frankie told her. "We're all old shoes. We'll be fine. And besides, it's kind of an adventure. NYU has a huge arts program, and yeah, will being in the city be weird? Maybe. But I can't wait to ride the subway or the ferry. I want to go and see all the sights. Play tourist when we're not busy. It'll be fun."

"All right, well then take this advice exactly as I intend it. You guys are all young, but you're smart and you're committed. This is fantastic. But you're all also at the very beginning of careers and lives. You're going to make choices sooner or later between what is good for all of you as a group and what's good for you personally."

Mom raised her hand before I could object.

"Just listen," she said solemnly. "This isn't a criticism or a judgment. It's simply me telling you to keep talking. Even when you think it's not a big deal, or when you think you shouldn't ask because you don't want to make someone feel bad. Some choices may pull you apart, not forever, but opportunities shouldn't be ignored either. If I'd had someone tell me that before I married your dad," she continued focusing on me, "I would have rolled my eyes. We were happy. We knew everything. We'd work it out because we loved each other. I still love him, Jake. I love him and I love Klara, but it didn't work in the long run because we kept trying too hard to protect each other from what we wanted personally, until all that bottled up resentment turned sour and spoiled what we had."

Frankie's hand slipped onto my thigh and squeezed. I frowned. The open honesty in Mom's voice promised me she believed every word. At the same time, it made me ache. If she still loved them and they broke up that…

"That's why I'm telling you to keep that communication open. It's so much easier to fix a small thing than it is a big one."

Frankie tilted her head to look up at me. "I think we can do that. We've already learned the hard way about what happens when you let the little things go and you don't talk about what's bothering you."

Wasn't that the fucking truth? I kissed Frankie's nose and then looked over at Mom. "Thanks, Mom."

She smiled at both of us. "You're very welcome, and, Frankie, one last thing. You deserve a mom who will be there at two in the morning if you ever need to vent. You can call me. I've got some practice with daughters. I'll always pick up. You can even complain about my angelic son."

"Hey," I protested, but Frankie had already pulled away and grabbed Mom for a hug, and I couldn't stop grinning. Hell, let her complain about me. "At least you called me angelic."

"Yes, the only thing holding up that halo are the two little horns sticking out of your head," Mom advised as she gave Frankie a squeeze. "Now, let's finish our dessert, and you kids can run away to do all the things I'm not supposed to mention because Jake is scandalized by the idea I've ever had sex."

Frankie frowned and looked at me. "She has four kids, of course she's had sex."

But the twinkling in her eyes betrayed her laughter, and I snorted. "Laugh it up." I could take it, especially if it made her smile. We ended up hanging out with Mom for a movie after dinner, and Frankie insisted we do the clean-up, so I sent her with Mom to sit while I did it. Then I cuddled her in my lap while we watched the latest superhero flick. Mom was behind, but Frankie loved these and I didn't mind watching them over and over.

When we finally left to head back to her apartment, Frankie couldn't stop yawning. "That was fun."

"Yeah?" I checked with her as I held open the door for her to climb inside. "I liked it. Mom really loves you."

"I really love your mom. I can't believe she did all that. It couldn't have been comfortable."

No, it hadn't been. "I'm going to call my dad after your birthday," I told her after I got into the driver's seat. "We have to do some finagling to schedule it. He has a regular call with the girls and I don't want to step on their time, but I also want to introduce him to you. Will you sit with me when I do it?"

"You sure you don't want to talk to him alone first?" But she was already reaching for my hand.

"We have some bridges to build. Not sure we will be successful but…I'm willing to try. Meeting you is part of that. I mean, he's met you obviously, but we were a lot younger then."

Frankie's laugh filled the interior of the car. "Yes, we were."

It wasn't until I pulled into her apartments that she added, "If I call my dad, will you be there for that too?"

No question. "Anything you need, Baby Girl. Anything you need."

Be Nice

"It smells like boys in here," Rachel complained as she followed me through the living room, where the guys sprawled on sofas and chairs, game controllers in their hands. "Oh look, boys."

"Oh look, it's the Cactus Queen," Jake said with a droll grin that only widened when she snorted. "Did you bring the boy toy?"

"There is no boy toy," she huffed and shot me a look.

"Now, now, Rachel, you can tell us," Coop told her, patting the sofa next to him. "Any bestie of Frankie's is a bestie of ours. I'm a vault."

Arms folded, she smirked. "I'll tell Frankie."

"Hey, Frankie doesn't spill anyone's secrets." Archie sounded almost incensed by the suggestion that I might.

"Exactly," Rachel said, all smug. "Now, as much fun as I have hanging out with you idiots, I came to see our girl and she's so much better looking and smelling."

I snickered. "Be nice."

Ian pursed his lips. "Our girl smells great." He winked at me. "See, nice."

Eyes rolling, Rachel turned to me, and I folded my arms and met her stare for stare. We had been playing telephone tag and texting for the last four weeks. We barely even caught up at school, and to be honest, we'd both been swamped.

But I'd missed her.

"Fine," she said with a huge huffing sigh and pivoted to look at the boys. They'd all paused their game and returned her stare, smirk for smirk. If I didn't think they enjoyed antagonizing each other so much, I'd be ripping my hair out. The silence elongated, and Rachel made a groaning sound before she finally said, "Bubba, your music kicks ass. Frankie let me hear one of the demos. You got skills."

"Thank you, Rachel, I appreciate the feedback." Ian's slow smile had me biting back a grin as Rachel considered the other guys.

Archie raised his eyebrows, and I could practically see that vicious tongue of his prepping, but Rachel surprised me. "Arch, you kicked ass with booting your dad out of Standish. Hats off, man. Remind me not to piss you off. At least without being prepared."

He laughed. "Maybe next time, I'll call you in for backup."

"Huh, I might answer that call."

Pressing my thumbs to my lips, I kept my hands clasped together as Rachel squinted at Jake.

"Great restraint today, I think anger management is really working for you."

Jake frowned. "Great restraint where?"

"At lunch, you didn't knock those freshmen on their asses. Good stuff." Pivoting she looked at Coop. "You don't stink." With that, she whirled to me all smiles. "There, I was nice."

Except now Jake was squinting at her and then over at the guys mouthing 'freshmen?' And I'd bet money there had been no freshmen but there might be.

"Yes, you were nice," I said. "Within reason. Now, true or false, do you have a boyfriend or girlfriend or both that you would like to have join us for a special event?" I'd been dying to ask her, but I wanted to ask her in person and the boys promised to not let it slip, particularly after how enthusiastic I had been about thanking them.

A week of almost nothing while I convalesced made me very horny. Good to know.

"Girl, you have a busy enough dating life, you do not need to worry about mine."

I made a face. "Rachel, I'm not asking for top secret data. Just yes or no?"

"No."

I frowned. "But I thought…"

"It's done."

"But…"

"It was an experiment, it's over. Nothing to see here. So, I'm free and clear. You may run away with me now."

Coop made a negative *bzzting* sound that earned him her middle finger. Pleased with her response, he fist-pumped.

I made a face. It was a good thing I loved them all.

"Whatever this thing is that you think I need a date for, I can borrow one of your guys, right? Or better, you and me can pair up." But behind that smirky smile and teasing look were shadows, and they were making me crazy.

I wasn't going to push it, not in front of the guys.

"That would be a negative, Ghost Rider," Jake said. "Frankie's very much taken. Coop can be your date."

"Hey," Coop said. "Don't I get a say?"

The guys started ribbing each other, but I focused on Rachel. "You don't need a date, but you absolutely have to come with us and you can't tell me no. I want you there."

"Done. Where are we going?"

"The Torched concert with backstage passes."

Everything in her expression froze, and then Rachel did the last thing I'd ever expect—she burst into tears and hugged me so tight, I couldn't breathe.

Chapter Twenty Three
IT'S MY BIRTHDAY

FRANKIE

My birthday fell on a school day. That was fine, it was also…bizarre. All week, awareness of the approaching day had been like a buzz under my skin. The guys surprised me with concert tickets. The fact we'd seen Torched in Colorado in no way diminished the fact we'd get to see them here. Archie had gotten us backstage passes and scored an extra couple so we could take Rachel and her SO.

Her tears when I told her had stunned me, and I'd never seen the guys move so fast. I swore they left cartoon like vapor trails as they scattered. Thank God they'd been happy tears. When Rachel realized she'd scared the guys off, her laughter had been epic. By unspoken accord, the guys never mentioned her tears, only asking me if she was okay and whether or not they needed to beat the shit out of someone.

I really loved them.

The plan, because of course they had a plan, was school—because blowing it off wasn't an option after my rather spectacular head cold—followed by grabbing food and then hitting the concert. Archie and the guys wanted to do a big splashy dinner the next day, and apparently, something else fun. The weekend, apparently, was going to be my birthday weekend.

No complaints from me. I just loved that I got to spend it with all of them and that they'd included Rachel. I'd missed her the last few weeks.

I woke up so early, it was still dark outside. Coop and Jake were both sound asleep on either side of me. Ian and Archie had crashed in the other room the night before. The best part of my day was having them all here. Maybe I was turning into a total sap, because I loved the fact they all stayed here. Every once in a while, I got an evening to myself. But even if I went to bed alone, I was never alone when I woke up.

Jake's arm was wrapped around my middle, and I had my back flush against his chest. We were even sharing the same pillow, and the tickle of his breath on the back of my neck made me smile. Though his face was hidden in the shadows, Coop faced me, one hand over mine where it rested on him.

The cats—two of them at least, I'd bet Tory had gone to sleep with Ian— were crashed out on the bed with us. Tiddles and Tabby were sleeping in the dip between my legs and Coop's. It was just warm, familiar, and safe.

And I'm eighteen.

Just like that.

I went to bed seventeen and woke up eighteen.

It was just another day, and at the same time it was… How long had I been waiting for this?

Emancipation had freed me from Maddy. Since that day at Standish, I hadn't seen or heard from her. As glad as I was for that, I couldn't help the twinge in my gut. When I was little, she would come in here on my birthday morning and tell me the story of the day I arrived in her life.

She'd always made it sound like a huge event. How she'd paced uncomfortably the day before. How she'd gone to bed aching, woke up an hour later with cramps. How she finally decided at midnight that she should call the doctor. They told her to go straight to the hospital, and she'd called a taxi to pick her up because she didn't think driving would be a great idea.

Then once she got to the hospital, her water had broken and what should have been a swift labor took all day. The staff had been attentive, holding her hand, sharing stories with her. They'd made her feel special, especially when she said she'd been there alone. Then I arrived, perfect. I looked like her even then, and from the moment they put me in her arms, it was her and I against the world.

Recounting the story, even in my own head, seemed anticlimactic. Maddy had stopped bursting into my room to tell me that story after I turned fourteen.

Made sense.

That next autumn, Archie arrived.

I thought it had more to do with high school, and I was being silly for missing it. She could be distant and volatile, but that one moment… I could still treasure those, even if they had probably been more about her than me. And enough about Maddy. Today was *not* about her. We had five weeks if that left of school, everything was about AP exams and getting ready for graduation, then we would spend our summer… Hell, I didn't even know what we were going to do this summer.

With care, I eased out from under Jake's arm and then slid out from the covers and off the bed. I'd gotten pretty good at disentangling myself, because I always ended up sleeping in the middle. No complaints, seriously. But a girl still needed to pee, and sometimes imagining the *Mission*: *Impossible* theme as I worked my way out amused me.

The cats followed me, the boys did not. After I peed, I washed my hands and face, then brushed my teeth. We'd all showered late last night and I'd probably shower before the concert, so I pulled my hair up into a messy ponytail before padding my way to the kitchen.

There were little signs everywhere of the guys. Game controllers on the coffee table. Jackets on the back of chairs. Backpacks scattered around the room. Sheet music on the side table. Ian's guitar sitting on a stand next to my own. The kitchen had similar touches. Pictures of us on the fridge held there by quirky magnets that just kept showing up, not that I was complaining. The little white board with notes, like what we needed from the grocery store, and all the takeout menus that officially had their own little drop box that Archie had stuck up there.

The kitchen table sported different things, including Jake's watch he'd taken off before helping with the dishes and the European history notes we'd been quizzing each other on. There was also a single rose in a vase with a card sitting in front of it.

That had *not* been there when I went to bed.

I waited until the coffee was brewing and the cats were fed, since they were cheerfully scolding me for taking so long, before I slit the card open. The front of the card was roses, chocolate, and wine with the words, *The best things…* I opened it to the rest of the message, …*become more valuable as they age.*

I chuckled. The sentiment was cute, but the actual note inside made me swoon.

Our darling Frankie,

We debated four cards, then we debated the message, we even debated whether to leave it for you to find in the morning or giving it to you ourselves. What we decided, however, was that since we love you together, we're going to celebrate you together. You're the best friend we've ever had, whether it was beating up punks on the playground, saving our lives with homework, making us smile with how you love to play, or just challenging us to be better because you only deserve the best.

This last year has been hard. For you and for us. It pushed us in all the right ways though, because look where we are! There is no place any of us would rather be. This is not our first birthday spent with you, but it is the first birthday of yours where we get to say we are celebrating our girlfriend.

Ours.

We cannot tell you how much it means to us that you not only wanted to date, but that you wanted all of us. We love you and we love having you. Even more, we love celebrating with you. So this weekend is not only all about you, it's all about us loving you. So brace yourself, babe, we have plans.

It was signed by all of them, and there was a hastily scrawled addition below their names.

P.S. I know I'm still your favorite - Coop

I burst out laughing and hugged the card to myself, even as I blinked back tears.

"Coop might think he's your favorite," Archie said softly from behind me. "But you don't have favorites."

I pivoted and found him leaning against the doorframe, his hair disheveled and dressed only in a pair of boxers. The rest of him just looked edible. "Hey."

"Hey, birthday girl," he murmured as he headed for me. I met him halfway and wrapped my arms around his neck, even as he slid his around my waist. He brushed a sweet, light kiss to my lips before hugging me tight. "Have I told you I loved you since you turned eighteen?"

"I might have read that," I teased him, and he chuckled. He pulled back and then wrapped something around my neck and clasped it. The metal was cool against the back of my neck. "Archie."

"Birthday girl gets what she wishes," he teased as he smoothed down the chain. "This is a gift that made me think of you instantly and what you do for us."

Glancing down, I found the infinity pendant in his palm as he held it up for me to see. The rose gold metal was soft and almost luminous in the half-light of the kitchen. The huge emerald in the center though had me catching my breath. Holy crap.

"Archie," I said, repeating the earlier sentiment.

"It's nowhere near as valuable as you are," he told me and traced his thumb around the double infinity loops. "This has been a bitch of a year, babe. Probably some of the worst and best moments happened during it. From when you shut us out to when you let us back in to when you said yes to dating to when you said yes to me."

Emotion clogged my throat as he pressed the pendant against my chest.

"Seventeen got off to a rocky start for you." He didn't have to explain why. It wasn't long after that birthday that Rachel dropped that bomb on me. "It kept trying to suck you under." When he cupped my nape and tilted my head so he could brush another kiss against my lips, I sighed. "You didn't sink."

"None of you let me," I reminded him.

"You didn't *need* us, babe. You are fucking amazing, but that will never ever stop me from wanting to be there and throwing you life line after life line. Because that's exactly what you do for us. You push me to be better…"

"Archie…" I choked out his name this time as tears welled. "You're going to make me cry."

"Can't have that," he whispered, but it was all there in his face. "Happy birthday, babe."

Then he claimed my mouth for a long kiss that had me arching up on my toes and clinging to him.

"Damn, I'm glad you two turned out to not be related," Jake drawled from by the door. "'Cause that's hot as sin. Not that I wouldn't have gone for the taboo if I'd had to."

I don't know which of us started laughing first, but I managed to flip Jake off before Archie did, so I'd take that as a win. Archie gave me a gentle nudge as he let me go, and I skipped over to give Jake a good morning hug. He picked me right up and claimed my mouth in a kiss that left me panting and ready to wrap my legs around him.

"We still have school, Don Juan," Coop said as he smacked Jake on the back. "And lemme have her. I need to give her my birthday kiss, too."

My nipples were so tight they hurt when Jake let me go, but instead of backing off, he sandwiched me right up against Coop and started kissing the back of my neck while Coop devoured my mouth.

"Oh, I can already see this is going to be a problem." Heat flushed me from head to toe, but when Coop tugged me away from Jake and then turned to pass me to Ian, I just sighed. "Happy birthday, Angel."

They all tasted minty. Every single one had hit the bathroom before coming out here, just like me, and kissing them was better for my wakefulness than coffee. As it was, I sighed against Ian's mouth as his tongue plunged against mine, teasing and coaxing. With warm hands, he cupped my ass and lifted me until I could wrap my legs around his hips.

"Hey," Jake called. "Don't start something we can't finish."

Ian chuckled against my lips as I groaned. "Pretty sure I wasn't the one that got her all wound up."

Somehow, I found myself sitting in Ian's lap with my back to his chest and my legs spread open and hooked over his thighs.

"And I don't think it's remotely fair to send the birthday girl to school all needy and wanting." The press of his erection against my ass had me wiggling, but the lightest of slaps against my hip stilled me. I leaned my head back to find him looking at me. "Be a good girl, and I'll take care of that for you."

When he slid his hand over my tank and cupped each breast, I groaned. Using both hands, he massaged them, flicking the nipples through the shirt until all I wanted to do was squirm. Sitting still was torture. Ian sucked against my earlobe as he dipped one hand between my legs and under the sleep shorts.

"Someone's very wet," he murmured as he pressed one finger against the labia and began to rub it back and forth along the slit, not quite touching anything. A moan slid out of me, and a sharp inhale had me opening my eyes.

Coop, Jake, and Archie all stared at me with hot and hungry eyes, and I'd barely registered that when Ian caught my clit between his thumb and forefinger, the pinch adding a sharp bite of pain, and then pleasure swamped me as he began circle the bud, pressure tipping me right over the edge.

I came, hips thrusting up against his hand the whole time as I stared at the guys, and holy crap. Ian petted me through it, slowing his caresses until I just lay there trembling. Bliss was a real place.

He nipped my ear again. "Better, Angel?"

"Oh, yeah." My heart hammered, and my legs were like putty. Ian was licking his fingers, and when he pressed one against my lips, I opened up to suck it clean. Archie let out a little curse and raked a hand through his hair. It was hard to miss the array of erections visible.

They were all so pretty.

All so mine.

"Coffee is ready for you, babe," Archie told me as he crossed over to where I was melted against Ian, and he shocked the hell out of me when he replaced Ian's finger with his lips and kissed me like he was trying to pull the taste of me from me. "I need a cold shower."

"Shit," Jake swore, following right behind him. "Me too."

"I can live with my boner," Coop called after both of them, and helpless laughter rushed up through me, along with heat flushing my cheeks. "Besides, Bubba's right—the only one who doesn't suffer today is you."

"What if I don't want you to suffer?" I dared him, and he put a hand over his dick in his boxers.

Not missing a beat, he said, "Birthday girl gets what she wants."

A shiver worked through me, and I glanced up at Ian.

"Whatever you want, Angel," he promised me, and I slid out of his lap on shaky legs, trembling as I moved to kneel between his thighs. But first, I tugged off the sleep shorts, and then I worked to free Ian's erection. Wrapping my hand around it, I glanced over my shoulder at Coop and wiggled my ass.

Bless him for reading my mind, because I'd barely closed my lips over Ian's tip when Coop began pressing inside of me. I was already soaked, thanks to Ian's generous orgasm-inducing play, so Coop didn't have to take much time to thrust deep. I groaned as I swallowed around Ian's cock. I began to suck, lick, and stroke like it was my favorite treat.

When he fisted my ponytail and gave it just a bare tug, I went loose. If he wanted to control it, I'd happily give him that. With gentle force, he urged me to move faster, and I softened my mouth so he could thrust deep. He always pulled back just as I began to gag. Coop held my hips as he powered into me. It was fierce, and every sharp push scraped more stars out of me. I was clenching around him, even as I kept swallowing.

"I'm going to come, Angel," Ian warned me, and I glanced up, holding his eyes as I sucked harder and deeper. He pressed all the way to my throat, and I could barely get a breath as he came. The low, husky groan he let loose had me shuddering. Coop had slowed his movements as I swallowed. As soon as I lifted my head and Ian slipped free, Coop banded an arm around me and pulled me back flush to his chest and his thrusts grew stronger, every single one sending me higher and higher.

When he skated his fingers over my clit, I came all over again and clamped down on him until he let out a shout. The hot rush of release left me shuddering.

"Fuck. Me." Jake's voice hit me from the hall, and I laughed.

"Give me a minute, and I'd be happy to," I promised. I was shaking, Coop was still inside me, and I could still taste Ian on my lips. This birthday was already the best ever.

"I'd take you up on that in a heartbeat," Jake said. "But you need a shower."

True…I did.

Rising on quaking legs, I shuddered as Coop slipped free. He groaned, and then I began the slow walk to the hall. Pressing a kiss to Jake's cheek, I murmured, "Library later?"

His eyes flashed hot, and he grinned. "Anything you want."

Excitement feathered through me, and I made it to the bathroom where Archie was showering. I found him with his hand wrapped around his dick, and when I leaned in, his whole expression lit up. "Birthday girl wants that," I told him, and he pulled his hand away and I grinned wider. My jaw was going to be so sore this morning.

Worth it.

We were a *little* late to school. It just meant we didn't hang out in the cafeteria. Worth it. I rode in on Ian's bike, body humming still. The weather was gorgeous. Sunny skies and cool breezes. I had on my Torched shirt, my ripped jeans, and all the jewelry they kept loading me up with. More, I was freaking floating. When we got there, Rachel was waiting.

Her hug was intense, and then she snagged my coffee before she pressed a wrapped box in my hands. The thing was heavy, and I stared at her. "Before you open that," she told me, "just remember, I adore you."

"Why does that worry me?" Archie asked as he slung an arm over my shoulder and glanced down at the rectangular present I was holding.

"Because you happen to be a highly intelligent man who is gifted at reading people," Rachel told him.

"Buttering me up or just calling it like you see it?" Just the barest amount of suspicion edged his words, and Rachel laughed.

"Why can't it be both?"

"Fair enough."

I snorted at both of them and moved over to Jake's SUV so I could set the box on the hood before I started tearing the wrapping paper off. I tried to follow the seams where the tape was to preserve the paper. She'd actually wrapped it in this really pretty rose foil paper.

"Oh my god, I forgot how anal you are about paper."

"It's not anal, Rach," Coop told her as he slung an arm around her shoulders. "She thinks the paper is gorgeous, or she wouldn't try to save it."

"Hmm," was Rachel's only response.

Jake closed in nearby, and they all watched as I got the paper free, then opened the box inside. It was a scrapbook. I glanced over at Rachel, and she just gave me a little smile.

When I cracked open the first page, I let out a little breath. It was us.

All of us.

Images from the first day of senior year.

There was even a shot of me glaring at Coop as he dragged me into the cafeteria. The guys by themselves. The looks on their faces as they saw me. Every page that followed was like another chapter in our story. She even got shots of them at the party, and there was one of me sitting in the garden that night. When the hell had she taken that?

Pressed roses appeared on some pages. Copies of the notes she sent me.

More shots of the guys. Different quotes and lines from them. Some I could pick out just because of the wording.

The earlier tears were back. The dance. The Halloween party. Oh my god, she had pictures of us the morning after, sitting at the police station waiting for the guy. Rachel had written, "True love doesn't need a sentence or a charge, it just needs to be there."

Christmas photos I'd sent her. Some of my boudoir shots. More snap shots from when Archie and I went dress shopping. There were a lot of pictures. Some she'd clearly hijacked off social media, but more she'd taken herself. She had to have. There were quiet moments, intimate moments captured when we weren't paying attention.

Ian performing his song to ask me to Homecoming. Me hanging over Jake's shoulder as we watched some video on his phone. Another where Archie had a lock of my hair twirled around his finger as he read something on his phone. There was another of me and Coop horsing around somewhere.

There were so many. She even caught the guys unawares. Jake and Archie discussing something intently with plans spread out between them. Another with Ian writing what looked like music. Shots of the guys on days when I hadn't been at school. Including one she'd sent me about them being so forlorn.

It was magical.

I stared over at Rachel. "This is beautiful."

"There's a few open pages for graduation pics and for prom. I'll make sure you have the pictures for them." The sober expression on her face tugged at my heart. "I worried so much I blew this year for you when I told you about their rules."

"I'm really glad you did," I told her. "I mean it. If you hadn't…if you hadn't given me that push, we might not be here. All of us. This is where I want to be."

The guys didn't say anything, but Rachel glanced at all of them, then at me. "I'm not going to tell them I'm sorry. But I am sorry about the way I did it to you. I should have known you'd take it so hard. Your heart is way too open."

"Yes it is," Coop told her, but he gave her a squeeze and then kissed her temple, and Rachel froze. "Don't get all excited, Manning, just letting you know we forgive you. We all got Frankie, and it's her birthday, and what the birthday girl wants…"

Was for them to all be friends. Fuck. The tears started falling, and Rachel rescued me with a swift and fierce hug. "Love you, girl," she said in a quiet undertone. "And not just 'cause you're hot and taking me to a Torched concert."

That did it. I laughed, and it helped with the tears.

By the time I got my coffee back and had the album safely stowed in Jake's car, Archie snagged me with an arm around my waist. "Hold on to your hat, babe. This is just the beginning of your birthday weekend."

Chapter Twenty Four
GOTTA MAKE A WISH

The day flew past, probably because I was floating through most of my classes. Prom court was announced over lunch, and fuck me, my name had been called. They plied me with a mocha espresso chocolate mousse cake, and I had a mouthful of it when they said my name. Archie and Jake high-fived, and the guys laughed. Rachel's name was also called for the court, and I grinned at her.

All four of them got called for the guys side, and they looked a little on the stunned side. *Ha*, teach them to sign me up for something like that. Rachel winked at me. I gave her a one-armed hug and a chocolatey kiss to her check that had her shoving me off with a laugh.

Still, prom would be interesting. Honestly, between the card, the morning sex, the fact Jake and I had a date in the library right after lunch, and the concert that night, nothing was going to get me down.

Absolutely nothing.

Not even one half of bad meatloaf waiting for us at the apartment when we got there after school. Rachel had to run back to her place, but she would be here soon. I slid out of Jake's car with Archie, even as Coop and Jake spilled out. Bless Jake, he moved right in front of me and Archie both. Ian wasn't far behind as he pulled his bike in.

"Edward, how very unpleasant to see you here," Archie said by way of greeting. "Why don't you fuck right the hell off and skip the spoiling our day portion of the program."

I cut a glance around the lot, looking for his car on the off chance he had Maddy with him.

"She's not here," Edward said, pulling my attention back to him. "She doesn't even know I'm here."

"You know what, babe," Archie said over his shoulder. "Why don't you and the guys go up and get ready. I'll deal with this."

That would be great, except I wasn't leaving Archie to deal with his father. Interlacing my fingers with his, I leaned into him. "I'm good right here. We also have plans," I told Edward. "So whatever this is, make it snappy."

The corner of Archie's mouth curved upward. Jake didn't bother to hide his smile, he just folded his arms. "Yeah, Eddie. We're listening," he threw into the conversation. I didn't have to look at Coop or Ian to know they were ready to back us up.

Instead of being put off by the show of solidarity, Edward merely loosened his tie as he narrowed the gap between us. I had no idea how long he'd been waiting outside of our apartment. I didn't want to think about that.

"Happy birthday, Frankie," he said to me, and I just shrugged. "I'm sorry to intrude today, but I had a gift for you drawn up from before, and while I'm aware that there was apparently some deception on Maddy's part, it doesn't change the fact I'd like to make amends with you." Then he glanced at Archie. "And with you."

"Wow, can you say too little too late, Edward?" Archie told him.

"Archie, you can be pissed at me. You have every right."

"Thanks for your permission. Didn't need it before. Don't need it now."

Archie flexed his fingers around mine. The tension cording through him had me squeezing his hand and keeping a firm grip. I didn't want him lunging forward and punching Eddie. Even if I kind of wanted to do that myself.

"Fine, I got your message with the takeover."

Was he kidding with that shit right now?

"Maybe this will go a ways toward proving I would like to try and open a dialogue with you." He pulled an envelope out of his jacket and held it out to me. It even had my name on it. I would sooner stick my hand in a beehive.

"Is that a bribe?" Archie asked.

"No, it's a gift. It's the same one you got on your eighteenth."

"I'm not your daughter," I interrupted. "Why are you doing this? I get that you wanted it to be true for whatever reason, but it's not. And you're doing this to Archie? Why?"

"Babe, it's okay…"

"No, it really fucking isn't." I glared at Edward. "You're not my father. You're his father. You don't act like it. You want to be his father, then start listening to him and don't treat him like some goddamn afterthought. If you can't do more than that, then get the fuck out of here and go away."

Archie didn't deserve this shit from anyone.

Edward glanced down at the envelope in his hands and then back to Archie. "I can see why she means so much to you." With that, he set the envelope down on the stone wall nearest my apartment. "That's for you. For your birthday. Give it to Archie if you want. He'll know what to do with it." He paused another beat, then said, "It won't mean anything, to either of you, but Maddy lied and I have to accept that. I wanted to believe the lie because I made a lot of bad decisions, but you weren't a bad decision Archie. I know my behavior doesn't support that assertion, but you never were. Maybe in time, we can talk on neutral ground and you can let me try to get to know you."

"Or maybe you can keep going," Jake suggested when Archie said nothing.

"Yeah, 'cause you're utterly fucking with the vibe," Rachel added from behind us. "This is party time for the eighteen-year-olds. Everyone over thirty needs to jump off, and all douche canoe parents need to drown."

A faint snort escaped Archie at Rachel's proclamation, and I glanced at him to find him shaking his head, but smiling.

I bumped his hip, and he looked at me. The tension around his eyes softened, and his smile grew.

I mouthed 'I love you,' and he kissed me. Sweet, tender, and loving, and he didn't let up until a car door slammed and Jake muttered, "And he's out."

Blowing out a breath, Archie rested his forehead against mine. "You're a little vicious when provoked."

"She's a lot vicious," Coop told him as he slapped his shoulder on the way past. "Just be glad she didn't clock him."

"Yeah," Jake said. "'Cause she might have bruised her hand, and I would have had to kick his ass."

Ian chuckled as the three of them flowed ahead toward the apartment and Rachel followed. "Is it bad that I would pay to see that?" They left Archie and me alone, but neither of us moved until his father's car pulled away.

"You okay?" I asked him, and he ran his finger along the chain of the necklace he'd put on me that morning and tugged the pendant out. I'd hidden it under my shirt because as beautiful as it was, I didn't want to risk something happening to it.

"I'm fine, I don't want him spoiling your birthday."

"He can't spoil anything. We're together. We won."

He grinned wider and tugged me in for a hug. "Yeah, we won. I still want to punch him."

"Me too," I agreed, and he laughed. Side by side, we walked over to the letter on the wall, and I picked it up. "Trash it or open it?"

He studied me a moment. "You'd just throw it away without knowing what it is?"

"I don't want anything from him. The most valuable thing he ever did is standing right in front of me, and I already have you."

"Charmer," he teased, but I didn't miss the pleased smile he wore. "You realize that's my job."

"Birthday girl…" I reminded him, and he threw his head back and laughed.

"Open it, let's get the insanity out of the way, and then back to your magical birthday weekend."

"Magical is it?" I squinted at him as I slit the envelope open. "Hmm, you're taking me to a Torched concert. Again. Not sure you can top this, Mr. Sexy Pants."

He snickered. "Challenge accepted."

Inside the envelope was some weird contract looking thing. Great, the bad billionaire dad gave me some kind of legal contract? Archie held out a hand, and I passed it over.

A snort escaped him. "Damn, Grandpa, that was cold."

"What?"

"I get why Grandpa waited for the day he did. See the executable date here?" He pointed to the notarized date, which happened when we were on spring break.

"Okay, I don't get it."

"Grandpa pushed him out at Standish, and he didn't have the support or the shares to hold Grandpa off, partially because he gave me ten percent on my birthday and he just handed you ten percent today."

Ten percent?

"Of Standish?"

"Yep," Archie said, folding it closed and sliding it into the envelope. "Guess you can now take care of me in the style to which I want to become accustomed. However, you cannot hire Jeremy away. I'll keep paying for him."

I gawked at him.

"He can't just give me…"

"He did."

"But it's yours."

"I don't care."

"Archie."

"Babe," he teased me by mocking my tone. "Stop worrying about him or this. It's time to take the birthday girl to the concert. Especially since the quickies are now on hold since Rachel got here before we ditched him."

I laughed. "Subtle."

"Nothing subtle about it," he teased. "Birthday sex? Definitely on the menu."

"Good thing we already got a start on that," I teased him as we headed up the short steps to the door.

"And that we have all weekend."

A shiver went through me at the promise twining every syllable.

The next hour flew past as Rachel helped me with my makeup as we got ready. Through unspoken agreement, no one brought up Archie's dad, and we skipped on past to having fun.

"Live a little," Rachel insisted when she pulled one of the black skirts out of my closet. "You always wear jeans. Drive the boys nuts. Let them wonder if you're commando all night."

"Rachel," I scolded with a laugh.

"Trust me, it's your birthday. Make them work for it. Plus, it's going to get hot at the concert and the skirt will be easier than the jeans for cooling off."

She did have a point.

"I will if you will," I told her and she smirked.

Of course, she probably brought a skirt. "I intended to, we've got backstage passes and I have killer legs. Not as killer as yours, but since you have them all tied up in a game of Twister around those four, I'll be able to steal the show."

I went with one of the concert tank tops I'd gotten in Colorado and tied it so it bared a section of midriff, then paired it with a black skirt. Rachel dug into my closet and found a pair of boots I hadn't worn since sophomore year. But they were calf length and had a slight heel to them.

Thrusting them at me, she said, "Wear these. Do you have fishnet stockings?"

"No," I told her. "And I don't want any."

"True. Going commando would preclude any kind of stockings or tights."

"I'm not going commando."

"Live a little," Rachel teased. "You're eighteen and have four hot hunks ready to do you any where at any time. Can you imagine sexing it up during the concert? All that thumping music? Hot sweaty bodies moving? I bet you could sit right down on one of them and writhe your way to—"

I clapped a hand over her mouth. "Unless you plan on telling me about the dick you've been testing out, you're going to leave their dicks out of it."

She wrinkled her nose, then rolled her eyes and huffed. "Fine. Killjoy."

Bumping her with my hip, I finished getting ready. I half-wanted to leave the necklace here. It would kill me if something happened to it, but I'd also done emerald eye shadow to pair with it and some dark smoky thing Rachel did with eyeliner to make my eyes pop even more. It kind of looked more like a cat's eye, but that worked for me.

Charm bracelet on my wrist, ring on my hand, necklace on, and I glanced around the room.

"Hang on," Rachel said, with a pin between her teeth. "Turn."

I pivoted away and she tugged the strap on the tank, and then pinned something to my bra under it.

"Better. Now everyone can see the tattoo. No mistaking that you're taken. I don't really want to have to bail Jake out of jail tonight."

I made a face at her in the mirror. "You wouldn't have to. Archie would take care of that."

Laughing, she glanced at herself in the mirror then hooked her arm around my shoulders and stood side by side with me. "We look badass. You think the boys can handle all of this?"

A shiver went through me. I was pretty sure my guys could handle anything. A fact they disputed as soon as Rachel and I appeared in the living room. Jake dropped his game controller and raked a hand through his hair. "I'm going to jail."

"No you're not," Archie said. "No bodies, no crimes."

Ian gave me a once over followed by a slow approving nod. "Be worth it though."

"Oh yeah," Coop added. "Do we have to go to the concert? I mean, we could start the private party right here."

"Still present," Rachel reminded them, and Archie flashed a wicked grin.

"You'd be down for watching, don't give me that."

"Normally," she countered, "I'd agree with you, but this is Torched we're talking about and backstage passes. I will cut you if your dicks make us late."

"Rachel…"

"I said cut them…not cut their dicks off. I wouldn't do that to you. They'd live. And be fully functional."

I couldn't help it, I cracked up and I wasn't the only one laughing.

"Don't worry," Ian said as he rose. "Frankie's as excited about this as anything. We're not going to miss a moment." I bounced a little as he reached me and traced his fingers down my arm. "You want a jacket in case it gets cold?"

"I figured I'd just snuggle you guys if I got cold."

Rachel made a gagging noise, and I flipped her off behind Ian's back, which sent Coop into a fit of snickers.

"It's okay, Rach," Coop told her. "We'll make sure you have a jacket."

"Ass," she declared and I grinned without once looking away from Ian's heated gaze.

"You look good enough to eat," he murmured before stealing a kiss. Oh, it was a good thing I'd not taken Rachel's advice, because now my panties were damp. Thankfully, the bra was also padded so my nipples weren't on proud display, but considering how good the guys all looked in their jeans, concert

T-shirts, and relaxed, happy expressions? I was going to be horny as hell before we made it back.

Correction—hornier.

"Let's go," Rachel announced as she hooked my arm. "Down, girl. I promise to leave you alone to devour them later."

It wasn't until we were heading back out to the cars that it hit me. We weren't all going to fit in Jake's SUV. It was snug with just the five of us. I didn't think Archie had ordered a car tonight. "Don't worry, babe," he assured me. "We have this covered."

We did?

Instead of heading to his car or Jake's, he headed over toward a…*Tesla*. It was brand new and it had three rows of seats. Archie touched the handle and opened the door for me.

"Happy birthday, Baby Girl," Jake said with the widest, most shit-eating grin I'd ever seen. "Archie and I have been taking one of these apart and putting it back together for the last couple of months. We wanted to make sure it was the best, safest car for you, with the most room to do whatever you needed to do."

They got me a car.

I turned toward Archie, and he pressed a finger to my lips. "It's from us. All of us."

"It is?" Coop gawked. "Even if we weren't in on it?"

"You're not the engineer," Archie told him, not lowering his finger. "But you deserved the best car with the safest rating that fits who you are. This isn't flashy or bright, but it's you."

And it was red too.

Man.

"Do. Not. Cry," Rachel ordered. "What is wrong with you? We do all this makeup, and you want to make her cry?"

A watery laugh escaped me, and I twisted to look at the car. Archie wrapped his arms around me, but Jake stood just a half step away, his expression fierce and fixed on me.

"This has been your secret project?" I asked.

"Pretty much," Jake said. "We wanted to understand it, make sure it was everything they said. It's…pretty fucking impressive. But we also wanted to get in and change a few little things. We just needed to know what to do and how."

"Do you like it, babe?" Archie asked, and I laughed.

"How am I supposed to answer that? I love it."

"Yes," Jake said with a fist pump.

"I love that you guys went to so much trouble."

"Get in," Archie said, ushering me into the driver's seat. Now I realized why the rush to leave "early." The others climbed in, and there were three rows of seats, plenty of room for all of us. Holy crap. There was a huge screen, and with the car on, Archie pressed a button on the dash and it brought up a camera in the apartment. I could see Tiddles sitting on the middle of the coffee table, eating the last of one of the guy's snacks.

"Oh snap," Coop said. "Jake, you left your fries out."

He laughed, and so did I. There were so many bells and whistles. I didn't know what to play with first. Archie put in the address of the concert venue, and then a crisp voice came over the speakers.

It was Jeremy.

"You recorded Jeremy?" What the hell?

"We got him to provide the voice print. He's very soothing," Archie said with a grin. "Don't you think? I was going to do it, but then that didn't seem fair. Jake and I tried to work out how to make it all four of us, but that just got complicated and wasted like a week of dev time."

Jake snorted. "It was worth exploring."

"Not disagreeing," Archie said. "Just we wanted it to be perfect. I wanted it to protect you when you were in it, and I wanted you to feel safe and confident. And it's environmentally friendly, and there's some other perks." He switched the screen to a crackling fireplace and heat even puffed from the front vents.

"Romantic too."

I half-expected Rachel to make gagging noises, but she was curiously quiet. When I stole a look back at her, she was dabbing her eyes. She caught me looking, and I bit my lip. No, I wouldn't draw attention to it, the softy. But still…

I let out a little squee. I couldn't help it. It was a *brand-new* car, and it wasn't anything Maddy had ever owned. It was way too extravagant, and I probably shouldn't be so excited, but at the same time…

"Can you hear the mental argument?" Coop mused.

"Probably five-four in our favor right now," Jake said. "Or she'd have already said no."

"Shut up," Ian said firmly. "Let her decide her own reaction."

A laugh escaped me, and I glanced over at Archie, then twisted to look at the rest of them. "I should say no."

"Yes!" Archie said with a fist pump.

"I haven't said yes yet," I scolded him, still laughing.

"But you're going to," he said, his grin widening. "You said '*should* say no,' but that means you're not going to say no. You're going to take the car we want to give you, because we want to give it to you and for no other reason than we love you and want you safe."

It was really hard to argue with that. "Don't think you can always get away with this."

"Damn," Coop said with a laugh. "That's twenty bucks I can kiss goodbye."

"Pay up," Jake said. "I told you he can talk his way out of any trouble with her."

"You're all terrible, horrible, awful people," I announced, and Ian chuckled.

"All of us?"

"Yes, guilty by association." Then I grinned. "And I love you all. Now put your seatbelts on." I did a little dance in the seat.

I was eighteen, in love, I had a brand-new car, my boyfriends were with me and my best friend, and we were going to a Torched concert.

"You heard the lady," Archie said, and he switched the screen back to the GPS. The engine was practically silent as we glided out. "Want music, babe?"

"That's a dumb question, and you're a really smart guy."

He laughed and hit two buttons, and the next thing I knew, it was me and Ian singing in the car. I groaned, but Ian laughed and the guys cheered. Even Rachel did. We ended up listening to all our demo songs, even the one Coop and Ian had teased me through multiple orgasms during it playing.

The best part, the car could zoom, and the guys were laughing and cheering as Ian and I sang along. The car handled like a dream. When we switched to the Torched songs, I already imagined I'd be hoarse before the night was over.

I couldn't wait.

Chapter Twenty Five
SEAL IT WITH A KISS

f I thought the drive to the venue had been fun—I was in love with my car and making no pretenses about it—our arrival had me bouncing excitedly. It was comfortable outside, the guys were laughing, and even Rachel wore a smile. She hooked arms with me after I gave each of my guys a solid kiss in thank you for the car.

"Hey, I'll take the kiss," Ian teased. "But Coop and I weren't in on this."

"Yeah you were," Jake told him. "Course, you also write *songs* for her. So we have to be able to compete."

"What about me?" Coop protested.

"Cradle to grave, dude." Jake gave him a light punch in the arm. "You're the only one who gets to claim that."

Rachel rolled her eyes, but winked at me as Archie broke between us and slid an arm around each of us. "Come along, ladies, let the boys argue, we're going to go merchandise shopping. Please, give my credit card a workout."

"What am I going to do with you?" I scolded and then slowed, forcing both him and Rachel to stop. "And don't we have to lock the car?"

"It's automatic. If you don't have the key on you, it won't open."

I gaped then looked back at the car again.

"Trust me, babe, it's going to be fine, and I will make sure you have all the handbooks on it to review after this weekend."

Rachel snickered. "After the weekend. You don't want her distracted."

"No, I do not."

Coop caught up on my free side and caught my hand in his, while Jake flanked Rachel and Ian was on our far side. I wanted to bounce my way across the parking lot, but decorum and the heels on my boots, short as they were, said no.

Then again, as soon as we were in sight of the main doors and the long lines of fans, I couldn't resist the bouncing. The guys and Rachel laughed at me, and I really didn't care. This was going to be so amazing. Even more amazing, we had VIP tickets, which meant we didn't have to stand in the long line.

"I bet you're not scolding me in your head right now for spoiling you," Archie said as he wrapped himself against my back while we waited for our turn to go through the far shorter access point for VIP ticket holders. He walked us forward the two steps, and I giggled. "You're totally indulging me right now."

"I love you," I said, as if it was the answer to everything. "You make me happy. You all make me happy. And that car is way too much and so is the necklace, and you know what, probably wanting all of you is too much."

Ian glanced over to me on the last and brushed a finger down my nose before pressing it to my lips. I kissed the tip of his finger and he carried it back to his mouth, and I grinned.

"So if you can have us, why not everything else?" Archie mused. "That's solid logic and very practical."

I giggled. "It also makes you happy."

"That it does, babe."

"It's the perfect birthday."

"We're far from done, Angel," Ian said with a wink, and then it was our turn to go through. Archie showed his phone with the tickets, and one by one, we went through the scanner. I didn't have my wallet or anything else on me tonight. Coop had my driver's license if I needed it and Jake had my phone, but I hadn't even brought a bankcard.

Nope, I was totally in their hands. Rachel had a small purse she'd brought. We cleared security and received our special, holograph style cards with the band on one side and the name of their most recent album on the other. Even the lanyard it hung from glittered and gleamed.

Ian had his hands on my hips as we followed the roped off area away from the crowds toward the kiosks of merchandise. "We have about thirty minutes before they bring out the opening act," he said over the noise. "So if we want food or drinks, we should do it now."

"Water," I said, and the others agreed with me. I didn't think I could stomach food at the moment, I was way too excited. Jake peeled off from us to get the water while we went to look at the merch.

There were new shirts. I had two of the concert tees they had on display. But I didn't need everything they owned. Well, not to say I didn't want it all, but I didn't need it all. Rachel let out a sound vaguely like a squeal, and I worked my way over to her, aware that one of the guys moved with me at all times. They were adorable, and I wasn't complaining. There was a *lot* of people here.

The shirts she found had my eyes widening. Holy crap, I'd never seen ones like this before. Each one sported an artist's rendering of one of the girls in the group. The back of the shirts declared whose team you were on, with the Torched logo following it.

Team Kaitlin, Team Aubrey, and Team Yvette. "All three of these times two," Archie said from the side, and he gave our sizes. Rachel glared at him, and I poked her.

"Don't argue, he's really good at that. And those shirts are to die for." I grinned, and Rachel made a face at me, then laughed.

"Fine, but if we're getting all three, then we need the booty shorts to match." When she held up a pair that were just hip hugging, boot cupping shorts with the Torched roses on fire across the ass, Coop let out a whistle.

"Hey, Arch…"

"Already on it."

I laughed, and Ian pointed to a hoodie with a single microphone on it and musical notes on the back. It was simpler than the others, and when I nodded, he hooked it down and turned it around so I could see the front. Oh, it had the Torched logo over the breast. It was a plain zippered hoodie otherwise, but super soft.

"We're going to have to come up with a name for us," he said as I ran my finger over the logo and then glanced up at him.

Holy shit.

I twisted to look up at him. "I…"

"Not right now, Angel," he said with a laugh. "Just something to think about."

It hadn't occurred to me at all. I mean, I wanted to do this with Ian because he wanted me to do it. The entertainment lawyer had pushed back on the recording contract, so we hadn't signed anything yet. As long as Ian and Arch were content with waiting for better terms, I really didn't argue. There was already so much on our plates.

A name.

"I thought we'd just be Frankie and Ian," I admitted, and he grinned as he tugged the hoodie from my hands and pulled me over to the checkout. Archie was paying for our stuff, but Ian wouldn't surrender the hoodie. When Archie shrugged, we moved forward, and Ian paid for my hoodie.

"We can do that, or we can work on something else," he said. "I'm open."

I grinned at him. "You're the best."

He winked at me. With water and loot acquired, we followed the velvet ropes past the throngs and down to the floor of the arena. Apparently, our VIP tickets included seats near the front, and not just the front, right off one of the runways where the girls could dance and move when they sang. Oh, I was already bouncing again. This time, I had my hands on Jake's shoulders as I hopped down the steps.

"Don't break anything," he warned, even as Rachel laughed at me. I couldn't begin to describe just how awesome today was and in all the different ways that it was amazing. I didn't want to. I just wanted to bask in the feeling of having them all here, including Rachel, and of how happy and content everyone looked. We'd made it.

It was like crossing a finish line in a race I hadn't even realized I'd been running. It wasn't over, but at the same time, we had come so far.

We had almost a whole row to ourselves, though there were a few people down at the end where there were two extra seats. They put Rachel and I in the middle, with Coop on the other side of Rachel and Jake on the aisle. Archie was next to me, and Ian on the other side of him. Rachel reached over and pinched my thigh hard enough to make me jump.

"Ow, what the fuck was that for?" I asked as I swatted her hand.

She laughed. "Just making sure you knew this was real."

I rolled my eyes and then bumped my shoulder to hers. "I know it's real, and wait until you hear them up there. It's so much better."

"Yeah, yeah, rub it in."

"Don't pinch me next time."

It took an hour almost before the first act opened, and we swapped seats a few times so we could all talk. I was sitting between Coop and Ian when the opening act began, and it was just a girl with a guitar, all by herself.

Ian nudged me, and I stuck my tongue out at him but grinned. I got it. Solo performer, and he thought that might be me? Yeah, no. First of all, there were thousands of people here. Second of all, if he wasn't doing this without me, I sure as hell wasn't doing it without him.

The opening act was all ballads, but she segued into something faster with a rhythm that had us clapping along. She really had a sweet voice, but I swore she must have been nervous, because this close, there was no missing how her hands trembled, even while she played. I felt so damn bad for her, and I cut my gaze to the arena around us and then back to her.

Yeah. No.

When she finished, we applauded, and then the lights plunged down into near darkness. The silence stretched, then there was a clopping of boots like coming down the stairs playing over the speakers. Then a voice cut into the silence.

"We ready?" The deeper pitch to the feminine voice had to be Aubrey Miller. She was the bass player and sometimes switched out with Kaitlin Crosse on the piano if they used it.

"Oui." Yvette Chanteur. Her playful French accent was an affectation she used when teasing others, because everyone asked if she was French with her name. "Definitely ready. We're mic'd right?"

"Yes, we're mic'd." That was Kaitlin Crosse. "A little late to be asking that don't you think?"

Laughter rippled through the darkness, and I grinned.

"Never too late," Aubrey said. "Particularly when we have to make a big announcement tonight."

"Shh," Yvette cautioned with a laugh. "If we aren't careful, we'll blow our own secret."

More laughter rippled through the crowd. Surely they knew their mics were on, right?

"Girls," Kaitlin began, but a male voice cut her off calling, "Mics are hot."

"Well fuck." Kaitlin's words reverberated through the stadium. "Guess it's a good thing we're not on TV, right?"

A moment later, the lights exploded upward with sparklers as the three appeared on stage, headsets on and hands spread wide. Kaitlin's grin was fierce and full of good humor. Her blue hair looked even deeper and brighter than it had when we saw her in Colorado. Aubrey's deep black hair fell in down her back from the crown she'd braided around it at the top. Yvette had cut her hair, and it stood up all spiky and dangerous, kind of like her in those killer heels she was wearing.

Fuck, they made my feet hurt just thinking about it. Glitter shown on all of their faces. It sparkled along their arms and seemed to catch all the lights playing over them.

"Good evening, Texas!" Kaitlin said as she strutted toward the lip of the stage. I swore she wasn't more than fifteen feet from me, and my heart skipped a beat. "You guys ready to party?"

Even over the laughter and the cheers, her voice carried with the huge speakers, and I was on my feet with everyone else, screaming. She said something else with her hand over the microphone and laughed. A second later, the band kicked off with the first bars of the very first song of theirs I'd ever heard.

For the next hour, I stayed on my feet, dancing and singing along, and I wasn't the only one. Rachel had her phone out and I knew she snapped some pictures, but I made her dance with me anyway. I danced with all of them. Hell, I even danced with the girls sitting behind us.

Torched worked their way through their first two albums, and I was breathless when the music slowed and Kaitlin headed out toward the runway, shading her eyes as though trying to look through the lights. "Are you guys still out there?"

A roar greeted her.

"Not sure I heard that, let's try that again. Are you guys still out there?"

This time, the roar was considerably louder. I laughed at the wildness of it all.

"That's better! Now I know you know our music, we can hear you singing out there, so sing this one with us."

When she began the first lines of "Open Your Eyes," I let out a little sigh. This was one of my favorites. It was also so bittersweet. It begged the people around you to open their eyes and see you, because they didn't. All they saw was what they wanted to see. The girls sang it a capella. No band. No percussion. Just their voices and that of the audience. It was entrancing, especially when I could hear Ian as he wound his voice around mine.

There really were tears in my eyes when they were done and the whoops, applause, and whistles climbed.

"Well," Kaitlin said with a grin. "Guess you don't need us after all. You could do this concert."

A chorus of nos belted out, and she laughed.

"You know, we've been on this tour for months. We've performed all over the world. We've been really fortunate, and I can't tell you how much we love it and we love you. Before we get into our latest songs, the girls and I wanted to share a special announcement with you."

"Breaking news," Aubrey said. "You're all the first to hear."

"Because while we've been talking about it for a while, today was the day we made our decision," Yvette tacked on. They'd come up to stand on either side of Kaitlin, and all three girls were holding hands.

"So, you might want to get your phones out if you haven't already," Kaitlin cautioned. I frowned, but Rachel had her phone out and so did Jake. "As Torched, we have had some of the best times of our lives, but we have been touring pretty continuously for the last three years, and with just six more stops on this tour… We are taking a break for the next couple of years…"

I barely heard the rest of it.

Torched was taking a break? Did that mean they were breaking up? The band was going away? This sucked on so many levels. At the same time, the smiles on their faces were genuine, and the longer I stared at them, the more I saw the tired there. The audience was a mixture of cheers and shouts of "we love you" and "no" and everything else.

"Okay, enough with the sappy," Kaitlin said, then she kicked off their next song and the band joined them. It was impossible to not sing and cheer along with them, and at the same time, it was bittersweet. Even if they weren't breaking up, a break would mean no more music for a while. I laughed a little, 'cause I was making this about me and they sounded committed, so I did the only thing I really could—I danced and sang with them.

And by the time they finished their fourth encore, I was hoarse and flushed and sweaty. It was *amazing*. I sagged into a seat and accepted Coop's water bottle when he held it out. I'd already killed mine and had to resist the urge to kill his greedily.

"Okay," Archie said. "Let's head to the side stage door." He had his phone out and had been reading off of it. Oh fuck, the backstage passes. I'd almost forgotten. We formed a line, weaving in and around the seats as we made our way to a door on the far left of the staging area behind another row of seats. A security guard was right there, and Archie showed him something on the phone, then he scanned each of our badges before letting us through.

We had to follow another long series of velvet roped off areas and then up two flights of stairs before we found a much shorter queue of people and an open bar area where they were selling refreshments. Ian and Jake cut away from us and grabbed water bottles. Thankfully, I hadn't needed to pee yet. Though that would definitely happen before we made the drive home.

I was fanning myself with both hands, and Coop turned to me and started fanning me too. I laughed and bumped him with my hip. I should have put my hair up, I was sticky and sweaty and flushed. The air conditioning out here was *amazing* on my overheated skin. When Jake rolled an ice-cold bottle along my shoulder and up to my neck under my hair, I damn near groaned.

He chuckled. I could see the girls ahead of us, they were talking to people who were farther up in the line, taking pictures and signing things. Rachel downed all of the bottle Ian handed her, and when she finished it, he took it and tossed it in the recycle bin before handing her another. Apparently, we were the ones in desperate need of hydration, because Jake kept the icy cold one on my neck while I drank.

The guys had all our stuff, thankfully—I'd half forgotten it. The line moved, slowly, and we inched our way closer. It was cool to watch them interact. They seemed so larger than life on stage, and they were mostly their voices and how they made me feel on their albums, but from here, they were people.

The girls ribbed each other. Yvette must've made a lot of sarcastic remarks because Kaitlin rolled her eyes more than once, and twice, she elbowed her. Aubrey was so sweet, she leaned in and got really close for hugs with fans and photos. Yvette held back from that, and Kaitlin seemed to land in the middle. She didn't mind the posing for the pictures, but she didn't seem to be a hugger.

That was fine, I couldn't say I'd been a big hugger before. I mean, I hugged the guys and I'd hug Rachel, and that pretty much filled my quota. I cooled more the longer we stood here. When it was finally our turn, I had to actively restrain myself from squealing or bursting into tears.

"Hey," Aubrey greeted us all with warm smiles. "Thanks for coming to the show."

"It was kickass," I said, managing to find some words, and then laughed. "I mean, it was really good."

"Kickass works," she said with a wink. "Did you have a favorite moment?" She flicked her gaze behind me. "Or moments, since apparently you brought your own team with you."

I burst out laughing, but Rachel cut in and said, "We loved the whole show. Frankie's a huge fan, she has listened to every album a hundred times easily. You should have heard her singing along with you. She's amazing. And today's her birthday."

Note to self—kill Rachel.

Behind me, Ian coughed, and it had the element of being a chuckle as Aubrey focused on me. "Oh hey, it's this girl's birthday! Wait, what was your name?"

"Frankie," Rachel supplied and shot me a grin, then Kaitlin and Yvette were both looking at me. Okay, I could die now.

"Frankie. Okay, this is—" Aubrey began.

"Kaitlin and Yvette." Oh thank God I didn't stutter. "Rachel's not wrong—I've been listening since you dropped your first YouTube video."

Katilin made a face. "Garage Band?"

"No, Tire Shop."

Yvette laughed. "The illegal one we made and uploaded without telling our parents. You do go back."

I shrugged a little. It was weird to think of things to say to them and I half-figured the guys would join in, but they were all hanging back and grinning at me. Sweet and so not helpful. When I made a face at Coop, he took my picture.

"Oh, hey." Aubrey wrapped an arm around me and pulled me over between her and Kaitlin. "Picture with the birthday girl." We got a couple of them, and then I dragged Rachel over and they put her between Kaitlin and Yvette. The guys were all snapping shots, and when I asked them to sign one of my concert shirts, they did. Then we had to move on 'cause they had other people waiting.

"Hey," Kaitlin said as I started to go. "Did your friend say you were a singer too?"

"Just getting started, nothing like you guys."

"She's phenomenal," Ian contributed. "Don't let her fool you. She's the best signing partner a guy could have."

Heat suffused my face. I couldn't kill Ian, but I might dump water over his head later.

Probably get me spanked.

Worth it.

"Cool," Kaitlin said. "Hang on, I want to give you an email address. It's not one we share a lot, and it goes to all three of us. Send us something you've sung. It'll be fun."

"Really?"

"Yeah," Kaitlin told me with a wink. "We all got started somewhere, and why not? I'm not promising anything."

"She's just nosy," Yvette said. "Especially since these boys aren't flirting with her."

"Shut up." Kaitlin snorted and elbowed her, and I burst out laughing. "That is not why I'm being nosy. Well, I am curious but no. So just send it, I'd love to hear it, and happy birthday."

I was delirious, but I managed to remember something before I got two steps away. "Hey," I said, and they glanced at me. Ian paused next to me. "Good luck with your break. I'll miss your new albums, but I hope it's everything you need."

"Thank you," Aubrey said with a wide grin. "We're looking forward to it. Some of us more than others." Kaitlin flipped her off, but there was so much genuine warmth there, I couldn't help but grin. I liked the fact they seemed like real friends.

That was really cool.

By the time we were outside, I did a twirl and laughed when Coop caught me and began dancing me backward. "Did you have fun?"

"Did I have fun?" I stared up at him. "Yes, I had fun."

He chuckled. I bounced up on my tiptoes and kissed him and then worked my way through each of them until I got to Archie last when we were by the car, and I kissed him fiercely. "Best. Birthday. Ever."

Everyone was laughing, and I glanced over at Rachel. When I turned to her, she raised her eyebrows and then I pinched her.

"Ow," she snapped with a laugh and swatted me. "What the fuck?"

"That's for throwing me under the bus in there."

"Girl, you need to seize opportunity when it's in front of you, and they were actually curious. So send them a song. Maybe nothing happens. Maybe something does. But you would never know if I hadn't said something."

She wasn't wrong, and at the same time, I was elated.

"You up for driving home?" Ian asked me, and I eyed my car. I'd just gotten this. Did I want anyone else to drive it?

"Actually," I said and looked at Archie, "do you mind? I am kind of giddy drunk on the music and the meeting and the everything…"

"Done," he said, and Jake tugged me into the backseat while he gave Rachel a gentle nudge toward the front. Archie snorted, but Coop followed and so did Ian. Jake and I were all the way in the back, and Ian and Coop were just in front of us.

Even with the seatbelt on, I nestled right up against Jake, and he hugged me and pressed his lips to my hair.

It really was the best birthday.

Even if the clock on the dash said it was after midnight and my birthday itself was over. The guys promised me all weekend.

Chapter Twenty Six

GIMME A SPANKING

The drive back to the apartment kind of drifted by on laughter, sleepy snuggles, and euphoria. I hadn't been kidding about feeling a little drunk on it all. Drunk even more on the fact that not only had I had a great time, I'd shared it with my favorite people. I found myself staring at Rachel's profile, or what I could see of it. I wished with everything I had that I could make her happy. The guys might even accept her if I swung that way, or at least they would work on it.

Maybe.

Man, I was drunk. I giggled to myself. At Jake's arched eyebrow, I'd just given him a kiss and snuggled closer. Despite all of that, I was still half-asleep by the time we got back to the apartment. I offered a bed or the sofa to Rachel if she didn't want to drive home, but she just laughed at me.

"Hey," I said as I hugged her tight. "I don't know what's going on with you, but I'm here and I really wish you'd let me help."

"You help more than you know." She pressed a kiss to my cheek and then blew a raspberry that made me laugh before she pulled back. "Have a great weekend. I'll talk to you Monday. Just make sure you hydrate."

"She'll be fine, Angel," Ian told me as I watched her go. "When she's ready, she'll tell you." Yeah, except I had a feeling in this, Rachel was like me. She wouldn't say anything until she was pushed. I let him tug me inside. It was almost two in the morning, and I was swaying on my feet. We washed up, checked on the cats, and I fell into bed, wearing a pair of panties and a clean T-shirt that Jake had dragged on me. As much as I thought about climbing one or all of them like a tree, I was out before my head hit the pillow.

Some vague part of my brain acknowledged the soft laughter and kisses as I sank into sleep still smiling. I roused when arms wrapped around me and then drifted back off with my nose pressed into Coop's neck. The next time I opened my eyes, I was too hot. I was pressed right up against Coop, and the sleepy part of my brain said Archie was on my other side. I tried to doze back off, but it was almost too warm.

It took some doing, but I extracted myself, even though Tiddles gave an unhappy meow as he leapt off the bed. Yawning hard enough to make my jaw crack, I headed to the bathroom. After I peed, I washed my hands and splashed cold water on my face. It was almost too warm in the apartment. Half-stumbling, I headed for the A/C and turned it on. The hum of the motor kicking in promised it would cool down. I wanted to cuddle the guys but not get cooked by them.

In the kitchen, I filled a glass with water and leaned against the counter as I sipped it. My eyes were half-shut, but the day before played out like a movie in my head. Everything from waking up, to all the playful sex before school, to the blowjob I gave Jake in the library. I loved watching them fall apart. I loved being the reason they did. Then going to the concert. Not even the arrival of half of bad meatloaf could diminish the day.

"What's a beautiful girl like you doing out of bed?" Jake asked in a sleepy half-rumble that made my toes curl.

"Hot," I admitted and glanced over at him. He was all rumpled hair and stubbled face where he stood in the doorway. The single light over the stove offered a dull yellow cast, enough to see by and not trip over the cats, but it was also easy on the eyes.

"You're always hot," he teased, and I chuckled at the easy compliment and play on words.

"Beauty is in the eye of the beholder," I reminded him.

"And I behold a really beautiful fucking girl." The firmness in his words sent a curl of heat to lick through me and warmed me from the inside out. He narrowed the distance between us and took the glass from my fingertips and refilled it before setting it on the counter and boxing me in. "Do you know how gorgeous you are?"

I traced one of my fingers up the ridges of his abs to his chest. "If I'm half as good looking as you, I'd be okay with that."

He snorted as I explored lazily. The dark hair dusting his lower abs before arrowing beneath his boxers was always so soft. Dipping his head, he brushed his lips along my throat, and I sighed as I moved my head to let him have better access. The air conditioning had come on, and a breeze of cool air washed over my arms and flushed skin, eliciting goosebumps. I shivered both from the air and the way he nibbled his way along my throat.

Sliding his big hands under my shirt, he massaged my sides and back before cupping my ass and dragging me forward, just as his mouth closed over mine. It was a slow, easy kiss. It demanded nothing. The stroke of his lips, the brush of his tongue. Teasing, testing, tasting. It was the kind of kiss that had me straining to get closer, and at the same time, savoring the play. When he lifted me, I wrapped my legs around his hips.

The slow grind of his boxer clad erection against the seam of my panties made me groan. So close, yet the friction was a delicious promise of what was to come. My shirt tickled my nipples as I rolled my hips and rubbed against him. He tightened one of the hands on my ass as he slid the other up to fist my hair.

Never once letting me up for air, he maneuvered us out of the kitchen and into the living room. The softness of the sofa brushed my legs as he lowered me to it. With a light slap against my ass, he murmured for me to let go, and I groaned. But from the contact and the command. He lifted his head and stared down at me.

With only the light behind him, I couldn't make out his face, but the weight of his stare rolled over me like a caress. Gently, he tugged my shirt up and then brushed his lips against my abdomen and followed the fabric up as he uncovered more flesh. When he reached my breasts, I let out a little sigh. He didn't quite touch my nipples, kissing around them until they were tight and straining. When I arched my hips, he gave my hip a sharp little slap that had me gasping.

"Baby Girl," he began in a voice so heavy and thick, it sent another shudder through me. "Do you want a birthday spanking?"

A shudder washed over me at the offer. It had been a while since Ian actually spanked me, and Jake had given me the occasional slap, but not a real spanking. I swore my whole body went liquid at the offer as he rubbed the spot he'd slapped, spreading the heat out.

"You're going to have to use your words," he told me. "I've been reading and we've all been talking, but you haven't told me exactly what you want from me in something like this."

"I don't want you to do anything you don't want to do," I whispered and reached down to cup his face. "But what I do with Ian is I surrender, I let him have the control. It's nice. He wants to take care of me, and I let him do it. Sometimes, that's a spanking, other times, it's teasing me until I'm crying with the need to come. But there's always bliss, and he's always there to catch me."

He rubbed his stubbly chin against my nipple as I confessed. Some parts of our relationships were always private. But this I could share with him. Because it was what I got from it, what Ian gave to me when I let him. It was always up to me to allow him, and there was a strength and power in that I'd never imagined.

"I want to give you what you want and what you need," Jake promised, but there was something else there. Something deeper. An uncertainty? Jake had never sounded uncertain. Not once. But I honed in on that note and curled upward, and he met me halfway and then urged me back before blanketing me on the sofa. I wrapped my legs around him.

"Jake, you give me what I need. You love me."

"I do," he said, then kissed along my jaw before raising his head as he brought his hands up to cradle my face. "I love you so much. But I never want to let you down. You've been going to Bubba for that release when you're too wound up. You go to Coop when you need comfort because he knows you so well. And you and Archie have been clinging so tightly to each other ever since that asshole dropped that bomb on both of you. They love you too and they take care of you, I just worry sometimes I'm not doing enough."

"*You* are Jake," I whispered, sinking my fingers into his hair. If he was cupping my face to keep his gaze on mine, then I gripped his hair so he couldn't slide away. "You protect me all the time. I am so safe with you. You're teaching me to fight and to be stronger on my own, but I know I don't have to be. I know you'll protect me. You, Jake. I love them, but none of them are you. If you want me to submit to you and to surrender, you have it. You have me."

I could almost taste the wonder in how he sucked in a breath.

"You can ask me for anything, and I'd do my best to give it to you. If I've been ignoring you—"

"No, Baby Girl, shh, no." He pressed his lips to mine with each word, kissing me as though trying to soothe a hurt. "You haven't. This is me being awake at four in the morning and I want to give you the world, but I don't want to smother you. Sometimes, I don't know what it is you need, and I never want to clip your wings. Never again."

I bit down on his lower lip and then laved the hurt before kissing him fiercely and trying to pour all of the complicated feelings into it. Yes, I needed the others. I needed them all. We worked, we were home, and I wanted to be that for each of them fiercely. Never did I want them to doubt that. None of them should ever feel a moment of doubt, but if they did…then I wanted to chase it away.

When he took control of the kiss and then dominated my mouth, I let out a little sound that echoed his groan as he ground his dick against me. A laugh bubbled up as I remembered grinding on each other that very first time, but there was something else I could show him. At my gentle nudge to his shoulders, he lifted upward and pulled back as I squirmed out from under him.

Only after I was standing did I shed my shirt and then pushed my panties down my legs. Turning away, I went to my knees and pulled my hair around to bare my left shoulder. "You're a part of me, remember?"

The heat of his hand tracing my tattoo made me shiver, and then he pressed a kiss to it and I closed my eyes. "I remember, you don't have to prove anything to me."

"And you never have to prove anything to me." Head bowed, I settled my hands on my thighs. "I'm yours, Jake. I'm all of yours."

He let out a little groan and gripped my shoulders gently as he pressed another kiss to my throat. Everywhere his stubble rasped, the burn prickled my skin. It would leave redness behind, but right now, I craved every mark he would give me.

"Let me have you?" he whispered against my throat, and I smiled, relief and desire combining to turn me to putty against him.

"All of me," I promised. "Anything you want."

He nipped my throat, and maybe I shouldn't have been so open with the offer, but I had zero regret. Nothing they could ask me for would be too much. If Jake wanted to be who I needed, I wanted to be who he needed. He moved me back to the sofa and urged me to lean against the cushions with a pillow beneath my knees and another under my hips. It had my ass jutting out, and with my legs spread, it allowed him an unimpeded view.

He stroked a hand over my back and then over my ass and back up again.

"Don't move," he murmured before leaving a kiss on my shoulder over the tattoo again and vanishing from behind me. I closed my eyes and relaxed into the cushions, even with the cooler air blowing on me and leaving me a little chilled. I wasn't in a hurry. I meant it when I said I trusted them.

He didn't keep me waiting long. He ran his hands up and down my back, massaging and soothing. I swore muscles I hadn't even realized were tensed unlocked, and I melted down against the sofa. Then he landed a crisp slap against one ass cheek, and heat flared through my whole system. Then another. The spanks came in an uneven rhythm, never quite letting me anticipate when it was coming. He'd massage the heat, spread it out, and then land it again. Lips pressed against my shoulder as a lubed finger teased my ass and began to press past the ring of muscle.

He eased a hand between me and the cushion so he could trace his fingers around my clit as he worked a second finger into my ass, and then there was another slap and my whole body vibrated.

Three hands.

Jake didn't have three hands. He pinched my clit though, and an orgasm hit me out of nowhere as another hand landed against my ass. This time, the spanking felt far more familiar and it pushed, the sting and the heat and my body softening to all of it as tears slid down my cheeks and gasps broke from me.

"So good for us, Angel," Ian crooned, and I swore I melted. Jake had three fingers stretching me, even as he toyed with my pussy, and I was soaking my thighs. "Such a good girl."

Jake had gotten Ian, and I let out a little sigh as he massaged my ass, then Jake pulled back and eased his fingers out. The familiar snap of a condom rippled over me, and when I would have lifted my head, Ian closed his hand on my nape.

"Condoms for ass play today, Angel," Ian murmured against my ear. "Keep your hands where they are and stay loose for him. Jake wants to have your ass first, but we're all suiting up for that so we keep your pussy nice and safe."

They were all planning to have my ass today. Oh, a shudder rippled up and down my spine. Oh yes please. I swore wetness slicked my thighs and I wanted to rub them together, but I didn't dare.

"Do you remember the word to use if it gets to be too much?" Ian asked, and I shivered again.

"Yes. Stop."

"That's right, just that one word, and everything stops until we know what you need." Another kiss. Then something soft passed over my eyes as he lifted my head. With gentle thumbs, he swiped away the tears. "You ready for more, Angel?"

I grinned. "Yes please, Sir Ian." He nipped my earlobe. "And yes, please, Sir Jake."

There was a soft chuckle behind me, followed by a, "Fuck that's hot."

"Can you take more here?" Ian asked as he rubbed his hand over my ass. It was definitely warm, but not remotely sore.

"Yes, please."

"Good girl, count them out for me... We're going to ten."

Okay, a dizzy part of my brain tried to focus on the numbers as he started. The first two were so light, they barely stung. He more rubbed his hand and then slapped.

"Three..." A little heavier, there was more of a sting, but he rubbed it away until the heat was sinking into my bones.

"Four, five, six..." Alternated from one cheek to the other in rapid succession. I swore every strike pushed my nipples against the upholstery of the sofa. It was soft and harsh and teasing, and I was so sensitive to every touch.

"Seven." The strike changed, and that distant part of my mind recognized Jake as he cupped his hand with the slap. It robbed the sting and left only the heat.

"Eight, nine..." I was on fire now, and the heat in my ass was a real thing, just this side of not fun, and despite the tears soaking my blindfold, I didn't want it to stop. "Ten."

I barely got the last syllable out, and then Jake pushed into me. The tip of his cock was past the ring of muscle and pressing deeper into me, and I let out a cry. The rub of his hips to my stinging ass and the way he filled me shredded me in the most delicious ways. I let go and just rode those sensations.

Rarely had they done the ass play without someone sinking into my pussy at the same time. It had been almost wholly reserved to Jake and Coop, but Ian had been testing it some, and Archie often played with my ass, even if he hadn't taken it yet.

A shiver.

Today.

Those thoughts scattered as Jake found a rhythm that rocked me and sent me spiraling in ways I couldn't imagine. I clawed at the sofa as he chased his release and pushed me toward another one. The tension coiling inside of me grew tighter and tighter. I needed… He shifted the angle, and suddenly, I saw stars. Oh, even with the stretch, or maybe because of the stretch, I came on a scream.

I swore I floated there, aware of Jake as he collapsed against my sweaty back, kissing and teasing along my shoulders. Words of praise tickled my ears, but all I heard were the voices of the men I loved.

"Angel," Ian murmured as he cupped my face and turned me toward him. I tried to open my eyes, but it didn't matter. The blindfold blocked everything. "You back with us?"

"Hi," I said, and I slurred the word, but oh, I felt so good and so loose.

"There she is. You good, Angel? We have more we can do. We've been planning this for a few days."

More?

Dazzled, I sucked the finger he brushed against my lips. Oh, that wasn't Ian. Archie. The callouses on his thumbs as he stroked my jaw, they were so familiar.

"You don't always like to share," I whispered. He had been experimenting, but Archie had his own reservations. I didn't want anyone to be uncomfortable. I was floating back down to earth almost gently, not falling. Maybe because there were now three sets of hands on me, rubbing and soothing.

We also weren't in the living room anymore. There was a soft comforter beneath my back. A lazy kiss pressed against my abdomen, then a little gentle suck like someone leaving a hickey. He ruined the effect with a bit of a raspberry at the end, and a laugh bubbled up through me.

Coop.

They were all here.

"Birthday girl gets what she wants," Archie said.

"And we talked about it, Baby Girl," Jake continued.

"All of us," Coop supplied. "We figured some things out. Everyone's on board."

Relief threaded through me, but what about Ian?

"I don't know that we'll do this all the time, Angel, but your birthday is definitely the one time where we can shower you with everything."

That lazy spark of lust rekindled as he cupped my cheek and then kissed me, softly and gently.

"Does that sound good to the birthday girl?" That last question had me shuddering.

I went with the only answer I had for this. "I'm yours."

"This stays on," Ian told me. "I want you to focus on what you're feeling and your pleasure. Not us. Let us give that to you."

This time, I did rub my legs together, but a warm hand pressed between my thighs. "Fuck, you're soaked, babe. Already ready for our dicks, aren't you? You get as much as you want, as often as you want. We're going to fuck you until you see stars."

I was already seeing them, but when he pushed my thighs apart and replaced his hand with his mouth, I arched upward. The lick and nip of his tongue and teeth was so fucking welcome as he devoured me like his favorite treat. A mouth claimed mine, even as I cried out, and another mouth locked over one of my nipples.

Fuck, the overload of sensory data had me straining against Archie's mouth, even as he kept me pinned with his hands. My own were trapped above my head, shackled in a warm grip that kept me still. I didn't even try to fight the orgasm as it hit me, screaming into the kiss and flexing my thighs as everything in me bucked.

They gave me a few seconds of reprieve as they moved around me, and then a cock brushed my lips and I opened to him immediately. I'd know Coop anywhere. I knew they wanted me to have the blindfold on to just concentrate on what I was feeling, but how could I not know them? A hand on my thigh pressed it up until my foot rested on a shoulder, and then a cock pushed into me with a rock of his hips.

Archie.

He lifted my other leg until they were both against his chest, and he hugged them as he fucked me at an angle and with a rhythm that struck sparks with every push. Coop gripped my hair as I swallowed around his cock. It was hard to focus on one or the other. I wanted them both. Someone sucked my fingers into their lips and lapped at them, and it was another sensation and I couldn't keep up. I relaxed my jaw, and Coop pressed deeper as I arched my hips to meet Archie's rhythm.

When someone began to tease my nipples, thumbing them, then squeezing, I spasmed. I clamped down on Archie, even as I tried to swallow Coop's cock into my throat. He let out an abrupt shout and came. It sounded like a surprise to him, and I fought not to choke on it as he whispered, "Sorry, sorry."

Then he pulled out, and I arched again as Archie's thrusts kept shoving me up and over, not quite letting me come down, and I swore my darkened vision utterly whitened out when he gave a shout and heat flooded into me. I was boneless and floating. There was soft laughter and stroking hands on me.

I thought I might have fallen asleep, because I woke to find Ian checking my eyes and a low light on. Oh, we were in the master bedroom, some part of my brain belatedly recognized. Ian said something but I didn't quite catch it, and then Archie was bundling me into his lap. Oh, I'd been in Ian's. He held a glass of water up for me to drink, and I drained it down. I was so thirsty, and my throat was so dry.

Coop sat at the end of the bed, and Jake stood next to it. They were both gloriously naked. Ian crossed from the bathroom with another glass of water, and so was he.

"Take it easy," he cautioned. "You fainted, so we may have to go a little slower."

I fainted?

Holy shit.

"I totally rocked your world, babe," Archie said against my ear, his voice smug and pleased.

I laughed and stretched. Someone had bundled me into a blanket, and I loved the hugging, but I was getting hot. "I can take more," I whispered, because man, was my voice hoarse. I didn't know if it was from the sex screaming or the singing the night before. Maybe both.

"Oh, you're getting more, Baby Girl," Jake promised me.

"We have all weekend, Angel," Ian said with a slow grin. "And we're not going anywhere."

Okay, I could legit die happy right now. When Archie pressed the new glass of water into my hands, I took it and then shivered at all the hot gazes on me. Definitely the best birthday ever.

Chapter Twenty Seven
START THE DAY OFF RIGHT

The guys hadn't been kidding about extending my birthday to the whole weekend, and I lost track of how many times I'd come. It had grown so intense at times, that they had to seriously push me to make it happen, and they took up that challenge willingly. There were breaks—oh thank fuck we had breaks—usually to ply me with food and water.

I ended up *fainting* a couple more times. Coop was so damn pleased with himself when he was the next one to knock me out. It was impossible to be irritated with any of them for anything, even when they got smug. They joked with each other, they teased each other, but mostly, they spent their time alternating between driving me absolutely mad and taking care of me.

More than once, they'd gone for cool, damp washcloths to clean me up and sooth my soreness. My ass was getting more of a workout than I expected, but they all took such extreme care that even that soreness was bearable. When Ian ran a bath that first afternoon, he sat beside the tub and actually fed me while I soaked. The guys had gone for more food and supplies, as well as to strip and change the beds.

Apparently, when I wasn't looking, they'd pushed the two big queens together, and it had more than enough room for all four of us. Ian had even worked out a way to bind me to the bed, but so far, we hadn't used that. One of them would restrain me while the others played, and twice now, I'd been sandwiched between Coop and Jake or Ian and Coop, but Archie had avoided that for the most part.

Or at least he had until Sunday afternoon when it was just Ian, Archie, and I, now in my bedroom because we'd run out of clean sheets in the other room and the guys were messy. Coop and Jake had gone for food, and I was straddling Ian, riding him slowly. Bruised and full as I was, it felt oh so good to just writhe over him. The press of Archie against my back had me tipping my head to rest against his shoulder.

To be honest, I didn't know how the hell I planned on walking the next day. I couldn't walk now. They'd gotten really good at carrying me, and I was too boneless to argue. I could feel them everywhere. The little bite marks and bruises from hickeys. The scrape of teeth. My nipples were sore to the point of perfect pain, and if you'd asked me what that meant even a week ago, I didn't think I would have known.

Ian feathered his hands over my hips as he began to move me. My buttery legs were having none of it, but I wanted to feel him. He pushed up with his hips, helping to hit that spot. Archie nipped at my neck as he massaged my breasts, his warm palms almost soothing to tenderness of the nipples.

I wanted more. I wanted all of them.

"Can you handle it, babe?" Archie asked. Had I said that out loud? Apparently. "You're moving slow."

"It feels good," I whispered, because my voice really was shot. "So fucking good." It did. I could roll my hips, even if I could barely lift my legs, and Ian could balance me. I met his gaze and then he flicked a look past me to Archie, even as I stretched an arm up and behind me to wrap around Archie's neck.

It had to be all right with them. They'd already given me so much this weekend. I didn't need to be greedy.

"It's okay…"

"Shh, babe." Archie bit me, and I laughed at the scrape of his teeth. It barely registered as pain so much as sharp kiss. "We're thinking."

I softened against the command, and it was kind of funny how easily they could relax me now. My body just let go, and my mind didn't obsess. They'd chased away every single worry, there wasn't room for much of anything past them.

"Her ass is too sore," Ian warned.

"Yeah, but there are other ways," Archie added, and they kept rocking me up and down on Ian's cock. The little sparks radiating through my system had me clenching around him. It was a slow, almost torturous build up, but I was enjoying how my clit rubbed against him each time he pulled me flush to him.

"You comfortable with that?" Ian asked.

"I am if you are."

"I'll try anything once," Ian murmured, his voice soothing, even as Archie urged me forward, and then Ian kissed me as I splayed against his chest. He slowed the motion, and I half-expected Archie to push into my ass, but he didn't. A finger traced the edge where Ian connected with me, and he gave a grunt. "Don't get too touchy feely."

"Just checking, not you I want to feel up." Then he pressed his finger in, and the stretch was intense but not unbearable. If anything, it had me gasping for a whole new kind of pressure.

"You up for it, Angel?" Ian asked me as he pushed the hair off my face. Then it hit me. Both of them. At once.

I'd…

"Both of you?"

"Hmm-hmm," Archie said. "Both of our cocks in this sweet pussy. You've had Jake and Coop sandwich you, I know you've let us take your ass and your pussy at the same time. Have they fucked this pussy together?"

A whole body shiver racked me. "No…"

"Oh, so a virgin for two cocks at once," Ian mused, and something in the way he said that just turned me inside out.

"I'm very good with a virgin Frankie," Archie said, and his words alone stroked memories to the surface. "Can we have that pussy together, babe? Both of us? Fucking you together?"

"Fuck yes," I said, all in. Everything in me shuddered. Two days ago, I'd probably have had to think about it. Hell, maybe even the day before. But I was so languid and soft for them that I could take it. I could take anything they gave me.

"Relax," Archie murmured. "Relax and let us fill you up with two dicks, stretching that pussy until the only thing you feel is us."

Fuck. That mouth of his.

Ian chuckled. "You like giving her instructions."

"And you don't?" Archie countered. "You may use prettier words, but I'm just calling it like I see it. This pretty pink pussy is all flushed and hot and like a vise around our cocks, and she can't get enough, but we're going to stuff you so full, you won't ever imagine anyone that isn't us. Our pussy. Our girl."

And on that last word, he pushed in. Oh fuck. Oh fuck.

Oh fuck.

I couldn't breathe. It was too much. I fisted the covers, half aware of their soothing words and the easy strokes of their hands. Archie pulled back and then pushed in again, Ian grunted, and I opened my mouth, but the only thing that escaped was a keening sound.

It felt so fucking good, I couldn't even form words. Ian fisted my hair and pulled my gaze up to his. The strain around his face was visible too. I hoped it wasn't…

"Fuck," Archie groaned. "You're so fucking tight, but you can take us both in that perfect pussy."

As he pushed in again, my vision frayed and I lost everything to feeling.

Ian pushed up, and they alternated who pulled back and pushed in. I couldn't imagine how it felt for them, but I couldn't stop the spasming once it started. I swore that one orgasm just fell over the other and the next until I was shaking like a leaf.

"Touch yourself," Archie ordered. "Come on, babe, you really need to come now."

Wait…hadn't I already been?

"You can do it, Angel," Ian told me, and the stress in his voice told me he was close. They both were, and I writhed between them, the pressure unbearable and perfect. With a shaking hand, I slipped it between us, and I could feel where Ian pressed into me and behind him, Archie. My brain threatened to short circuit at the image. I wish I had a picture.

"Fuck," Archie grunted as he shuddered. "Come on, babe, I need you to come."

Ian's hand joined mine, and he tangled our fingers together. We barely touched my clit, and I swear it was like I detonated. I clamped down on both of them as I shook for real, and my vision whited out as I screamed. Pleasure spiraled through me, and Ian kept the pressure up on my clit as he sucked my tongue into his mouth and swallowed my cries.

They followed me with shouts, and the mess was going to be incredible. I swore I had to be gushing, and I floated on a wave of bliss as I collapsed against Ian and Archie flattened against my back. Beneath me, Ian groaned. Then Archie let out a similar sound.

I wanted to laugh, but I just didn't have the energy.

When Archie rolled off carefully, I hissed out a breath as my nerves jangled and lit up. My hand and Ian's were still trapped between us, and he twitched his fingers. The brush against my clit made me wince and whimper. He eased his hand away and then carefully rolled so we were on our sides, and then he eased out of me.

Oh shit.

"I think you broke my vagina," I mumbled.

There was a beat of absolute silence, but I waited for it. There was no way they could resist, and I was too damn deliriously happy to care about setting up that joke.

A smothered snort of laughter from behind me was the first fissure in the dam. A calloused hand moved over my stomach as Archie hugged me from behind. "Is it *broken* broken? Or just needs a little TLC broken?"

The snicker from in front of me pulled the rest of my smile out. "Maybe you can build her a new one."

"You're the one with the magic fingers," Archie snarked. "Write her a song and sing it back to health."

"I know," Ian said. "You can talk to her pussy. You can convince her of anything, right?"

"Hmm."

Oh God. Suddenly, I was flat on my back, and Archie eased my legs apart. "Hello, pretty girl, are you feeling all abused and overused? Maybe you just need some TLC?"

I died.

Laughter swelled out of me.

"Dead," I told them as I gave Archie a shove. "I'm dead. I cry uncle. I give."

I couldn't stop laughing though, because Archie was promising my pussy all kinds of things to get better soon, and when I glanced up at Ian, his eyes were warm, full of mirth, and his smile was tender.

"Thank you," I whispered to him and touched his jaw. Then I glanced down at Archie. His brown eyes shone, and his disheveled hair fell over his forehead. There was a carefreeness to him that I hadn't seen in a long time. "Thank you both."

"You're welcome, Angel," Ian told me, pressing a kiss to my temple. Archie pressed a similar one to my thigh. And at some point, I would need to move. "Though I think we're gonna have to change the sheets, and I'm pretty sure we've run out of them."

"I'll call—"

I didn't know I had it in me to move, but I was up and pressing my fingers to Archie's lips, ignoring the throbbing pulse I could feel in my pussy. Dude, I really thought they had broken it.

Worth it.

"If you say you're going to call Jeremy, I will…I will…I will pin you down and do something terrible to you." I didn't even have a real threat in me.

"Jeremy's not going to care, babe," he said. "He just likes looking after us."

"You cannot ask him to come wash sheets covered in cum and sweat and everything else from the last two days. I will not survive."

"Shh," Ian soothed, sitting up and pulling me into his lap. "Archie's not going to call Jeremy. We know how to use the washing machine."

"Yeah," Archie said. "Or I can call Jake and Coop and tell them to buy us more. 'Cause you know, we've proven we don't have enough."

Ian snorted, and I closed my eyes.

Yep. Dead.

Damn.

The guys were still laughing at me a few hours later as I soaked in another tub, sprawled against Coop, who'd climbed in to just hold me. Probably a great idea, 'cause all I wanted to do was sleep.

"Next time," Archie said. "We need a bigger tub."

"Hot tub," Jake agreed.

"Yeah, more room to maneuver," Ian said. "Definitely more frequent breaks."

"Are they really discussing the next time we do this?" I asked Coop in a hushed voice as Archie started discussing the different types of hot tubs.

"Yep," Coop said. "Shh, don't want to scare them off."

I grinned.

God, I loved them.

The weekend was going to go down in history. Even if I was tender as hell for the next three or four days. Not even my period showing up added to my discomfort. I was already sore, and one of the nice things about the implant, it reduced a lot of my issues from three or four days to one to two. Totally doable.

We were drilling down more at school. They had a practice run for how we would do our graduation walks. I'd started receiving my cords from different classes, including the all A honor roll.

Final class ranks were posted.

I'd done it—I'd edged up. I was in the top twenty with Jake and Archie. Ian and Coop weren't that far behind. Rachel scored a spot in the top ten. She smirked at me when I saw it, and I laughed my ass off. Sneaky bitch. But still, I was super proud of her, even if she still hemmed and hawed about which college she wanted to go to.

I pulled for NYU, but then, I was being greedy. I wanted her to stick close to us.

By the next weekend, Jake and I were drilling once a day on our European history facts. Archie and I had government and economics down, it was mostly terms and applications, but we'd been surprising each other with pop quizzes. Ian and I did practice tests for calculus, and Rachel and I practiced French either texting or when we talked or video chatted.

I had to do that when Coop wasn't home, because the last time Rachel and I got going, Coop ended up half stripping before he realized that we were on video chat. Then he just grabbed the phone and said, "Sorry, I need to fuck my girl. She'll talk to you later."

I don't know who laughed harder, me or Rachel.

Still, it was fun.

And I got to drive my car, a lot. We needed milk from the store? I went and got it. Wanted to run over and pick up something from Jake's? I'd drive him there. Trina needed a ride, I was all in. The guys laughed at me, but the car was fricking cool, and I *loved* taking it to a charging station.

Prom was right around the corner. AP exams were coming. Our graduation robes came in, and true to his word, Jake had gotten me a set. I was actually looking forward to walking, which was weird. I mean, it was just a ritual right? No big deal? They didn't even give you the real diploma.

Still, it was fun.

Archie had lined up a couple of places for us to look at, but he was also talking to his grandfather about their brownstone. Apparently, there was also an apartment, but he and Jake both nixed that.

Work was even fun, though I let Marsha off the hook and turned in my notice before mid-April. The scholarship was locked, and she had her new waitress up to speed. I was making plenty from my delivery job, which I got to use my new car for. I told Coop I was still finishing paying off the car I'd gotten from Maddy, and if he wanted, we could store it for Trina.

I'd thought about Jake's sisters, but Jake said there was already a plan in place for them with his parents, so Trina won that flip. Then there was the bit about my trust fund. Apparently, on my eighteenth birthday, true to their word, my grandparents transferred the first twenty-five percent to my control. I'd get another twenty-five percent when I graduated college or turned twenty-five, whichever came first, and another twenty-five when I turned thirty or got married—also whichever came first. The last twenty-five percent would be made available on my thirty-fifth birthday or when I had a child.

The terms seemed weird on the surface, but I kind of appreciated they were an 'either or' and not an 'if only.' Wittaker handled all of my side of it and worked with their family attorney. I'd also started having weekly phone calls with them.

It was strange, not just the generational and money gap, but the everything gap. They didn't quite understand my interests, and when I brought up the singing thing, they'd pushed back pretty hard. The dismissiveness irked me more than stung, so I just changed the subject. They were excited that I was going to college, but they offered to work with Harvard to get me in there or at Columbia rather than NYU. I turned down the offer.

We had a plan, and I was sticking to it.

One night, when it was just Jake and I, we sat down in front of his laptop while he video chatted his father. I hadn't seen Jake's dad in years. It was kind of impressive how much the colonel and his son looked and didn't look alike. He had his mother's coloring, but his father's eyes. Jake's dad was blond where he wasn't silver and gray. There was an agedness at his eyes, and the conversation between them was terse and uncomfortable at first.

Then Jake introduced me and they started talking more, through and around me. There was a lot of hurt from the sounds of it, on both sides. I leaned my head against Jake's shoulder as they discussed college and the opportunities Jake was looking for. When his father brought up enlistment, Jake stiffened, but I squeezed his hand.

"No, sir," he said slowly. "I understand the opportunities available through enlistment and service. But I've chosen a different path."

I really hoped his dad let it go. All he said was, "We can revisit it in a few years. After college then. You'd do well. You have all the right qualities and qualifications. Good way to take care of your family."

"As you've told me many times."

On the screen, a woman came into view, and if you'd asked me to describe Klara, I wouldn't have picked her out in a million years, but she was the babysitter. The one who looked after the girls and Jake on some weekends when his parents went away. I didn't see her often at other times, and I guessed she wasn't the babysitter, she was just who I'd thought was the babysitter.

"Hello, Jake," she said, greeting him as she took a seat next to the colonel. Unlike him, she was dressed in more relaxed civilian clothes. Her hair was dark like Jake's and his mom's, but it was cut short like a pixie.

"Klara," he said, and with a squeeze to my hand, he added, "It's good to see you. I'm sorry I've been a stranger. I had—" He cut a glance to his father, but I kept my gaze on Jake. "I had to work through some things."

"We understand. And I mean that. The girls tell us all about your exploits, and I'm so glad we're finally getting to see you again. Frankie, I'm afraid I still remembered a girl with dirt on her face and skinned knees who got in as many fights as Jake did."

I laughed. "Well, he probably wins that now, but mostly 'cause he doesn't let me fight."

"Damn right," Jake said in the same breath as his father, and they both grinned. It was the first moment of real accord that I'd seen, and something in me relaxed. After a few more minutes, I kissed Jake's forehead and excused myself, even as Klara did the same. It was good to let the two of them talk on their own.

I went out to the living room, and I was halfway through the third book about Madison Kate and discovering what Steele had done with a piercing when Jake emerged. Somehow, I didn't think he'd go for it, but now I was curious. "How did it go?"

"Good," he said, scooping me up and glancing at my Kindle. He frowned, then pulled it to read a few lines. I snuggled against him as he paged back once and grimaced. "I love you, but fuck no, Baby Girl. Talk to Coop, I bet he'd do it."

I burst out laughing, and he kissed me.

Then of course, we had to go back to the first book in the series, 'cause Jake wanted to read it too. It was only when we were getting ready for bed that he asked me about calling my father. Well, sperm donor.

The guy who fucked Maddy and the result was me.

Yeah, none of those sounded particularly attractive.

"I don't know," I admitted. "I go back and forth on it, and…he's married, Jake." I crawled up the bed on my knees as he dragged the covers back, and then we slid under them. We were alone tonight because of the call to his dad, though

I had no doubt Coop would show up. Jake dragged me into the middle of the bed, so he probably figured the same thing.

He turned out the lights, and I tucked my cheek against his chest as he rubbed my shoulder. "Talk to me?"

"He's married and he's got three kids—an older boy and fraternal twins. Wittaker spoke to him. So he knows about me now and he wants to talk to me, but I don't know. It's…he seems like a nice guy I guess, and maybe he never knew or maybe he did. He says he didn't, or at least that's what he told Wittaker."

"You don't believe him?"

"I don't *know* him. He has a whole other family." Why would he want me? Why did I want him? Did I even want him?

"Well, if he didn't know about you, then you're as much a surprise to him as he is to you. The fact he wants to talk to you says good things about him. That he's not immediately dismissing you." Kind of hard when we had the DNA tests, but I got his point. "You're never going to know unless you talk to him or meet him."

"What if he turns out to be a jerk like Edward or Maddy?" I grimaced. "I mean, Patience and Eugene aren't awesome, but they're not horrible either. Just really deluded in some ways and hard to talk to."

They never asked about Maddy, thankfully, and neither did I. After that day at their house, they didn't compare me to her either.

"Then we'll kick him to the curb like we did them," Jake said softly. "But what if he turns out to be cool and supportive and the kind of man who would be proud to call you his daughter? I mean, have you looked at you? You're pretty fricking awesome."

I laughed. "You're biased."

"Damn straight, and you're perfect. Can't convince me otherwise."

I sighed. I had two brothers and a sister I'd never met and who had no idea I existed. Or at least I didn't think they had. Maybe he'd told them. And he had a wife. I had a stepmother.

My track record with mothers wasn't stellar.

I groaned and snuggled closer to him.

"You don't have to decide right now, Baby Girl. When you're ready, you tell me or any of us. We got you."

That, more than anything, was something I could hold onto and believe.

"I'll think about it."

I kept turning his name over in my head.

Henry Jackson. Hank. Professor of humanities at Harvard University.

Of all the gin joints in all the towns. He was a professor at the one school I'd always wanted to go to.

Made sense why Maddy hadn't wanted me to go there. Even if she'd graduated from it herself.

Bitch.

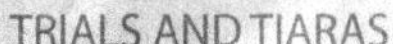

Chapter Twenty Eight
I NEVER WANTED THE FAIRY-TALE

I never dreamed of being the princess in the tower. In fact, the only princess I ever wanted to be was Princess Leia 'cause she kicked ass. The first time we watched *Star Wars*, Jake wanted to be Han, I wanted to be Leia, and Coop wanted to be Luke. That worked, until Luke turned out to be Leia's brother. Something Jake used to tease him about. Still, I never changed my mind about Leia. She was a badass.

That said, as I got dressed for prom, I couldn't help but think about those fairy tales and movies. All the princesses wanted to find their prince. Blegh. I had four of them right now, and they weren't what I dreamed of, they were who I dreamed *with*. The only rule for today had been no homework and no studying. Rachel and I had gone out to get our hair and nails done. My shoes were glittery and had open toes so better to have my toenails a matching shade with my dress. It was ridiculous and fun.

We laughed. We relaxed. And for the first time in weeks, Rachel seemed like her. She wasn't going to prom though, or she hadn't been until I begged her to go. I'd even dance with her if she came with. Part of her didn't want to deal with the whole prom court and expectations. It was too heteronormative, and I got that.

"But you're important to me, and I want you to be there too. You don't have to stay, and if it gets too uncomfortable, you tell me who is being bad to you and I'll sic Jake on them. Or I'll punch them myself."

Rachel laughed. "You'd do it too."

"Damn straight. C'mon Rachel, do you know how much you've saved my life this year?"

"You saved yourself," she scolded. "I got to be there to cheer you on, and if we're being honest, you saved mine too."

"I didn't do anything."

Her smile held all kinds of secrets. "That you know of, but you did plenty. Trust me."

"You don't have to come tonight if you don't want to." I still didn't know what had happened with her girl or her guy or both of them.

"I'll be there. I don't see the guys throwing their usual end of the school year blowout, and this might be our last time to party until we get to college."

"You have to come to New York for that."

"Funny, I accepted my admission to NYU…" I didn't let her finish as I pitched myself at her, and they had to fix my nails 'cause I messed them up.

We were going to have so much fun.

I'd asked the guys to pick her up, and Archie promised we'd swing by in the limo. Of course he ordered a limo. Then again, the last time he'd gotten us one was for going to Homecoming…

No, this would be nothing like Homecoming. First, we were all firm and together. We'd still been on uneven ground then, and Ian and I had broken up. Second, this was a date Archie had asked me for months and months ago. The guys were all in on it too. I love that they weren't wrestling over the fact Archie asked or that they were going too, but it was Archie's date.

A knock on the door pulled my attention, and I glanced over to find Archie leaning on the door frame in his suit. Damn, he looked so good. He looked me over, and I did a little spin. I loved the flare of the skirt. The lady at the salon had left my hair down, but worked it into the wild curls the guys loved.

I had on my charm bracelet on one wrist, but the single charm of the gear on the other wrist. The class ring and then the emerald drop necklace. Archie grinned slowly as he raked his gaze over me.

"Damn, you really do look like a princess."

I laughed. "Warrior princess."

"Works for me. Though if you do that yayaya thing that Xena did, make sure I have my phone out so I can record it." The perfect aplomb and cool delivery sent a ripple of laughter through me, and I cracked up.

"I promise," I said as I walked toward him. He held out his hand, and I slid my fingers across his, and when he lifted our arms and twirled me again, I chuckled. Only when he stopped, he held out a little jewelry box. "Archie."

"Yeah, I know," he told me, all deep brown eyes and playful smirk. "I really can't help myself."

"Did you even try?"

"Nope."

I giggled, but he popped the box open, and there was a pair of emerald earrings to match the pendant, right down to the double infinity knots.

"They are perfect for us," he said. "All of us. It's not just from me, you know."

The corner of my mouth kicked up. "That excuse is only going to fly for so long."

"As long as it flies, babe, we're golden."

With a roll of my eyes, I took the box and gave him a kiss before I headed over to the mirror on the dresser so I could get the earrings in. "You do know that I may start to retaliate for these gifts."

"You can retaliate on me anytime you want."

The earrings fit neatly and you couldn't really see them with my hair, but

I knew they were there. Just like I knew the tattoos were on the guys and on me. Like I knew that I had on a pair of red solid lace panties and no bra, because it would have left lines where it gathered over my chest. Just like I knew there was a hickey on the inside of my thigh, a matching set from the man standing right behind me with his hands in his pockets and a delighted smile on his face.

"Last big high school hurrah," I said.

"Nope."

I turned to face him. "No?"

"Last one is when we walk across that stage and get our faux diplomas and switch our tassels from one side to the other."

I chuckled. "That's more perfunctory."

"Life is full of rituals, babe. Rituals are important. Sure, there's no real diploma in the leather folder they give you. That's not the point of it. The point is to walk across that stage because for twelve years, we've followed the rules, dotted all the i's, crossed all the t's, and fulfilled our obligation to be educated. Our obligation ends right there. It's that last stab at our childhood and getting the acknowledgement that we made it."

He narrowed the distance.

"But it's just like everything else you wanted to experience…you wanted a boyfriend, dates, you wanted parties, and games, and you wanted love…"

My heart sped up a little.

"You deserved love."

"I had love," I told him. "I had all of you. I just didn't see it, not the right way, and now I do. Now I have you and…"

"That's it, babe," he whispered, cupping my chin and smiling. "You do have us. You're stuck with us. Us with burritos. Us without. Us on a tear with a new video game. Us working on projects."

"Us dealing with our families and going to college."

"Fuck the families, the only family we need is right here. Fine. We can keep the guys' families."

"And Grandpa," I reminded him.

"And Jeremy," he agreed. "I'll make a special allowance for your grandparents, but that's totally probationary and I reserve the right to get rid of them."

I laughed.

"See, we have our family and we have our own rituals."

I glanced around the room. The signs of the guys that lingered in here, just like they did everywhere in the apartment. Tiddles stared at me from the window ledge, and I tilted my head back to gaze at Archie. "Okay, you've convinced me, and I don't want to cry because Rachel will scold me for messing up my makeup."

Holding out his arm, he said, "Well, we can't have that."

Out in the living room, the other guys were waiting, and they all looked great in their suits. They'd gone for somewhat matching—Archie and Jake were in deep gray suits, while Coop and Ian had on almost black. They looked amazing.

"I need a picture."

"We'll get them there," Jake said, but I shook my head.

"No, I want a picture here, with you four together. I want that picture for me."

Archie brushed a kiss to my cheek, and they indulged me as I snapped a few photos of them. I pulled out my ID, and Archie tucked that into his wallet for me, then Jake took my phone. I didn't bother with anything else, because if I knew Archie, he already had my overnight bag secreted away somewhere.

I adored him, and he usually thought of everything.

"You got your lipstick?" Coop asked, and Jake turned to stare at him.

"Did you get a vagina when we weren't looking?"

Coop and I both flipped him off while I chuckled. "No, but you're right. I'll get it." Because they'd kiss it off me otherwise.

Ian caught my arm, then brushed a kiss to my cheek. "Because the numbnuts over there forgot to mention it, you look beautiful."

"Numbnuts would not be me," Archie chimed in. "I told her exactly how beautiful she was."

"Frankie doesn't need us to tell her that just because she's all dressed up," Coop said. "She's beautiful every day."

"Smooth," Jake said with a chuckle, but his eyes twinkled when he met my gaze. "He's not wrong though, Baby Girl. You're always beautiful."

I laughed. "Okay, you know I'm a sure thing, so no need to suck up."

That earned me a swat on the ass from Ian, but oh so worth it.

The limo ride over, we laughed and there was actually champagne in the back of the car. I stared at Archie, and he just grinned as he poured our glasses. Jake held his up. "To senior year, because who would have thought this is where we'd be?"

I laughed. "To Archie," Coop said, "because he was the one who said we corner her on Monday. We find out what the hell is going on."

Another round of laughter threaded through the car. "Well, in that case," Archie said. "To Coop, because you're the one who got her there."

"And to Frankie," Ian added, "for not giving up on us."

"Hey," I sniffed. "Don't start the tear things again. Besides, you guys didn't give up on me, so I think it works out pretty even."

"Fine, we're all awesome and we're not making her cry," Jake said. "So here's to great sex, good music, and a lot of laughter."

On that, we clinked our glasses and drank. Between the five of us, we killed the one bottle of champagne and I was barely tipsy, but I was loose and happy. Prom was different from Homecoming. One, it *wasn't* at the same hotel that Homecoming had been held at. They changed the venue, and for that, I was grateful. We just needed no reminders of that night.

Second, it was far more formal in some ways than Homecoming was. It was one of the few really traditional *rituals* I supposed that still lingered from decades past. The point of school dances had been to teach young men and women how to socialize with each other. How to interact at formal occasions. There were rules for a reason, not that we paid attention to most of them now.

The two big things tonight would be the music and the crowning. There would be some awards handed out. Prom was for the seniors and the juniors. Underclassmen were not allowed to attend, unless they had permission from a parent and had been invited by a senior. It was a whole thing.

There was also a spring dance that took place that was open to the whole school. Most juniors attended that rather than prom. That dance was the following weekend and happened *at* the school and not the party barn where our prom was being held. Despite the colorful name, the party barn was a great location with nothing close by, which meant we didn't have to turn down the music and, at the same time, there was no hotel for the seniors to sneak off into. Kind of win-win for the administration, I supposed. It also featured an outdoor deck that in good weather—like tonight—could be opened for party-goers to spill out on.

As the limo pulled in, I was grinning from ear to ear. The guys had been laughing and joking about putting up with me during AP test week. I ignored them. Pretty much how I planned to deal with them during AP test week too.

It was good practice.

Ian and Jake were out first, and then Ian held out a hand to help me. Coop and Archie followed. Music spilled through the wide open doors. Ian lifted my fingers to kiss and winked. "Dance with me later?"

"Absolutely."

"Tonight is all about fun," Archie said, his grin wide as he crooked his elbow to me and I threaded my arm through his. "You ready?"

We went through the doors together, and there was a picture stop just inside for the seniors. I made all the guys get in the shot with us, and then got one with each of them. They put me in different positions for the picture, and we hammed it up. I spotted Rachel right at the end and actually put my fingers to my lips and whistled. She pivoted and laughed as she sauntered over to us in a strapless painted on dark gold dress that looked fantastic. While we were holding up the other arrivals, I managed to get a snap with Rachel too.

It was pretty crowded and there were football players waving to the guys. A girl in our French class wandered over to me and Rachel, then Archie tugged me away to dance. I'd half-expected a slow dance for our first one, but nope, Archie chose "Uptown Funk." When it segued from that to the next song, I wasn't surprised when Coop slipped up behind me and joined us to dance.

When Rachel let Jake drag her over to us and Ian followed, there was a split-second reminder from Homecoming, but I shook it off. This was our night.

From Bruno Mars to Justin Timberlake to 50 Cent to Eminem and AC/DC and Queen, we didn't leave the dance floor, save for once to get water and for Rachel and I to hit the bathroom together. If you thought the guys were right outside the door, you would be right. Not that I cared. When they played Cyndi Lauper, Rachel and I hit the dance floor again, then it was cool down time and more water. They cut the music for a brief announcement of some awards.

I got to whistle and clap for Jake as he got a scholarship for being in the top percentage of STEM students. Archie's name got called, but to acknowledge that he'd donated his scholarship back to someone else on the list, and there was a lot of whistles and applause for him. Ian got an award from his coach for valuable player. Rachel got called up and out for Outstanding Achievement and Service.

It was rare to see her blush, but she did, and the guys and I were cheering her on. Merit scholarships came next, and Coop did a whoop when my name was called. Coop got one for Spirit of Community, which surprised him too. Those were all teacher nominated awards. But they were fun. We clapped and cheered as seniors were congratulated and awarded, and when it came to crowning the prom court, I had to bite back a groan.

The guys looked entirely too pleased with themselves. The princesses were named off, leaving only Rachel and I for the queen spot, and I cut a look at her and pointed at her. She snorted and flipped me off. See, she really did get me.

"But we have something a little unusual this year, and we decided that it shouldn't be." Ms. Fajardo had the honor of handing these out. "We had a dead tie in votes, but those votes were more than all the votes received in entirety for the guys. If you think we don't know a coordinated effort when we see one, kids, you'd be wrong."

I laughed and glanced over at Archie. He just kept grinning, smug and pleased. What the hell had they done? Coop and Jake wore equally smug looks, and Ian just seemed at peace.

"With that in mind, we've decided to honor the write-in votes and we will not be having a prom king this year."

I glared at the boys. They did *not* get to get out of that.

"But instead, we're crowning two queens."

Two…

Rachel threw her head back and laughed. Archie whistled, and so did Jake. Then everyone was stomping their feet and standing as they applauded. I stood up and curtseyed to Rachel with a smirk. Fine, the boys could get out of it. Rachel's reaction was worth it. We went up and got our crowns together, posed for pictures, and then the rest of the court joined us.

Jake slipped his arms around my waist and murmured, "We did good, yeah?"

I laughed. "You did great."

We danced for another hour, and I had to keep a hand on the tiara they stuck on my head until Rachel did something with pins. Archie kept eyeing it, and I had a feeling I was gonna get another one of these but not quite so plastic or cheap.

Not today though. Today, this one was perfect, and I even got in a few slow dances, one with each of them. Kind of perfect, and even though we didn't stay until the party was over, we left when we were ready, and instead of heading to a hotel right away, we invited Rachel to dinner with us and raided a diner in all our finery.

It was the best breakfast at eleven at night meal I'd had in forever.

And I wasn't wrong about the hotel, Archie had the car drop us off first, and I kissed the guys goodnight and Jake winked. He'd come get us the next day. Then it was me and Archie heading up to a room in the same hotel we'd stayed at for his birthday.

A perfect end for a perfect evening and an imperfect year.

When he wanted to dance again, I leaned into his arms and let him take the lead. It wasn't long before we were naked, but we still took our time, and by request, I kept the sparkly heels on.

Archie's grin was adorable.

And I got my first NSFW pic of him to keep on my phone.

He got several.

Win. Win.

Chapter Twenty Nine
GUESS WHO'S COMING TO DINNER

ARCHIE

AP exam week was always brutal. We had different assigned times for different tests. Frankie went into blinders mode. Nothing would break her concentration. The fact she could shut us all out so efficiently probably shouldn't have impressed me so much, but it did. The only time she emerged was to eat—usually because one of us made her—and to participate in quizzing.

By silent agreement and with no complaints from Frankie, I asked Jeremy to give us a hand this week. That meant the fridge was stocked with study snacks, hot dinners waiting each evening, and the apartment cleaned and straightened. He'd even hung out with us one evening, quizzing Frankie in French. Sometimes, I forgot he spoke a couple of languages.

Of the five of us, she and Jake had the most AP exams. Five each. They had a specialized time for the AP European history exam because they were the only two students. Frankie and I had AP economics and government back-to-back.

I didn't think a test could hurt my brain. I was wrong.

Still, we made it work. All of us.

What I wasn't expecting was the call from Edward or the request to see me. Rather than worry Frankie when she had so many tests, I went to see him on my own. He was at the house, shocker. Since moving in with Maddy, he hadn't been back that I knew of, other than to pick up some of his suits. Jeremy had sent the rest of his things to him upon request.

"He's out back on the deck," Jeremy told me when I got there. "I've got supper ready, and I'll be taking it over within the hour. Do you want me to stay?"

"I'm good, Jere. Go look after our girl. You know she loves your roast."

"I'll be here for at least another half hour," he informed me with a firm nod. Jeremy always had my back. But I wasn't that worried about Edward.

Grandpa said he'd been out for blood, but so far, the only thing he'd done was hand Frankie ten percent of Standish. Something she still hadn't decided what she wanted to do with. I took the stairs up to the next level and then out to the deck. It was already dipping toward summer. It wasn't quite hitting the nineties yet, but it was warm enough out here that Edward had shed his jacket and rolled up his shirtsleeves. I slid my sunglasses back on before stepping fully out.

He turned at my arrival and nodded. "Archie."

"Edward." Sliding my hands into my pockets, I strolled out. I could probably have gotten a drink before coming out here, but I didn't intend to linger. He wanted to talk, so I'd give him a few minutes, then get back to my life.

That was about all I intended to spare, and he was lucky to get that much.

"Thanks for agreeing to this."

"What do you want?"

"Can't I just want to talk to you?"

I scoffed. "Seriously?"

"Fine," Edward said after downing his drink. "I deserve that."

And so much more.

I'd made my point, so I didn't say another word. I just waited.

"I want to talk to you about Standish and your grandfather."

Coop

The first half of the week had been brutal, but I only had two sets of AP exams, which meant I took point on keeping an eye on everyone else. Bubba was doing the same. Frankie had exams every single day that week, and two on some of them. The funny part about it was despite the dedicated focus she had, we could see her wilting, only to relax with relief as she finished each test.

Late on Friday, I waited for her after school. She and Rachel had their French exam. It was the last one. Jake and Bubba had gone to a team thing, the last one where they handed off stuff to the new team. Hopefully some wisdom, like 'don't be a dick.'

Archie had something else going on with his grandfather, but he hadn't given us much in the way of details. Probably about where we were staying when we got to New York. We also had to discuss our summer trip, because last summer before college? Yeah, we were taking some time and doing something, even if we ended up following Bubba and Frankie to wherever they were recording.

The door opened, and kids started to trickle out. Frankie and Rachel were among the first, and boy did they look wasted. It was hot out, and I was glad I'd gone with shorts and a T-shirt. When Frankie saw me, she added a little skip to her step and said something to Rachel, who just gave her a playful shove before giving me a two-finger salute and heading away to her own car.

I caught Frankie as she flung herself at me and picked her up.

"I'm dead," she mumbled against my neck. "Dead. My mind is tapioca. I literally can't brain anymore. I haz the dumb."

Cradling her, I chuckled. "Well, does that mean I get to do all the thinking?"

She paused. Long enough, I tweaked her, and she giggled as she lifted her head. Despite where we were in the parking lot, she made no move to get down. "I'm good with you doing all the thinking."

"Excellent, 'cause I'm thinking about four pounds of barbecue wings, mozzarella sticks, some sodas, and ice cream for dessert while we do a full *Fast and the Furious* marathon." Her eyes lit up.

"All of them?"

The dumbest movies ever made.

She *loved* them.

"All of them."

She laughed and hugged me. "You're the best."

"And your favorite," I quipped. When she kissed me, she deepened it almost immediately, and there was a whistle from across the parking lot.

Yeah yeah.

PDAs at school.

I nipped her lower lip. "Gotta save that for the apartment and food. But no more homework. No more studying. No more brain."

"Just hot food, hot guys, and hot cars." Her grin widened.

"So glad you think I'm hot," I told her as I set her down and looped an arm over her shoulders to walk her to the car.

"You?" She batted innocent eyes at me.

"Remember how I'm doing all the thinking?"

"True. You're right. You're the hottest."

"Yes," I said with a fist-pump. We actually made it through four of the eight before she passed out, sprawled against my chest. I didn't even bother to move to the bedroom. The sofa was damn comfy.

Ian

Weekly dinners with my parents had actually proven to be a lot of fun. Mom and Dad made a real effort with Frankie, and what tension I'd worried about initially evaporated after the first dinner. They just went back to treating her like they always had, favored daughter status, which worked. The guys were over for the first group dinner with all of us.

Timing hadn't been ideal, and with the rush to finish the year and AP exams, we'd had to push it off. But tests were done, and school wasn't really about actual education. Hell, most of us were on reduced schedules. Grades locked this week, and it was all about make up work if you had it. We didn't.

So Mom played the Mom card, and I gathered up the guys along with Frankie for dinner. Dad grilled, and we were all out by the pool. Frankie wore the bandage bathing suit from spring break, and damn if it didn't look even better on her right now than it had then.

Of course, I had to not *focus* on her in it. Swim trunks were not good at disguising erections, and no one needed to give Mom any more fodder for teasing. Frankie and Coop were playing in the pool, while Dad gave Archie a grilling lesson.

I didn't know whether to feel sorry for him or to laugh. The guy tried, I'd give him that. But I thought we might be better off if we designated cooking off limits to him. I had a feeling those burgers were going to be burnt or raw when we got them.

"So Jake," Mom said as she put the covered salad on the table. We were all going to eat outside. "I talked to your mom, and she told me the girls weren't all going to Germany until later in the summer?"

"Yeah, Dad might get new orders, he's TDY somewhere in Italy right now, and he has another assignment. So until we know he's back at his base or reassigned here…they're waiting."

"Oh that's a shame." She glanced over at Frankie and Coop. "You two should start getting dried off for food." Then in a lower voice, she added in a half-whisper, "If they don't burn it."

Not laughing proved difficult.

"Ian, go help your brother boyfriend. I do want to eat this evening, and we have a lot to talk about."

Jake choked and sputtered. "His what now?"

Fuck.

Mom grinned, and I shook my head. She was never letting this go. I made my escape to "help" Archie and Dad. Coop's sudden laughter rolled over from the other side of the pool, and Archie glanced at me.

"What's so funny?"

"Oh, Sara's probably explaining brother boyfriends to them," Dad said without missing a beat, then shot me an apologetic look. "Sorry, I tried."

The burger Archie had been flipping broke apart as he dropped it. "The what now?"

Yep.

Never. Going. Away.

Jake

After dinner at Bubba's place and "brother boyfriends," I wasn't quite ready for the big family dinner "surprise" that was thrown for us. Mom, Bubba's parents, Coop's mom and his dad, all the siblings, and Jeremy sprang it on us the last weekend of the last week of school. We really only had "classes" on Monday, then graduation prep on Tuesday, and on Wednesday, Frankie, me, and the guys would walk her old elementary school in our graduation caps and gowns and visit with the kindergarteners before we were out. While we—as in Archie, Bubba, and I— hadn't started there, we could still go if we volunteered, and we wanted to do it with Frankie and Coop.

Graduation was Saturday.

The Saturday night before, Jeremy informed us we had to show up at Archie's place for dinner, no excuses. So we'd gone, only to find the rest of our families there. The only ones not present were bad meatloaf—thank fuck—and Archie's mom.

It was like a huge holiday meal with courses, and toasts, and laughter. It was also about congratulating all of us on graduating and getting ready for college the next year. Mom and Sara pulled Frankie aside at one point along with Carly, and when I would have gone to rescue her, Joe stopped me and Bubba both.

"Let them have their moment." At my quizzical look, he just gave me a patient smile and waved us back over to the others. Coop's dad was trying, and while there was still a definite chill in the air between Coop and his dad, Coop seemed to be relaxed.

It turned out the moms had gotten together and gotten Frankie a graduation present. In addition to a diamond bracelet, they'd also volunteered to be a 'mom' if she needed it. It amused me that they would pinch hit for her to call if she had boy issues. Like she could call my mom if she had an issue with the other guys, and call Carly or Sara if the issue was with me.

As cute as I thought it was, it was also very sweet, and Frankie had been kind of sniffly afterward. I found her outside in the garden after dinner. She'd disappeared, and I had a feeling the noise and laughter might have been too much.

Some days, I had to wonder why my mother hadn't drowned my sisters at birth, yet here we were.

"You okay?"

She glanced over at me and smiled. "I'm good, just thinking."

"About whether to call Jackson?" I wouldn't call him her dad, not right now.

"Do you have like some secret idiot's guide to handling Frankie?" The exasperation in her voice made me smile as I crossed over to her.

Wrapping my arms around her, I pulled her back to my chest and tucked my hands over her stomach. We didn't spend as much time at Archie's place as we used to, and sometimes it was weird to think of it as his "place" when we pretty much lived at the apartment. Still… "If I did, I couldn't tell you because it'd be classified eyes only, top secret."

She laughed and leaned back against me. Some of the tension drained out of her.

"And there's a lot of family stuff going on inside."

"Yeah," she said softly. "I've had his name for weeks, you know, and I still don't know whether I should call him."

"I'm right here if you decide you want to."

And I'd be right here. No matter what she decided.

Two days later, she called him while we sat in her living room. None of us spoke while the phone rang. It went to voicemail, and I grimaced. But Frankie actually looked relieved, and she left a message and then hung up.

"Out of my hands now," she said. "I called."

"Yeah you did."

Friday night before graduation, we'd just gotten the pizza in and cued up the next round of *Fast and Furious* movies that Coop and Frankie wanted to finish when there was a knock at the door.

"I got it." I made it there and pulled it open. The man standing there looked a bit surprised, and I raised my brows. "Can I help you?"

"I was looking for Frankie Curtis," he said. "I'm Henry Jackson."

* * *

Frankie and the boys' story continues in Graduation and Gifts!

To keep up with Heather and all her series join her reader's group:

Https://www.facebook.com/groups/HeathersPack/

Afterword

Hopefully, this was a much softer landing than last time. And yet, in some ways, this is also the end of the road too. The end of high school. It's both thrilling and bittersweet. When I first envisioned this series, I didn't imagine spending all these books set in senior year. Now? Now I'm so glad I did.

I love seeing how far they've come from the first day to the last. I love how they fought to understand, to connect, to communicate, and ultimately to commit. I love how they share and support not only Frankie, but each other. From Frankie and the guys to Frankie and Rachel, to Rachel and the boys sharing a tacit kind of peace, I continue to savor every step they take.

Their journey is far from over. Happily ever after is a work in progress, remember? Life after high school has its own challenges from college to moving to what happens next in their personal and professional lives.

They're a unit, they can handle what life throws at them and they are adapting and shifting around in the relationship as they all find their footing in this dynamic. Curveballs and sucker punches are not the end of the road.

Thank you again for being on this journey with me. I am so excited to see where we go next.

xoxo

Heather

About Heather Long

USA Today bestselling author, Heather Long, likes long walks in the park, science fiction, superheroes, Marines, and men who aren't douche bags. Her books are filled with heroes and heroines tangled in romance as hot as Texas summertime. From paranormal historical westerns to contemporary military romance, Heather might switch genres, but one thing is true in all of her stories—her characters drive the books. When she's not wrangling her menagerie of animals, she devotes her time to family and friends she considers family. She believes if you like your heroes so real you could lick the grit off their chest, and your heroines so likable, you're sure you've been friends with women just like them, you'll enjoy her worlds as much as she does.

Follow Heather & Sign up for her newsletter:
www.heatherlong.net

Also by Heather Long

UNTOUCHABLE

Rules and Roses

Changes and Chocolates

Keys and Kisses

Whispers and Wishes

Hangovers and Holidays

Brazen and Breathless

Trials and Tiaras

Graduation and Gifts

Defiance and Dedication

82ND STREET VANDALS

Savage Vandal

Vicious Rebel

Ruthless Traitor

Dirty Devil

ALWAYS A MARINE SERIES

Once Her Man, Always Her Man

Retreat Hell! She Just Got Here

Tell It to the Marine

Proud to Serve Her

Her Marine

No Regrets, No Surrender

The Marine Cowboy

The Two and the Proud

A Marine and a Gentleman

Combat Barbie

Whiskey Tango Foxtrot

What Part of Marine Don't You Understand?

A Marine Affair

Marine Ever After

Marine in the Wind

Marine with Benefits

A Marine of Plenty

A Candle for a Marine

Marine under the Mistletoe

Have Yourself a Marine Christmas

Lest Old Marines Be Forgot

Her Marine Bodyguard

Smoke & Marines

BRAVO TEAM WOLF

When Danger Bites

Bitten Under Fire

BOOMERS

The Judas Contact

Deadly Genesis

Unstoppable

Chance Monroe

Earth Witches Aren't Easy

Plan Witch from Out of Town

Bad Witch Rising

Her Elite Assets

Featuring:

Pure Copper

Target: Tungsten

Asset: Arsenic

Fevered Hearts

Marshal of Hel Dorado

Brave are the Lonely

Micah & Mrs. Miller

A Fistful of Dreams

Raising Kane

Wanted: Fevered or Alive

Wild and Fevered

The Quick & The Fevered

A Man Called Wyatt

Going Royal

Some Like It Royal

Some Like It Scandalous

Some Like It Deadly

Some Like it Secret

Some Like it Easy

Her Marine Prince

Blocked

HEART OF THE NEBULA
Queenmaker

Deal Breaker

Throne Taker

LONE STAR LEATHERNECKS
Semper Fi Cowboy

As You Were, Cowboy

MADISON, THE WITCH HUNTER
Every Witch Way But Floosey's

MAGIC & MAYHEM
The Witch Singer

Bridget's Witch's Diary

The Witched Away Bride

Mongrels

Mongrels, Mischief & Mayhem

SHACKLED SOULS
Succubus Chained

Succubus Unchained

Succubus Blessed

SPACE COWBOY
Space Cowboy Survival Guide

WOLVES OF WILLOW BEND
Wolf at Law

Wolf Bite

Caged Wolf

Wolf Claim

Wolf Next Door

Rogue Wolf

Bayou Wolf

Untamed Wolf

Wolf with Benefits

River Wolf

Single Wicked Wolf

Desert Wolf

Snow Wolf

Wolf on Board

Holly Jolly Wolf

Shadow Wolf

His Moonstruck Wolf

Thunder Wolf

Ghost Wolf

Outlaw Wolves

Wolf Unleashed